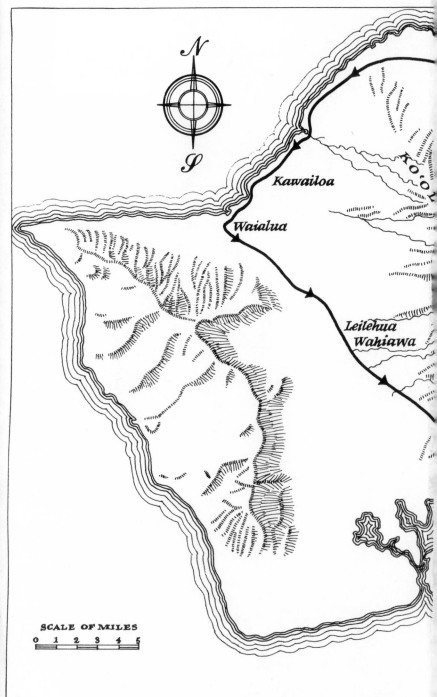

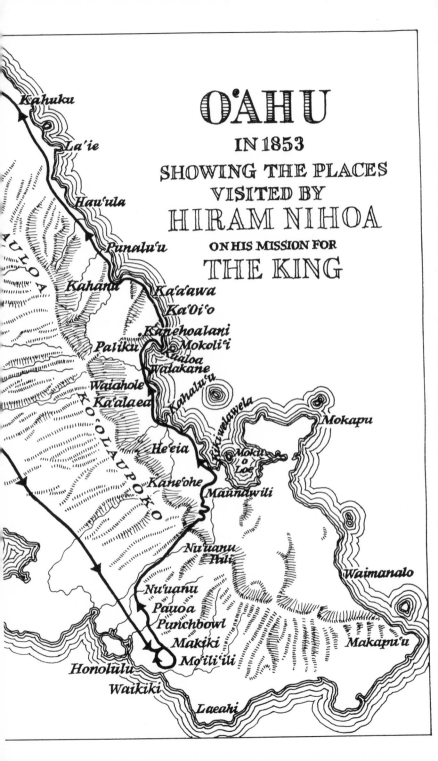

KA'A'AWA

A

NOVEL

ABOUT

HAWAII IN THE 1850s

O. A. BUSHNELL

UNIVERSITY OF HAWAII PRESS

HONOLULU

The translation of *Maika'i Waipi'o* is the work of
Alfons Korn and is used with his permission.

Copyright © 1972 by O. A. Bushnell
All rights reserved
Library of Congress Catalog Card Number 72-83490
ISBN 0–8248–0729–4
Manufactured in the United States of America
Designed by Dave Comstock

First printing 1972
Second printing 1973
Paperback edition 1980
06   05   04   9   8   7

CONTENTS

HIRAM NIHOA

SAUL BRISTOL

VIII

HIRAM NIHOA

(TRANSLATED FROM THE HAWAIIAN)

KAPU KAPU KAPU KAPU KAPU KAPU

THE

HISTORY

OF A

JOURNEY

AROUND

OʻAHU

FOR

THE KING,

KAUIKEAOULI KIWALAʻO,

KAMEHAMEHA III,

IN THE YEAR 1853.

———

WRITTEN BY HAND

BY

HIRAM NIHOA,

OF HONOLULU, OF KAHANA, OF OʻAHU,

IN THE KINGDOM OF HAWAIʻI

KAPU KAPU KAPU KAPU KAPU KAPU

CHAPTER 1.

IN WHICH A MAN RATHER TOO CURIOUS
IS CALLED TO SERVE HIS KING

The messenger came in secret, in the shadows of evening, without runners to cry the way or guards to show who sent him. Quietly, as a friend or neighbor might, he rode into the yard of my country house at Makiki, in the hills above Honolulu, where we had fled from the sickness which was afflicting the people in the town.

We were sitting on the front verandah, my wife and I, with our daughters and sons. The cooking-fires had been put out, the lamps were not yet lighted, and we were talking of little things while we watched the colors changing in the sky above, upon the earth and the sea below. Red the sky had been, from its eastern arch beyond Diamond Head to its western arch beyond the mountains of Wai-'anae, red the color of blood, the color sacred to the great gods of old. Yet even as we exclaimed over the beauty of the heavens we gave no thought to the ancient gods or to the Jehovah who has taken their place. In our Christian household, we did not abide in fear either of the gods of our ancestors or of Him whose power is proclaimed in the glory of the firmament.

No. We were happy then, laughing at the game Daniel, our youngest son, was playing for our pleasure. Like a ship's captain he stood at the porch railing, holding a long curved piece of sugarcane to his eye as a mariner holds a telescope. "Red at night, sailor's delight," he was telling us with a big voice, in words learned from his father, "red in the morning, sailors take warning." And we were laughing because the little fellow was so comical, with his telescope pointing to the ground rather than to the horizon, and because of our contentment each with the other, when Paliku came into the yard.

I did not know it was he, for my eyes are somewhat weak with aging, and the sky's brightness did not help them to see clearly. But, as is proper with a hospitable man, I went at once to greet him.

"Good evening," I called in English, thinking he was a foreigner coming up from town to see me on business. The error was a natural one. He was dressed in a black suit, he had a tall hat upon his head and black boots upon his feet. Furthermore, evening is the time when foreigners make their visits, whereas Hawaiians come early in the day, the earlier the better, so they can partake of at least two meals as guests before they must go home again—if they go home. This is but one of the many differences between natives and foreigners. Some say that it is the difference between an open hand and a closed purse, but I do not think this is the reason, for I have found most foreigners to be generous enough in other ways.

"Good evening," he answered in our native speech as he dismounted. "Paliku is here, Paliku of 'Ewa."

While my mind wondered what this stranger could want with me, my tongue did its duty, my arm invited him to the house. "Welcome, Paliku of 'Ewa. Come in, come in. You have traveled far to find me."

"No," he said firmly, "we will talk here. This place is safer." Coming close, he showed me the back of his left hand. Written in black ink upon the brown skin were three words: Kauikeaouli, Ka Mo'i: Kauikeaouli, the King.

"You understand?" asked Paliku.

Recognizing the writing of the King's own hand—how many times I have seen it—I bowed, as much to it as to the messenger. "And what does my King wish of me?" I whispered, starting to tremble. Not for two years had I seen His Majesty, not for five years had he spoken a word to me. For five years I had thought I was out of grace with him, no longer of use to him. And now, suddenly, as fast as a shark appears beside a wounded swimmer, did he rise up out of the past to worry me. A man has the right to tremble when he sees the gape of a shark.

"He wishes to talk with you. Tonight. He is at 'Ainahau in Waikiki. I will take you to him." Even as he spoke the King's messenger was removing the sacred writing from his skin, with spit and sweat and the rubbing of fingers. In the days of the great Kamehameha, father to Kauikeaouli, I was thinking, this herald would have been killed for such an act. So upset had he made me, so stupid for the moment, that I did not remember how, in those days before the missionaries came from America, neither Kamehameha nor any man of our race could put his name down in writing.

I am not a warrior, alas, not a man of bravery. I do not think I am entirely a coward, but no matter. I am indeed a man of great imagination: at that moment I could almost feel this shark's teeth scraping against my rib cage, where the heart is, and the liver. "Now?" I asked, trying to make my voice sound like a grown man's. "Alas, alas!

And what have I done, that he calls me to meet him in the dark of night?" Like a sailor in a foreign port when constables approach, I strove to remember what crime I might have committed, what offense against the King or his laws. No crimes could I recall, and only the paltriest of sins. And these were committed so seldom, with Maria in our house in Palama! Surely he wasn't calling me to account for her?

The summoners of kings must learn very early how they deliver fright along with their messages. Paliku of 'Ewa, a just man at heart if not an affable one, quieted me. "Would he tell me this?—But do not fear. Your friend is with him: the Prince Liholiho."

"Alex is there?—Ahh, then I have no fear." Paliku knew what everyone in Hawai'i Nei must know: that Alex is like a firstborn son to me, who attended him during the years of his childhood. And like a foster-father does he regard me. How, then, could I remain afraid? I ceased to tremble, my voice box was no longer tight around the sounds it made. "Come in, and rest a while. My wife will fix you a cup of tea, while I change my clothes." And now, entering into my mind, pushing fear aside, came curiosity. What does the King want with me?

"No," said Paliku, this man of stubbornness. "I shall wait here. Tell no one where you go. And do not put on the clothes you would wear to the Palace."

I heard him in amazement. "You talk like a man who has no wife! How can I just go away from here—like a wisp of black smoke drifting in a dark night?"

He waved my problem away impatiently. "Tell your wife what all husbands tell their wives when they must go from home in the night. Tell her that you are called away on business. Tell her that you are needed at a meeting.

Tell her that you are called to the bedside of a friend who is sick."

"Chah!" I grumbled as I hurried back to the house. It is easy for him to talk so smoothly. But no other man can have a wife like mine. A mountain of suspicion is she, this green-eyed woman to whom I am wed. How can I tell her such a story, even if it is the truth? The last time I was late for supper she tracked me to the house in Kewalo where I thought I was dallying safely with Abigail Moepono. Such a screaming of women, such a rending of clothing and shattering of furniture I never want to hear again. And my crooked arm: in cold weather it still pains me where the bones were not set aright. "Next time I will break your head," she said grimly, as she took me in her carriage to Dr. Newcomb, for him to fix my arm. But he, poor man, to fortify himself against his awe of her, drank so much of the whiskey which was meant to sustain me, that neither of us noticed how ill-set the bones were.

There they waited, all of them, sitting, standing, reclining, hanging from the porch rail, expecting me to explain this mysterious visitor: four daughters, five sons, and one wife, the bosom of my family. Ten pairs of eyes turned upon me, questioning as judges in a courthouse. Ten pairs of big ears, pricked up like the ears of jackasses. I loved my family, as a good father should, but they were too much with me, up there in the hills of Makiki. Once again I wished I were still a carefree sailor, drunk in a faraway port, not yet a bounden husband, not yet the parent of so many inquisitive children. *Niele, niele* they were, every one of them, I fretted, not willing to admit that they came by this talent naturally.

"Mama," I began, putting a hesitant foot upon the first step of the stairs, looking up at her with my most innocent face.—O Lord! What shall I tell her? How can I find a reasonable excuse?—But no new thought came to my aid. Remembering Paliku's lies, I used one of them whole. "Dear . . . It is a message from Noah Mahoe.—You remember Noah?—He is taken with the sickness." Just in time I recalled the name of this latest of the new plagues the foreigners have brought among us. "You know: the influenza. He asks that I come to see him—to help him with the making of a will, perhaps. I must go . . ."

She did not believe me. I knew she did not. I could tell by the set of those lips, by the steadiness of that gaze as she looked down at me, and weighed my words, and threw them away, like rubbish. While she measured me, one of the boys asked another, his eyes as rounded as a Frenchman's: "Who is this Noah Mahoe? Do we know him?" "Yes," said my wife, still looking straight through me, "he is a good friend of your father's." A very honorable woman is my wife. She does not tell untruths. The children asked no more questions. Putting her plump hands upon the rail of the porch, she raised herself up. Massive as a cliff garbed in a Mother Hubbard, she stood above me, a thin and scrawny pole of bamboo, waiting to be crushed by the flow of her anger. "If you are needed," she said quietly, "then you must go. I will help you to make ready."

A very remarkable woman is she, a true aristocrat in manner as she is in blood. She it was, not I, who remembered to tell Abel, our oldest son, to saddle Papa's horse, who sent Elisabeta to fetch a clean shirt from the clothespress, who reminded me to put on my shoes, helped me to don my black alpaca coat. She it was who tied my neckcloth in a comely bow when, nervous as a racing pony, I stood on the verandah while, one after the other, each of our children gave me a farewell kiss upon the cheek. And she it was who said, when she kissed me goodbye, "Do not hurry home. The making of wills can take much time. I shall not wait up for you." Then, with a gentle pat, she turned me toward the stairs.

Aye, unsettled though I was that evening, I remembered to be proud of her, and grateful for her care. Love of the flesh between us has long since ended, as she has grown older and heavier, and as I, in the way of men who are neither priests nor missionaries, have sought my comforting in other beds. But affection still abides. And respect. Of all the women who are mothers to my children, she is the one who is the best mother.

She has never told this to me, but I think that in virtuousness she is trying to live down the reputation of her family for loose living and harlotry and mischievous sleeping. "The Forrests of Kealakekua: so easily are they felled" is a saying about that notorious clan which is well known throughout the islands of this Kingdom, from Ni'ihau to Hawai'i.

Yet about Rebekah Nihoa, wife to Hiram Nihoa, nothing evil can be said. And with this I am well content. For this is the way things should be, is it not?

CHAPTER 2.

IN WHICH A LOYAL SERVANT IS SEVERELY TRIED AND SORELY TESTED

Soft and gray was the light of evening when Paliku and I left my family, calling their goodbyes to me. At the gate, after I put up the wooden poles which shut out roaming cows and horses from our yard, he turned to the east, toward Punahou, not to the south, toward Kaka'ako. At Kaka'ako the long causeway begins that leads across the swamps between Honolulu and Waikiki.

"Ho, Paliku," I called, checking my mount. "Here is the way to Kaka'ako." I had in mind not only the best road to Waikiki but also the pretense of going to Noah Mahoe's house, which is not reached by riding toward Punahou.

"And do I not know this?" he said. "Tonight we take a shorter way."

"Through the swamps?" I cried, not wanting to believe him.

"Be quiet!" he barked. "And hurry!"

Never, since I have become a grown man, has anyone spoken to me so rudely. When I drew up beside him he growled, "Would you tell the whole city where we are going?"

Inasmuch as my house sits half a furlong inside its yard, and my nearest neighbors are half a mile away, I thought Paliku was being more officious than reasonable. Nonetheless, I kept my peace, not being a man who holds grievances. Who am I to know where big ears may be listening and big eyes may be watching? And besides, I remembered the lesson every Hawaiian learns when he is very young: "Kick down, not up," our elders teach us, which is to say, do not question a chief or the servant of a chief who has a higher rank than your own. My excitable father, alas, did not heed these wise words. Because he questioned in anger the right of Kahanaumaikaʻi, tax collector of the great Kamehameha, to take away our biggest sow, he died a young man, before I could know him— offered up in sacrifice he was, along with the sow, that time Kamehameha with his mighty army and vast fleet of canoes was gathering for the second time on Oʻahu to invade Kauaʻi. I, who have ever been soft with my answers, I hope to die a very old man, in my very own bed.

With Paliku, also, meekness softened wrath. "Do you not worry," he said after a few minutes. "I know the way, even in the dark of night." These were the last words he spoke during that terrible ride. No doubt he was a troubled man, as servants of kings often are.

Out of regard for my brittle bones, he set our mounts an easy pace. For a while I tried to enjoy the last traces of the evening's loveliness, the excitement of my adventure, putting off in these my worries about Moʻiliʻili's swamps and the King's intentions. To our left the valley of wide Manoa opened up, the high tops of its mountains hung with clouds. "As springs in the sky are the clouds of

Manoa," says an old chant, and I believe it. Almost never does sunlight touch the uplands in that place of rains and waterfalls. People can not live there, because of the lung fever such wetness causes; and wild cattle, the learned say, have grown webbed feet, like ducks, to keep them from sinking in the mud.

At the mouth of the valley, still distant from us across the plain, like stars lying upon the ground, twinkled the lights of the American missionaries' children's school at Punahou. Only there, with water flowing forth from the precious spring, or along the banks of streams issuing from the valleys, or in Mo'ili'ili's swamps, can people live, can they make Honolulu's earth yield them food for their bellies. Everywhere else upon this long plain of Kona, from Punchbowl to Koko Head, is only dust or sparse grass, cropped by horses and cattle which find no other forage. If trees grew here once upon a time, they were cut down for firewood long ago, by adzes of stone or by axes of steel.

And then the darkness was complete. But Paliku knew the way. After we had cantered for about half an hour, he slowed to a walk. We came to clumps of bushes, small shrubs, more like shadows standing up than things of stems and leaves. This sharp-eyed Paliku: his spirit-guardian must be 'Iole the rat. In a place I could not have found at midday he turned to the right, toward the distant seashore. My obedient horse followed, deaf to my moans. Trusting to him, I let the reins fall loose, thanking first Jehovah, then Kane, Ku, Lono, and Kanaloa, the four great gods, and the forty lesser gods, and the four hundred, the four thousand, the forty thousand, the four hundred thousand little gods, that my Spanish saddle had a pommel I could clutch in my tight hands. From either side came the sounds of water, of flowing, gurgling, sighing water, yearning to embrace me when, with a single misstep, my horse and I would be thrown into the swamp, to sink in its mud and drown. Frogs croaked, night birds screeched, my stomach burned, my teeth chattered, and on we plodded in the dark. Miserable, dizzy, I clung to my pommel like a shipwrecked sailor to a spar, calling on all the spirit-guardians in my family's line to help me in this journeying through the ink sack of a squid.

How could they not hear the clamor I raised? In their mercy they sent Mahina to comfort me. Out from behind the wall of Manoa's clouds she came forth for a long moment. Not yet in her full glory, she was like a pale cowry shell, or a China bowl, tipped in the heavens, to pour the rains of Ka'ele upon Manoa below. But the moment was enough.

Just before the clouds covered her kind face again, she revealed to me a gift from the greatest gods: there, growing out of the earth beside the path, was a whole clump of *ki* plants. Swiftly I reached out and pulled from their stalk a handful of the long cool leaves. According to custom I should have tucked one of these leaves into my trousers, to protect the sacred organs of generation wherein lies my *mana* and that of my line. But I did not have time to follow the ancient law, and I hoped that Kane would not mind if I thrust the leaf under the bosom of my shirt. From other leaves I fashioned wreaths to place around my wrists, forehead, and shoulders. The last two leaves I tied together, to make a *lei* for the horse. With such protection, the evil spirits, the demons in mud and water, those malicious beings from the other world who bring accident and sickness and sudden death, could not touch me or cause me harm. Nor could the great gods punish me for being a proudful traveler when I bore the amulets which asked their favor. Ahh, it is a good thing for a man to have about him the things of old, to give him comfort in times of jeopardy.

As I became more confident in the care of the gods, the ordinary things of earth, with which the gods do not bother themselves, began to afflict me. I itched, where the underdrawers we must wear these days were all bunched up, where the horse's flanks rubbed against the woolen trousers covering my legs. And the mosquitoes! A new kind of demon are they, another present from our generous foreigners. In my youth we did not have mosquitoes in Hawai'i Nei, nor scorpions, centipedes, cockroaches, or frogs. But now they are everywhere, like foreigners, poking their long noses or their sharp tails into every place, making their loud noises, beyond chasing out because they are so many. Sour as David Malo used to be, when he protested against foreigners at the Council of the Chiefs, I rode along, wishing I struck at foreigners as I slapped at mosquitoes.

And another thing!—Oh, how the anger in me swelled. —Why am I riding like this, through the swamps of Mo'ili'ili, in the dark of night? In peril to my health, if not to my very life? Were I at home now, comfortable in my parlor, I would be reading a good book, or dozing in a soft chair, thinking of a softer bed. In the dining room, seated around the big table beneath the bright whale-oil lamps, my children would be studying their school books, my wife would be sewing while she kept them at their lessons. As I thought of them, my four pretty daughters, my five handsome sons, my good and devoted wife—ahh, I longed to be with them again, I vowed I would be a better father and husband when I returned.

If I returned.—Ah, ah, I sighed again. What does the

King want of me? This was the greatest worry. I skirted about it, running around it as a hunting dog runs around on a mountainside, sniffing for the scent of boar.—And why is His Majesty staying out there in Waikiki, when he has a fine palace in Honolulu to do business in? Why doesn't he—

"No, no, I take that back," I mumbled, touching my *ki* leaves as a Papist would finger his beads. *Kick down, not up.*—Needing a safer target, I found it in something utterly useless: "What is this Waikiki?" I addressed the air, full of swamp stinks and harmful vapors. "A sandspit bestuck with coconut palms and bedaubed with bird dung. A shoal of coral, caught between the vomit of the sea and the muck of Moʻiliʻili."

Really, the gods are very patient, long-suffering indeed. There I was, tongue clacking inside my head, hands waving in the dark, thinking mean thoughts about everything and everyone, yet expecting only the kindest of treatment from both gods and men. A little breeze, perchance the very least of the littlest gods, was sent to warn me: lifting a bit of the frayed *lei* upon my shoulders, it tickled my ear. All right, I yielded. I understand, I shall be careful.

No doubt at one time, when Honolulu did not exist, before these foreigners came in their sailing ships and found the harbor of Kou for an anchorage, perhaps then this Waikiki was an important place, the home of Oʻahu's kings. But now, with half of Oʻahu's people dead in their graves, with almost all the surviving half clustered around the wharves and warehouses, the grogshops and whorehouses of Honolulu, Waikiki too is dead. It will never amount to anything. A breeding place for mosquitoes and frogs and rats it may be, but of no use to people. They do not come here anymore, to swim or to ride their long boards in the waters of the sea, as we did when I was a

youth. Forbidden by the missionaries are these disport-
ings in the sea because they are heathen pastimes, and because the nakedness of swimmers is an invitation to sins
of the flesh, is an anathema. Alas, alas! Such narrow
minds, such dirty thoughts, those Christians have. I can
not remember being more lustful when I swam naked than
I have been since I was girded about with clothing and ar-
mored with commandments. And what is sin, anyway?—

Cha! As peevish as a man trapped in an outhouse without leaf, shirttail, or piece of paper, I endured, swatting
at mosquitoes, snapping at stinging thoughts. What a marvel is a man, that he should survive despite the gods' annoyance! Perhaps he lives because the gods hope that,
with time, he will learn to be forbearing. Just as, in their
patience, they have tried to teach me to be forbearing. Not
wisdom do they ask, certainly not silence.—I should choke
to death if they did.—Only kindness, from a man to other
men, from a man to his gods: this is all they wish.

As we moved farther from the mountains the clouds
were left behind, and Mahina lighted up the rest of our
way. To the left, a dark battlement, rose Diamond Head.
The narrow path underfoot widened to become a muddy
road. The wild bulrushes, the swamp weeds, fell behind
and watery plantations of taro took their place. On little
islands raised above the level of the mud, clusters of
thatched huts, domes of trees, barking dogs, gave proof
that we were coming again into the world of people.
Straight ahead the glow of fires showed, a beacon in the
desert of night. Soon I could see the flickering torches, the
plumed crowns of palms in the coconut grove where kings
reside when they wish to be undisturbed. Mingling with
the sweet scent of burning candlenuts came the stronger
smells of seaweed, of the salty ocean.

With a suddenness that surprised not only me, we reached the end of our journey. A startled guard, naked as a farmer in his taro patch, ran toward us, shouting "Stand!—Who comes here?" From behind the stakes topped with globes of white *kapa* which mark the boundaries of a royal *kapu* other guards appeared. Some were naked, some wore the loincloth, none was clad in the uniform all are forced to wear in town. In the shadows under the trees, upon outspread mats, women sat up to see who interrupted their pleasures of love.—O you of the worrying mind, I smiled to myself. It has not changed, this Waikiki . . .

Paliku stopped his horse, lifted a hand to halt mine. "Be easy," he called to the sentry, "Paliku of 'Ewa is here. Returning as I departed, by the quiet path of Mo-'ili'ili."

"Ah, it is you," said the guard, beckoning him in. "Then welcome back from your little ride. You were not gone for long." As we moved forward into the light he burst out laughing. A most unsoldierly man is he, I was thinking, and is this the proper manner for a guard to the King? "Wait a moment," he bawled. "And who is this *kahuna* coming here with you? Have you plucked him from out of the swamp, perhaps?" Then I knew why he laughed. The loud-mouthed gossipmonger! May his stones shrivel in their bag, may moths be his seed! Many of the soldiers, who only a moment before were returning to their mats, gathered around, teeth and eyes flashing, fingers pointing at me, at the leafy *lei* I had forgotten to remove. "*E!* He is a jungle on horseback," said one. "Nah, nah, a parrot is he," said another, "a bird of many colors." "A *kahuna 'ana'ana*, beyond doubt," jeered still another. "Old man, what sorcery do you make tonight?" "*E*, womanless one," shouted a fourth at a companion, thereby changing his laughter to frowns, "ask him to make a love-potion for to end your lonely days and nights."

A *kahuna*, indeed! They knew as well as I did, how the law of this Christian land forbids the practice of the evil arts of sorcery and even the kinder rites of magic for the sake of love. Feeling like a fool, I could do nothing but scowl at them, miserable as only an older man can be when he is taunted by the young. Something is wrong with the young men and women of today. When I was a youth, we had more respect for our elders. Never would we have mocked an old man or an old woman, never would we have dared to laugh at a *kahuna 'ana'ana*. But the young folk of today: alas for them. No wonder the nation is wasting away, no wonder we are beset with troubles from far and near.

Keeping my peace, I strove to keep my dignity. I intended nothing else, but I could mark the instant when dread entered among my tormenters. "*Auwe!*" wailed one, as he backed away, no longer laughing. "Forgive," murmured others, "forgive us." In the flick of a fly whisk they were gone, slinking away to the darkness under the trees. All of them went save one, the womanless youth who was in need of a love-potion. "Great is your *mana*," he proclaimed loudly, taking the bridle reins from my hand. Somewhat pleased with this effect—I think it must be the first reward for silence I have ever won—I looked toward Paliku, to share a little smile with him. But he did not see it, he was hurrying forward to help me from my horse.

"Now will we go to the house of the King," he said, when I stood upon the ground. While we walked along the path I removed the *ki* leaves. Not daring to throw them into the bushes, I tucked them into my shirt, where the other one lay warm against my belly. Cool they were, for a few moments, soothing against the place where my heart was beginning to quicken. The same dread which had quieted the jeering soldiers was stirring now in me. For greatest of all among the gods on earth are the Kamehameha. Very great is their *mana*, burning is their *kapu*. And deep, profound, was my fear of the King.

CHAPTER 3.

IN WHICH GOSSIP IS MADE HISTORY, AND HISTORY IS SHOWN TO BE SOMETHING MORE THAN GOSSIP

The house of the King was a disappointment: a very ordinary beach cottage, it differed from the huts of commoners only in having walls made of wood. A thatch of dried coarse grass covered its roof, and plaited palm fronds protected the wooden planking from the salt air. At the front and along the two sides of the house was a narrow verandah. It is a mean place, I sniffed, a dwelling for fishermen.

Yet the signs were there which set it apart from houses of ordinary men: the many *kukui*-nut torches lighting up the space surrounding it; the tall *kapu*-sticks thrust into the sand at either side of the stairs; and, taller still, two soldiers in uniform, each bearing a heavy musket.

Paliku of 'Ewa delivered me into their care, then disappeared into the night. While one soldier barred my way with his body, the other performed the stiff and graceless dance whereby he managed to turn around upon a space the size of a penny and clumped heavily up the stairs to the house. I have always thought this military business to be silly, a waste of time. It is understandable, perhaps, in front of the palace where the Queen of England lives, who is ruler of such a warring country, or in the Spanish colonies of America, where they are always fighting for some reason or other. But here in this little Kingdom of Hawai'i, where we wish to live in peace and could not chase off a school of hungry fish, it is ridiculous. It is all a part of this children's game, of fancy uniforms and three-cornered hats, of gold braid and colored ribbons, which the crazy *haole* who is our Foreign Minister tells us we must play. Forever talking about "court etiquette" and "the Congress of Vienna," Mr. Wyllie says that we must do as other nations do, if we wish to "command the respect of foreigners for the style and state of His Majesty Kauikeaouli, Kamehameha III, King, by the Grace of God, of the Hawaiian Islands." Hoo, this mad Scotsman! Because he enjoys dressing up like an actor on a stage, because he loves even more to play with the magic of words, all the rest of us must look and act like fools, from Kauikeaouli, wilting in his Windsor coat, to the lowliest soldier, hurting in his boots.

Spitting my disgust into the ferns beside the path, I turned toward the sea. Beyond the leaning trunks of the coconut palms, beyond the long curve of the beach, it filled the great space between the far horizon and the mountain Lae'ahi. In that place, on that special night, I refused to call it Diamond Head, the meaningless name foreigners have given our proud mountain.

Just as the old song says, "the cool land breeze of 'Ainahau moved gently in," rustling the palm leaves overhead, bringing ease to us below. Lured by the moon, the waves of the sea lifted and broke, roaring with anger when they fell upon the reef, sighing with love when they caressed the breast of the land. In the distance, near Lae'ahi, fishermen with spears and flaring torches hunted among the coral heads for squid and lobsters and eels. Closer to me, where the surf was breaking, sounded the laughter of men delighting in their game. Naked they were, I knew, as their ancestors were and mine, as men should be when they ride their long heavy boards upon the rushing waves of the sea.—Ahh, they have not forgotten, I rejoiced, they will never forget, no matter what those missionaries preach from their pulpits. I was composing a prayer of thanks to Mahina, who revealed all this beauty to me, and to Kanaloa, who rules the sea, when the guard returned.

Behind him walked a tall man I know very well. He greeted me with outstretched arms and the friendly grin he always shares with me. "Niele!" he cried, taking me into a brother's embrace. "These old eyes delight to see you again.—Kauikeaouli sends me to talk with you for a while, until the servants clear the table. We have only now finished with our supper.—You haven't changed a bit. How do you keep so young?"

Looking up into his face, I observed how he had changed. The light red-hued skin, the reddish tint to his hair, for which he was so admired, were faded now, the lean, wide-shouldered body, which in his youth was acknowledged to be the handsomest in all Hawai'i, was bending now, curving in the back under the weight of the massive head, the pull of the swelling belly. With him, as with me, the toll of our years was showing. "You know my prescription," I answered, "and you seem to have been following it: you have not changed much either, since last we met." Old men's lies these were, as both of us knew, lies to life as well as to our mirrors, given not as deceits but as comforts, because, having been young once, how could we bear to acknowledge that we were grown old?

"Same old Niele," he laughed, "always joking.—Tell me: by following this prescription of yours, how many children have you made by now?"

"Who can say?" I shrugged. "The ones I know about are twenty-two. Perhaps twenty-three, if Kupua's birthing has gone well."

He shook his head, admiration touched with envy. "Some men have all the luck. How is it possible for you to have so many, for others to have none? And you being such a sinner, too.—Do you still own that whorehouse down on Mauna Kea Street?"

"Of course. It is a very good business, indeed. And ideally located, next to the Britishers' Mess. Only now you will please refer to it as a 'hotel.' "

"Ah, yes. So it is.—I had forgotten that we must now use such a fancy name."

"As a matter of fact, I own three such 'hotels.' One new place, just opened, on Fid Street. The other, a more settled establishment, in Iwilei, just off Cow Bay. They are more convenient to sailors." I was not boasting. I was only acquainting an old friend with my enterprise. Even if he was the High Chief Abner Paki, Chamberlain to the Court and His Majesty's very best friend, he and I have shared thoughts, money, food, secrets, griefs, sometimes even our women, since we were lads in the household of Ka‘ahumanu the Queen. Even so, I did not think that this was the time or the place to report upon the grogshops, Chinese bakeries, *hula* schools, food stores, and vegetable farms I own. One of the great lessons I learned during my years as a sailor is this: a man who serves the mind or the spirit of his fellowmen can starve to death in the midst of plenty, but a man who serves the body's needs will become rich. Because I remembered this lesson when I returned to port for the last time, I am a wealthy man. Abner Paki, better than anyone, knows my philosophy, and the foundation of my fortune.

"And Rebekah? Does she know about these—ah, these little 'hotels'?"

"Oh, may Heaven forfend! No, she does not." My alarm was not pretended. "Did she know of them, she would pull the hair from my head and break the bones in my legs. Even worse! She would force me to sell those makers of good money."

"Ah, ah, ah. Then she, too, has not changed with the years. She was always a good woman."

"Aye, a very good woman: a cornerstone to the church, a very carriageful of respectability. But—very hard to live with."

"So," he smiled and sighed in the same breath, thinking beyond my Rebekah to his Konia. "Is it not so with all wives in these new times? The good old days: they are gone."

Well do I know the story about why Abner Paki and Konia were wed. Someday, perhaps, I shall tell it. On second thought, I shall tell it now, for it is too good a story to leave untold, and I may forget to come back to it later.

In the years of their youth Kauikeaouli and Paki were closest friends. "Like sea and shore are they," people said then, "for where one is, there is the other." In those days, as was only natural, Kauikeaouli was more interested in pleasure than in statecraft, even though he had been King since his tenth year, when 'Iolani Liholiho his brother died of the measles in London. But, as everyone in Hawai'i knew, Kauikeaouli was given little chance to be the ruling chief while Ka'ahumanu of the iron will lived. She was the Regent, appointed by the Council of Chiefs, and she was the ruler of the Kingdom.

Respecting Ka'ahumanu, yet resenting her, Kauikea-ouli bided his time until she died, and Kina'u succeeded her as Regent. Then Kauikeaouli set up his own household, apart from Kina'u, where he lived in idleness and debauchery with many young companions, both male and female, drawn from families of both chiefs and commoners. There food and drink were plentiful, the pounding of *hula* drums was heard every night, the pleasures of love abounded. Leading the way in this rebellion of youth against frowning older chiefs and horrified missionaries were Kauikeaouli and Paki. So great was the affection of one for the other that they shared the same house, the same *poi* bowl, the same drinking cup, and, often enough, the same willing woman. No cloud dimmed the light of the single sun shining down upon those two young gourds swelling upon the vine.

Kauikeaouli's favorite residence was Pohukaina, near the eastern shore of the bay of Honolulu, the stone house that Kalanimoku had built when he was prime minister and which, when death approached, he bequeathed to the young King. There, at Pohukaina, the Place of Ordered Calm, all those young people were enjoying themselves, without let or stay, without fears for today or worry for tomorrow. Until the time came when Kauikeaouli was smitten with love.

Kalama was the one who awoke this love in him, thereby kindling the fire of jealousy as well as the sting of desire. "She is mine," Kauikeaouli said in the hearing of all his companions, "let no other man touch her." His companions agreed readily enough to this *kapu*, for Kalama was plain, by no means the most beautiful of the women

who were drawn to that palace of pleasure, and other com-
forters were easily found. So, for a while, their life of
indulgence went on as before.

But, as is the way with jealous lovers, Kauikeaouli
could not be at peace. He brooded in his thoughts, suspecting every man of stealing in secret the prize he had
ignored before the *kapu* was placed upon it. Most of all
did Kauikeaouli suspect Paki, the companion he knew
so well.

Did he imagine that Paki broke the *kapu*? Or did his
friend betray him? No one knows, for no one ever found
Paki together with Kalama. No matter. It is enough to
know that one day Kauikeaouli burst out of the house,
half-mad with rage and rum, crying that he must have
Paki's life. Summoning all the young chiefs to a council,
including Paki, he demanded Paki's death. In vain did
the young chiefs plead with Kauikeaouli to give up this
demand, to banish Paki if he wished, but not to end his
life. Kauikeaouli would not relent. "Death!" he insisted.
"Do you decide how it must come." Not one word did Paki
say in his defense. And in vain did Kalama rush in, when
she heard of Kauikeaouli's madness, to throw herself at
his feet and, with tears and wailing, to tell him that she
and Paki had not broken the *kapu*. He would not believe, and ordered her to be dragged away from the
meetinghouse.

This is how they decided Paki would die: he should be
tied with ropes of sennit to a stake in the courtyard of
Pohukaina, there to stand until his spirit fled from its
body. No one was to give him food or drink, on pain of
death.

And so it was done. For two days and two nights Paki
stood there, without so much as a loincloth to shelter him
from the sun, uttering neither word nor groan. Laughter

was heard no more at Pohukaina, the *hula* drums did not throb in the warm nights. Servants went about their tasks with downcast eyes. The young chiefs and chiefesses kept apart, having no interest in the games of love.

But in the dark of each night Kalama and her friend Konia would bring food and water to Paki, while the servants, the guards, the populace of that great household turned away, not seeing them.

On the first day Kauikeaouli would not speak of Paki or look upon him. On the second day, as his rage weakened, he peered at his suffering friend from the doorway of the house the two had shared.

On the morning of the third day Kauikeaouli and the young chiefs stood before Paki, held up only by the ropes which bound him to the stake. Long did Kauikeaouli gaze at his friend, waiting for an admission of guilt, a cry for mercy, for any sign that would give him an excuse to relent. Paki made no sound, gave no sign. Loyal to his King, he hung there, lips shut, eyes closed, a willing sacrifice to his friend's twisted love.

Kauikeaouli was not as strong. "This is no way for a man to die," he shouted. "Unbind him—and take him to the shore." Servants crept forward, to untie the ropes, to rub Paki's arms and legs until the blood flowed again and he could walk.

They went to the shore nearby, the entire household, men and women, chiefs and commoners together, all except Kauikeaouli wondering what was to be done with Paki. At the water's edge Kauikeaouli lifted his hand, pointing toward the deep sea. "Go!" he commanded, "swim out. And do not come back." From the people around them went up a great wail of dismay, a high keening of grief.

Without hesitation Paki went into the shallow water,

wading out over the reef toward the depths beyond. In the space of a single breath Kalama stepped forth from the crowd to follow Paki. The people gasped. Kauikeaouli cried out in despair. Then Konia stepped forth, loyal to her friend Kalama, faithful to Paki, the love of her heart. Whereupon, by ones, by twos, by fives and by tens, the young chiefesses, the young commoner women of the court, the servant women of the household, all the women on the shore who at one time or another had known pleasure from the embrace of Paki or who had yearned for such joy, went into the water.

As Kalama went out Kauikeaouli had cried in sorrow. But when all the others followed her, and the coral of the reef was covered more with women than with water, he laughed in relief. "Come back! Come back!" he called, wading out after them, weeping, laughing, calling to them, all at the same time. "Paki! Kalama! Konia! Come back! —I have learned. I am humbled." Hearing this, the men on the shore sent up a loud cheer and, themselves filled with relief and joy, went laughing upon the reef to lead the women home.

When Kauikeaouli came up to Kalama, Konia, and Paki, they knew that his jealousy was ended, was burned out. With tears of happiness they embraced, as Kauikeaouli asked their forgiveness and was forgiven. United now in bonds of love and trust that nothing save death will break, they returned to the land and to life.

This is the true story of how, in a most brave way, Kalama proved her love for Kauikeaouli, the true story of how Konia declared her love for Paki. I was not there at Pohukaina to witness this event, but I know the story to be true because Paki himself was the one who told it to me.

Not long after this taming of Kauikeaouli the household at Pohukaina was broken up when, on his twenty-first birthday, he determined to be a good man and a proper King. Soon Paki and Konia were married in the Christian style, by Hiram Bingham at Kawaiahaʻo Church. But, because of her low rank, Kalama was not wed to Kauikeaouli until three more years had passed. Not until Nahiʻenaʻena, Kauikeaouli's own full sister, had died, without bearing him a child of the highest possible rank, would the Council of Chiefs permit a marriage between Kauikeaouli and Kalama.

But that, as the tellers of tales would say, is another story, for someone else to relate.

I have not known Konia well, but, from listening to Rebekah, I have learned about the succession of sorrows little and great in Konia's life of many laments. Because Paki had asked about my spouse, I politely inquired about his. "Oh, she is healthy, I thank you. But she is still unforgiving about Pauahi's marriage to that American boy. I keep telling her: 'Mama: she has married the man of her choice. She is happy. Then let us forgive her, and welcome her to our home once more.' 'Never!' she answers me. 'It is easy for you to say this, you who are not her father. But I —I am her mother . . .' And then she weeps. You remember how quick she is to shed tears. Perhaps she is right, that it is easier for me to say this about Pauahi. But I do not think so. Even though she is not my daughter, I have always loved her as though she were my own."

For this I can vouch. In the old days, when no child in Hawaiʻi was considered to be a bastard, Pauahi was never dishonored because her true father—that same Henry A. Peirce who is now a great man in Boston as well as in Honolulu—was not married in the Christian manner to Konia. Far from it. The issue of such a union—and there were many such unions in the old days, as there are even now—was called a child of love, and was not made to suffer. But now, suddenly, since we are become a Christian nation, such a child is despised and rejected, is denied the love of two parents because at least one of them, as the preachers say, has "committted a sin." Such is the thinking of the Christian mind, the feeling of the charitable Christian heart. I can not understand this kind of cruelty. Neither can Paki, who is renowned for the love he has shown to Konia's only child.

" 'Never!' she says," Paki continued with Konia's plaint. " 'When she could have married Lot Kamehameha, why did she go and marry that cold fish, that Charlie Bishop?' To this question I have no answer. For, indeed, he is something of a cold fish. Good to look upon, perhaps, in his pale, thin, Yankee way, and very smart in matters of money.—As you know, he is being quite successful in his new job as Collector of Customs for Dr. Judd.—But, between us, I do not think that he is made of flesh and blood, like us. A thing of northern ice is he, like the snow from Oregon which comes here in the holds of ships. Cold to talk to, cold to the touch. And this is Konia's unspoken worry. If Pauahi and Charlie would make a child for her to love, then I think she would forgive their marriage. You know how Konia longs for children in the house. Even to the point of taking Caesar Kapa'akea's oldest daughter, Kamaka'eha, to live with us."

"Ah, that one! I know her too well from her visits to my house. She is a terror."

"Oh, she is not so bad," said the patient man, victim of so many women, in and out of his household. "Proud and sassy she is, sometimes, as if she were born to be the wife of a king. But I can handle her well enough, with a few tickles, a few jokes, and a kiss or two at the right time. Although Konia tells me this too must stop, now that the girl is growing into a woman. I suppose she is right," he grinned, reminding me of the days when we were young. "Times have changed . . ."

Because he told me nothing new, because I did not know how to console him, I turned our conversation to a problem great enough for the two of us to share. "Children and grandchildren: a man wishes for them, a woman yearns for them, but the nation cries out for them. Where are the children of our land? Where are the young people who will be the mothers and fathers to the next generation of our race? And who will care for our persons when we are aged, who will save our bones when we are dead?"

"You have said it," he answered. "Samuel Kamakau is saying it, in the churches, in the streets, in the Legislature: 'Thriving seedlings did the people of old bear, great gourds filled with seeds they were. But the people of today are poison gourds, empty of seeds, and bitter to the taste.' "

"Nah, nah: wait a moment. This Preacher Samuel: he rumbles forth a churchman's sermon, but he does not tell the truth. The seeds are here. And—as I should know— they are plentifully sown, far and wide. And the seedlings: believe me, they come forth. But they do not live, Paki, they do not thrive. This is Hawai'i's sorrow. Why is it that, in 1778, when Captain Cook and his ships discovered these islands, about 300,000 of our people dwelled upon them, whereas today we number no more than 80,-000? Why is it that, in 1848, when only 1500 children were born to our people, not one of those infants lived to see its third year? Today, if we searched from Hawai'i, where the sun rises, to Kaua'i, where the sun is lodged, you would not find a five-year-old child."

"Yes, I know this. And he knows," Paki nodded toward the house, "and he worries with the rest of us. 'What,' he asks, 'is the reason for this falling-away?' Do you have the answer?"

"Who can tell? I think there are many reasons. The missionaries say it is because we are a lewd and a sinful race, given to lust and to laziness. This I do not believe. Not all of us are such lustful sinners."

He held up his hands in protest. "Your Rebekah, my Konia, many others like them: I do not think that even Hiram Bingham, if he were here still, could call them lustful and lazy."

"He would praise them, these good wives who are an affliction to men like us.—But then, are we different from the men of our parents' time? No, we are not. And they bore many children. Then is the nation's childlessness the punishment of Jehovah for our sinfulness? Perhaps it is so, but I for one can not believe that this loving God can destroy a whole nation for the sins of a few. Look at this argument in another way. I am a creature of lusts and lewdness, perhaps, yet I am gifted with many children. I am doing my best to preserve the race, but I can not do it all by myself!"

Paki did not laugh at my jest. "Take care," he warned, crossing his fingers, rolling his eyes in fear, "lest the gods think you proud."

"How can I be proud, when death stares me in the face? When year after year these new sicknesses sweep through our people as rakes through fallen leaves? When each morning, as I awaken, I must make a count to see if I have lost a child during the night?—No, I am not proud in this way. But I can believe the doctors when they say that sickness is the reason for our dwindling. For I have seen some of my little ones perish, of the diphtheria, of the scarlet fever. But so also have I seen older people perish, and children of missionaries, and missionaries themselves.

And children and parents die in other countries, so sickness can not be the only reason for our falling-away. I have wondered, I have worried, about other reasons, and I will tell you my thought about what I think is the greatest reason. Here is my thought: the *mana* of the nation is weakened because the *mana* of the great chiefs is being weakened. When their *mana* is weakened, the gods turn away. Only by strengthening the *mana* of the chiefs can we bring back the favor of the gods. When the favor of the gods is restored, then will the life of the land be restored."

"Aye, perhaps you are right, perhaps you have said it. This is a new thought to me."

"How can it not be so?" I persisted. "Of all the great chiefs in the land today, how many have borne children in the last five years—no, even in the last ten years? Let us begin with you, Paki of Moloka'i and O'ahu: how many have sprung up from the seed of your gourd?"

"Alas," he sighed, "not one, not one."

"And from the Kaumuali'i lines of Kaua'i?"

"Not one."

"And from the Kalanikupule and Kahekili chiefs of O'ahu and Maui?"

"Alas, they are gone: their lines are ended."

"Then, from the greatest chiefs of all, the Kamehameha?"

He groaned. "Only one.—And, in the eyes of foreigners, he can not be counted. . ."

Weighted down with our knowledge we faced each other, having nothing more to say. The breeze of 'Ainahau, the laughter of the men riding the surf, the flickering torches under the sheltering palms: they brought us no solace.

Then the door of the house opened wide, bright light streamed out upon the *lanai*, flowed down the stairs to the earth at our feet. Framed in the glowing doorway stood a young man, tall and slender. His features were hidden in shadow, but I knew who he was.

"There," I whispered to my friend, "there is the hope of our race."

"Aye," he answered. "Those two: they are the hope of our race."

"Those two?" For me there was only one.

"Aye," he said. "Kapuaiwa also is here."

CHAPTER 4.

IN WHICH THE BURDEN IS PLACED IN
WILLING HANDS

Alex greeted me with affection. "Kahu," he called, hastening down the steps into the yard. "I am happy to see you. Thank you for coming here on such short notice." Taking my hand, he drew me with him toward the house.

He has not changed, I was thinking, he is still as a son to me, the child of my heart, dearer to me than are the children of my own flesh and blood. I have cherished him since first he was put into my arms, when he was a newborn babe. "Do you be the *kahu* to my son," said Elisabeta Kina'u, his mother, as she gave him into my keeping, according to the custom. I was a grown man when she chose me for this honor, a sailor-wanderer who had spent almost half his life upon the sea or in foreign lands. And therefore, she believed, a fitting guardian for her son in these new times.

And in the shelter of my arms and of my heart did I raise this young prince. I was the one who fed him, who washed and dressed him, who burned his body's wastes and his worn-out clothing to prevent sorcerers from doing him harm. Nurse to him in his sicknesses, companion to him in his child's games I have been, watcher, warden, teacher. In the embrace of my arms did he learn to walk and to swim. With the aid of my sharp eyes did he pick out the stars in the sky, learn to name the creatures of land and sea and air. From the example of my strong limbs did he learn to run and jump, to throw the spear, to box in the honorable English style, not in the bone-breaking way of robber-fighters. Sitting on my lap, in the shaded room of the Chiefs' Children's School, he studied (as I did with him) the reading and the writing of the English language. In my shadow did he, as a little fellow, seek shelter from the teasings of older children. Out from that shadow did I send him, when he was old enough to fend for himself. From my mouth, but never from my hands, he received the correcting of his little boy's little faults, the judgments of larger offenses as he was changing from a boy to a man. From my hands he took the rewards for his goodness, the choicest parts of a dog or a pig, pieces of sugarcane or of baked *ki* root in the early years, sweeter cakes and candies when foreigners in Honolulu began to sell these good things in their shops filled with marvels from the world beyond. Under my care he grew from a soft and helpless babe to a tall and handsome youth. Father and mother I have been to him, more meaningful than were the lordly Kekuanao'a and the queenly Kina'u who begat him. And for this service does he regard me with fondness, as a grateful son regards a devoted father. Ah, is there a happiness to compare with the gladness of one who finds that he has raised up a noble man? As I walked beside him at 'Ainahau that evening, my heart swelled again with thankfulness, my eyes were wet for joy.

"Do not enter in fear," he said softly. "He is not angry

with you anymore. That is forgotten." How like Alex it is, to have given me this assurance. Five years before that fateful night at 'Ainahau had Kauikeaouli turned his mind against me, because I was bold enough to speak out against the proposals being made to him, that all lands in his Kingdom should be divided into three parts: one for the Crown, a second for the chiefs to share, the third for commoners and foreigners to buy. The American missionaries were saying that commoners would plan a future for themselves and their offspring only when they owned the farmlands upon which they lived and labored. Foreign merchants, supported by their noisy consuls, were arguing that without ownership of land *haole* businesses could not thrive, the *haole* and their money would not stay, and the Kingdom could not prosper. Caught between the old ways and the new, Kauikeaouli was uncertain how to decide. The great chiefs grumbled among themselves but, for this reason or for that, they did not speak up in Council. Of all the lesser chiefs, I was the only one to stand up and speak against this division of lands. My concern for Alex made me do it: what would happen to him when he was King, I asked, if two-thirds of his Kingdom had been given away? My concern for Alex did not harm me, but the fact that I dared to speak of the time when Kauikeaouli would be dead was held to be ill-omened. He frowned, and smiled no more upon me.

But he was not so cruel as to take Alex away from me then. Only later, in 1849, did he do so, with a reason against which even I could not protest. This was when he sent Alex and Lot with Dr. Judd as his envoys to governments in America and Europe. Alex was not yet fifteen years old, but he was ready to take his place among men, and willingly I cut the bonds that tied us each to the other.

David Malo and Samuel Kamakau, who are not even

lesser chiefs, but only commoners educated by the missionaries at Lahainaluna Seminary, they too stood up with me because of their worry for the people. "Do not shelter foreigners," warned these two, "for they are graspers of land. Entertaining foreigners is the beginning which will lead to the government's coming into the hands of the foreigners, and the Hawaiian people becoming their servants to work for them. And by-and-by you will see the truth of it. We shall see that the strangers will complain of the natives of Hawai'i as stupid, ignorant, and good-for-nothing, and say all such evil things of us, and this will embitter the race and degrade it and cause the chiefs to go after the stranger and cast off their own race."

Of the foreigners only Dr. Gerrit P. Judd, who was adviser then to the Council of Chiefs, sided with us, because he too feared the newcomers' hunger for land. But we four, and those few who thought as we did, were like people talking under water: only rumblings were heard, only bubbles of air were seen. The *Mahele* was decreed, the lands were divided up. I must admit that, until now, the consequences have been good for the people and for the nation. But sour David Malo has not changed his mind. From the exile's home he has sought at Keokea on Maui, where he hides for shame from the world because of that bitch second wife of his, he writes to me, saying, "Wait and see." From my perches in Honolulu I wait and watch.

With his fingers upon my arm Alex brought me to the King. I, who while lying flat upon the ground have seen great chiefs crawl naked into the presence of the first Kamehameha, who myself have crawled into the presence of the second Kamehameha, I walked upright now, with the full honor of a man, into the presence of the third, guided by the hand of the prince who one day would be Kamehameha the Fourth. This grace of dignity, this recognition of the worth of a man, be he chief or commoner, is surely the greatest blessing the foreigners have brought to us who are Hawaiians. All others of their benefits and their troubles are as nothing, compared with this supremest boon.

Even so, I am old enough to be marked forever with a remembrance of the old ways, to feel the ancient awe. My spirit trembled as I entered the brilliantly lighted room. How full of *mana* was that house! With the three greatest princes of the nation in it, who were attended by a fourth chief of almost as great a lineage, the room seemed to draw its light not from lamps but from the spirit-power of the gods, gathered there in those men who were their sons.

"My Father," Alex said, addressing the man who was mother's brother to him, adoptive father, and Sovereign, "here is Hiram Nihoa." As would any mortal man in the parlor of his home, the King came forward, offered me his hand to shake, saying "*Aloha* to you, Hiram. I am happy to see you again." With a nod and a smile he indicated Alex's older brother. "You know Lot, of course." Sprawled upon a settee, Lot Kapuaiwa Kamehameha did not bother to sit up. Whereas the King and Alex and Paki had put on frock coats to receive me, Lot was still in his shirt-sleeves. This Lot, this bored and cynical boy: he is not one of my favorite chiefs. We two have known this ever since I banged his head against the trunk of a tree one day at the Chiefs' Children's School, when I could stand no more the way he was teasing my little Alex. Thereafter we have lived in a wary sort of peace. "*Aloha*, Kahu," he said, granting me half a smile, a flip of his long fingers.

For me, as for so many people, Lot is a puzzle. With an excellent mind, he rarely speaks; with an athlete's body, he moves as little as possible; with great ability, he does only what he must; with the same parents as Alex, he has inherited their handsomeness but little of their charm. He is not lazy. Rather he is indifferent, aloof. He acts like a man who wishes he had not been born, because he can find so little in life to interest him. For this reason, I suspect, Kauikeaouli must be relieved that, many years ago, he chose Alexander Liholiho to be the Heir Apparent. This accident of fate, hurtful as it might be to most elder brothers, does not seem to have affronted Lot in the least.

"Come, let us sit down over here, near Lot," said the King. "Paki: do you join us also. In this way we can have the benefit of Lot's wisdom without causing him to lift either his feet or his voice." They were at ease each with the other, this uncle and his kinsmen. And, with their round heads, high cheekbones, pouting lips, their hooded eyes, they looked like each other, as all Kamehameha do, stamped with the features passed on to them by the great one who was their ancestor. But, unlike the boys, Kauikeaouli was short and stocky. And he was aging unseasonably: years of drinking and debauchery, begun in his youth and continued even now despite the pleas of his wife, the scoldings of missionaries, and his unsteady resolve, were exacting their due. I was shocked by the changes I found in him.

He waited until we were seated in a circle, each equal in place to the others, before he began. "This, I suppose, is a Council of War—without the Secretary of War."

"*Auwe!*" I was unable to hold back my surprise. "And what has happened?" I stared from one to the next, only to see them chuckling at the King's little joke and at my big worry.

"Nothing yet. That's the problem," he went on. "We do not know if there is cause for war. And we do not know who the enemy is—if, indeed, there is one. This is why we have asked you to help us, Hiram. From the beginning

Alex has said that you are the best man in the islands for us to call upon. But I did not like to disturb you in—well, in the management of your many business ventures, to ask you to go on a journey which, at the least will be tiring, at the worst may be dangerous. Until today. Now, after another talk with Mr. Wyllie, this morning before we came here to Waikiki, I am disturbed enough to accept Alex's suggestion.—I see that you are mystified by all this. Let me assure you that each of us here is equally mystified. Alex and I think that this whole business is the work of Mr. Wyllie's very active fancy. You know him well enough, I believe, to understand how inventive that fancy can be. But Lot says, 'How do you know? Go and see.' And Paki agrees with him. We ourselves can not go and see. Nor does Mr. Wyllie think we can safely send someone from our households, or from any of the government ministries. Alex thinks of you as a man we can trust. So does Mr. Wyllie. And so do I."

Oh, my goodness me! Questions rushed into my mind faster than raindrops are whipped by the winds through the pass of Nuʻuanu. With the gesture of a servant to great chiefs, I lifted my opened hands before me. Of course, they said: these hands are yours to command, as is the person to whom they belong: tell this person what he must do.

The great chief understood. "Good. I will let Alex place our burden in your hands."

"Do you remember," Alex began, "a year ago and more, when we of Honolulu lived in fear because of the filibusterers from California? How for months we waited for them to come, in many ships and with many fierce men, to seize these islands from us and to establish a government of their own?"

"Indeed, I do remember. And I remember, also, how

when they came at last, their navy was made up of only one unarmed ship. And their fierce warriors were the politest of men, who fired no guns, and who spent much good California gold in the town." Those had been fine weeks for us, the merchants and whoremasters of Honolulu, an unexpected time of prosperity in the months when the whaling ships were off at sea, and after our brisk trade with the hungry gold-miners around San Francisco had come to a quick end.

"Exactly. Most of us, like you, were much relieved by their amiable behavior. A few, I believe, were almost disappointed. Mr. Wyllie," Alex allowed himself a smile for the man at whom most of us laugh, "was one of those, I think. No chance to put on his general's uniform, to lead his soldiers in the defense of Honolulu. To die, sword in hand, a hero in a great and bloody battle for Punchbowl. —Even so, all of us were glad to see Sam Brannon, the *Gamecock*, and its polite crew sail away again."

"And I to send our militia home again," said the King. "Keeping an army is very expensive. Our treasury cannot afford more than one such extravagance."

"Especially when they don't know how to fight in the first place," said Lot.

"We are hoping that Brannon and his gang will not return," Alex resumed. "But Mr. Wyllie is afraid that they will. And perhaps he is right in this. He believes that last year only a scouting expedition came here, to spy on us, to determine where our defenses are, how many soldiers we can muster, who will be our generals. This year, he says, they will return in great force.—And, he insists, we must be prepared to defend ourselves when they arrive. And of course we must be ready. Even though we are a weak and peaceful nation, even though the burden of our defense would be very heavy, we must repel them!"

"Why do we bother?" asked Lot soberly. Slouching on the settee, his long legs resting more on its velvet cushions than on the floor, he showed none of the determination which armed the other grandson of Kamehameha the Conqueror. "If they don't take us now, then sooner or later the British will, or the French, or the Americans. Perhaps it would be better for all of us to let these free-booters seize the place. Get it over with, the whole thieving grab. Then Uncle could have his wish: to be the captain of a ship, instead of being the ruler of these hapless isles. Think of the prizes he could capture if he too became a pirate. Think how rich he would be—for a change."

Such traitorous talk horrified me, but Kauikeaouli and Alex only laughed. "Ah, come on, Lot," his brother protested, "this is serious business."

"That would be fun, perhaps—while it lasted," said His Majesty, "but I have no wish to end my days hanging from the yardarm of a frigate."

"And furthermore, brother," said Alex, "what would you and I do in this pirates' kingdom?"

"Hah!" Lot was so taken with his thought that he almost sat up. "Me, I would build a railroad. And I would so run it that pirates and Hawaiians would sit in the seats, and white folks would have to stand in the back. Like niggahs in America," he finished bitterly. With Lot you can never know where his thoughts are leading when he starts to speak. He is a dangerous man.

"That may be a good reason for you," said Alex, keeping his patience, "but it is not reason enough to give up our country without a fight.—And who can say that those filibusterers would not treat all of us like niggers?" He pronounced the word as though it dirtied his mouth.

Once again I sorrowed for them, smarting still under

the insult of that ignorant trainman in the city of Washington in the republican country of America. Two handsome young princes they were, who had been received with honors and with courtesy by great statesmen and gentlefolk in England, in France, and in the United States. And they were full of *aloha* for the people of those powerful countries until the day in Washington, when that conductor yelled at them, "Get out of here, you niggahs! This car is not for you."

We sat in embarrassment, searching for words to carry us away from this picking at sores upon the spirit. I who am an old man, a traveler of some acquaintance with the world, I longed to tell these boys that not all the world's people are as full of fear as was the conductor in Washington. Yet how could I say this, preaching like an old *kahu*, in the presence of the King? I looked to him for his wise man's counsel, but he said nothing. Worried and tired, the receiver of abuse from foreigners to a degree Alex and Lot had never known, he stroked his mustache, waiting for Alex to speak.

"No," Alex was easy again with his thoughts, "that is not the way. When we have a railroad here, in this land of the Kamehameha, all the people in it, young and old, Hawaiian and foreign, will sit in its cars wherever they please."

"Excellent!" cried this sassy Lot, "smart Alex! Grandfather gave us the Law of the Splintered Paddle. You give us the Law of the Classless Asses.—Very good!—And when that train comes, where will we sit, Uncle and you and I?"

"Why, that is easy," Alex said, grinning. "Uncle will drive the engine, you will throw wood upon the fire, and I —I will be the conductor. Then each of us will be doing what he likes best. Now come on, Lot. Stop interrupting.

Let's get on with our immediate business." Kauikeaouli smiled approvingly, I beamed like an idol in a Canton joss house.

"By all means," agreed Lot, settling back into his lazyman's position. "Let us repel the invasion."

Mindful of the King's motto, Paki growled, " '*Onipa'a*! Stand firm!"

"Kahu," Alex turned to me. "This is what we ask of you: do you ride, as would an ordinary man of the people, through Ko'olaupoko and Ko'olauloa, along the windward coast of O'ahu, from Kane'ohe in the south to Kahuku in the north. As you ride along, look about you, listen to the countryfolk you will meet. These are the questions we would like you to answer. First: do you find, in any place along that coast, evidence that someone is readying a harbor, a fort, or an encampment to receive those filibusterers from California. Look especially at these places: the inner end of the deep bay of Kane'ohe, where a whole fleet of ships could find safe harbor; the far end of that same bay, near Kualoa, where Dr. Judd bought some land three years ago; the long narrow valley of Ka'a'awa, which lies next to Kualoa; the sheltered bay of Kahana, which follows after Ka'a'awa; and, finally, at the far tip of the island, look at the plain of Kahuku, where Mr. Hopkins has his ranch.—You know this country well, I do believe?"

"Indeed, I do.—As perhaps you know, Kahana is the valley of my birth, and many times have I traveled from and to that place. But—forgive me—I am disturbed by your mention of Dr. Judd and Mr. Hopkins. These are men high in the government. Do they conspire against it?"

"You are right to ask. This is the second reason why we have sent for you. Not one small piece of evidence do we have that Dr. Judd, or Mr. Hopkins, or any other man of

O'ahu conspires against us. Even Mr. Wyllie does not really believe that these two are guilty of treason. But he receives reports from people in Ko'olaupoko about strange happenings around Kualoa and Ka'a'awa. Great fires, with much smoke, are seen often. Are these signal fires to ships at sea? Or are they merely fires set by farmers, to burn the brush from their fields? Or are they fires set by filibusterers, as they build a fort? We do not know. But because Mr. Wyllie is alarmed, we must send to find out, as Lot has said. You may wonder why we do not talk about this mystery with Kauka Judd and Mr. Hopkins. The answer is simple: to do so would be embarrassing for all concerned. If they are innocent, we would hurt their feelings with our suspicions. If they are guilty—" He, who tries not to be unkind toward anyone, left the conclusion for me to imagine.

"We are caught in the middle," said the King. "As always we are when our *haole* fight with each other.—You know, I am sure, how Mr. Wyllie and Dr. Judd are not the best of friends."

"Oh, the Secretary-at-War seeks to purge us of the Minister of Finance," Lot chanted in the manner of a *kahuna* at prayer, "but the Minister of Finance swallows much—and passes nothing, not even the bills our wily warrior submits for his ministering." We burst out laughing, for Lot's drollery summed up exactly the latest dispute in the continuing feud between the King's most powerful ministers, each exceedingly jealous for his authority and position. They reminded us of two *kahuna 'ana'ana*, each trying to blight the other with prayers, spells, and assorted kinds of black magic, when neither had *mana* enough to triumph over the other. Meanwhile, the nation watched and wondered who would be the victor: the dealer in purges of morals and bowels? or the spewer of words,

the dueler with pens and papers?—There, now: I have
said it. And I do not know whether I should be proud of
my wit or ashamed of my jingle. But let it stand. It is
better than some things which have been printed in this
town.

Once again Alex brought us back to the reason for our
meeting. I do not mean to give the impression that he is
always so serious, so humorless. But on this occasion, like
the chairman of any gabble of committeemen, he tried to
keep the attention of its members fastened upon their
business. "The one who falls most under suspicion—and
it hurts me to say this—is the American who lives at
Ka'a'awa." Shifting in his chair, he looked wryly at me.
"Do you remember Saul Bristol?" Try as I might, I could
not recall the person. "Think back, to that day—oh, about
three years ago, I guess it was, just after Lot and I returned from our trip—when you and I went fishing at
Kaka'ako."

"Of course! I remember now.—The man in the sea?"

"That is the one. He works for "Polly" Hopkins, and he
lives now at Ka'a'awa. A strange and lonely fellow. The
people there abide in fear of him, I am told, because he is
so bitter. They call him 'the angry *haole*.' He is the one
Mr. Wyllie most suspects. And he is the one we ask you to
study most closely. I can not believe that he would do
anything to harm us, but—" he shrugged, and left unspoken the question about the man for whom he had done
so much. "There: now our story is ended. Will you do this
for us?"

"I will do it. And gladly, for your sakes and the nation's.—Not for nothing, as Paki can tell you, am I called
Niele. Inquisitive I was born, and inquisitive do I live.
I will put these sharp eyes, these big ears, this glib tongue,
to your service."

"Don't forget that long, sharp nose," Lot jeered. "Something stinks about this business, and it's not only woodsmoke. You may find a *haole* in the woodpile out there."

"This is why we called you," said the King soothingly. "Your name, we know, is well founded. And so, also, is your loyalty to our family. The one without the other would not be sufficient. Together, they make of you a *kahu* not only to Alex but to all of us." These were good words to hear, they filled me with pride. But before I could enjoy the moment fully Lot spoke from his couch.

"As Wyllie would say," he began in Hawaiian, finished in an imitation of the Laird of Rosebank, "a vurrrry Machiavelli must you be."

I stared at him in confusion. He made no sense. How could I be a "fearful purpose," even to please Mr. Wyllie? Paki, my good friend, joined me in this display of ignorance: "Who is this Makia Weli?" he asked. "Is he an O'ahu man?" Lot whooped with pleasure over the success of his baiting, showing the big white teeth, the blood-red gums. I shuddered: a shark among children is he, a thing to be feared.

"Machiavelli," thoughtfully he spelled the foreign name for us, "was an Italian in the days of old. A man who knew the art of controlling men, even though they were princes and kings, and therefore of controlling nations. He wrote a book about all this. If a man wants to be a success in statecraft, this smart *kahuna* wrote, then he has to be a greater scoundrel, all the time, than are his opponents. Obviously, old man Wyllie has not read the book." He smiled engagingly upon us. "I think I am the only one in Hawai'i Nei who has read it."

"Shoot!" I said, annoyed at his smugness, furious with

his interruption of the King's praise of me. "Does a man have to read a book to learn that lesson?" For Heaven's sake, I could have told him, but I didn't, this is the first thing any businessman learns—if he wants to stay in business.

"When do you plan to leave for the other side?" Alex was asking me in one ear, while with the other I heard Lot arguing with Paki. "You're crazy," Lot was saying, "a good man who is stupid can cause much more trouble than a bad man who is smart. Look at any one of the missionaries!" "I shall go in the morning," I answered, "because, it so happens, this is a good time to be away from my office." "Your family is well? You have escaped the influenza?" This was my considerate Alex. "Just think of what's happened here in Hawai'i since grandfather died." This was the contentious Lot. Goodness gracious! My *niele* ears were flapping, trying to keep up with two conversations at once. I was suddenly weary, wanting to go home, yearning for a little glass of rum, to strengthen me for the long ride. But I did not dare to mention it. Obviously, the King being as sober as he was, Alex had forbidden the servants to bring a drop of liquor into the house. "I shall return as soon as I can. In seven days, perhaps, in ten at the most." "Very good," Alex stood up, giving me the signal for my withdrawing. "I expect we'll be back in town before then. Send me a message when you have returned, and I will arrange a meeting."

"Good luck," Lot called cheerfully, "and good hunting. If you succeed in preventing an invasion, Wyllie will make you a duke. Niele, the first Duke of Nihoa!"

"No," said His Majesty, coming to bid me farewell. "That desert island is too far away from us: it would be like a place of banishment. Hiram Nihoa will deserve better thanks than that. And we shall put our minds to this matter while you are away. I, too, give you my good wishes, Hiram."

"Remember," Lot held up a finger as long as a dagger, "Makia Weli."

Alex accompanied me to the verandah. "Take care, Kahu. There may be dangers in this mission. I hope you will meet with none." As he shook my hand he said softly, "One more thing: when you see Saul Bristol, please give him my *aloha*."

I had much to think upon, much to be pleased about, as I rode home from 'Ainahau. This time my escort and I went along the causeway to Kaka'ako, and I did not have the dangers of Mo'ili'ili's swamps to worry me. But not until I was almost home did I remember that none of those mighty Kamehameha had said what would happen to me if I should fail them in their need.

As was only to be expected, my dreams that night were filled with warnings from the spirit-world: of foreign sailors running through the town, of burning houses and thousands of dying people, of red-mouthed sharks swimming through air gray with smoke, of myself hung from a leafless tree, pierced with slender daggers made of bone . . .

CHAPTER 5.

IN WHICH A SPY, DEPARTING UPON HIS MISSION, IS ESPIED BY A MAD MAGICIAN

In the morning, while we were still lying in our high four-poster bed, I told Rebekah where I had gone the evening before and where I must journey for the King. "I thought he was the one," she said, and when I asked her how she could have known she gave me a sidelong glance from those green eyes, bright even so early in the day. "No ordinary person who sent for you—even though, like Noah Mahoe, he lay on his deathbed—could have made you so nervous. Like a flea on a sheet you were, desperate to hop away." The bed began to shake: I thought an earthquake was coming until I heard her giggling. "Besides, I read in the paper only two or three days ago that Noah Mahoe and his family have sailed on the boat to Hilo, to visit his kinsmen there. You, my dear—I have told you this before, but you do not like to believe it—you are not a very good teller of untruths."

"Oh, my," I groaned, not knowing whether to laugh or to cry over this deficiency, "may this tongue fall out of my mouth if ever I—"

"Wait a moment," she put her fingers to my lips, "a promise you can not keep is a promise you can not give.— And what would you be, I would like to know, without that much-used tongue? Certainly not the husband I know so well."

Sitting up against the pillows, she began to braid her hair. This long, thick, reddish-brown hair, which is her only vanity, was turning gray now near the temples. She was a beautiful girl when we were wed and, as I foresaw those eighteen years ago, she had become a handsome woman. As always, because I delight in their grace, I watched those nimble fingers do their work of braiding, of pinning the heavy coils into a crown upon her head. For her patience with me during our life together, I thought, for her goodness to our children, I pray that she will wear a crown in Heaven.

"You will need food and water, until you reach Ka-ne'ohe," she said, thrusting the last long hairpins into place.

Thinking of her goodness, faintly troubled still by the burden of my dreams, I wanted to give thanks here on earth. "It is a lovely sunny day," I said, looking beyond the lace curtains to the sky above Waikiki. "Why don't you and the children ride in the carriage as far as the Pali? There we can eat a lunch, before I go down the other side."

"It is a nice thought," she said as she slipped out from the bed. "The children and I would enjoy the ride. But I think we should not go. They will ask too many questions. The older boys will want to know why they cannot ride with you to Kahana. And Esther will cry when her beloved Papa goes away in that frightening place. No: it is much better for you to go by yourself this morning, just as though you were riding into town. And tonight, at supper, I shall tell them why you do not return."

"What will you tell them?"

"Only what is true. That you have gone to Kahana to visit your relatives there. Have you forgotten them?"

"Good Lord!—I have indeed. How long has it been since I have seen them? Eight—no, ten—years have passed since last I visited Kahana."

"Then the time has come when you should return."

"Mama: I have said it before, I say it again: you are a very smart woman."

"Ah, ah, ah," she lifted a plump hand, "remember that tongue," she said before disappearing into the closet to change her clothes. Twelve children has she presented me with, in the years of our marriage, yet I have never seen her body. Sometimes I think the missionaries have taught our women to behave as if they had been born fully clothed.

As she ordered my departure so was it done. After the family had taken breakfast together, the children were sent into the nearby forest, the girls to pick herbs for medicines, the boys to gather wood for the cookstove. While Rebekah and the housemaids packed my saddlebags with food and a small earthen jug of spring water, I prepared Lokelani, the most docile mare in my barn.

Being a provident man, I try to think ahead, anticipating my needs. To protect myself against the rain I borrowed Abel's Mexican poncho from its hook in the barn; to ward off the catching of a cold I fetched a bottle of French brandy from its hiding-place under the oats-bin. The one I wrapped in the other, and both I tied behind the saddle. "All right, Rose-of-Heaven, my fragrant flower," I sang to the patient beast, patting her on the muzzle, above the flaring pink nostrils which had suggested her name to my daughter Miriam, "let us be on our way." At the barn door, just as I touched the nailed-up horseshoe for good luck, I remembered something else. "Wait, my dear, wait. Papa has forgotten his money belt." That was indeed a very early stroke of good fortune. Hurrying back to the saddle-room, I felt along the beam where I hide the thing, above the hanging bridles, strips of old leather, and parted cinches, in the hope that my boys will never find it. If ever they do, I shall disclaim any knowledge of it. Needless to say, it does not hold only money.

At the house Rebekah met me with the saddlebags and a message to deliver: "If you see Eben, pull his ears for me. Tell him to leave that woman who has put a ring through his nose. Tell him to go home to his wife."

"Yes, Mama," I replied meekly, not having the least intention of delivering such a command to a man who is twice as big as I am, in every part and dimension. "But is it likely that I shall see him?"

"She is out there, wandering around the countryside like a loose cow," said my wife, who has more information than newspapers ever print, "and where she is, there he is. Do you tell him what I have told you.—And do you take care of yourself. And don't forget to come home." She gave me a farewell kiss, the parting words of a good wife: "*Ahui hou aku.* Until we meet again." At the gate I turned to wave to her, standing alone on the verandah. Sturdier than the house she seemed, and more enduring.

Lokelani wanted to go to town, but I persuaded her to follow the cart-road which cuts across the back of Punchbowl, where it meets the hillside which nowadays is called Ka Papakolea, which is to say Plover Flat. "Everything is being named anew," I grumbled aloud. Talking helps to pass the time, for one thing, and a horse, I find, is a very satisfying listener: much better than a wife, of course, considerably better than most acquaintances. Many a speech I have polished while rambling along on horseback, many a clever business arrangement I have planned. "Would you believe it, Lokelani? When first I came to live in Honolulu, this place called Ka Papakolea had another name: Kewalo it was called then. That hill called Punchbowl—there is another of those ugly *haole* names, my dear—was Pu'u-o-haina, the Hill-of-Sacrifice, where men were slain to appease the bloodlust of Ku. Right there, where the long black cannons of the fort are sticking out, where the flag pole rises up: that is where the altar stood, upon which the bodies of the dead men were laid. When I was a lad, grass grew on the slopes of the Hill-of-Sacrifice, and many trees. Behold it now: bare as a dead man's skull, as empty of life as its eye sockets. Between them, soldiers from the fort, people from the town below, have stripped it cleaner than a limpet given to ants.

When we came closer to Ka Papakolea, I saw that the wandering plovers were there in great numbers, among the weeds and the rocks, for this is the season of their visiting. "Ka'elo is the month, the plovers are fat," as the old song remembers. Where they come from, where they go, no one can say. Trappers and snarers, too, were there, seeking to catch the golden birds. Their meat is eaten by the very poor and by the rich, their feathers are used to make *lei* for commoners and foreigners, as is the fashion now that feathers are no longer reserved to the chiefs. The birds of old Hawai'i which yielded up their plumage for the chiefs: they are gone, vanished as are so many of the great chiefs who wore those gorgeous feathered cloaks and helmets, whose tall nodding *kahili* were held above them as they moved, as they sat, as they lived, and as they died. Dead they are, those chiefs, and dying, everything is changed, is changing still. And on Ka Papakolea's lowest slopes I saw the latest of these signs of change: scattered among the dry rocks and thirsting weeds, like rubbish blown by the wind, were the hovels of those *kolea* among men—the poor, the sick, the outcasts of Honolulu.

Happy to put Ka Papakolea behind us, we descended the naked backside of Pu'uohaina into the valley of Pauoa. "Divided are the mountains at Pauoa," I sang the words of the old chant, "opened like the legs of a woman ready for love. And faithful to beautiful Pauoa is Kane, generous with the water of life." The fruits of their love are the many fields of taro, watered by springs and a flowing stream, the many tall trees which cast their shade upon the houses of people who live in this cool place. Who would think, looking at Punchbowl from the sea, that this little pocket of greenness, hidden in the cleft of the mountains, lies so close to the dirty, dusty sprawl of houses which is Honolulu?

Wanting to linger, I urged Lokelani to go on. We were greeted cheerfully by farmers carrying their harvests of taro to markets in town, were scarcely noticed by woodcutters toiling with their mules toward the forests. Almost as great as the hunger of men for food is the hunger of their cooking-stoves for wood. Each year the edge of the forest moves farther away. Soon these hills, these mountainsides and ridges, will be robbed of their trees. Then the grass and the ferns will turn brown in the sun, as are the hills of California, and Honolulu will be no different to look upon than are San Pedro and San Diego. And the bounty of Kane, scouring the body of our Earth Mother, will cover the reefs with mud. Those filibusterers: alas, they are not our only enemies . . .

Beyond the far end of Pauoa's narrow mouth my path

met the wide muddy thoroughfare which we of Honolulu are pleased to call Nuʻuanu Street. At the harbor, where it begins, this street is paved with cobblestones, to help horses and oxen in the moving of freight to and from sailing vessels warped in close to the stinking beach. Long ago, before it was befouled by beasts and men, this beach was called Nihoa. Not after me or my family was it so named, but because of the marks in the sand made by the hulls of canoes and by the keels of small boats when they were drawn up on the shore. Notched and jagged, as though raked by teeth: that is the meaning of *nihoa*. But who remembers this beach now? Who cares for the past, when the rubbish of today mounts up? Who can find anymore, beneath the harbor-fort of Ke Kua Noho, the stones of Lono's temple of Pakaka? Who knows that, beneath the sail lofts and warehouses of foreigners along the waterfront, lie the sacred grounds where once the first Kamehameha dwelled? Who can see, in the black mud of Nuʻuanu's beach, the white sand whereon chiefs and chiefesses did rest when they were weary of riding the surf in the bay of Mamala, beyond the harbor of Kou?

"The marketplace," my fellow members in Honolulu's Chamber of Commerce call Nuʻuanu Street, hearing the bustle of trade, the music of gold, in the rattle of wagons across the cobblestones, in the clink of chains upon those beasts of burden. It is Hawaiʻi's treasury, this marketplace —as its mint is the whorehouses which surround it. But this Fid Street, as sailors call it, although it is paved with cobblestones, is bounded with warehouses, stores, grogshops, and brothels. It is no thing of beauty. Not for the first time I felt ashamed of the ugliness to my eyes of my grogshops and fleshpots, the ugliness to my spirit of the businesses by which I am made a man of worth. "This Ma-

kia Weli," I muttered, not wanting even Lokelani to hear,
"he is not a worthy man."

I turned my back upon that city of commerce in bodies
and in spirits, lifting my face toward the beckoning mountains. And, as often happens when I am leaving the dirty
town for the clean country, I was reminded of the fan-
tastical poem Alex (and therefore I) had to learn by rote
for an elocution exercise at the Chiefs' Children's School.
Oh, how we labored over this funny thing, which we found
in a battered old book in the schoolhouse. Oh, how everyone laughed—Mrs. Cooke most of all—while, stiff and
scared, his arms moving like pumphandles, poor Alex
tried to chant his way through this string of noises. The
laughing was so loud that he never did finish: Mr. Cooke
thanked him by letting him sit down before his time
was up.

> Fly the rank city, shun its turbid air:
> Breathe not the chaos of eternal smoke
> And volatile corruption.
> And (tho' the lungs abhor
> To drink the dun fuliginous abyss)
> Did not the acid vigor of the mine,
> Roll'd from so many thund'ring chimneys, tame
> The putrid salts that overswarm the sky;
> This caustic venom would perhaps corrode
> Those tender cells that draw the vital air,
> In vain with all their unctuous rills bedew'd;
> Or by the drunken venous tubes, that yawn
> In countless pores o'er all the pervious skin.
> Imbib'd, would poison the balsamic blood,
> And rouse the heart to every fever's rage.
> While yet you breathe, away! the rural wilds
> Invite . . .

To this day I haven't the slightest idea what most of
that stuff means. But I like to repeat it because it is so

fancy, and I remember it because it is so fine an example of the way some people can talk much and say nothing that anyone can understand.

The rural wilds invited me, while yet I breathed . . . A bridge of heavy planks covers Nuʻuanu's waters where the stream completes its curving from the Pauoa side of the valley and enters its last run, straight across the plain, along the western edge of town, to its muddy mouth in the harbor. Like the cobblestones, the bridge is not beautiful. But, unlike them, it leads up to beauty. And the people who built this bridge have found this beauty.

Halfway up the little hill which rises above the stream is the new house of Asher Bates, who is brother-in-law to Dr. Judd. And at the top of the hill is the residence of Dr. Judd himself and his family. This was the first of the big mansions in the foreign style to be raised in Honolulu. And what gossiping there was among the townsfolk, six or seven years ago, when Kauka bought this land and started to build his spacious home. The missionaries at Kawaiahaʻo were annoyed because he chose a place so far removed from them. Hawaiians were fretted because they feared his house would be bigger and fancier than Hoʻihoʻi Ea, the King's new palace down in town. Everybody wondered how Kauka could afford to build such a mansion. No one was pleased to learn that he had pledged his future to borrow the money from merchants. And, in the crowded town, where almost everyone lived with somebody else, few could understand why Kauka did such a haughty thing, even after the poor man explained that he was tired of living with other families, as he had been forced to do for almost twenty years, that now he just wanted to live with his wife and children, in peace and quiet, in a house of their own.

And there it was, on the brow of the hill, peaceful and

quiet, set far back from the road, upon a green lawn dotted with *kukui*, tamarind, and orange trees. Cows and goats grazed in a pasture beyond, chickens wandered about the yard, not a person was to be seen, not a sound could be heard. I have never cared much for the house itself. It is a little too severe for my taste, too much like a missionary's house (and, to tell the truth, much too close to the new graveyard for foreigners which has been put in next door). But it certainly is not fancier that Hoʻihoʻi Ea, which is rich with green paint and gleaming white pillars and a widow's walk upon its roof. Nor is it bigger than other mansions, such as Paki's, which have sprung up following Kauka's example. But it is a refuge where this busy man can find rest from his labors for the government.

"A sensible man is Kauka Judd," I saluted him and his dwelling as we passed the big gate with its nameplate. "Sweet Home," it reads, a reminder to others as it is to the Judds of the happy life they hope to find there. "If only people would leave them alone, Lokelani, they could be happy there. Envy it is, impurest envy mixed with malice, my dear, which makes people write letters to the newspapers. And poems, to show about in secret."

One can not ride along Nuʻuanu Street anymore without being reminded of those vicious verses which Anthony Ten Eyck wrote a few years ago. No great man was safe from his ill will, not even the King. Even now I burn with anger to remember what he said of His Majesty:

> Should a *Monkey* wear a crown,
> Must we tremble at his frown?
> Could we not, through all his ermine,
> Spy the strutting, chattering vermin?

Those verses cost Ten Eyck his position as United States Commissioner to His Majesty's court—but only after everyone in Honolulu had read them. And, I fear, they will be recounted long after Ten Eyck himself is forgotten. Like Prince Lot's judgments, some were too close to the truth to be ignored; but, like all innuendoes, they did not hold enough truth to be fair:

> Should a *Doctor* leave his shop,
> And mount a Throne in one hop?
> Could we not, in all he did,
> Spy the firm of Jalap and Fid?

No: it was not fair, this verse. A good man at heart is Doctor Judd, if somewhat overbearing at times, and exceedingly righteous. He is a man best admired from a distance, I have learned, and because I keep apart I have had no difficulties with him. Perhaps this is why I could be more charitable toward him than I was to the memory of tempestuous Tony Ten Eyck, who, like all American officials—and British and French too—gave everyone in Honolulu a lot of trouble.

"A sensible man, a sensible man, is Kauka," I warbled for Lokelani's instruction, admiring the neat yard, the rock wall already spotted with ferns and lichens, the glossy leaves of the cinnamon tree imported from Java, the rarest plant in Hawaii. "Maybe we should do what he has done, *e*, Lokelani? How would you like to live up here in cool Nu'uanu, instead of down there, in that hot and noisy place of ours on Beretania Street?" The need to spend most of my time with the young Alex in Hali'imaile, the house on Richards Street he shared with Lot, had made me establish my family nearby, on busy Beretania Street. Now—I felt again the hurt of separation that never ceased to amaze me—now, when I no longer served him as *kahu*, only habit kept me there.

Averting my gaze, I kicked Loke into a trot, speeding past the foreigners' cemetery. Too many of my friends lie there already, silent neighbors to Dr. Judd. Rather than count tombstones, I looked to the right, observing the houses of the living. Spaced out along the valley road, among the dwellings of native families, were the residences of other eminent foreigners: of Theophilus H. Davies and E. O. Hall, who were prosperous merchants, of the Reverend Artemas Bishop, a member of the second company of American missionaries who had arrived in 1823, and of many others. Two of these *haole* had not escaped the attention of tender Tony.

One of these victims was the Reverend Lorrin Andrews. Too honest to be hypocritical as a minister, he had withdrawn from the Congregational mission because it receives some of its support from people in America who own slaves. In order to keep him alive in the land he had come to love, Kauikeaouli and Dr. Judd had appointed Lorrin a judge, to assist Governor Kekuanao'a in the maintaining of law and order on O'ahu. For his striving to be honest as a man, before ever he became a judge, he drew the poet's scorn:

> Should a *Judge* put on a sack,
> Ne'er designed to fit his back?
> Could we not, through all the wool,
> Spy the Doctor at the pull?

Never was there a man who less deserved such abuse. I know Lorrin well: on many occasions he has asked me to help him with words and meanings for the dictionary of the Hawaiian language which he has been compiling for twenty years. A man who spends all his spare time writing a dictionary must be, by definition, an honest man.

But the next man on this street: hah! Now there was a beast of a different hue and cry:

> Should an *Ass* put on a skin,
> Nature ne'er designed for him?

Could we not, when he's fed highly,
Spy the fool—as well as Wily?

With this verse I found no fault. And I was reciting it, for Lokelani's amusement and my own as, just above Kapena falls, an uncordial half-mile or so beyond Dr. Judd's place, we drew near Rosebank, the house of this newcomer whom I've never been able to credit with having any sense at all.

There we were, riding happily along, minding our business, enjoying the day, when—all of a sudden, from behind Rosebank's high stone wall, came the most awful shrieks and screams I've ever heard in my life. Lokelani reared in fright, I bleated in terror. *Ghosts*! was my first thought. *Murder*! was my second. This is no place for me, was my decision. Startled from scalp to sole, I was commanding Loke to put her forefeet back on the ground and run, dammit, run, when—Blast my eyes! Out from the gate danced a crazy procession: a mad old foreign woman, followed by a mob of gleeful screaming children of all sizes and complexions. The old hag wore the shortest dress seen in Hawaii since the missionaries converted us to virtue: *indecent* it was, exposing her thin shanks to the knees. And, through one of its unfleshed legs, she was blowing her lungs' air into the carcass of an animal dead beyond all reviving.

They stopped short when they saw me, hanging for my life to Loke's mane. "Hey!" the urchins squealed, pointing and prancing about, "the horse is dancing! He likes our music!" The madwoman let fall the legbone from her lips, releasing a whole barnyardful of squawks, groans, sobs, and sighs from the dead creature clutched to her breast. I swore every oath I knew, in all the languages of land and sea, adding a few others of my own invention. The children clapped their hands and shrilled their pleasure, while Lokelani and I, like a pair of drunken clowns at a Mexican fiesta, bucked and cavorted all over the wide road. I was so furious at this insane old female and her unruly brats that I could think only of beating the wits back into her and snarling some manners back into them.

At last, when Lokelani was calmed enough, I leaped to the ground and ran back to the clutch of imbeciles. In the old days I could have hit them with sticks. Now, because we are civilized here, I could lash them only with my tongue. But even as I started it in motion, the old woman called out: "Oh, I say! Have we given ye a frrright?" By then I was close enough to see the bearded chin, the freckled balding scalp under the flat and floppy cap.

"Oh, my goodness!" I blurted, "Mr. Wyllie!" Unclenched were my fists, back into my spleen did I squeeze its rage.

"We are terrribly sorrry," he said, rolling his r's and his bright blue eyes. "We are being Scotsmen this morning and—" He waved his hands vaguely, explaining thereby the womanish skirt, the bag of hairy skin hung like a *malo*-flap before his crotch, the shapeless hat upon his head. "The children love the music of the bagpipe—" Very genteely, the thing belched forthwith, the children whooped for joy, and Hawai'i's Secretary-at-War tittered. A few feet away, with a most marvelous loudness, Lokelani pissed into the mud of Nu'uanu Street.

"Isn't it a lovely day!" exclaimed the helmsman of my country, lifting his face in rapture to the sun.

What could I do but laugh? "Indeed, a lovely day," I burbled, "a beautiful day." So must all days be to the mad man who can play so happily with children as this one does. So should this day be to me, saved from madness by the antics of a crazy man.

"Now, if you'll excuse us," he said courteously, smiling

benignly, twinkling those blue eyes, "we must get on with our ceremony. We are piping in the *poi*. It's almost time for our picnic, you know."

"Of course," I bowed in my most courtly manner, "please do not let me delay you."

"Ready, my dears?" he asked the moppets.

"Yes, yes," they twittered, a choir of hungry birds. A few of them I recognized, offspring of better families in town, foreign, half-white, and native. Others, judging by their ragged clothes and muddy feet, were poor folks' children, recruited from the neighborhood.

Clutching the bagpipe under his arm, like an old woman hoisting a sagging teat, Mr. Wyllie began to blow air into the shriveled sack. Biting my lips to keep from laughing, I was preparing to back from the presence of this mad minister. "Oh, yes," he said, interrupting the process, while the kids and I sagged in disappointment. All that air wasted, I lamented, as the sack collapsed, sighing over his neglect. "You almost forgot," he scolded himself. Turning toward the gate, he called: "Emma? Emma, my dear. Please bring the umbrella for this gentleman. I think he will have use for it."

While I protested that I did not need an umbrella, could not possibly use one on such a lovely day, such a beautiful sunny morn, he started once more to blow into that incredible instrument. Reluctantly, from beyond the stone wall where she had been hiding, Emma Rooke glided forth, bearing a furled umbrella. A beautiful young woman is she, not a child, and I could understand why she would want to hide from strangers rather than let them see her in the company of this Pied Piper. Shyly she presented the umbrella to me, quickly she fled to her shelter.

"Dear Emma," the master of music said, this time trapping the air in the bellows with his fingers upon its vents.

"She is so modest—doesn't want you to see her without shoes and—I, myself, I think it is dreadful that any one in this comfortable land should have to imprison his feet in— Yes, yes . . ."

This old fool, I thought, this idiot who has such a passion for words that he will take ten pages to write what can be conveyed in one, he can not speak a complete sentence.

"Ready, children?" While they lined up in pairs he puffed a few more breaths into the swollen bagpipe. Watching them, without looking at me, he said softly, for only me to hear, "Good day, Mr. Nihoa.—And good hunting."

Then, with a squeaking and a squealing that, to my ears, sounded more like mocking laughter than music, he and the children went off in their parade—leaving me standing in the empty road, slack of jaw, open-mouthed, the most deflated bag of wind in the entire Kingdom of Hawai'i.

CHAPTER 6.

IN WHICH AN UNNERVED SPY, WORRYING ABOUT HIS FUTURE, IS ASSAILED BY GHOSTS FROM THE PAST

After that everything went wrong. It was as though Mr. Wyllie, like a most powerful sorcerer of old, had stolen my *mana* away from me and made it captive in that leathern bag he held in the crook of his arm. "How can it be?" I enquired more than once of Lokelani, of the attending air. "How does he know me for the King's man?"

Oh, it was easy enough for me to imagine that Alex, or His Majesty, had sent a messenger to tell him that I had been chosen to perform the King's mission. After all, keeping him informed was the proper thing to do. What I could not understand was Mr. Wyllie's recognizing me. We had never met, even in as small a place as Honolulu. And, as best I could remember, he had never seen me, the one and only Hiram Nihoa. To be well known was the price he paid for his position in the King's government. But how could he know me, a nothing, a less than nothing, in the King's eyes, until yesterday?

This was not the only worry which nagged me. "Worse than the biting of mosquitoes," says a new Hawaiian proverb, "is the stinging of a guilty conscience." Sitting small and shrunken on Lokelani's broad back, like a wineskin from which all the good wine has been drained —I refuse to compare myself to an unwinded bagpipe— I remembered my uncharitable opinion of Mr. Wyllie. "This crazy *haole*" was my favorite epithet for him, as it was for so many of us who talked about the personage without knowing the man. We thought him mad because of his love for show, for costumes and ceremonies. How full of jokes we were when he stuffed small Kauikeaouli and mountainous chiefs alike into Windsor uniforms, stuck three-cornered hats upon their heads, taught them to sip tea from tiny China cups when they preferred to swig rum from coffee mugs, and instructed them in the intricacies of a quadrille. "*U-iii, ka* fancy!" we had cried in our vulgar masses, crowding around to see the show, but never admitting even to ourselves how impressed we were by the elegance, how pleased we were with the dignity which the King and his state acquired with such ceremony.

And how we had whispered, from one end of the town to the other, when this wealthy, middle-aged bachelor, newly arrived in Honolulu, showed no interest in women, whether they were chaste or purchased, or in boys, whether they were free or for hire. We thought we had him catalogued when he began to arrange those little parties for children at his new villa in Nuʻuanu. "Ah," we sniggered, raising eyebrows, smacking lips, "now we know." Among the contingents of watchful mothers and innocent children who went to the first of those parties, we placed a few knowing ones of both sexes and different ages, in order to hurry our expectations to their unnatural conclusions.

And how our tongues hung limp in our big mouths when those wise ones reported back. "No, he pinched no bottoms," said one pretty lad, "not even cheeks did he touch." A girl who works for me now in Iwilei gave us the most likely explanation: "I t'ink maybe he *pi'alu*," she declared with a pout. "How is it possible for a man so young to be impotent?" we asked, shaken with unexpected sympathy. "If it is so," we wondered, "why does he go on living?"

Founded or not, the opinion spread quickly, and he has been beyond suspicion ever since. Nowadays mothers and fathers are honored when their offspring are invited to a party at Rosebank. "Isn't it nice how fond of children Mr. Wyllie is," we gush, expressing only praise in the remark. Most of the kids, as my own have told me, are just as pleased as their parents. "We have fun there," says Daniel, my youngest one, "and many good things to eat. Not like at home." What more does a parent need to know about Mr. Wyllie?

And yet there is a mystery to this man which some of us can not fathom. He came to Honolulu a rich traveler, sailing in his own ship. After settling here, and spending great sums of money, he remains a rich man. But where does this money come from? From his business enterprises in Mexico and Chile, as he has declared? Or from the office of the Foreign Secretary in London, as his enemies maintain? He is devoted, he says, to the Kamehameha dynasty and to the independence of their Kingdom. Alex himself has told me that he believes this. And yet the man writes many long messages to the Foreign Secretary in London, and to Mr. St. Julian, that scheming republican in Sydney. Dr. Judd himself has told me this, and he should know because his clerk pays the postage for all those many fat letters Wyllie writes. Those who like him say that he is safe, at worst a harmless romantical man who thinks life in Hawai'i is a lovely masquerade at an unending children's party, at best a shrewd diplomat who plays the great powers one against the other in his unceasing labors to keep our little Kingdom out of their grasp. Those who mistrust him say that London has sent him here to seize these islands for Britain at the first opportunity, just as Lord George Paulet did ten years ago. "But this time," they warn, whispering behind the cover of lifted hands, "Beretania will not give them back to us. This time the life of the land will not be restored in righteousness."

If this is true, I was forced to conclude, then Wyllie is the greatest Machiavelli of us all. He is a spider, spinning his web from Rosebank, with its ends in Makiki, Kahana, Kahuku—even, Heaven help him, in London, Sydney, Paris, and Washington. Need I wonder, then, how he had caught me, an inquisitive little gnat, in this web of his weaving? A few minutes ago I was calling him a crazy man. Now I was struggling in the wondrous net this artful *kahuna* had put up, not knowing whether it was spun to protect me from other dangers or to strangle me.

But then—the question was inescapable, once I began to think about these things—if Wyllie is a master spy, what of that other one, what of Dr. Judd? As the Minister of Finance—and, even more important, as the virtual Prime Minister of the Kingdom—he has sent his spies all over the town, as everyone knows who ever tried to smuggle in a cask of French brandy or a hogshead of Virginia tobacco. If those informers can detect a fisherman from Kaka'ako who paddles his canoe to shore with a bottle of rum hidden beneath the nets, then surely they will know all about me and my commission from the King.

Slowly, slowly, as Lokelani and I plodded along, I

began to understand the loneliness, nay the helplessness, of a spy. And, being helpless, I began to suspect everyone. Who could have told Mr. Wyllie? Who had informed Dr. Judd? Was it Paliku of 'Ewa, that surly man? Was it the quiet guard who accompanied me home last night? Or was it some unseen pair of eyes outside my house, some unheard pair of ears listening beneath my window this morning, as, foolishly, oh, so trustingly, I talked with Rebekah?

For a frightened second I suspected even her. But "No!" I shouted at Lokelani's bobbing head, "why should she want to be rid of me?" Most uncomfortably, the reasons bubbled up in my mind why indeed she might want to order me killed, to have my body dragged into the jungle somewhere, there to be devoured by wild pigs and mountain rats, never to be seen again— "Impossible!" I bellowed in relief, "she wouldn't have had time to betray me." But who did, then? I still needed to know. Who can I trust?—Even worse! Who should I not trust? The clop of Lokelani's forefeet in Nu'uanu's mud asked me "Who?"; the sough of her hindfeet asked me "Why?" And into my anxious mind a cruel verse stole, making me wince:

> Should an *Old Fool* leave his station,
> For the sake of King and Nation?
> Could we not, despite his guise,
> Espy the spy who is not wise?

Huddled in the saddle, shivering like a man taken with the ague, I could find answers to none of these questions. When fear rose in me to the level where it was a bitterness in the mouth, I wanted to go home, to lie down in my bed. But I did not turn back. I knew even then why I did not do so. Not pride, nor a greater fear, nor trust in gods old or new, made me go on. Nor was it courage, for as I have said very little of that virtue was put into me when I was made.

Deep in thought, I scarcely noticed the countryfolk along the way, bringing their wares to market from Kaneʻohe. I had no eyes to see the beauty of Nuʻuanu's steep mountains closing in the valley at either side, no awareness of the road the army of Kamehameha the Conqueror took on its way to meet the army of Kalanikupule, when he was Oʻahu's king. Without noticing it, I went right past the place, just above Johnny Lewis' big white house Hanaikamalama, where the valley widens again after having been narrow for a while. There, at Puʻiwa, Kalanikupule's waiting warriors were startled to hear the thunder of Kamehameha's cannons, beginning the battle of Nuʻuanu. They were so astonished that, ever since the fatal day, the very name of Puʻiwa reminds us of their surprise.

But never, since I was a boy, have I passed Laʻimi without fear, without seeming to hear the shouting of warriors in the heat of battle, the cries of victory as Kamehameha's hundreds broke the lines of Kalanikupule's scores of men, the wailing of Oʻahu's women as their husbands, sons, brothers, lovers, wavered and broke and fell or fled. Terrible was the slaughter, dreadful was *la ʻimi*, the day of searching, as the victors hunted down the vanquished, on the field of battle or in the forests upon Nuʻuanu's ridges and peaks, to slay them or to take them prisoners for sacrifice in the temples of Kukaʻilimoku, Kamehameha's feathered god of war. Drenched was the earth with blood, as with rain; and loud with the groans of wandering spirits is the air of Laʻimi to this day.

I have heard them before, these ghostly shouts, these screams and groans and sighs of the unburied dead. I heard them again on this day of my journeying—at the

very wall of stones where Ka'iana 'Ahu'ula was slain.
This great and handsome chief of Kaua'i, people are told
today, he who had been Kamehameha's ally in the conquest of Hawai'i, Maui, and Moloka'i, was driven by
vanity and ambition to betray his lord while the Invader's
fleet was crossing from Moloka'i to O'ahu. In the wave-
roughened channel, Ka'iana and his warriors turned their
canoes upon another course, and went over to the side of
Kalanikupule. For this treachery, it is said, Kamehameha
ordered his men to kill Ka'iana upon sight, wherever they
might find him.

They found him in this valley of Nu'uanu, in the midst
of his warriors, fighting for O'ahu's king. Wearing his
long cloak of yellow feathers and his towering feathered
helmet, Ka'iana was the target of many spears, of uncounted stones hurled from slings. But they could not
touch him. A cannonball, fired from a gun aimed by John
Young and Isaac Davis, those first foreigners to work for
Kamehameha, did what the weapons of old could not do.
That cannonball hit the top of the stone wall behind which
Ka'iana stood directing his soldiers, and splinters of rock
killed him together with many of his men. When they died
O'ahu's warriors lost heart: they were routed, and they
were destroyed.

"Such is the fate of traitors," say the righteous historians of the Kamehameha family. "Do you not believe
them," said my grandfather to me in secret, when first he
took me to La'imi. "Ka'iana was no traitor to us of O'ahu.
Loyal was he, to Kalanikupule his kinsman, loyal unto
death. And for his loyalty to us, and to a cause he knew
was foredoomed, do we of O'ahu honor him." Since the
day I heard this account from my grandfather I have done
two things: I have questioned the words of historians with
a fierce doubt; and whenever I pass it I pause at the stone

wall where Ka'iana died to say a little prayer in memory of him.

But how could Lokelani know this hidden loyalty of mine? She had not carried me this way before. And I, not noticing where we were, I had not bade her to stop. Yet there, by the side of the road near the stone wall, she stopped.

And there I heard the groaning, the sighing . . .

The hair on my head stood up like the feathered crest of a helmet. The breath was squeezed from my lungs by a heart suddenly grown big. "Run, Loke, run," I begged. She would not move, the stupid beast. I lashed her with the reins, she nibbled at the tender grass. I swore, I kicked, I slapped her. Still she would not budge. In desperation I pulled out Mr. Wyllie's umbrella and whacked her across the rump. With a yelp of pained surprise, she ran.

But before we left that haunted place these old eyes had time enough to see, rising up above the bushes beyond the wall, a startled naked girl and her naked lover, very much annoyed.

CHAPTER 7.

IN WHICH A RECRUITED HERO RESOLVES TO STAND FIRM

Rose-of-Heaven ran swiftly, once she started. Even so, I flogged her with the umbrella—because I was mad at her, at the lovers in the bushes, at everyone in the whole wide world. A man must always have something to flog or to kick when he has been both frightened and fooled.

"—Damned Wyllie!" I swore, "how the hell did I ever get involved in that crazyman's mess? Damned kids! The missionaries are right: the only thing us *kanaka* can think about is the pleasures of love. Morning, noon, and night, any hour in between, love, love, love. In the bed, on the ground, in the sea, up in the trees. Every woman a whore, every man a boar. Not even the haunted places, the sacred places, are safe from our lusting . . ."

By the time I worked this out of my system I arrived at the only possible verdict for a *kanaka* who most definitely is not a missionary. "Lucky Hawaiians," I grinned, "Stand firm!" I said, raising the umbrella in salute. The words of the old love song came to my lips: "This is the way things should be, wouldn't you say?" Whereupon the world and most of the people in it were set aright again. And, like that mad Spanish knight journeying on his quest, I trotted along on mine, with such brilliant thoughts in my brain and a furled umbrella for a lance.

So, of course, before we had gone a dozen paces farther Lokelani cast a shoe. We had to limp along for more than a mile until, in one of those miserable run-down farms along the way, I found a country man who would bother to trouble himself to nail the shoe in place. He was a huge and mean-looking fellow, shaped like the trunk of a tree, and made as hard. Not a word did he say when he listened to my request or while he did the work. I thought he must be deaf and dumb. But he had words enough when, the simple job being finished, he led Lokelani to me. "Two dollars," he said with utmost clarity, holding out a hand bigger than two of Loke's hooves. One look at that hand and the screams died in my throat. I paid. "Cheap nails," he sneered. Feeling dreadfully ashamed of the cheap city nails holding her other three shoes upon those dainty feet, Loke and I slunk away.

This eloquent man who knows the value of a dollar commits his robberies near Luakaha, where the King has a country retreat. At Luakaha, Lono-of-the-Clouds decided to give his burden of water over to Kane. These two gods were exceedingly provident that day to dwellers in Nu'uanu, and very playful with travelers. First the rain fell in torrents, as though the sharp peaks of Lanihuli were tearing open the floor of heaven, to let out all the water Lono was storing there. Then, when the road was so filled that it seemed to be a muddy stream in flood, and trees and shrubs and grasses were bent under the weight of raindrops, Lono would stop up the leaks, his clouds would drift down the valley, Kane's sun would shine, and everything was as before—only muddier and wetter. After ten minutes or so, their game would begin again, the rainbow would give its warning, the rain would pour down as it must have during Noah's flood, the shallow stream of Nuʻuanu Street would flow, and Lokelani and I would be in misery for a while. Abel's poncho and Mr. Wyllie's umbrella gave little service. We were wet to the hide, as if we had gone swimming together in one of Nuʻuanu's many pools. When the sun came out we steamed like sodden garments hung above a hot stove. Only frequent applications of brandy, administered internally, saved me from taking a cold.

Yet I did not complain. I rode like a man enchanted, seeing my world anew, as though I ventured into it after a long time of being blind. That was the morning when I understood at last how beautiful is a fall of rain, and how great a mystery. This veil of softness, woven of mist and air, yet louder in its advance than the roaring of cannons: how can I describe it, as it swept down the slope of Nuʻuanu from the heights above? How can I describe the numbers of raindrops, floating, shifting, sinking, rising, soaring, shining, like birds on the wing, like fish in the sea, each drop a thing alive, a separate thing, a thing apart and yet a part of the whole? Pierced to the liver I was, as I saw their grace while yet they soared, not ready to fall, as I saw the willingness with which they made their swift plunge to earth as the moment arrived when separateness must end. "Ah, ah," I cried, joyful in the revelation, "they are like people!" For is not each of us a thing apart, clinging to life, unwilling to fall into death, not knowing that, in dying, each will begin a new life—just as, in dying, each drop of rain begins a new life, in the earth into which it sinks, in the streams, in the sea, in the plant or in the animal which drinks it up?

Toward midday Lono and Kane tired of their sport: the clouds disappeared, the sun shone in splendor upon Nu-ʻuanu. On either side, in all the little ravines which score the proud cliffs of Lanihuli on the left, of Konahuanui on the right, waterfalls poured down, hundreds of them, like ribbons of soft white *kapa* adorning the green *pali*. But almost above us, on the flank of Lanihuli, the flowing water could not fall: up it went, up into the air, blown by strong winds rushing through the pass of Nuʻuanu.

I grew soft with love for this island of my birth. "Praise God," I said. "Praise God from Whom all blessings flow," I sang, standing up in the stirrups to make my homage the more seemly. My, how I like that grand music! I sang it over again, in the Hawaiian translation Hiram Bingham made when he first came to Honolulu, and then, because the older gods were near—after all, did they not live in these blessed isles long before Bingham and Jehovah came?—I praised them too with a verse in our native tongue:

> *Hoʻonani i na Akua mau,*
> *i Kane, Ku, ame Lono no,*
> *na Akua mau—hoʻomaikaʻi pu,*
> *ko keia ao, ke kela ao.*

Strong was the spirit, but weaker grew the flesh: in the presence of beauty, the belly still growls with emptiness. Knowing how gusty the wind would be at the pass, I stopped about a quarter of a mile below it, turning off to a grove of *hau* trees a few yards removed from the road. After easing the bit out of Lokelani's mouth, to let her graze in the damp grass, I ate the good things Rebekah had prepared for me. Because the ground was wet, I sat like a monkey in the tangled branches, all mixed up with themselves in their eagerness to grow. One branch was my seat, another the table, a third my footrest. All the others overhead were canopy against wind and sun. Upon the table I laid the bowl of soured *poi*, the dried squid, steamed fish, green onions, the red salt.

Auwe noho'i e! What else does a man need to make him content with his lot? Only a sleeping-mat, or a sailor's hammock, would have made perfect my resting-place. Yet, as I learned long ago, a traveler must make shift with whatever he finds along the way. In that *hau* tree, with its branches going off in all directions, a whole forest growing out of a single root, I did not have to seek at all before I found one suitable for my rump to rest upon, others for head, shoulders, and legs. I settled in place. I slept.

After a good nap, to let the heat of the liver consume the meal I had eaten, turning it into solid flesh and firm bone and coursing red blood, I awoke refreshed. The sun stood high in its heaven, birds sang, Lokelani dozed. Swinging down from the tree, I carefully gathered up the uneaten portions of my meal, the leaves used as napkins, the pieces of newspaper in which Rebekah had wrapped the foods, and went off with them into the bushes far away from the road. There, while uttering a prayer of apology to the great gods, the lesser gods, and especially to the little gods who live in the neighborhood, I buried in a hole dug with a fallen twig the wastes from my table and those coarser ventings from myself. The gods and the spirits of Nu'uanu, I could honestly claim, would not be offended by my brief stay among them. Nor could a *kahuna 'ana'ana* who wished to do me harm find those portions of me to use as bait for the ghosts and evil spirits he might command to attack me.

After covering this cat-hole with dead leaves and mossy stones, I washed my hands in little pools of rainwater. Cleansed within and without, I was almost ready to depart. Only one more thing was needed to protect me against the dangers of the Pali. This time I placed the potent *ki* leaf where it should be worn. Other leaves I plucked as offerings to Kaneholopali, the guardian god of the pass, and put them in a pocket of my jacket.

"OK, Lokelani, OK," I sang, using this new expression without which Americans can not possibly talk these days. What it stands for, where it comes from, they do not know, but they chant it incessantly, in every imaginable situation, as though they invoked some primitive god whose name they have reduced to these magical letters. Most Americans, I have noticed, know almost nothing about the history of their country. Some do not even remember the names of their grandfathers. I thought they were making fun of me when they told me this, but they persuaded me that they spoke the truth. Yet they refused to believe that I spoke the truth when I told them that I know the names of my ancestors for eighty generations.

"OK, my dear, OK. Time for us to go," I said, rubbing her nose, thinking to wake her gently before I slipped the bit into place. She did not lift an eyelid. She does not understand American very well, I am afraid, being a young and sheltered mare. So I entreated her in the words of a Hawaiian father's song to his child: "Enough, enough, O my beloved child. Sleep is ended. Wake, it is light, it is bright." And lo, she was awake.

We were in good spirits, we two, when we returned to the road, to climb the last gentle slope to the Pali of Nu'uanu. Behind us were the mishaps of the morning, ahead were the hopes of a shining afternoon. In my liver my harried spirit rested at ease once more. I could laugh at the frights of the morning, certain that they would not come again. "You imagine troubles too easily, my friend," I scolded me. "Aye," I defended myself, "so it has always been with me. This comes from knowing too much. From knowing the lore of ancient times as well as the ways of the new times. From traveling too much in a world too full of troubles. From reading too much in those newspapers and books the foreigners have brought among us."

This, indeed, is a weakness, a vice which I hide from my friends. A room in my house on Beretania Street (but not at my office in town) is full of books from England and America. I have read all of them, and I hunger for more. As some men spend money on whiskeys and wines, or upon fine furniture, so do I spend money on books. "But no more!" I vowed for the gods to hear. No, I did not mean that I would read no more books. I can not live without them. I meant that no more would I let this imagination of mine throw me into fear and confusion. From this moment I would stand firm, making the King's motto my very own, using the brain the gods and my ancestors have given me to keep myself from falling into trouble. Proud of my resolve, I sat straight again in the saddle, eager to continue my journey for the King.

We were halfway up the slope when, from behind us, came the shouting and yelling of many men. Turning to see who made these noises, I saw, far down the road, the dark shapes of a whole troop of horsemen riding furiously toward me. *Auwe, auwe!* I shuddered, they are coming for me! The new resolve, the decision to stand firm: it sped into the air with my first breath. Fear was couched in my bowels, more devouring than worms. I wanted to run away, to hide. But where could I go? On that treeless, shrubless hill there was no place to hide.

The earth shook with the pounding of hooves, the air crackled with shouts of triumph. "There he is!" they yelled, "Get him! Beat him!" Slumping in the saddle, I waited for them to fling themselves upon me, to drag me down into the mud, to kill me. "Alas for this raindrop," I sobbed, "now is its time to fall . . ."

Lashing their mounts, shrieking with bloodlust, they charged up the hill like savage Indians attacking a lone plainsman. At the last instant, just before they were upon me, Lokelani backed featly to the side of the road. Whooping, shouting, swearing, their mounts flecked with mud and foam, their bodies and clothes spattered with mud from head to foot, the mad Jehus swept right past me, up to the brink of the Pali. Borne on the wind, their laughter came back to me, where I sat small and still.

But the gods were kind: no one else was near to see my shame.

CHAPTER 8.

IN WHICH A HISTORIAN, UPON HEARING THE AUTHENTIC VOICE OF THE PRESENT, ADJURES IT TO HEED THE VOICE OF THE PAST

When I reached the narrow open space which is the pass across the Ko'olau mountains, those boisterous fellows were swarming all over the place. Some stood on the very edge of the cliff, peering into its depths, others threw pebbles into the abyss, or scratched their names upon the softer rocks of the mountain. A few were leaning backwards against the pushing wind, their clothes bellying like sails in a spanking breeze. One muscular chap was trying to push from its place the great upright stone which is the manifestation of Kaneholopali, the god who decides whether travelers over Nu'uanu's mighty precipice will live or die. No one paid any attention to me.

I dismounted and tied Lokelani next to the other horses at the hitching rail. This rail is another evidence of *haole* shrewdness. No Hawaiian would have thought to put such a thing there, or in any public place for that matter. But one of our Yankee businessmen in Honolulu has done it.

Still visible on its face, among the names and initials carved into the wood by scores of visitors, was a painted sign: FOR THIS CONVENIENCE, THANK MATTHEW BRADY AT THE FLYING FISH.

"Well, I declare!" I moved instinctively to whisk Loke away from a service offered by one of my competitors. "But wait a moment! This Flying Fish . . . " Straight from my spirit-guardian the thought came: this Matthew Brady is a smart man, from whom I may learn a thing or two. When I return to town I shall go to thank him at the Flying Fish—with my eyes opened wide. Whereupon I permitted Loke to be his guest.

The energetic lads were Americans, sailors off some ship in Honolulu, who were out seeing the sights of Oʻahu. I have always felt a great liking for Americans, having sailed with many of them aboard their merchant ships and spent much of my shore-time in their strange and fascinating country.

It is full of interesting things, great cities, enormous buildings, fantastic machines to do the work of many men. But what I liked best about America was its rivers, wide and deep, cold and clean and strong, flowing silently to the sea. What an immense country it is, that can make rivers so broad and so mighty! Even so, it was an alien land to me. I could not feel at home there, where the plants, the animals, even the grasses in their fields, are different from those of Hawaiʻi Nei. Only the kindness of the people made me stay among them as long as I did. Yet always the heart yearned for home: foreigners wander, but natives return. This native is glad that he came home again.

Those young men at the Pali were no different from other Americans I have known. They were so eager and lively and good-humored—and I do not except that foolish one grappling and straining with the rock of Kane. He was not the first, nor will he be the last, to try the impossible task of moving that immovable image. Muddy though they were, smelling of sweat, they were clean inside, as I could tell from their laughter and from their behavior when finally they noticed me. "Afternoon, sir," they said, every one. A few, with shy grins, added a considerate "*Alo'a*." To each I responded with smiles and a crisp "*Aloha ia 'oe*." I liked those lads, some no older than is Abel, my firstborn son.

But I could not make my offering to Kaneholopali while they swirled about, like leaves caught up by the wind. Think of what their folks at home would say if these boys told about the old *kanaka* they'd seen at "the Pally" making a heathen sacrifice in this Christian land! Rather than give scandal to such innocents, I decided to wait until they had gone. And, remembering how, except in schoolrooms, young people are embarrassed by the presence of the old, I kept apart from them as best I could.

Standing a body's length away from the precipice, respecting it most carefully because I know how sheer the cliff is, how far below the bottom lies, I was holding the *lauhala* hat upon my head with one hand, clutching my jacket with the other, looking out upon the awesome scene. I was *makaleha*, as we say: gazing with eyebrows raised in astonishment at such beauty. Never, even after all the times I have seen it, does this place fail to humble me, to make me marvel that the earth, the sky, and the sea can meet in such grandness. Silence, I believe, the silence of prayer, is the only manner in which a visitor can show his respect for such a gift. In a silence of my own, unbroken by the rush of the wind or the shouts of the sailorboys, I stood like a pilgrim in a holy place, offering up my tribute to the beauty beyond.

On either side the great cliffs rise to their jagged peaks. To the left, a rampart of mountains thousands of feet high, green with mosses and ferns, they stand up in pride as far as the eye can see. To the right—black, gray, brown, red, green—they form the massive body of Konahuanui, whose summit is the highest point in this long lofty range of the Koʻolau. Clouds and mist swoop up over the mountain wall, like waves in the sea rising to break. The strong winds, which ruffle the hair of people and pull upon their clothes, have bent ferns and shrubs to their will. Below, stretching from the feet of the cliffs to the fringing sea, is the green plain of Kaneʻohe. Blue, deep blue, is the plain of the sea. And, far in the distance, thrusting into the ocean from the body of Oʻahu, is the fantastic, the unbelievable, the impossible ridge of Kanehoalani. Like painted scenery upon a stage it seems, the work of an artist's brush upon the canvas of the sky, put there to fool the eye into thinking that it sees the handiwork of man, not the glory of the gods.

Forth from my love, sudden as a cloud forming in a clear sky, came a poem, a song of joy:

> Fair, fair indeed, is Oʻahu,
> And green, cool green, is the color of my land,
>   this island beloved of the sun,
>   this land which holds my heart . . .

"Is this the place where that Kammy-hayma-hayma —or whatever his name was—fought that big battle?" Shouted above the wind, the sailor's question broke in upon my *mele-aloha* for Oʻahu.

"Yeh, yeh. Right o'heah," the answer came, in the unmistakable accents of a local boy. "Heem an' hees sojahs: dey wen' poosh 'um ovah da Pali. W'en dey all dead, Kamehameha he da boss."

Too curious to resist, I turned to examine this learned guide. He was one of those waterfront lads whom the livery stables will send along with a group of visitors and their rented horses, to make sure that the horses come home again. Very young, eager to please, this one was decorated with the usual white teeth, flirting eyes, waving arms, and dirt. I know his kind very well. In a few years he would be pale and balding and running to fat, from too much hanging around grogshops and whorehouses. Diseased he would be, of course, and none too clean. But now he was at the beginning of his career, an apprentice in everything, a master of nothing, not even of lies.

"Gosh," said the sailor, looking warily at the brink of the cliff. "That ain't no way to fight a battle.—How far did those soldiers fall?"

"I dunno. About one mile, I guess."

"And how many soldiers were killed, do you s'pose?" asked another.

"Oh, t'ousands, t'ousands of 'um," the fountain of knowledge assured his audience. "Get plenny bones down dea," he waved a grimy hand in the direction of Kane'ohe. "All pile' up on top each uddah. Like one mountain, al- mos'... An' dis Kamehameha: you know w'at he wen' do, w'en da battle all feenish?" Cunningly he looked from one to the other of his charges, teasing their interest. "He wen' peeck up da keeng of dees islan'—I fohget hees name—an' he wen' t'row da buggah right ovah da cleef too, ontop all da res'." Cackling like a clown, slapping his knee, the boy did not seem to know the meaning of death.

But one of the sailors knew, a tall gaunt fellow: he closed his eyes, turned his back upon the void. "When did all this happen? How many years ago?" the first sailor asked.

"Oh, long time a'ready. I dunno. One hundred, coupla hundred yeahs, maybe. Befoah my time."

This was too much! "Gonfon it!" I swore in waterfront language the guide was certain to understand. Forgetting my determination to keep out of their way, forgetting even my respect for the place, I pushed into the startled group, shaking my finger under the stableboy's nose. Because my anger was reserved for him I spoke in Hawaiian: "You stupid fish-head, you! You son of a son of a mud-shrimp, you! May you eat moths for meat. May your flesh crawl with maggots while you live. May your bones rot longer than the bones of all the warriors of O'ahu who were slain in battle."

"*Auwe, auwe!*" the poor fellow wailed. He did not know much English, but he knew Hawaiian well enough to recognize a *kahuna*'s curses. "And what have I done, that you should be so angry with me?"

"You tell lies!" I snarled, baring my sharp teeth. "You who know nothing about the olden times, you stand here and talk like a schoolmaster full of learning. If you do not know the truth about the old days, why do you not learn it? Then you could tell these strangers the facts, instead of filling them with fables." Oh, my, I was mad! Had he not been so greasy I would have slapped his giddy head.

"Aw, grandfather," he started to defend himself.

"What's the old guy got his wind up for?" a sailor asked.

Neither of us had time to answer him. "Aw, *kuku*," the apprentice pimp entreated, "where would I learn these things? Who could tell me about the olden days? No one knows about them anymore, they happened so long ago."

"Here again you talk nonsense! Is fifty-eight years such a long time, even to you? Many a man who remembers the battle of Nu'uanu still lives today in Honolulu."

"Only fifty-eight years?" Eyes popping, he stared at me as if I were the teller of lies. "Is that all?"

"Aye, that is all. And he could tell you that the battle was fought not here but near La'imi—"

"La'imi? That place!—My goodness! That is near where I live, where my own grandfather lives."

A husky, red-haired, freckled seaman, the kind who loves to start fights, tugged at the boy's arm. "What's he fussing about? You need help?"

"Nah, nah, dass OK.—We oney talking. About da olden days."

"He sure sounds wrought up," said Red, not at all convinced.

"You have a grandfather who lives near La'imi," I continued, not ready to let my victim escape. "And you do not ask him about the old days?" My anger was waning, I was beginning to enjoy this chance to save a thoughtless youth from ignorance.

"No. Who can talk to an old man?"

Back surged my anger. It is always the way. The old have the wisdom, the young have the fun, and neither can share these prizes with the other. "God damn it, boy!" I shouted in the clearest of American, waving my hands in exasperation. Off flew my hat, out flapped my coattails, in jumped Red.

"Hey! This old buck giving you trouble? Maybe we should throw him over the cliff too?"

Pretending not to understand, I drew myself up, pointed a commanding finger toward the road to Honolulu. "Then do you go back to the town," I instructed the unhappy boy. "But do not spend all your time hanging around grogshops, drinking wine and pimping for harlots. Ask your grandfather, ask any old man, to tell you about the olden days. Hear from them that no warrior of Oʻahu was pushed over the Pali—but that, indeed, perhaps thirty or forty chose to jump from this place out of loyalty to their King. That perhaps as many others, trapped here on the cliffs, chose to jump because they did not want to be captured for sacrifice to Kukaʻilimoku.''

"Come on, let's get outta here," said Red. "Can't make head nor tail outta all this heathen gabble."

"Naw, let 'em finish," said the pale thin one. "Sound's like the old man's gotta get something off his mind."

Sharp as a teacher's stick, my finger pointed now at the stableboy. "And learn how that same King—Kalanikupule was his name: remember it!—escaped with his wife from Kamehameha's soldiers, by climbing up the side of Lanihuli.—You know which one is Lanihuli? That one, that highest one right up there.—And learn how they hid for eleven months in these mountains of Koʻolaupoko. How they were hunted down and were captured at Waipiʻo near ʻAiea in ʻEwa. And how, at the end, they were offered in sacrifice upon the altar of Kukaʻilimoku in his temple at Moanalua." He listened to every word, interested beyond any doubt in what I was telling him. He was not such a stupid fellow after all. It was the moment for me to end with a moral my torment of his unused mind. "If the young do not ask the old about the ancient times, how will the young ever learn about the things of which they should be proud?"

"You are right, grandfather," he said meekly. "I will do as you say." Raising his head, he looked beyond me to the heights of Lanihuli, to the distant jagged mountains where Kalanikupule had fled. "I did not know," he said,

"I did not know." The sailors looked up too, but they did not see what he was seeing.

"OK, you guys," he cried, "time foh go. Getting late."

"What did the old guy say?" they wanted to know as they walked away. "What's he so mad about?"

"I tell you bimeby," the lad tried to hush them. "He's one *kahuna*, I t'ink."

They must have been impressed. As they clattered off, some called "*Aloha*," others lifted a couple of fingers in farewell.

Until they were gone from sight I stood straight and grim, as I imagined they would want a *kahuna* to stand. My mind was enjoying the drama of the moment, my vanity was hoping that the light at my back showed me to be the mysterious and fierce survivor of ancient times whom they would remember for the rest of their lives. But deep within me my heart was sore with the knowledge that few people are left who know about the olden days, and that even fewer care.

CHAPTER 9.

IN WHICH A FEARFUL PILGRIM DESCENDS INTO THE VALLEY OF THE SHADOW

At the feet of Kaneholopali I placed my offering: a *ki* leaf, a *hau* leaf, a *kukui* leaf, brought from my resting-place, the three weighted down by a single stone. Other sacrifices had been laid there before mine, others would follow in time. To this visible tribute I added a brief prayer, asking the protection of all the gods, great and small, and most especially of the flying fish, who is my own family's totem-spirit. Knowing what was to come, and that I must help the gods to assist me, I removed boots and stockings and rolled up the legs of my trousers. A *malo* would have been more practical, of course, but, in common with most citified Hawaiians who fear the missionaries, I wear the "indecent loincloth" only in the privacy of my country houses. Then I was ready to make the perilous descent.

This trail down the windward side of Konahuanui is older than the memory of man. Some say that the gods hewed it out of the mountain, as a gift to puny mortals. Others say that the *menehune* made it, those small, strong, dark people who lived in these islands long before the ancestors of our race came with Hawai'i-loa from Kahiki-across-the-Sea. Perhaps they did, or perhaps our people made it, but I do not think the gods can be held responsible for such a poor job. What they do they do well, I have found. People are the ones who make mistakes.

Until foreigners brought us horses, mules, and oxen as beasts-of-burden, this was only a narrow footpath for chiefs and commoners to walk upon. Today it is a little bit wider in certain places, for the sake of those pack-animals the foreigners have taught us how to use. The widening of the way was a thank-offering from some American missionaries who were going to Oregon a few years ago, to bring word of Jehovah to the Indians of that cold country. While they waited in Honolulu for their ship to be readied, those good men spent their time trying to improve the Pali trail. Even so, it is still a narrow and dangerous path, where only the sure-footed among men or beasts may go. No wagon or carriage will ever be drawn down the face of this tremendous cliff.

In its steeper places the path is paved with stones. From around many of these the mud has been washed away by rains. Some of the bigger rocks are fixed in place, a part of the mountain. Most are loose and slippery, quick to roll out from under the careless step. A man who misses his footing, a beast which stumbles, unless he falls against the wall of the mountain, will plunge over the edge of the trail to certain death below. The bones of Kalanikupule's warriors are not the only ones which lie mouldering at the bottom of Nu'uanu's *pali*.

For the first mile of the way, where the trail is highest and narrowest, I did not ride. No one rides there. Clinging to the mountain with fingers and toes and eyelashes, never looking up from the stony path, I crept along, with Lokelani following behind. Whenever rocks and boulders, loosened by wind and rain, rolled down from the slopes above, I crouched against the mountain wall until, many seconds later, they crashed into treetops far below. I did not mind these falling rocks, because I knew they would hurtle over me, but I dreaded the landslides they might start, the quick silent rush of mud and dirt which could bury me where I knelt. This is the manner of dying I fear the most. Death itself I do not fear so much. But the manner of dying—ahh, the thought of this is what makes me so cautious a man.

At long last we came to the spot where the precipice ends, where Konahuanui's sides slope more gently, the path becomes wide, the dangers cease. While Loke cropped grass and leaves, I sat for a while, breathing deep again, easing the trembling in my legs. Only later did I have time to look out over the land to the sharp points of Olomana, as jagged as a broken back-tooth, to the marching cliffs that join Konahuanui with the steep-sided mountains of Maunawili and Waimanalo which end in the sea at distant Makapu'u, to the peaks and pinnacles above Kane'ohe which join Lanihuli to the long backbone of O'ahu. Up above me travelers were gathering at the pass, preparing to make their way down the trail, some as carefully as I, others perhaps more swiftly. These were the people of Kane'ohe, coming home from market in Honolulu. They make this journey two or three times a week, and for them it can hold few terrors.

Almost at the foot of the trail, where a ruffle of hills joins Konahuanui to Kane'ohe's plain, the path crosses a little ravine which carries off the water flowing down from the mountain. There, since before the days of my youth, a grass house with a small *lanai* has been perched upon a little ledge beside the singing stream. Although it is not halfway to any place, whether up, down, or across, everyone calls it "Halfway House." And, although it is not an inn, every passerby stops there to rest, to sip a drink of water from the cold stream, to barter one thing for another, or simply to gossip with other wayfarers or with members of the family who dwell in this convenient place. Long ago, when I went more frequently to and from Kahana, the head of this household was a fine-looking man of some learning, who had an excellent reputation as a physician. Travelers paid for his medicines or thanked him for his hospitality by leaving a sweet potato or a taro root, a small fish perhaps, or a dab of *poi*, a bit of this or a bit of that, sometimes even a small foreign coin put quietly into a cracked calabash hung in a net on the *lanai*.

Because I have pleasant memories of the place—many a young fellow has met an agreeable Kaneʻohe girl there, and I am no exception—I looked forward to stopping for a while at Halfway House, to wash the mud from my hands and feet in the stream and, while they were drying, to sip a cup of *koʻokoʻolau* tea with the physician, if he still lived.

I was dismayed when I saw the place. The house sagged with age and rot, its grass thatch was black with mildew, no longer able to shed the rain. Only the posts of the *lanai* stood up, dead man's fingers pointing to the sky. Weeds and ferns grew thick upon the stone platform where travelers used to sit. A dead house it was, abandoned—

But no: someone lived there still. A thin and naked boy, six or seven years old perhaps, stood before the door of the ruined house, staring at me with suspicion. "Hello," I called cheerfully, as Loke bore me across the stream, "and where is everyone?" For answer he reached behind and pulled forth a heavy stick. With my friendliest smile I asked: "May I rest here for a while? I wish to wash my—" Unsmiling, he pointed with the stick to the pool farthest away from the house. "Thank you, boy, thank you," I said, "you are very kind." He was too young to hear the sourness in my voice.

When I was clean and booted again, ready to depart, he was still guarding the forlorn place. Already I had put one foot in its stirrup when the thought came to me. I do not know why it arrived so slowly. Perhaps I was weary, or too disapproving of that unfriendly boy, to listen any sooner to the message from my *'aumakua*. "Help him," it commanded me, "this is a household in trouble." But the messages of spirit-guardians, I have learned, are not always easy to distinguish from the fancies of my own mind. This one, I cautioned myself, must be tested. Leaving Lokelani, I walked toward the boy. "Do you have something to eat?" I called to him, above the babble of the stream. "I am hungry," I was going to continue, but he gave me no chance to say it. Suspicion gave way to rage. He burst into tears, threw the stick at me, and fled into the house. Now I knew.

I ran up the path to the door of the hut. "Boy! Come here!—I want to talk with you. I will do you no harm." He did not come out, but even above the stream's noise I could hear his wailing. Bending low, I entered through the opening into the darkness within. When my eyes could see again in the dim light they found him. Choking back his tears, he stood in a far corner, beside a pile of sleeping-mats. Warily I moved toward him, watching him with one eye, peering at the bed with the other. Under a sheet of tattered *kapa* lay the swollen corpse of an old woman. I did not need to look twice to see that she was dead. "*Auwe, auwe*," I said, kneeling before the lad, taking him into my arms to comfort him. He put his head upon my shoulder and wept. The hot tears fell upon my heart. I held him close, murmuring "Cry, boy, cry. Tears will wash away the sorrow." Out of the same little holes in the corners of the eyes through which the spirit escapes from the body issue the tears which cleanse the living of grief.

While the boy clung to me I saw another body lying on mats at the far end of the house. But—I stiffened in horror—this one's eyes were open: gleaming in the half-light, they were watching me. Carrying the boy in my arms, I forced myself to approach that second bed. An old man lay upon it, very close to death. Unbelievably thin he was, little more than a bundle of bones held together by wrinkled skin. From him, too, came the smell of death, the stink of excrement, of unwashed rotting flesh.

"Take him," he whispered as I knelt by his side, "take him . . ."

"I will do it," I promised, "into my own family will I take him."

"Thank you," he sighed, closing his eyes. "You are kind. Now I die content."

"Is there another way to live?" I answered with the old expression, the words of one good man to another.

"Kuku," the boy wailed, touching his head to his grandfather's brow, "I do not want to go . . ."

"Tell me," I begged, for he was slipping fast away, "your name? His name?" A man bears a name, a sacred name, and his sons, his grandsons, and all the men of his line must honor that name with their lives and their remembrance.

With a faint smile the dying man said, "He knows. Take him away . . ."

But how could we go? If we left him to die alone, instead of staying to ease his passage into the pit of Milu, the realm of death, his spirit would be lost upon the way. It would become a wandering ghost, night-vomit, angered with us for our neglect of the body in which it had dwelled for so many years, and it might haunt us for all the days and nights of our lives. I knew what to do to help his spirit depart in peace, to help his grandson live untroubled. "Boy," I said gently, lifting him up, "now is the time to do your greatest service for your grandfather."

"I know," he answered, "he has told me what I must do."

Within four breaths he had run out the doorway and returned bearing the wooden bowl in one hand, the stalk of *ki* leaves in the other. "Here," he commanded, giving the leaves to me. For the second time in the course of a day I fashioned amulets to gain safe passage for a frightened spirit. This time the sacred bands were to be tied around the arms and the head of a man whose spirit was going upon a journey mine would not be taking for yet a while. As I prepared the *lei*, the boy sprinkled the sacred water, compounded of stream water, salt, and turmeric, upon the head of his grandfather, over the *kapa* sheet which covered the shrunken body. When he was done with the anointing he took the *lei* from me and put them in their proper places. "Thank you," the dying man sighed, and we knew that he was content. Then the boy put his mouth upon the pale lips of his ancestor and drew from him, in his breath, the *mana* which the old man would no longer need. It was the boy's now, the *mana* of his line, given from his ancestor to him, for him to keep as long as he should live.

We sat beside the old man until he died. With remnants of the *ki* plant the boy fanned away hungry flies, already gathered for their feast. We did not wait for long. He went so quietly that I did not know when he left us.

"Come," I said softly, "now we must leave him."

"Not yet," he replied, "one more thing must be done."

Before I could question him he dashed through the door. Before I could follow he was throwing pieces of wood through the thatch opposite the door. Logs, branches, twigs, they fell upon the earthen floor as fast as he could toss them in. When I saw what he planned I went to help him. Together we heaped the wood above the bodies of his grandfather and grandmother. Only once did I stop him, to ask two questions: "Are any papers kept in this house? And where are your clothes?" To the first he answered, "None." To the second he replied with a scowl, "I will take nothing from this house."

From a stoppered gourd he shook its last few grains of red salt into the little mouth of the dead man's navel, into the wide open mouth of each withered armpit. Now was he readied for his long journey into the land of the dead. "And what of her?" I asked, speaking of the bloated corpse across the room. "For her it was done yesterday," he said, laying the empty gourd at the old man's feet.

With flint and steel he struck the sparks which caused the tinder to glow. I gave him the sheaf of dried grass to set ablaze. Full of admiration for this boy, I stood at his side while he lighted the navel-thatch above the door. When it caught fire and promised to burn until the house and all it held were consumed, he reached for my hand, saying, "Now we will go." Full of pride for this stalwart naked boy, I took his hand in mine. What a son has been given to me in this one, I rejoiced, as we ran down the path, away from the burning house.

Near Lokelani, neighing and kicking with fear of the crackling flames and billowing smoke, we stood together to watch the funeral fire. It burned furiously: nothing would be left when the last ember had cooled to ashes.

"It is good," said the boy.

"Aye, it is good," I said, seeing him clearly for the first

time. "Fire purifies, fire makes clean," I finished, "it consumes grief, as it does flesh."

Under the dust and the dirt from the firewood, under the tear-streaks marking his face, he was a most handsome lad. Broad in the shoulders, narrow in the hips, already he gave promise of being a very handsome man. But his was the most remarkable face I've ever seen on a boy: long and lean, with a high thin nose, high cheekbones, firm chin, and great dark eyes sunk deep under the arches of their brows, it was the fierce, proud countenance of a man who has seen much sorrow, not the soft, unformed face of a child. Sorrow he has known, and hunger, I said to myself, half in pity, half in wonder, but that is not all which has given shape to this boy's body or beauty to his countenance. There is good blood in this lad. A man can tell these things, if he but looks. Aye, and something more, I was thinking, my *niele* self delighting in the discovery of this new mystery which now I could explore, when down the trail from the Pali came a crowd of people, running in great haste.

The boy pulled his hand from mine. "I will go to bathe in the river," he said quickly. "Do not tell them about me."

They ran up to me, with their gabble and their questions. A loutish lot of countryfolk they were, half-a-dozen skinny men and a couple of fat women, all reeking of taro-patch mud and sweat. Any other time I could have been more tolerant, I vow, but on this occasion I thought I had every reason to be angry with them.

"And what has happened?" they wanted to know, as though they could not see for themselves. "Is anyone in there?" "Why does it burn?" "Who did it?" Out of long experience, I let them ask all their questions before I told them that it was a funeral fire, which I had lighted at the request of the old man who had just died. I did not mention the boy.

"Is it so?" they exclaimed.

"It is a strange way, not the way of common folk," a grizzled farmer allowed, watching the flames and the smoke soar up. "But they were strange people."

"Strange they may have been," I said severely, "but was that reason enough for you to let them starve to death in their helplessness?"

"Alas!" they quavered, all but one, "is that the manner of their dying?"

The larger of the women, who could never have known hunger, glared at me. "How do you know that they starved to death? How do you know that it was not this foreign sickness which carried them off?—Are you a doctor, perhaps?"

If ever there was a time for kicking down, this was it. "Cha! A blind man could have known that it was hunger. The flesh of their bodies was wasted away: their bones stood out like those of a fish when you have finished picking away its meat."

"Aye," admitted the other woman, "we should have been more neighborly. We should have helped them more than we did."

"Jehovah in his heaven will remember how we tried," the fat bitch insisted. "And I have not forgotten how that proud woman chased us away from her door." Defiantly she turned upon me. "We tried, all of us here, and many others who pass this house. Months ago, when the old man became sick and could not rise from his mat. We stopped one day to ask about him—" A true female, she began to weep with indignation, her voice choked. "Ioane," she commanded the grizzled farmer, "do you tell this doubting city man—"

Soberly he took up the story. "This old man's wife: ahh, always she was a proud one, never were we comfortable when she was near. But we would visit with them for the sake of the husband. He was a good man, a kind man."

"And a good physician for our needs," put in another fellow.

"Yes, that too. But then he fell sick. And the greater was their need for us, the bigger grew her pride. Did we leave gifts of food, she would throw them back at us, screaming that they did not need our cast-off things. After a few beatings from her hard tongue we did not stop, we left no food. Later we forgot them, out of habit. To us they were already dead, long ago."

"So do not blame us for their dying," said the angry woman, lifting a clenched fist toward me, the hated outsider.

"How can I blame you, now that I know the story?" I assured them. "Now that I understand, I ask your forgiveness for my suspicions. I did not know those two, I did not know you. But surely you can understand how I felt when, by chance, I found them in that house of death?"

"No trouble, no trouble," the old man spoke for all except the unforgiving fat female, "you have asked what needed to be asked."

She, the bloated cow, continued to mutter under her breath, to give me the angry eye. She would have rejoiced if I had dropped dead on the spot, felled by her dislike. Smiling sweetly upon her, I hoped she would drown in the next mud puddle she tried to waddle through.

"Now, if you will excuse us," said the polite old man, "we have far to go."

"I am grateful for your help," I waved them on, "farewell until we meet again."

Taking up their bundles, all save one bade me a pleasant farewell. She pushed ahead, like a pig heading for the food trough. And good riddance to you, O taro-munching sow, I spat, may we never meet again.

As soon as they were out of sight, beyond the next turn in the trail, I called to the boy. He did not come, he did not answer. Thinking that he could not hear me above the music of the stream, I went in search of him along its bank, in the bushes lining its course. He was not there. Frantic with worry, I shouted: "Boy! Boy! Where are you?" I did not even know his name. Running beside the stream like a crazy man, shouting "Boy! Boy!" at every step, I knew how unbearable would be my loss if he did not return. But he did not return.

Retracing my steps, I looked into every pool in the stream, fearing to find his body in one of them, dead because his spirit yearned to be united with his grandparents'. I did not find him.

Heavy-hearted, almost unable to walk, I went back to Lokelani. Slowly I pulled myself up into the saddle, turned to take one last look at the burning pyre, in hope that he would be near it. Only the blazing wood, the bright sparks rising into the air, were there. "He is gone, Lokelani," I mourned, my voice breaking, my eyes filling with tears, "he is lost to us. Now let us go away from here, from this sad place. From this place of evil." Willingly did she bear me away, down the path the countryfolk had taken only a short time before.

And happily did she whinny when we came to the bend in the path, and joyfully did I call out! For there he was, riding toward us on an old nag, coming up the slope of the mountain from the singing stream below. Naked still, clean and radiant as sunlight streaming over the mountains, he rode up to us, bringing me the gift of joy. "I went to get Pueo," he explained. I could not speak: I could only nod, as though, of course, I had known this all the time. Motioning to him to lead the way, I willingly fell into place behind him.

Handsome he was, proud as a high chief he sat. And like a great chief did he lead me toward Kaneʻohe.

CHAPTER 10.

IN WHICH A NEW-FOUND BOY ENTERS UPON A NEW LIFE

Where the trail becomes a road again, among the little rounded hills of Kaneʻohe, we two could ride side by side. I had so many questions to ask of this mystifying child that I did not know where to begin. Yet, time after time, as a new one started to tickle my tongue, the lad's silence forced me to put the question back into its storehouse. He was not ready to talk. Sitting like a young lord upon his steed, he looked out upon the land of Koʻolaupoko as if it were his domain, which he was visiting for the first time. For once in my life I was sensible enough of a companion's wish for silence to respect it. This is how wondrously the boy affected me. Silence may be golden to Englishmen, but to me it is like a lid put upon a pot of boiling water: unless the steam escapes, the pot will blow up.

Just in time to save me from being scattered in bits and pieces along the way, he spoke: "Where are we going?"

Pent-up air rushed from me like steam through a spout: "To Kaneʻohe first, then to Heʻeia, Kahaluʻu, Waiahole, Waiakane, Hakipuʻu, Kualoa, Kaʻaʻawa . . ." I recited the lovely names, right around the whole island back to Honolulu again. Eager to keep him talking, I hurried on. "You know these places?"

"Only by their names," he answered gravely. "Never before have I gone this far away from home."

I could not believe my ears. "What? You have never been to Kaneʻohe? Not even to this place which is so close to home?"

He turned that astonishingly serious countenance upon me. "My grandmother would not let me go."

Ahh, that proud woman, I reviled her in my thoughts. A barking bitch-dog she must have been, to her miserable husband, to this unfortunate boy.

"By what name are you called?" he asked me, the man who was dying of curiosity to learn his name. Quickly I told him, hastening toward the point where I could put the question to him. Again he forestalled me: "And by what name will you call me?"

"Oh, my goodness, boy! Do you not have a name? How is it possible for—"

"Until today I have had a name. But my grandfather told me that I must not use it when I left his house. It must die with him, burned up in the fire. My grandmother said it was trash, and like trash should be burned. So now it is gone, the name I bore. And I am in need of another."

"Wait," I begged, "you go too fast for me." Deeper than my disappointment at not learning his name and lineage was my pity for this boy whose past was wiped out so completely by his grandparents' hatred for the present. "This can not be! A boy has ancestors of whom he should be proud. A boy will grow into a man who will have children who will respect him. —Tell me: your father, your mother: where are they?"

"They are dead. Long ago. I did not know them."

I groaned to hear once again the story of our race. "And their kinfolk? Are they still alive?"

"Perhaps. I do not know.—Now you are the only one I know. That is why you must give me a name."

"I can not believe it!—Do you know no other people, no neighbors from the lands around here? No children with whom you have played?"

"None. My grandparents kept me hidden away. I have seen some people, passing on the trail, but they have not seen me. This is the reason I went today to hide in the stream. Until today I have spoken only to my grandfather and my grandmother. You are the third one to see me— and to speak with me."

"O great gods!" I cried into heaven, "what evil has been done to this child."

"What is evil?" he asked. "I do not know this word."

"Later, later," I said gently. "Evil is an ugliness, a hurt. You will come to know it soon enough, in its many meanings. For now, let us talk of better things. And let us first above all give you a new name. It must be a good one, worthy of you, when we choose it."

"I will like it so," he replied, with the gravity of an aged man.

"Do you know how it was, in the olden days?" I enquired, "in the times before the years were numbered according to the new foreign style?—Wait: first, let me ask you another question: do you know the foreign calendar? And that, in their style, this is the year 1853?" As I suspected, he knew no English words and had never so much as seen a foreigner, although he did know about their presence in Hawai'i and about some of the things they had brought. But his Hawaiian was excellent. It was somewhat old-fashioned—he used many words and expressions that I had not heard since I was a child—and far more learned than might be expected of an ordinary boy his age. Because his grandparents were the only teachers he had known, their ancient mode of speech combined with his seriousness made him seem older than he was.

"Well, then, let us return to our consideration of the olden days. Often, in those times, a child was given a name which referred to a great event or to some unusual circumstance that happened about the time he was born. In this manner his family and friends were helped to remember the year and the season of his birth. It was not an exact method, of course, as is the foreign way, but it was better than nothing. In such a manner did I receive my name.— But you would never guess that I was so named because, on the day I arrived in this beautiful world, my father was bitten by one of the first horses to come to Oʻahu. That inquisitive man, in his determination to look upon those strange new beasts, those long-legged dogs with iron feet, he pressed too close. A stallion, frightened by all those shouting, pushing people, bit my father on the arm. It was not a serious wound, but for several days thereafter those toothmarks, notched and jagged, were a part of him. Because he was the first man in Honolulu to bear such marks, his family and friends said, 'Lo! Your spirit-guardian has spoken: the child's name is given. Let him be called Naniho.' But my mother held to a different opinion. 'No child of mine,' she cried out, 'is going to be called just plain old *teeth*!' They argued, they fought, everybody shouting and yelling and waving hands at once, some agreeing with my mother, some supporting my father. Until at last, in great annoyance with this tumult, my mother's brother, who was a teacher of the *hula* and a poet as well, suggested that they should call me Nihoa. My father was delighted with this elegant name. My mother, much relieved, gave her consent.—From my father, I might add, I get my curiosity, and my other name, Niele. From my mother I receive my stubbornness, perhaps, but also, I like to think, a portion of the poet's soul which flowered in her brother. From the stallion I got—well, never mind that for now . . . As I was saying, the screaming and the fighting stopped, if only for a while, and everybody except me and my attendants went merrily off to the feasting that celebrated my birth and my naming.—That, my dear boy, was how things were done 'way back in 1803."

He was amused by my tale, which in truth was not much exaggerated. I think it must have been the first time he had laughed in many weeks. But he was not to be diverted from his purpose. "And your other name: Hailama. I do not know what this means."

"Oh, that one. —It is my missionary name, one I was given much later, when I was a grown man almost. The Queen Ka'ahumanu: when, as a favor to the missionaries, she became a Christian, she commanded all who were members of her household to become Christians also. The chief of the missionary preachers at that time was called Hiram Bingham. Being a smart man by then, I took his name and thereby pleased both her and him. But, to tell you the truth, I do not know what it means. These foreign names, I have learned, have no meanings: they are just strange noises, even to foreigners. Would you believe it?"

"Even so," he said politely, "it has a good sound.— But what are Christians? What are missionaries?"

"Oh, those.—Someday, when we have lots of time, I will tell you what I know about Christians and other foreigners. For now let us think of a name for you."

I looked intently at him, the boy from whom I could not look away. "It must be a name that will be yours alone. —How old are you?"

"In the month of Makali'i I was born, almost seven years ago."

I rummaged through my memories of that uneventful year, that unnoticed month. "Too long ago," I dismissed them, "without meaning for us now. Then we must look to this day for your name, to this day when a new life begins for you.—Ah, ah! Wait a moment! It has been revealed, without my thinking. Your spirit-guardian has spoken to mine, to bring the message to my mouth." It was, indeed, a most fitting name, a name of good omen, and I throbbed in the thighbones at the nearness of our spirit-guardians. "Try it in your mouth, my boy. See if you like it as much as I do."

"I have tried it," he answered happily, "I, too, heard our spirit-guardians when they spoke. And I thank them for giving this good name to me."

"And let us thank the gods also," I said loudly, that they might hear. For me, too, a new life begins this day, I understood them to be saying: a *kahu* to this boy I must be, as once I was *kahu* to Alexander Liholiho, that other favored son of the gods.

"Eahou," I called to him, thereby making the name his forever. For words bind, and words make free: and words uttered are binding forever. "Only one more thing is lacking on this your name-day."

"And what is this thing?"

"A name-song, to explain the meaning of your name, to praise the charms of your person, to ask the blessings of the gods upon your life. I shall compose one for you now, as we ride along, and when it is done I shall say it for you. Many a name-song have I created in my time, but never have I made one so gladly."

"Then I shall make no more noise than a shrimp in a stream, until you are done."

The first line was easy, because it is prescribed:

Eahou no he mele-inoa: a name-song for Eahou

But the lines immediately thereafter were the most difficult of all: they should refer to his family, to the illustriousness of his line. But these were unknown to me, if not to him, and by his wish they were put behind him. Behind us, when I turned to seek a sign there, rose the steep dark cliffs of Nu'uanu and, white against them, the thin column of smoke where the sorrowful past was being burned away.

> Of Eahou, the spirit-son of Kaneholopali,
> Of Kaneholopali, the guardian-god of Nu'uanu,
> The guardian-god of travelers upon the narrow path of life.

Before us lay the green and lovely land of Kane'ohe, bathed in the golden light of Kane the Sun, Kane-the-Giver-of-Life, going now to his sleep beyond the wall of high mountains. From dwellings among the hills and upon the plain the smoke of cooking-fires ascended into the quiet air, sent forth from the fires that sustain life:

> Look not back, O new-born one:
> The steep cliffs are behind, the dangers are passed.
> Nothing is there, nothing is lost,
> The treasure has been brought away.
> It is here, it is safe.
> Look to the front!
> From here the path is wide and long.
> Breathe deep! The spirit of Kane is here.
> And bright is the light of Kane,
> The Giver of New Life to you,
> New-born in Kane'ohe,
> O Eahou,
> The breath of Kane,
> The life of Kane,
> The son of Kane in the years to come.

The rest came like water issuing from a spring: I had only to look upon him, upon his perfection, from the gloss of his long black hair to the arch of his slender foot, to find reasons for a chant that need have no end.

> You are the treasure, O twice-born son,
> For past and future, gods and men,
> Are met in you.
> Great is your *mana*,
>   a heritage from gods and men.
> Noble is your mind,
>   a grace to gods and men.
> And handsome is your body,
>   a delight to gods and men.
> Straight is your back,
>   firm as is the *koa* tree which gives the warrior his name,
> Wide are your shoulders, narrow your hips,
> Long are your legs, strong your arms.
> Fashioned to be loved and to love are you,
> O Eahou.
> And from this day forth, O perfect one,
> Men and women will seek your love,
> O my Eahou.

Endless were his charms. I could have gone on for thousands of lines, and I promised myself that someday, when I gave the words of his name-song to a chanter, to be set to music, I would recount them all, every one. But for now these few would be enough.

Repeating the song to myself, I examined it carefully, word by word, verse by verse. Did it hold words of ill omen which, once they issued from my mouth, would be forever beyond recalling? No: I could find no such harmful word. Did it do justice to the art of poets? Yes: as name-songs go, it was not a poem I need be ashamed of. Did it do justice to the boy? No, I sighed. Nothing I or any poet might compose would ever do him justice. But the gods, and he, must be content with knowing that I had done the best I could. Was it so proud, then, so presumptuous, in its praise of a mortal boy that the jealous gods would be offended? No, I could not think so, if only because I was convinced in my heart that he whom I praised was indeed a descendant of the gods. Yet, just to be safe, I prayed that if unwittingly the name-song or any part of it offended them, their wrath would fall upon me, not upon him: "Strike me, O you just rulers over the destinies of men," I implored, "not him, not him."

"Now it is done," I called out. Piercing as the point of a warrior's spear was his glance when he looked at me. Oh, those eyes! How many hearts will he break, I wondered, how many willing victims will he command, when he is a youth, when he is a man? I should have warned him then that he must learn to veil those weapons, that he must never go abroad without covering them up with a hat, low on his brow, or with a strip of cloth, or even those ugly spectacles of colored glass which some foreigners put on to shield their eyes from the bright sun.

"Then, please, do you tell it to me," he said.

So, as the shadows of mountains and trees and of our own two selves were lengthening upon the plain, as the air was turning blue with woodsmoke and the cool of evening, I recited Eahou's name-song for him.

When it was ended he said, with that honesty I was only beginning to discover in him, "I do not understand all the words. But those words I do understand, and the way you say them: those things I like. And," he paused, looking up into heaven before he finished, "I am glad that you have given me to Kane for a son."

"Kane is father to us all," I said, "but you will be a most special son to him." I wanted to say more, to express the thought that lay very close to my heart: as you will be a most special son to me. Yet something warned me to hold this back. At the time I did not know why, although the thought was conceived, the words could not be born. But now I know: the gods were telling me that this honor was not mine to claim.

Suddenly the world was bleak. I shivered. "Are you cold, Eahou?" I asked, full of concern for the unclothed child. He seemed surprised that I should put the question to him.

"No, the day is still warm."

Then I saw why I shivered. We were passing a graveyard. The ghosts of the unhappy dead were making the air cold with the breath of their lamentations. To feel the breath of the dead is an omen of ill. "Night is near. Let us hurry," I urged, kicking Lokelani into a trot. Pueo followed Loke's lead and soon we were carried past that haunted place.

Even so, uneasiness persisted. And I needed no graves or ghosts to tell me why. The countryside through which we rode was a land of desolation. This lovely fertile district, where once so many people lived, was almost emptied now. Where are all the people gone, I wondered, until I remembered the graveyard, crowded to its walls with the dead of Kaneʻohe, covered from end to end with strawflowers, those ugly dry blossoms that even as they are opening feel dead to the touch. Many houses were rotting away, others had long since fallen in upon their foundations of rocks and stamped earth. Cooking-fires marking the abodes of the living were few and spaced far apart. Fields and pastures were overgrown with weeds, not with the old familiar plants but with new ones, brought in by foreigners: the strawflowers from America, the Peruvian guava, the Mexican lantana, the blue-flowered Jamaican tea, the Spanish needle, the spiny amaranth, blankets of vines, and high-tufted grasses. Each plant was the parent of a million seeds, and every one of those was quick to sprout, that they might overrun our native earth and smother in their exuberance our native plants.

Grieving at the change which ten years had brought, I rode in dismay through the deepening gloom. Even though I had known in my mind that my people were dying away, I was not prepared for this. Thinned they were, I had thought, stripped like old leaves from the trees by a searing wind. Yet the trees still live, I had thought, and they will bear young leaves again, and fruit. Now I saw how even the trees were dead, that no leaves and no fruit would grow again from those lifeless branches, from this invaded earth.

We came to the place where the Panoa family had lived. Always it has been the custom for traveling members of my family to spend the night with the Panoa of Kane'ohe, for wandering Panoa to find hospitality with us at Kahana. I stared in unbelief: it was a dead house, sinking under the weight of morning-glory vines and heavy runners of *honohono* grass. Beyond the stone wall the yard was waist-high with weeds. Eahou's house had been a palace, full of life, compared with this ruin. "*Auwe, auwe,*" I moaned, wondering if he were a Panoa trying to warn me whose cold breath I had felt at the graveyard. "Where are the people?" asked Eahou. I could not answer him, who had seen enough of death in this day of his re-birth.

"We shall find a place to stay in the village," I promised, showing a bravery I did not feel. Hungry and tired, we rode down the long dark slope that leads to Kane'ohe's stream. In the last flush of evening I saw the thin white steeple of the missionary church standing above the trees

which fill the ravine. "Of course," I said. "I was forgetting the mission here. Tonight we shall rest with the good
Reverend Parker and his family."

We forded the stream and started to climb its farther
bank. The certainty of Christian hospitality restored my
humor. Seeing the milling crowd of people and the torches
in the village, I could even make jokes. "Well! There seem
to be people enough in this muddy town. Do you suppose
their Chamber of Commerce has sent a delegation to welcome us?"

"What is this Chamber of Commerce?" asked Eahou.

All handwavings and eloquence, I was busying trying
to explain to him this Yankee peculiarity, paying not the
slightest notice to the people ahead, when we reached the
top of the bank and found our way blocked by a barrier of
very serious citizens. "My goodness!" I said. "It *is* a committee."

"Halt!" cried a loud-voiced fellow, somewhat unneces-
sarily inasmuch as their very presence had stopped us.

"Well, this is a surprise!" I said for all to hear. "How
did you know?"

"You're under arrest!" roared the great big voice of
the great big policeman, as he stepped forward to pull
the reins from our hands.

I'm afraid I laughed. "Under arrest? Good heavens!
Whatever for?"

"Under suspicion of murder!" the policeman bawled,
very much aware of the dangers he ran from two such
desperadoes as we.

"Murder?" This was indeed a surprise. "But I have
only now arrived. How could I have committed a murder
in your fair town?" With the courage of innocence, I was
not even afraid.

"Nah, nah," he bellowed, "don't get smart with us, just

because you come from the city. Back there on the Pali, we mean. At Halfway House."

"Ah, ah, ah, now I understand." This time I laughed in scorn. "And where is that pouting lump of taro-patch mud? That sow with lice in her ears who, because she is angry with me, itches to say I am a murderer?"

"I am here," she spoke up forthrightly. And there she was in fact, standing solidly in the front row of the mob, arms folded upon her big belly, lips closed tight as the halves of a threatened oyster, the very picture of Justice determined to exact retribution. A pillar of Reverend Parker's church she was, I knew at once, and a smiter of heathens and backsliders for miles around. How did I know? Because she looked exactly like Rebekah at her sanctimonious worst. Oh, these Christian women of Hawai'i! They are worse than whips and scorpions when they are aroused.

"Does she say that you are a murderer?" the policeman labored through his exercise in logic. "Do I say it? No. We say only that you should be questioned about what happened back there at Halfway House." Faceless voices mumbled approval of his brilliance in the law. Voiceless faces, looking like masks in the torchlight, leered in malice. Irritated beyond endurance by the woman's self-righteousness, by the policeman's large idea of his importance, I determined to bring this farcical performance to a quick end.

"And I am willing to tell you what I know—once again," I began politely enough. "But before we start, let me ask you if you think it is possible that I should be a murderer and a breaker of the law. I, Hiram Nihoa, *kahu* to His Royal Highness the Prince Alexander Liholiho in his boyhood, trusted adviser to His Majesty the King, a respected—" I know my countrymen: at the mere mention of my connection with the ruling chiefs they were defeated. When I named the King, my accuser uttered a good old-fashioned heathen wail that would have collapsed the Congregational church about her head.

The policeman dropped our reins, held up two defensive hands. "Enough! Enough!" he cried. "We ask your forgiveness. Go in peace—and do not think unkindly of us as you ride away."

"Have no fear," I assured them, feeling sorry now for their shattered self-esteem. "You were but doing your duty. His majesty will be pleased to hear from my mouth how law-abiding are the people of Kaneʻohe, how courageous is their policeman."

"I told you he was an important man," a voice filled the silence, "but would you listen?"

"And now, if you will be so kind," I said, "please do you tell me where we can find the Reverend Parker's house. We are weary, my son and I."

"Ho! I myself will lead you there," announced the policeman. "It is not far."

"And we will light the way," called one of the torchmen in the crowd.

Like great chiefs in the days of old, preceded by runners to clear the way, surrounded by retainers and torchbearers, Eahou and I were taken to the mission. They left us in the yard before the simple wooden house, calling "*Aloha*" and "Good luck" as they backed away. I was well pleased—until I heard that monument to virtue having the last word. Loud and clear her parting shot came back to me: "That naked boy. You would think he'd have sense enough to clothe him decently." You fat busybody! I wanted to screech after her, you slitted slut! Go back to your bamboo husband, and let it keep your mind off other people's affairs. But it was too late for this crude retort. Mr. Parker was waiting for us by the door, and she got away before I could even the score.

He was tall and thin, and very kind—and even more weary than we were. The house was full of sick people suffering from the influenza, he explained, and he thought we would be uncomfortable among them. But if we did not mind sleeping in the barn, he could shelter us there for the night. For him, too, I found a fitting answer: "If a stable was good enough for the child Jesus, it will be more than enough for us." Often I have slept in stables, and in worse places, and that night I would have been content to lie my body down upon the earth itself, if only it were dry.

In the barn, by the light of a lantern, we ate the supper he brought to us: cold boiled taro sweetened with black molasses, ship's hardtack, ripe bananas, and milk still warm and frothy from the cow. "It is not much," the harried preacher apologized, "but it is all I can find in the cookhouse." Indeed, it was a poor man's meal, but it eased our hunger-pangs.

"What is this?" asked Eahou, pointing to the milk, that strange American food. He did not like it, as I do not, but we choked it down because the missionary poured it for us with his own hands. The boy was much impressed by the mere sight of this tall, stooped foreigner, with the long brown beard, the enormous hands and feet, and, withal, the very gentle manner. He would have drunk sea water, I think, if Benjamin Parker had served it to us.

"And who is the boy?" he enquired. I was amused at the way in which he managed to see only Eahou's head. Although he speaks fluent Hawaiian I answered in English, explaining what I knew of Eahou and about how he came to be with me, finishing my account with the inevitable question. "I know so little about them," he replied, shaking his head sadly. "A proud woman, a bitter man, who shut themselves off from the community. I think they had two or three sons, who have died—or, at any rate, who have disappeared, somehow. And a daughter who ran away, I was told, although I can not vouch for this, and went to live in sin in Honolulu. Perhaps this boy is the fruit of her sinning?" This would be how he would look upon Eahou, I had to admit, but even so I resented it. The boy was good fruit, whether or not he was a fatherless child. But who can argue this point with a Christian missionary? I slipped past the issue to ask the family's name. "I have forgotten, if ever I knew it.—You see, I never did meet them, because we never go up the Pali. When we must go to Honolulu, we go by canoe, around Makapuʻu.—I will ask the people hereabouts and let you know what I may learn. But now I must return to my duties in the house, so I will bid you goodnight. Sleep well."

Side by side, on our two beds of dried grass covered with the poncho, Eahou and I laid ourselves down to sleep. But sleep did not come at once, to either of us. Into my mind, suggested by the presence of the animals who shared that shelter with us, crept some silly words: "with sleepy cows and asses." And, of course, I could not rout them out again until I'd traced them to their source. It was not an easy task, until the simple tune to which they are sung came to my aid. Then the verses followed complete and, smiling in the dark, I remembered my children singing the hymn at Christmastide:

> Cradled in a stall was he
> With sleepy cows and asses,
> But the very beasts could see
> That he all men surpasses.

Ah, I thought, satisfied at last. The Christ-child: he too was given his name-song on the day when he was born.

But the words that were sung for him: could they not also be sung—in this world of human beings, I hurriedly explained to the proud Jehovah and his listening son—in praise of the child who rested beside me?

And what of that twice-born one beside me? I should have known, I should have sensed his need. This serious lad, who had behaved more like a man than like a boy in the few hours I had known him, he was still a very young child in his heart. In the darkness I heard him stirring on his pallet.

"Are you cold, Eahou?"

"No."

"Are you still hungry, perhaps?"

"No."

"Are you frightened?"

"No."

"Then what is the trouble that you can not go to sleep?"

"I wish to be closer to you."

"Then do you come here," I said gently, reaching out for him. And he was here, nestled in the crook of my arm, warm against the length of my side, just as, each in turn, my littlest son or daughter has come from the cradle to snuggle up against a fond papa. He was different from all those children of mine, and yet he was no different.

"Is this better?" I asked.

"Yes," he said. After a little while, he whispered, "I have thought of my name for you."

"And what is it?"

"I will call you Makuahou."

Makuahou: new father. "I like this name," I said softly, after a long moment. "It is good."

It is good. It is my greatest gift.

CHAPTER 11.

IN WHICH A HAPPY MAN SINGS A SONG OF LOVE FOR O'AHU

We woke up with the chickens—and with the cows, horses, goats, pigeons, mice, and lizards who were kind enough to share that inn with us. Not counting fleas and cockroaches, the living creatures crowded into that barn were more numerous, I think, than all the people in the entire district of Kane'ohe. And loud enough to arouse the entire district was the morning-song they raised. Unable to endure it, Eahou and I fled outside to the shelter of a huge mango tree. The last thing to get up that morning was the sun.

While we were at the watering trough, washing away the sleep and the barn dust, Mr. Parker appeared. In one hand he carried a wooden bowl containing our breakfast, the same assortment of victuals we had eaten the night before. This time, in the cool dawn, they were less appetizing. In the other hand he clutched a bundle of faded garments. "Here are some of Henry's clothes," he said, placing them on a corner of the trough. "They may be too small for the boy, but they will cover his nakedness."

Having no gratitude for the clothes, I thanked him for his thoughtfulness. Bare as a plucked cockerel, Eahou was peering into the food-bowl, happily unaware of the preacher's determination to garb him in decency.

I asked the poor man how his sick ones fared. "We didn't get much sleep, I'm afraid. I'll be glad when this is over. At least they've stopped vomiting. But the headaches, the sore muscles, are with us still."

"Ah, then, may I suggest a remedy for these ills, which I have used often." I did not have much hope that he would accept my recommendation, but I felt that I should offer it.

"And what is that?" he asked, combing the tangled beard with his fingers.

"A strong tea made with roots and stems of the *'uhaloa.* Something is in it, I do not know what, which eases aches and pains." I wasted my breath. These foreigners have long ago decided that our Hawaiian medicines are useless, because they are heathen. These *haole* would rather die, I believe, than ask the help of a native physician. They will physick themselves with the horrible stuff they call castor oil, but they will not swallow a pinch of the flesh from a bitter gourd, or even of a single *kukui* nut, which we have found are better purgatives and far kinder to the taste as well as to the bowels. Americans especially carry to extremes this disdain for native things. Take, for only one example, the luscious red-skinned fruit called the love apple (which, for some reason known only to themselves, they prefer to call the tomato): this juicy, tart berry, with its green and golden seeds, its pink flesh, we find delicious as both food and medicine. But they look upon it with suspicion, considering it poisonous, turning pale at the thought of taking into their precious bodies a substance we eat every day without harm to ourselves.

"Yes, yes," he said, as polite in the matter of my gift of a medicine as I had been with his present of clothes. "Thank you. I will think about it.—And now, if you'll excuse me, I must get on with my labors. I pray you'll have a pleasant journey—and I hope that when you return this way we'll be sufficiently recovered to offer you more comfortable lodging." With a handshake for me, and a pat on the head for Eahou, the only part of the lad I'm sure he ever saw, he hurried back to the house. A good man at heart he is, I have no doubt, but—like all missionaries —somewhat small-minded.

After we had eaten and had washed the food-bowl I helped Eahou to dress. "*Auwe*," he picked in dismay at those strange garments, "do I have to?"

"Yes, my boy, you have to," I decreed, as hardheaded as any Yankee. "Sometimes we must do things we do not like, for the sake of other people. But I promise you this: the instant we have left Kane'ohe behind us, you may take off these silly things if you wish."

"Then let us go fast," he begged. "I do not like to wear even a *malo*. How can I bear the weight of all these heavy things?"

The woolen underdrawers, covering him from waist to shins, he hated on sight and complained about immediately. The pantalons—too small, as the giver had suspected—I denounced as an added insult to that perfect body. The undershirt I stuffed beneath my saddle, as being unnecessary. But the shirt! Both of us laughed at the ridiculous thing, with its wide collar, its long sleeves, the many little buttons.

"It tickles me," he giggled, while we forced him into it. "How can I breathe? I am choking . . ." I saw that he was more embarrassed than balky, so I did not lose patience as I would have done had my son Daniel been jigging about with these same objections. "Just be glad you don't have to wear shoes. They are the worst torment of all."

"Never will I wear shoes," he vowed.

"Wait and see," I advised, remembering how the small Alex had made this same promise to everyone within hearing. And look at him now: the best-dressed beau in Honolulu, with shoes, boots, and dancing-pumps to match the elegant wardrobe he finds so necessary to his pleasures.

Exhibiting Eahou decent, we rode close to the Parker house on our way out of the mission yard. I had not been able to get the boy to tuck shirt into trousers—"How can I," he wanted to know, "where is the space?"—but I hoped that Mr. Parker would be so pleased with the overall effect that he would not notice details. Whether or not he saw us we will never know. Not a curtain was lifted, not a hand was waved, on our departure. Probably the poor man was busying applying cold vinegar compresses to the brows of his suffering ones, while 'uhaloa plants flourished almost at his doorstep.

And not a person was abroad in Kane'ohe's single street to see Eahou in his finery. For the whole stretch of that muddy miserable hamlet, all of two city blocks in length, not a thing stirred, not even a pig wallowing in a ditch. So much for decency, I huffed. Somewhere in this little episode there must be a moral, but I'm not quite sure what it is. As we passed the last discolored disconsolate house Eahou looked at me expectantly. "Now," I agreed. He leaped to the ground, peeled those bits and pieces of faded cloth from his body, and stood free again. He was about to hurl the clothes into the nearest weed-patch when I stopped him. "Nah, nah, nah! Not yet. Better save them. We may need them again, when we come to another missionary station." "Is there more than one?"

he cried. Even so, he gave the bundle to me, to stow in my saddlebags.

Not far beyond this place of Eahou's freeing is the summit of a little hill overlooking the long bay of Kaneʻohe. Mindful of my purpose, I said, "Let us pause to look about us. We are not in such a hurry that we can not spend a moment here, a moment there, enjoying the beauty of our island." Shading my eyes against the sun, now riding only a little higher than the round-backed crater of Ulupaʻu, which sticks out from Oʻahu like the thumb of the left hand, I searched for the signs Alex had told me to seek. I found nothing to suspect, no ships in the bay, no new clearings, no fort. The land was green and peaceful, the sea lay calm and undisturbed. From the shore below us a solitary fisherman paddled his small canoe to the flat, treeless, waterless islet of Loʻe. He left no wake upon the unruffled surface of the bay.

"Where is he going?" asked Eahou. "Why, to catch fish, or to spear lobsters, perhaps, or squid." He was full of questions about the big world into which he was going. I was ready with answers, and with questions of my own. He knew a great deal about the native trees and plants growing along the way, distinguishing those which were useful for healing sores from those for binding broken bones, and the ones which were good for costiveness from the ones which closed up the loosened bowel. He was a physician in the making. Perceiving this, I concluded at last what I had not recognized the day before: the physician of Halfway House and Eahou's grandfather were one and the same man. Yesterday, in that wasted dying body—as indeed in the active lad riding beside me today —I could not detect the features of the physician whom I had known so long ago. My memory might have failed me, I had to admit: a man can forget much in ten years.

And an old man can change much in ten years, I countered, especially when he takes a long time to die.

But then, looking at Eahou, riding beside me in all his perfection, I saw that he was the mystery, not the man who died. And I could not believe that Eahou was the child of commoners. The bearing of chiefs, the lineaments of princes, were in him: he was the culmination of a long line of noblemen, with all the *mana* of a hundred generations of high chiefs centered now in him. And great was his *mana*: I could see it, I could feel it.

Then who were the lords of whom he was the issue? Here my fancy went riotously to work. For what Hawaiian does not know the tale of 'Umi, son of Liloa, high chief of Kohala? And of how 'Umi, because he was the child of a commoner woman, was hidden by his mother until he was a youth, strong enough and clever enough to claim his birthright from Liloa's own hands. And what Hawaiian does not know the history of the first Kamehameha? Of how he was born in Kohala on a stormy night during a time of strife, when the kingdom of Keawe his grandfather was being stolen by the usurper Alapa'i. And of how the young Kamehameha was hidden for many years until, between them, Ke'oua his father and Kalaniopu'u his uncle won back their kingdom from Keawe'opala, the brutish son of Alapa'i.

Thinking of such heroes' stories as these, I studied Eahou once again. Much as I wanted him to be one, he was no Kamehameha: he did not have their big bones, their pouting lips and heavy-lidded eyes. Kauikeaouli had done his best, when he was younger, to scatter his seed far and wide. But of his few seedlings, only one still lives; and this little love-child, this Albert Kunuiakea, looks exactly like his father. And, although Lot and Alex, as is to be expected, are thumping many a melon throughout the land, neither of them, as far as I know, has sired a child. Much as I would have rejoiced to find that Alex was Eahou's father, I had to concede that this was impossible: I, of all people, should know that when Alex was ten years old he was using his little spiggot only to make water through.

Then who remained? Of all the chiefs I knew, Abner Paki was the only one who resembled Eahou. For Paki's sake I hoped this would prove to be his son—even though I could imagine the difficulties with Konia when Paki brought the boy home. And like a knife twisting in my liver was jealousy: how could I give him up to Paki, when I wanted to keep this boy to be my son? Yet I knew that, out of loyalty to both, I would give him up if he were Paki's son. But what if Paki were not the one? What then?

Tormented and happy at once, like a man in love who is uncertain of his mistress's love, I rode through O'ahu's countryside, wondering, scheming, questioning, deciding, undeciding, starting all over again upon the puzzle—and never reaching a conclusion. It was not an unpleasant occupation, I confess, and it certainly helped to pass the time. But honesty compels me to add this little bit of wisdom learned from the experience: the curse of the inquisitive man is not his curiosity but his flightiness. Always in search of new delights to entertain his thoughts, like a honeycreeper in search of nectar, he does not linger long enough to collect the facts upon which to support his fancies. Cha! If I were in need of a spy, I would never employ an inquisitive man. The best use I can think of for a *niele* man is to send him along as a guide with a bunch of visitors riding out to see the scenery of O'ahu.

Just as flitsome as was my counterpart from the livery stables—although somewhat better informed, I insist— I undertook to give Eahou the grand tour of O'ahu. I pointed out the many fishponds, built by the people of old in coves and inlets along the shores of Kaneʻohe bay. I showed him one of my favorite sights: the half-waterfall hung upon the upper cliffs of Haʻiku. I told him how fish are caught, the fishnets are made. I instructed him in the methods by which the stone walls were built which enclose the shallow fishponds, how clean water and fingerling fish can come and go through the barred gates in the walls, how the ponds are cleaned. He was well on his way to becoming either a mighty expert or a very bored boy when we came to Kikiwelawela, the place where Kaneʻohe adjoins Heʻeia. There a sluggish stream flows into the bay, through a marsh overgrown with bulrushes and other water-loving plants. No narrow path such as Paliku took me along at Moʻiliʻili crosses this swamp: the people of old had sense enough to make their road go around the edge of these foul-smelling lowlands.

Where the stream meets the bay they had enclosed the largest of Kaneʻohe's fishponds. "Eahou," I said, "let us continue your education by showing you a fish or two." We turned in upon a path leading toward the pond. Upon the muddy shore two fishermen, as free of clothing as was Eahou, were pulling up weeds and bulrushes, throwing them upon the land to dry. The men lifted their hands in welcome, and one of them came toward us, washing the mud from his body as he splashed through the water.

"*Aloha* to you two," he said, "and how can we help you?"

He was a fine strapping young fellow, burned almost black by being so much in the sun. "We have here a mountain boy," I explained, "one who has never seen a fish. I have told him that you could show him some. Will you be so kind?"

"Is it possible that a boy can live so long without knowing a mullet from a file-fish? Then come in, come in. Not only will we show you some. We will also show you how to catch them."

For the next hour, while I dozed in the shade of a *hala* tree, these two good country men willingly instructed Eahou in the art of casting a throw-net, told him the names of the fish they caught, and how to distinguish them one from another, and brought him back to me encrusted with mud and full of their learning.

"He will make a good fisherman," they declared, with winks and smiles and no need for lies. "If ever he wishes to work with us, do you bring him. We will take him."

As a parting gift they presented him with four fat mullet, neatly held in a basket plaited of fresh bulrushes. "A boy who has never seen a fish," said the elder man, "can not have tasted one. Take these, and think of us when you eat them." This kindness of heart, much more than the sight or taste of fish, was the experience I had hoped they would give to Eahou.

The lesson was not lost on him. As we rode away he said, "Those were good men. Not like—"

"Yes, my son? Go on, do not stop. The thought must be spoken. Else it will lie in your mind like the barb of a sea urchin in your foot, festering, causing pain."

"Not like the people on the path to the Pali."

"Can you be certain of this?" I asked, very gently, like a physician probing in a wound for the barb. "I have found that if one is kind to people, these people will be kind to him. This is the way of good people, not only here in Hawai'i Nei but in all the lands across the seas."

"I understand," he said, looking unhappily at the ground, "and I shall remember." After a long pause he said the most hurtful thing I hoped he would ever have to say. "My grandmother: she was not kind." I said nothing.

Each alone with his thoughts, we rode in silence around the marsh. I saved for another time my disquisitions about the logs of hard *'ohi'a*, put to soak in the swamp water in order to soften them for cutting, and about the bundles of paper-mulberry bark, put to soak in order to loosen the fibers from which *kapa* would be made. At the crest of Kikiwelawela's little cape, where one can look back over the plain to Konahuanui, to the deep cleft of Nu'uanu's pass, we did not look back. We looked ahead. We raced past the King's country house at the tip of the point, and hurried down the far side of the hill to meet the sea.

This is not the ocean in all its mightiness: here it is a gentled sea, tamed by the width of Kane'ohe's bay, of which He'eia's shore is only a small part. But the tide was high, little waves were rolling in, curling and breaking as though they were small brothers to the surfers' waves at Waikiki—and this was Eahou's first meeting with salt water. So we hastened down to the beach, gleeful as a pair of backsliders escaping from a Sabbath-day's third sermon.

The road through He'eia is the hard-packed sand, when the tide is out. When the tide is in, the road is gone. "No trouble," we Hawaiians say; "we get plenny time foa wait," as the lad from the livery stable would have said. The day was young, and I did not need the example of the other wayfarers who were frolicking in the warm water until the road was revealed. "Let us go for a swim, Eahou my friend. It is time you learned about the sea." While he tied the horses and the bundle of fish to the branch of a *milo* tree, I undressed and hung my townsman's garments upon other convenient branches, reciting as I did so the words to an ancient chant, "famed is the strand of He'eia, for its clusters of *milo*, growing in abundance even to the water's edge."

We had much fun. Eahou splashed and kicked, struggled and sank, swallowed the usual amount of salty water, and eventually learned to float without my having to hold him. This, I thought, was achievement enough for one morning. Yet, like every other boy at the beach, he wanted to stay longer. As though they would have some great effect upon my decision, I considered the brilliant sun, the sparkling water, the lapping waves, soft as puppy-dogs against our legs. He was right: why should we hurry away from such a pleasing place? "As you wish, so shall it be. Do you splash around then, while I go and talk with those people yonder."

The water was so shallow that it did not reach to my knees, the deep holes in the reef, marked by their green and blue coloring, were far away. He was not endangered. Nevertheless, worry made me sharp. The very name of He'eia is a warning to the unwary: "slipped away," it means, because here long ago, during a battle between the people from this district and invaders from leeward O'ahu, a great wave washed the residents out to sea. "But do not go where you can not stand up, you hear? And watch for big waves, you understand?"

"Alright," he agreed, blinking those salt-stung eyes, almost as red as his lips, "I will follow at your heels, like a fish." Feeling better because of my discretion, I waded stiff-legged through the warm sea, over to the other bathers. After all, this is a good-omened place, I thought: that great wave, in washing the people of He'eia back to shore again, had given them victory over their enemies, thus fulfilling an ancient prophecy.—If you can believe the tales of history, that is.

They were a happy little family, those other swimmers: a small thin man and his small plump wife, each with a little child in arms, each crooning "ui-ha, ui-ha" to distract the child as each tiny wave came past; a grandmother about my age; and two young girls, about ten and twelve years old.

At the seashore everyone is a commoner, as the first Kamehameha learned to his enlightenment that time a fisherman of Puna broke a canoe paddle over his head. The family greeted me as though I were a neighbor and old friend. They were not waiting for the tide to go out, but had come from their home in Kane'ohe just to enjoy a good time together.

"Next week," the husband said, rather grimly, "and only the good God knows how long thereafter, we shall be working hard, without rest."

"Yes," his wife agreed, adding the shrug and the sniff with which women express annoyance with the state of things, "next week we'll have no time for swimming."

"And what is happening then, that will keep you so bent of back?" I wanted to know.

"Heavens above!" she exclaimed, "and where have you been that you have not heard? All of Ko'olaupoko has been told."

"Forgive me for being so stupid. I am from Honolulu, where nobody knows anything."

"Well, then," she said, laughing, "fortunate are the people of Honolulu, in their ignorance."

"Ah, fortunate indeed are the people of Honolulu," said the grandmother sadly, the corners of her mouth turned down, "to be ignorant of the days of labor."

"The days of labor!" I repeated. "But that old rule is ended. Have you not heard? No longer do the people have to give time and labor to the chiefs."

Wife sniffed, Grandmother shrugged, Husband sighed. "Ahh, they are not called 'landlord days' anymore," he explained. "Now we are told to bring gifts. And next week is our turn to bring tribute to the Princess Keʻelikolani and her army of hungry dogs."

"Ah, ah, I see, I see.—And is that mighty one near by, then?"

"Too close," he said. "Just around that point she is, in Kahaluʻu."

"And while she and her robbers feast," the wife said bitterly, "Kahaluʻu's people go hungry."

"That is why today we eat and play," the man said. "This may be the last time we can be together as a family. Among the army of dogs are some who leap. No woman, no girl, is safe. Even boys are in danger. Tomorrow we send Kuku and our daughters into the mountains above Haʻiku, until those hounds have passed beyond the borders of Kaneʻohe. But, living there, in the cold wet forest with little to eat and little to shelter them from the rain except a roof of ferns: that will be hard for them."

"Of only one thing can we be certain," said the old woman, looking beyond us to the empty bay. "Not many other people will go with us into the mountains, as in the days of old."

"What a pity," I said. "I have noticed how few are the people who remain."

"Aye," said the wife, "perhaps next time Her Highness and her dogs come sniffing this way they will starve to death, because no one will be alive to bring them tribute."

"Terrible, terrible," I clucked, regretting both their helplessness and their discontent with the ruling chiefs. When the people complain, the chiefs are not doing their duty. And when they do not care for their people, the chiefs are endangered. I saw that I must report to Kauikeaouli this burden the Princess Ruth was placing upon his people. He would not like this message, I knew; but I knew also that I must warn him of as great a danger to the security of his Kingdom as is the threat of filibusterers from across the ocean. This one, closer to home, he himself must correct, for even an apprentice Machiavelli could understand that a king who does not restrain the behavior of his relatives and his ministers makes himself their ally in the eyes of his people.

"*E*, Mama," said the man, "although we may be hungry next week, let us not deny ourselves today. I am hungry now, so let us eat." Smiling shyly, his eyes soft with kindness, he turned to me. "Do you and your grandson be our guests. Do not fear: we have plenty. What is ours is yours."

Never have I been so touched by a man's courtesy. "You are very kind, and I am grateful. We shall join you with pleasure—and bring a morsel of fish to add to the feast."

This good family was well met: Ka'aha'aina was their name, which is to say "the feast." He was called Abraham, she Sarah. Upon *lauhala* mats spread upon the sand beyond the reach of waves, we ate our meal. It was simple fare by city standards, but it was by far the best I had eaten since I left home. Eahou's eyes stood out like the stalked eyes of a crab when he saw so many things laid upon the mats. Never in his whole life had he eaten so well. The women were his slaves, naturally, and they plied him with five times as much food as I thought his body could hold. "Eat, eat," they urged, "a growing boy must eat." He obliged them, and amazed me: when he was done his belly was swollen as tight as that of an overfed puppy.

As the meal reached its end the sandy road of He'eia was only a few inches under water. And for us the moment was approaching when "the eyes blink drowsily, the desire for effort is gone," as the old song says. "This impatient person can wait no longer for time or tide," I resisted their invitation to stay and nap with them. "After this generous repast, I should want to sleep until evening."

Abraham accompanied us to our horses. While I put on my clothes he said, in a low voice: "Your Eahou is a fine-looking boy. I am thinking that perhaps it would be wise for you to send him to the mountains. He is welcome to go with Kuku and our daughters, if you wish."

"I thank you, my friend, for your kind thought. But no, he must go with me."

"Then do you guard him well against those hunting dogs."

"I shall guard him well. He will be safe with me." Such trust I had in my ability to ward off all perils to him or to me.

"Then go with God," said gentle Abraham, making the sign of the cross in the air between us.

My goodness me, I thought, as our horses splashed through the ebbing waters of Heʻeia. How sinful I have been today, how many abominations I have committed. Swimming in the sea, exposing myself in nakedness, giving scandal to little ones, consorting with Papists—and naked ones at that. Not to mention the sins of hypocrisy and of gluttony, and perhaps a few others I couldn't bother to sort out—or couldn't recognize, in my ignorance. Every last missionary and his wife would have swooned dead away had they seen us, sitting unclothed around the eating-mat, half the foreigners in Honolulu would have cut me from their lists. How is it possible then, I asked, for a man so sinful to feel so happy? The answer, I knew, lay not only in my innocence but also in the innocence of Eahou and of my people. And our innocence, our enjoyment of the good things of life, is only a part of our reward for living on this beautiful island, the fairest of all islands in the great Pacific sea, this bower of loveliness which is Oʻahu ...

O most fortunate of men, I thought, this is the way it should be, wouldn't you say? Wanting to express my joy, I sang the charming song which celebrates the beauties of Waipi'o—and of another beauty who was encountered there:

> On all sides of Waipi'o the cliffs face each other,
> The cliffs enfold Waipi'o everywhere
> Except on that one side of Waipi'o turned to the water—
> Toward that other beauty,
> Another splendor,
> That gleams in from the open sea.

Too full of happiness to be drowsy, I chanted at the top of my voice, much to Eahou's amusement. The village of Kahalu'u, the dogs of Ke'elikolani, were still far away. Why should I worry yet about them? Why should I not sing?

> The ascent to rugged Koa'e-kea is steep,
> The climb onward to Ka-holo-kuaiwa is steeper still.
> At the Hi'ilawe falls a white cascade spills
> Sparkling from above and over the cliff, dropping down,
> Down into the pool of Ha'i—
> Ha'i, the woman there, Ha'i of the sacred pool.
> This is the way it should be, wouldn't you say?
> For me a little water, please—then let us eat and eat well!

When we left the sands of He'eia, to climb the little hill which lifts the road to the slopes above the in-curving bay of Kahalu'u, I was nearing the end of this long and subtle love-song:

> Now the trees of Makawao grow sturdy and erect:
> Now their young bark thickens:
> Now the tall cliff of Kokomo,
> The broad cliff,
> The cliff of glowing Kokomo
> Enfolds, in a way of her own, all the quiet charms of Ha'iku.

To our right, far across the bay, proud and majestic, rose up the high-standing ridge of Kanehoalani, "the heavenly companion of Kane," deserving of its name. Interrupting my song, I cried out: "Look! Look, Eahou, at the beauty of Kanehoalani. Look upon the loveliness of Oʻahu. And rejoice with me, that we live in a land so fair."

Never have I been so happy, I the most fortunate of men. Returning to the love-song, I took up its refrain:

This, too, is the way it should be, wouldn't you say?
For me a little water, please—then let all eat and
   eat well, again and ag—

Before I knew they were near, the hunting dogs of Keʻelikolani rose up to bar our way.

CHAPTER 12.

IN WHICH TRUSTING TRAVELERS ARE
THROWN UPON THE MERCY OF
A FIERCE PRINCESS

Yet, what are hunting dogs to commoners may be fawning dogs to chiefs. The Princess's watchmen were not as fearsome as Sarah and Abraham believed. Countryfolk, like city people, are more easily swayed by rumor than taught by experience. The four men who stopped us with upraised arms and apologetic smiles were not brutal soldiers, but seemed rather to be hewers of wood and drawers of water who had been told by the Princess's chamberlain to stand watch for a while over her privacy. The Kalani, as is well known, does not like to be bothered by petitioners, memorials from tenants on her vast properties, or other such dull business, when she is making one of her progresses. Other affairs are occupying her time and attention.

The watchmen took my measure and seemed to be favorably impressed. "*Aloha* to you two," said their leader, rising from his couch of ferns, drifting toward us as the blossom-kissing mist flows down a mountainside. Everything about him was soft and smooth: voice, skin, hands, lips, budding breasts, rounded hips beneath the sash of his loincloth, the walk, all proclaimed a *mahu*, one of those womanly men who make excellent dancers and musicians for all of us to appreciate, and comfortable lovers for men of a certain inclination to enjoy. Ke'eli-kolani is famed for her entertainers, and he, I suspected, used those long, supple fingers for nothing more arduous than tapping out upon gourds and sharkskin drums the rhythms for her *hula* dancers.

"And what brings you along this road?" he asked politely. The inquiry was for me, but his gaze was fixed upon Eahou.

"We are travelers on the way," I replied firmly, resolving not to let Eahou out of my sight while this soft-eyed pointer with a nose for delicacies was nigh. "We go to Kahana," I persisted, trying to draw his attention from the boy, sitting upon Pueo like Cupid, that *haole* godlet of love.

"What a pity," sighed the smitten one, smiling upon Eahou innocently smiling back at him. Recalling himself to duty, he lifted an arm as unjointed as that of a squid. "Then do you take the lower path, the one beside the shore."

Gladly would I have gone at once, but more than I feared the nearness of this tempter did I dread the temper of my wife in Honolulu. "Tell me," I leaned toward him, as one man asking a great confidence of another, "in the Kalani's company on this journey: is there a person named Eben Forrest?"

"Aye, he is here indeed. In the Kalani's sight, there is no other man." How nicely he put it, without the vulgar smirks or eye-rollings with which ordinary folk refer to the current favorite of Ke'elikolani.

"He is wife's brother to me," I said. Now at last he turned those dewy eyes upon me. "And she sends him a message which I must deliver. Is it possible, do you think, that I may speak with him for just the shortest of moments?—I do not wish to disturb Her Royal Highness."

"I think it can be done. Unless, of course," he peered upward into the trees, seeking the sun, "they are—well, resting. One never knows. Let us go to see. I myself will take you to him." Aware now of my importance, he stared no more at Eahou. Taking the reins, as sign that we were in his keeping, he led us along the upper path, into the shade under the tall *koa* trees.

Within a few minutes we came to the place where the hilly slopes become more gentle, where long ago the forest was burned away to make some farmer's sweet-potato patch perhaps. In this wide clearing the retainers of Princess Ruth had set up a village of grass huts, canvas tents, low sheds thatched with *ki* leaves, and other kinds of temporary shelters. Dozens of servants were laboring for their chiefess. All were dressed in the manner of olden days, the men in *malo*, the women in *pa'u*, for Ke'eliko-lani does not suffer gladly either foreigners or their garments. Smoke from fires for heating the stones to be used in the many earth-ovens made our noses twitch, enormous heaps of foodstuffs of every kind made our eyes open wide, the braying of mules, the squealing of hogs, the clamor of busy workers caused our ears to ring. The Princess Ke'elikolani journeyed in great state. Not since the days when Ka'ahumanu and the Reverend Hiram Bingham, with hundreds of attendants, traveled around the island, bringing the word of the New God to people of the countryside, could O'ahu have seen anything like this.

"And who is this important woman?" Eahou asked.

"None other than the greatest chiefess in the Kingdom,

and, after the King himself, the greatest landowner. The Princess Ruth Keʻelikolani is she, great-granddaughter to Kamehameha the Conquerer, niece's daughter to Kaui-keaouli, our King—long may he reign!—and half-sister to the Prince Alexander Liholiho, the Prince Lot Kamehameha, and the Princess Victoria Kamamalu—about whom I shall tell you some other time." I love to recount the genealogies of our important families and, wanting to interest him, I continued: "The High Chief Matthew Kekuanaoʻa is father to these four. Keʻelikolani is his child by Pauahi, a granddaughter to the first Kamehameha through his wife Kanekapolei. After Pauahi died, in giving birth to Keʻelikolani, Kekuanaoʻa was wed to Kinaʻu, a daughter to the Conqueror by his wife Kaheiheimalie-kaniu. In permitting these marriages, the Kamehameha family showed how wise they were. For Kekuanaoʻa is the son of Nahiolea, brother to that same Kaʻiana who died at Laʻimi, fighting for Oʻahu's King."

To my astonishment Eahou spat with disgust, saying: "These Kamehameha! These droppings of Ku! They are everywhere, like pig dung along a muddy trail."

"Hush, boy, hush," I pointed in alarm at our guide. "You must not say such things. You must not even think such things." But our graceful escort continued upon his way, giving no indication that he had heard, and I thanked my spirit-guardian for confounding his ears with camp noises. Yet no amount of noise could deafen the questions set loose in my mind by the boy's behavior.

I was still unnerved when the guide brought us to the end of our path. Highest of all the shelters in the village, built above all others so that the shadow of no commoner could fall upon either her dwelling or her head, was the pleasure-house of Keʻelikolani. It was a large grass hut, such as is erected in each of her resting-places, as is burned to the ground when she departs, so that no commoner may live in it to defile it. At the front, sticking out like the foredeck of a schooner, was a *lanai* covered over with white sailcloth. And in the cool shade of this airy pavilion, lying upon soft mats and silken cushions like two great whales stranded upon a reef, were Her Royal Highness and my brother-in-law.

Before the *kapu* signs our leader dropped to his knees. From beside the *lanai* a chamberlain came running, all bent over like a scuttling crab, hissing in exasperation. "What have you done?" he muttered, "bringing visitors here, when the Kalani rests." Unperturbed, the *mahu* explained who I was, what I wanted. His face furrowed with uncertainty, the unfortunate chamberlain looked with despair at me, with terror upon the recumbent Highness.

"Do not bother," I said in the lowest possible voice, "we will go away." No more than he did I want to draw her wrath upon our heads.

"Goddammit!" the roar billowed forth. She hates foreigners, but she uses their oaths with wondrous ease and no regard for their source. "What's the reason for all this noise?" The chamberlain cringed, I ducked, the *mahu* winked at Eahou. On their mats the two whales thrashed about, struggling to sit up. In this contest of gaspings and heavings my tactful brother-in-law allowed her to win. Leaning on an arm of molded fat, she glared out at us, an assemblage of blanched faces and unmoving ligaments. "Ah, it is you," she bellowed, while time stood still. The wide mouth broke into a friendly smile. "*Aloha* to you two. Come in, come in and eat!" Breathing began again, blood resumed its flowing, even the horses knew that we had been spared. While beyond her Eben grinned his welcome, her free hand fell like the limb of a tree upon his belly. "Hey, sleepyhead! Wake up. Company is here."

"Yes, my dear, so I see," said my brother-in-law, never one to be excited by anything, least of all by the husband of his domineering sister. "Hello, Hiram. Come aboard," he said, friendly enough.

In an explosion of relief, the chamberlain rushed to help me get down from Lokelani. The musician, leaving languor in the dust, hastened to lift Eahou from Pueo, taking much longer to do so than was necessary. Too annoyed with that mincing minion to thank either of those servants for their help, I grabbed Eahou's arm and pulled him toward the *lanai*. Not knowing whether to walk or to crawl, I settled into the chamberlain's crouch, trying to push Eahou into the same ignoble posture. "Walk like men!" she commanded. Like men we entered into the presence of this most formidable of all the Kamehameha.

"Sit down," she pointed toward a place on the mat opposite the two of them. I sat. Eahou did not obey quickly enough to escape her very close attention. "And who is this little man with you?" she asked, sweeping him to her side with a massive arm. "He is a handsome one!" While I stuttered away, saying "he is my son . . . his name is Eahou . . . ," she fondled his buttocks, put her lips to his belly, his nipples, to the little gourd of his boyhood, exclaiming between kisses, "Oh, my! Such a man he will be!" He, poor lad, taut with embarrassment, tried to pull away, beseeching me with his eyes to rescue him. But what could I do? Eben was laughing, knowing too well how fond she is of handsome men, how—as every one knows—she worships the gourd of a man as her greatest god.

Her tribute to the god in the boy being ended, she released him. As he fled to my side, she said, "Bring him back in ten years.—By that time this Eben here will be worn out."

My brother-in-law, the shame of my wife, the pride of all other Forrests of Kealakekua, smiled good-naturedly. "The hardwood firestick will outlast the softwood rubbing-board, I think."

"Indeed, you seem to be standing up very well," I cackled, thinking it was my turn to join their ribaldry.

Whereupon she laughed mightily, patted his huge thigh with a heavy hand, and conceded, "This Eben! I tell you: he is a man."

They were well matched, those two, looking upon each other with the fondness of lovers, not with the boredom of mates. She was never a thing of beauty, at least in my opinion, being too generously supplied with every item that makes a woman: her lips were too thick, her breasts too big, the nose was too flat, the waist too wide. Everything in excess: that is Ke'elikolani, The Leafbud-of-Heaven. And, worst of all, under the abundance of flesh, there burned in her the fire that does not consume, the itch that can never be appeased.

Even so, she has never lacked for handsome men. Her husband, Lele'iohoku, son of that Kalanimoku who was prime minister to Kamehameha I, was gained in a marriage of state, of course, but he soon died. Of her uncounted lovers, some no doubt were attracted more by her great wealth and high rank than by her charms, but many were willing captives of her generosity in largess and in love. Yet each of them knows that sooner or later her ardor will cool, her eyes (or her spies) will find another man of proportions generous enough to please her, and that when the new man appears at her side the old lover is supposed to take his leave. If he goes gracefully, as most of them do, he is showered with gifts and keeps the sisterly affection of the woman who has tired of him as a lover but remembers him well as a friend. If he refuses to depart with good grace, she commands her servants to throw him into the nearest cesspit.

Only one man, according to the gossips of Honolulu, has ever surpassed her. He was a country youth, from Hauʻula of Oʻahu I believe, who, upon being brought to her, proved to be—But no: I can not go on. The missionaries have unmanned me for this tale about that man of parts. Suffice it to say, this superlative youth lives (and probably will die) an unwed man. Those gossips also say that, when her astonished retainers escorted him home again, he carried with him a bar of gold of a certain shape and of enormous size and weight, in token of her esteem. Upon this gold bar was inscribed the one word *Minamina*, that is to say, "grief for something that is lost." I think the story is imagined. Whatever would he have done with a bar of gold in remote Hauʻula? She, a most sensible woman, would have given him a more practical gift than that.

Her servants were most attentive, in all things. When Eahou and I arrived she had said "come and eat." Now the food appeared—deep calabashes of *poi*, fish steamed in *ki* leaves, morsels of tender pig, crisp seaweeds from the bay: a light repast—and silver bowls of scented water for us to wash our fingers in. We Hawaiians are a clean people: we eat not unless first we wash. And, alas, some Hawaiians are also a gluttonous lot: although all of us had eaten only an hour or so earlier, we fell upon that collation as though we had not tasted food for several days.

Between dainty dippings of her fingers into the *poi* she asked, "And how is that Christian wife of yours? Has she sent you to tell Eben to go home?"

Oh, my, these Kamehameha! They are shrewd ones.

And of them all she and Lot most nearly resemble that shrewdest one, the founder of their line. "Not really," I replied, thinking to lie my way out of this trap, until I saw the half-smile, the glint in her eyes, and Eben, waiting for my answer. "Well, yes, you have said it," she compelled me to admit, "that is one of the messages I am to deliver."

"Cha! I thought as much," she nodded, ripping the backbone whole from a steamed 'opakapaka, as if it were Rebekah in her grasp. "Those women! They can never let me enjoy the life they wish they too could live. Though they may feel the itch, they do not have the guts to do as I do."

"And a good thing, too," laughed Eben. "What would happen to Hawai'i Nei if all its women were like you?"

"You are right, my firestick. This way *I* can claim the best.—And the other messages?" she demanded of me.

"The others?—Oh. Oh.—They are not for Eben. I go to Kahana, to visit my family there. I have not seen them in about ten years."

"A mistake," she decreed. "Relatives are best endured when they are most unseen. I never look upon mine unless I must.—Why do you take this boy of yours with you?"

"To keep me company on the way, for one thing. To meet my relatives, for another.—And because I go to prepare my resting-place there. He will care for my bones, when the time comes." I do not know why I thought of this reason, but the words came before I could stop them. Yet to talk of death at a feast is an unforgivable breach of manners, an even more dreadful omen. I sat as if already I were stricken with several mortal illnesses.

"Ah," she said, unexpectedly kind, "this is a reason I can understand."

Eben offered a true friend's comforting: "Nah, nah.

You are too young yet to worry about such things. You do not look ready for a grave.—How old are you now?"

"Fifty," I said, feeling like I was a hundred, wishing I'd never had this grim thought, wondering why my spirit-guardian had thrust it into my mind, and bitter because these lovers were only half my age while I was so close to the dark path of night.

"And then?" she pushed me past my waiting grave in Kahana, and for once I was grateful for her directness.

"I think I will go home by way of Kahuku. I am to give greetings from people in town to 'Polly' Hopkins, if he is there.—And, oh yes, I almost forgot: the same to Saul Bristol in Ka'a'awa, if he is there."

"You will see the one, perhaps, but not the other," said Eben. "Hopkins has gone back to town by now, I think. Bristol never leaves Ka'a'awa. Even so, you may not see him. He is a strange man."

"Indeed," said Princess Ruth. "He *hides*. Like an eel in his hole. When we went past Ka'a'awa he was gone. So were the people who live in that lonely place. Never have I been so offended. Deserted it was, like one of your whorehouses when the night is ended." Laughing loudly at my embarrassment, she pointed at me with a moist finger. "You are not the only inquisitive one in Hawai'i, my friend. But no matter: the gifts at Ka'a'awa were plentiful, for a valley inhabited by ghosts."

"Before he hid himself away, and the people with him," Eben explained, "Bristol sent us steers and calves. They were a welcome change from the usual pork and fish."

Yawning mightily, she washed her fingers. "Now it is time to sleep," she declared. The waiting servants crawled in to remove the remnants of our meal. Amid a contagion of yawns from all of us, she gathered a pile of cushions at her side. "Do you sleep also. In the house right over there. Later, when the sun has gone beyond the mountains, we shall have a feast. Tonight is Mahealani. The dancing will be good, I promise you. We are not bothered here by missionaries."

Quite aside from the fact that one does not decline an invitation from Her Royal Highness, I was delighted to accept. Townsfolk such as I am rarely are given the chance to see her dancers and to hear her musicians.

Even as the solicitous chamberlain escorted us to our sleeping-place, the gigantic pair settled back among their pillows. Eahou and I were glad to fall upon our mats.

When I awoke, late in the afternoon, Eahou was not on his bed. That long-fingered musician! was my first thought. Rushing out of the house, I almost stepped upon the boy. He was sitting on my saddle, which someone had placed beside the door, watching the people at their many tasks. While I finished the slow business of restoring wakefulness to mind and limbs, I sat beside him, answering his questions about what the Kalani's retainers were doing. From our vantage we could see them wandering about on the land and in the sea, as they did every day for their imperious lady. They were not working very hard. "They have a good life," I concluded. "They eat well, they travel about, they see different places, meet different people. They have an interesting life." I forgot to consider that they might miss the company of their children—if they had any children waiting for them in Honolulu.

"Makuahou," the boy began slowly, looking out across the bay to the mountain of Kanehoalani, "are you going soon to the pit of Milu?"

"Hah! Not if I can help it!—I like this land of the

living too well to exchange it for the land of the dead."

"Then why did you tell her what you said—about going to Kahana?"

Aye, this was a puzzle, most of all to me. I could not really say that I had lied to her. Nor could I say that I had not lied. "Because," I replied soberly, remembering how many a truth is discovered by mistake, "it is a good and proper thing for a man of my age to think about where his bones will rest, when at last his spirit must depart for the realm of Milu.—Did not your grandfather think this thought, while he lay there on his bed?"

"He did.—But I do not want you to leave me, as he has left me."

Full of love for this boy who was so much in need of love, I drew him into my lap, nuzzling the top of his head, the back of his neck, the ears. "Bless you, my son. For your sake, and for mine, I will not leave you too soon." Not for a long time could I see clearly again. And for a longer time we sat in peace, comforted by more than the light of the sun.

After a while he spoke of another worry: "I am thinking that I should put on those clothes of the missionary boy."

"But why?—I thought you did not like to wear clothes, not even a *malo*."

"For to cover me from the sight of that woman. I do not like the way she looks at me.—Is she an evil?"

"No," I laughed, "she is not evil. She is an honest woman. And honesty is not an evil—although sometimes it can hurt like evil." But, I thought, the loss of this boy's innocence is evil. Now he is like Adam, after he did taste of the fruit in Eden. Yet I knew that, sooner or later, this awakening must come to Eahou as it does to every boy. And I wished that his Eve might have been someone more beguiling than that huge sensual woman. Then, remembering the musician with his wanton glances, very well aware that the serpent can command so many helpmates, I said, "I think perhaps you are right. We shall find you a *malo*." Just then Eben, stretching and scratching, came out from the Kalani's house. "And I know exactly where to ask for one."

He is a big man, this Eben. One of his loincloths would make a dozen for Eahou, with enough left over for a cape and sheets for his bed. The friendly giant ambled toward us. There was so much of this Forrest, that we could not see the trees behind him. Almost beyond recapturing in this hulking man, padded now with fat and flesh, was my memory of Eben as a youth: lean and slender he had been, with the body and the interests of an athlete, and little time to spare from the sea for the women who swooned over his handsomeness. But now his thighs were thick, the folds of his belly hung down over the *malo*'s sash, the weight of those heavy legs slowed his pace. Ah, Eben, Eben, I sighed to myself, by living with her you have lost more than you have gained.

"I am going to the place of the wilted grass," he called cheerfully. "Do you come along, and we will talk." As we walked beside him he said, "Would you believe it? Only when I go to relieve myself am I alone. For I alone can use this place. My exalted position even has me pissing above the rest of mankind. I, who am a commoner at heart, I do not enjoy this as much as I should, perhaps.—Now you must tell me about Rebekah and your family. But spare me her special message. I have heard it before, you must know."

"They are well, I thank you for asking. And that is enough about them.—But tell me: what am I going to say to Rebekah when she asks if I have seen you?"

He stopped, looking down at me with the patience one grants a child who is not very smart. "Hiram, my friend: look about you." Like a high chief he indicated with outstretched arm the busy village below. "And tell me how I can leave all this sooner than I must. This life is better than any I have known. Certainly it is better in every way than the life I led as a policeman in Kona. And she— Eahou, my boy," with a single hand he took the lad by the neck, lifted him above the path, put him down again, facing toward the valley of Kahaluʻu. "I am sorry we have no children in this camp for you to play with. But do you go over there for a while and look at the chickens and the pigs, while I talk with your father."

"But do not go far," I said, the worried parent, "and when we go back, do you come with us."

As the boy sped off Eben clapped me on the shoulder. "I see no Forrest blood in him. Surely Rebekah is not his mother?—No?—Ah, you rascal, you. How many gift-children do you have?"

"Oh, ten or twelve, I guess. I can never be sure."

"You old cock, you. A fine one you are to be bringing me messages that I must cease to scratch about in a barnyard with but one hen."

"Eben, my friend, surely you realize that giving you this message is not my idea?"

"To be sure, I know this well enough. Only an older sister like Rebekah would try to pry this limpet from his rock.—But seriously now, how can I leave? I am the prisoner not only of this woman's wealth but also of her lust—and of my own. I please her, as few men can. She pleases me, as no other woman has. Is not this reason enough for us to live together for a time? So I shall stay with her while she is content with me. But be assured: it will not last long. It never does with her. She will find another cock to please her, I will be sent away. Then perhaps I shall return to Lukila and the life of a poor man in Kealakekua. I endured it once, before Keʻelikolani found me, I can endure it again.—Tell me: have you heard how Lukila is, and the child? Lukila does not write to me. For which I do not blame her."

"They are well, Rebekah has told me. The girl goes to school now, at Hoʻokena."

"I am glad to hear this. But I do not miss them, I confess. There is little love now between me and Lukila, as I think you have heard. And I hardly know the girl: her mother has made us almost strangers. But I would stay at home more, I think, if Lukila had made me a son. Or if, even now, she would let me take an adopted son, to go fishing with, to talk with as a man can talk with a manchild.—You who have so many: why do you not give me a son to have for my own? Give me this one, I ask you. He is a fine boy. Keʻelikolani thinks so too. Already she has told me how she would like to betroth him to her daughter—"

"No!" I cried, more fiercely than this unhappy man deserved, not even thinking of the great honor the Kalani would bestow upon the boy and me with such a marriage. "Eahou is promised to another.—But I have several other gift-sons in Honolulu. When you are ready to go home to Kealakekua, then I will give you one to be your own."

Stopping in the path, he took my hand in his, binding me to the promise. "Hiram, those are good words to hear. Do not forget them."

"I shall not forget," I answered in good faith, even as I saw a way to help both him and me. "In fact, I have in mind the very one for you. His mother is dead, he lives with his grandmother, and she is too old to care for him. He is a little rascal. Nine years old, full of the devil, and readier to go fishing than to attend school."

"Good, good. He is the one I need, the very one."

"Then he is yours. When you are ready, you shall have Caleb to take home with you."

When, later, we parted before the *kapu* signs, Eben said, "Caleb . . . I like that name. I shall like the boy. When the time comes for me to leave all this, he will make my going easier."

CHAPTER 13.

IN WHICH CAPTIVE GUESTS ARE
ENTERTAINED IN A
PLEASURE-PAVILION

The feast began in the cool of evening, just as Kane-in-the-Eye-of-the-Sun disappeared behind the mountains, on his way to the lands of the west. Because this was to be Mahealani, the night of the full moon, Princess Ruth ordered a ceremony of great state, that we might give honor to Mahina, the goddess of the moon.

The solemn note of a conch shell, blown by a young musician, quieted everyone in the village. Thereafter they should make no noise, no needless movement, until the Kalani and her guests were seated. The stewards who prepared the foods for her eating-mat worked in silence. All others gathered at the bounds of the open space before her pleasure-house and sat cross-legged upon the ground, uttering neither word nor sigh.

In our little hut Eahou and I listened for the second call of the conch. Instructed by the head chamberlain, and dressed by servants under his supervision, we scarcely breathed. Each of us was girded in a loincloth of *kapa*

scented with powdered sandalwood, was draped in a cape
of matching *kapa* tied over the right shoulder, leaving the
other bare. These were gifts from Eben, cut by the stewards to fit our smaller bodies. In the darkening house,
awaiting our summons, we stood stiff as carven images.

As the herald's second signal wafted over the hillside,
Ke'elikolani and Eben came forth to take their places beside the feast-mat.

"Do I have to go?" Eahou whispered. "I am not hungry . . ."

"Do not be worried," I tried to soothe him. "You will
recover your appetite, once we are there. And I think that
you will like the dances which will follow the feast."

A lesser chamberlain appeared at our door, murmuring "Now is the time." Quickly we followed him to the
pavilion, making our bows to the Princess and to Eben as
we approached.

"Good evening," she called out, "come in, come in. Be
at ease. Never mind all this formality. It is for the sake
of the people, not for us."

As with all the folk in her train, she was dressed in the
ancient style: a *pa'u* covered her bulk from waist to knee,
a *kihei* hid one sloping shoulder, one full breast. Around
the neck she wore the whaletusk hung from a *lei* of braided
human hair that was the sign of her rank; and in her hair,
like a coronet, rested a *lei* of yellow feathers. Not since
the time of Kina'u had I seen in public a royal princess
dressed in the style of our ancestors.

We were honored indeed: the chamberlain escorted us,
like high chiefs, to places at the same mat with her. She
pulled Eahou close, exclaiming "My, my! You are a
handsome one, even with clothes on." As fussy as any
doting mother, she rearranged the folds of his cape,
smoothed the mane of his hair, while he scowled at the

touch of her unrelenting hand. "Now let us enjoy the evening," she commanded, pulling him down beside her, "let us eat."

The mat, almost hidden under fresh leaves, ferns, and flowers, was laden with fruits and vegetables of every kind the lands of O'ahu could offer. From far and near they were gathered in: coconuts, sugarcane, pineapples, oranges, watermelons, guavas, bananas, mangoes, bowls full of the red prickly pears of the cactus plant, freed of their spiny skins and bathed in their blood-colored juices; pyramids of baked taro, sweet potatoes, white potatoes, and breadfruits, of raw cabbages, love apples, onions both green and round, chile peppers, radishes, alligator pears, and wooden bowls holding a dozen different kinds of seaweeds. At the center of the mat was a forest of bottles, decanters, and jugs, holding every kind of beverage: springwater, coconut water, orange juice, coffee, and tea; German beer, English ale, and French wines; strong liquors such as gins, whiskies, rums, and brandies; and, most powerful of all, our island-made spirit, 'okolehao, distilled from a mash made of fermented ki roots. Already awaiting each of us were a huge calabash full of poi; platters of dried beef, dried fish, and dried squid; a coconut-shell cup holding crystals of red salt; another full of that delectable relish prepared by mixing fragments of baked kukui nutmeats with rock salt and crisp red seaweed; a silver fingerbowl with yellow 'ilima flowers floating upon the water; a nest of sparkling glasses to hold any drink we might choose. "My goodness me!" Eahou and I said at the same moment. "Eat!" the Kalani ordered, presenting with her own fingers a slice of sweet pineapple to the bedazzled boy.

Now, coming before us almost on their knees, a long line of servers brought in bowls and trenchers of hot meats, still steaming from the earth-ovens in which they had been cooked: tender flesh of pig, dog, beef, veal, mutton, and lamb, rich with gobbets of fat and flakes of crusted skin; coveys of whole chickens, pigeons, and plovers arranged around native ducks and geese. Then came the provender of the sea: raw or cooked, baked or steamed, whole or broken, they were more numerous than were the meats and fowls: mullet, *'opelu*, *kawakawa*, *aholehole*, *'opakapaka*, *'a'awa*, *ulua*, and *papio*, several kinds of tunas, *mahimahi*, eels, squid, crabs, lobsters, *'opihi*, *pipipi*, *wana*, sea cucumbers, even that new and costly delicacy, salted salmon imported from Oregon. Never in my whole life had my nose been treated to so many enticing aromas, my stomach to so many assaults upon its strength.

Each dish was presented first to her, then to us, finally to Eben. And, as was only polite, each took a portion from each savory viand, placing it upon the clean *ki* leaf which served for a plate. Every now and then, as a mark of favor, when something especially fine arrived she would put a bit of it upon Eahou's leaf or upon mine, saying "This looks delicious," or "Try this: it is quite rare." Soon before each of us was heaped three times as much food as he could ever manage to swallow. Eahou, who had never been tested so heroically, was wise enough to cry, "Stop, stop! Enough, enough!" But only when the last servant had passed did she desist. "Now let us eat, and eat well," she said, dipping her fingers into the *poi*. "The gods have given us all these good things. So let us enjoy them."

"In the name of Kane," I called to Eben between tastings and lip-smackings, "do you dine this way every night?"

"No, thanks be to Kane," he replied, "if we did, I could not walk. Only when we have guests do we fare so well.—Or when the chamberlain thinks the time has come to cook everything in the camp, before the foods can spoil."

"Nothing is wasted," she assured me, in the tones of a thrifty housewife. "What we do not eat, my people will. In a few minutes they will have their turn, out there."

This much I knew, of course, from having been among the retainers of other chiefs at many another feast. According to our rank and position did we have the chance to pick among the remnants from the eating-mats and cooking-ovens of our lords. The cooks always fared best. They never went hungry, which is why, in my youth, I was ever willing to lend a hand with the preparing and serving of meals. Most of the time there would be enough for everyone, even the lowliest commoner, in a chief's following. A good chief, through his chamberlains and stewards, must be a good provider if he wants to keep his people content. Rarely, even in the largest retinues—such as the hundreds of folk who attended upon the first Kamehameha or upon Ka'ahumanu when she was Queen Regent—was anyone forced to lick the *ki* leaves in which dog or pig had been cooked, and even when that happened he had enough fish and *poi* with which to satisfy his hunger. This was the rule, except in time of famine. Then everyone was hungry, except for the greatest chiefs. They must be fed, said the law, in order to preserve them and their lines who were the children of the gods.

Thinking not of her people but of gentle Abraham Ka'aha'aina and his Sarah, I ventured to say, "All these servants: they must need so much to eat."

She sensed my meaning at once. Her head went up, she threw the morsel of fish upon the mat. "You will find no hungry ones among my people," she said coldly. "Most of my money is spent upon feeding them, not me."

This was not the answer I expected. "You buy all this food?" I asked, unable to reckon the immense cost of sustaining such a horde.

"Most of it. How else do you suppose it would come to us, in these new times? The days of labor for the chiefs are ended. Surely you must know that, my friend.—Or have you been living in the city for so long that you do not know how smart in matters of money our countryfolk have become? All that you see before you—except for the seaweeds and perhaps the limpets and sea urchins, which are gathered by my people because I trust no one else to take them fresh—is paid for in good *haole* gold."

She was well on the way to being angry; I was wishing I could crawl under the flowers and ferns to escape her wrath, when Eben saved me. "Tell Hiram and Eahou about the gift-offering the other day," he suggested, offering her a sip from his glass of gin.

"Ah, yes, the people of Ka'alaea," she said with a big smile, her good humor seeming to return at his bidding. "The old people have not forgotten the old ways. They are the ones for whom my liver is saddened. They want to bring gifts, they want to do things in the right way, but most of them can not. Often they are too poor, and this I can believe. Others say that a son or a daughter begrudges them the gift they would like to bring, and this too I can understand. Even so, when they come to the side of the road with nothing but bunches of *ki* leaves and wreaths made of ferns in their hands, I stop to talk with them, to tell them that their *aloha* for me is gift enough. I may be a bitch, but I am not a greedy bitch. Am I, Eben?"

"A bitch only in bed, my sweet, not on the highway," said Eben, not looking up from the haunch of dog he was gnawing upon. "And that is all that matters."

"Oh, this Eben!" she cried. "Do you wonder that I like

him? He is not afraid of me, not even of my sharp tongue."
Patting him fondly on the knee, she begged, "Pour me
something to drink, my dear. All this talking and eating
gives me a thirst." Leaning toward me, she confided in a
voice the whole village must have heard, "How can I
scream in anger at a man who yawns at my temper?"

"Far worse than a screaming woman," said Eben com-
placently, while he poured her a glassful of whiskey, "is
the one who wanders from the subject of conversation.
What about the gift-giving, my dear?"

"Ah, the gift-giving!" she shrieked. "You see?" she
beamed at him, at me, who could only marvel at the ease
with which my brother-in-law bridled this force of nature.
"Where was I, in my story?—Oh, yes. At Kaʻalaea it was,
that place of swamps and mudflats, the poorest district on
Oʻahu perhaps. There the old people found a way to greet
me such as no other place has ever offered."

While she drained the draught of whiskey, Eben said,
"I have seen many offerings of gifts from people along
the road, but this one will live longest in my memory."

"And in mine," she agreed. "There they were, five old
women and three ancient men, people of my grandfather's
time, lined up beside the road. As we came up to them,
their leader, a frail and wrinkled person, stepped forward. 'Only the eyes have come,' he called out, standing
in the road before me. To myself I sighed, thinking this
was to be one more dull apology for empty hands, another
plea for forgiveness. Yet something about him made me
look twice. He was not the kind who whines, not the kind
who breaks his back with eager bowings. Good cheer came
from him and, as I looked at them, from his company.
'And our voices,' he said with a big smile and something
that was close to a very saucy wink. Whereupon they sang
an old chant of welcome, one that even I had not heard

before. When they were finished with that first one, they
sang others. Those white-haired old folk, the women with
their broken teeth and hanging breasts, the men with their
thin arms and empty loincloths, were full of jests and
surprises. They danced—a little stiffly, to be sure, and in
the old-fashioned style—but all their chants and dances
were happy ones, without a touch of sorrow. My people
gathered around to listen and to praise. Their people, seeing how we liked this gift-offering, came out of hiding-
places in the swamps and bushes. There in the road, between the mudflats and the bulrushes, we had a joyful
time. Not since Eben came to live with me have I been so
happy."

"They knew about me, too." Eben was pleased with
having been noticed. "Always it is a wonder to me, how
the news is spread about. Tell Hiram about the song in
honor of our—"

"No!" she stopped him, "how can I, with the boy here
so wide awake? But later, later, my people will sing it for
us. I told them to learn it, before we parted from those
good folk of Ka'alaea, and they have done so."

"Only their eyes came," said Eben, "but when they departed their bellies were full, and their hands."

"Nice, nice!" I burbled, enchanted by the tale and by
its tellers. This proud Princess and her hunting dogs: they
are not such robbers as I had been led to think.

"And why should I not thank them well?" she asked.
"They gave me something of great worth: a gift I never
thought to carry away from so poor a place. From any
place. When we were about to say farewell, I asked them
how they could be so high-spirited, so full of cheer. At
once, without need for thinking, their leader spoke: 'Because we live.' And behind him the others, with their tooth-

less gums and wisps of white hair, smiled and nodded in agreement."

"Ah," I said, touched not so much by the lesson, which I have discovered for myself, but by her response to it, "there spoke a wise man. He has understood what few people learn, even when they have grown old: that a man's life is his to make."

"You have said it," she looked at me for the first time with something like respect. I do believe that she was surprised to discover, lying within me, a core of good sense, which ordinarily I keep wrapped up in the levity of a joker. "Fortunate are those who, like him and like you, have seen this truth," she said softly. "Now, since I have learned this lesson, I am not so fearful anymore of growing old."

"I see no sign of aging," Eben pronounced cheerfully, toasting her in 'okolehao, "but you will waste away into a scrawny young woman, if you do not eat."

"Ah," she lifted her glass to him, "rather than lose my beauty in your eyes, my love, I shall eat, I shall drink."

Merry once more, we continued with our feasting. Below us, near the village, the lesser retainers sat at eating-mats, enjoying their portion of the repast. Beyond them the countryfolk were gathering, come to gaze upon the Kalani who dined in such splendor and to watch the entertainment which her people had promised them. Her musicians and dancers were famed throughout the Kingdom, as once Kauikeaouli's were, in the days of his youth, when he was in rebellion against the domination first of Ka'ahumanu and then, after she died, of Kina'u. Because they, in their turn, were influenced by the American missionaries, who hate and decry our heathen dances, Kauikeaouli asserted his independence of both missionaries and regents by surrounding himself with pleasure-loving companions and entertainers of all kinds. The more the missionaries protested by day, the louder did the *hula* drums sound by night. But now, alas, rebellion has been driven out of Kauikeaouli; and, of all the great nobles, only Ke'eliko-lani ignores the preachments of the missionaries.

At length the time came when we could eat no more, when we lay gasping beside the mat. Most of the good things spread before us were untouched. The stewards carried them away, to be consumed by those chamberlains and household attendants who were worthy to share those choicer viands. After the mat was cleared of its heavy burdens it was removed, leaves, flowers, and all, uncovering a clean one beneath. Upon this the beverages were placed, for us to draw from as we wished.

Slowly did the day depart, as though it were a guest unwilling to leave the feast. Soft was the dusk, and delicate as dyed *kapa* were the last touches of color in the western sky: pale pink and lemon yellow, and the green of seawater over sand they were, promising a fall of no more than dew in the mountains during the night. Above the unwrinkled waters of the bay, Kanehoalani stood up black, the forerunner of night, like a cresting wave poised to fall upon the little island of Mokoli'i. And from the east night stole in, covering sky, sea, and earth with her dark cloak.

It was a time of waiting, a time of mystery. And in completest silence did we sit, knowing what was to come.

CHAPTER 14.

IN WHICH THE NIGHT OF MAHEALANI IS
CELEBRATED IN SONG AND STORY

Within a few minutes the eastern horizon began to lighten. Brighter glowed the sky, more intense grew our hush of expectation, until—at last! the golden arc of the moon rose above the rim of the world. Amid cries of love and welcome from hundreds of throats was Mahina born anew.

Our fervor ended the instant she was revealed in the fullness of her glory. Out of the darkness on earth a chant was offered up to her:

> She is here, Hina is here,
> The goddess who dwells in the sky.
> She has come, Hina has come,
> The Mother in the heavens,
> To make bright the night of Mahealani.
>
> Where is heaven? Where are the stars,
>   on the night of Mahealani?
> They are there, they are not lost.
> They are above, they are in place,
> Showing the way for Mahina.

Out of the darkness under the trees a score of young men and young women danced into the space before Ke'elikolani's pavilion, timing their motions to the rhythms of the chant. Lighted only by Mahina, in their capes of white *kapa* they seemed to be shafts of moonlight, gliding slowly across this darkened earth. Beautiful they were, and pure, like a picture come to life, like music for the eyes. And I thrilled to see that in this ceremony, too, my people had not forgotten the ancient ways.

When the devotion to Mahina was ended, young men ran in from the corners of the village, each carrying a flaming brand. With these they lighted *kukui*-nut torches set into the ground in a half-circle before us. Beyond the torches, in their rows seated, kneeling, and standing, were the watchers. Within the ring of fire, facing us, stood the dancers and the musicians. Upon their heads and shoulders they wore *lei* made from strands of fragrant *maile* leaves.

As is the custom, the first song was an invocation to Laka, who is the guardian goddess to dancers, poets, singers, and musicians. Slow and worshipful, the hallowed words, the prescribed gestures, were given to her:

> A cluster of herbs, O Laka,
> An offering of growing things is here.
> Calling upon you, O Laka, we stand here.
> The prayer to Laka has power,
> The *maile* of Laka grows now anew.
> A freeing, grant us a freeing,
> A two-fold freeing.
> Free us, we ask, free us.
> A *kapu* profound is yours to keep.
> A freedom complete we ask for us.
> The goddess is *kapu* still.
> Now we who ask are freed!

The prayer being ended, the musicians sat down upon the grass, placing their instruments before them, drums of several sizes, gourds both small and large, feathered rattles holding seeds, lengths of bamboo, sticks of heavy wood. The dancers remained standing, waiting for the music to begin. It came at once, the accompaniment to a dance of noblest honor and dignity, telling of the journey of Hi'iaka, that time she went from Hawai'i to Kaua'i to bring the handsome Lohi'au to woo her sister Pele:

> In Ko'olau I met with rain:
> > it comes with lifting and tossing of dust,
> > advancing in columns, dashing along,
> > the rain, it sighs in the forest . . .

Smooth and supple and sweet was the voice of the chanter. I was not surprised to find that he was the *mahu* who had led Eahou and me into this village of delights. "A beautiful voice!" I declared when his song was ended, loud enough for him to hear my praise. "Who is he, this excellent singer?" I asked the Kalani more privately.

"The best in the Kingdom. Jared Pihana is his name. A man of Maui."

"Cha! That is no man," said Eben with a sneer that I did not expect of him.

"You! You!" she rebuked him with a slap upon the knee, "and why are you so small-minded? You snort like a missionary. Is it not enough that he should have such a fine voice?"

"If you say so, my gentle one," he agreed, pretending to fear heavier blows. "I was only warning Hiram, for his virtue's sake." Then it was my turn to snort. "Yet I suppose you are right, in a way," Eben went on, "about my being small-minded. He is, after all, the *aikane* of Peter Kahekili."

As it always does with natives, this word *aikane* set us to laughing. To us it means a bed-man to a chief, yet somehow or other the foreigners have taken it to mean a friend. In a sense, I concede, no one can be more of a friend than is a bed-man, but even so we're always wonderfully amused when some woman-chasing foreigner or an unsexed missionary hails a Hawaiian man as his *aikane*. It is one of the proofs of our cruelty, I believe, or perhaps of our vengefulness, that none of us has ever bothered to tell these foreigners how they misuse the word. There and then I promised myself that someday I would define the term for Lorrin Andrews, at the risk of scandalizing him. "You must understand, Lorrin," I could hear myself saying, "that while '*ai* does indeed mean a food, especially a vegetable food, *ai* means something very different . . ." Oh dear, how could I ever explain all these things to Lorrin?

"You know Pita, of course?" the Kalani was asking me.

"I have met him," I answered, "but I do not know him well enough to know this much about him." I could have guessed as much, however, from knowing some of the company he keeps. A scandal to ordinary folk are they, as well as to the virtuous—and damnably unfair competition to hotel-keepers in town.

"Does this make any difference to you, as it does to this bed-man of mine?" she persisted.

Really, I thought, she is frank to the point of indecency. Both embarrassed and worried because of the effect such loose talk might have upon Eahou, I wished she would give up this subject for another. Bright-eyed and perk-eared, that young gentleman was taking in every word we said. I could imagine him, when we were alone, asking about half-a-dozen interesting items in this conversation which I was not quite sure I could explain to a lad of such limited experience. Good Heavens! My mind reeled as, suddenly, I understood how immense was his innocence—

"The main thing," she lectured me, while she ignored the entertainers and the populace, who I was certain were watching our every action, "the main thing is to love— and to be loved."

"Of course, of course," I replied sincerely, as well I could because I hold the same belief. Anxious to get away from the subject and eager to watch the dancers, I said no more.

"Pita," she shook her head sadly, "is sick in town. I worry about him. He has some sores on his foot which do not heal. The medicines of foreign doctors and of native doctors do not help. I have told him to soak his foot in the urine of a red sow. This is a favored remedy among fishermen, who often have sores on the feet."

"Is it so?" I said politely, groaning inwardly at the uselessness of such a prescription. To heal sores something living is needed, something growing. "Has he tried a poultice made of the leaves of the *laukahi?*" I enquired, not really caring whether he kept his damned foot or not, but feeling that I must say something to guide them to the right path.

"He has done that first of all, I am sure. Everyone knows the value of *laukahi*. But these, it seems, are not ordinary sores, such as the *laukahi* can heal." I was about to pray to Laka, beseeching her to strike this talkative woman dumb for the rest of the evening, when her own mouth came to my rescue. Flicking her fingers along Eben's thigh, she said, "We are thirsting, my kegful of love. Please do you pour us something to drink."

Eben was attentive: thereafter our glasses were never empty. And at last, as was proper, we devoted ourselves to the entertainment, listening to the throbbing drums, the pounded gourds, the voices, sometimes alone sometimes in chorus, watching the graceful motions of the dancers. So decorous were they, at the beginning, that not even a missionary wife could have complained.

But after the fourth dance the sacred part of the evening was concluded. The dancers took off the capes, to cool their bodies and to free their arms, shoulders, and hips. "Wonderful!" I cried out at sight of the figures thus revealed. In the years since last I had seen the dances of olden times, I had forgotten the elegance of the clothing which is worn by entertainers to the court of a ruling chief. No simple skirt covered the loins of Ke'elikolani's artists. With a lavishness which only the very wealthy can afford, she had decreed that each of her dancers should be swathed in many yards of the most costly *kapa*. Wrapped tight around the hips, and only one layer thin at the front, it was built up from there, at the sides and at the back, with loopings, flounces, and great bows. The effect, instead of being decorous, was wondrously exciting: the eye of a beholder was drawn to those hips, to the gardens of love they enclosed, in a way that a mere *pa'u*, or completest nakedness, could not have done.

As in the old days, the women wore their head-hair short, brushed back from the brow, and bleached around the face with burned lime. The long hair of the men either fell free to their shoulders or was tied in loose curls upon the head, to stand up like the crown upon a helmet. The young men were tattooed in the ancient manner, upon the strong arms, the flat planes of the chest, upon the inner flesh of the thighs. Beautiful to see they were, those young women, handsome to behold they were, those young men. I could not contain my delight: "Ah, ah, such beauty! I did not dream that I would see it again," I said to her who has the sense of our past which is so lacking in young folk today. "They are like the people who danced before your mighty grandfather." And to Eahou I said, "Look well. Never again will your eyes gaze upon such a scene."

She was pleased with my testimony. "You are right. You will not see here one of those false things in the new style, such as they dance in town. You will not hear a single one of those sweet and sickening tunes sung in the manner of a missionary hymn. And if any stupid fool so much as brought one of those whining Spanish guitars among my people: ha! I would have him strangled to death with the strings ripped from that damned stuttering sea chest with holes in it!"

"Thanks be to Laka!" I replied bravely, "the old ways are best."

"You have said it," she nodded, a queen approving an established law. "A guest who knows so much about the olden days will always be welcome at my parties."

"I would sell my leg bones for *kahili* staffs, my ribs for fishhooks, to be invited again. I pray you, do not forget."

"I shall not forget. You shall see, when we return to town."

"And me, too?" asked Eahou eagerly.

"And you most of all, my stealer of hearts," she said, hugging him fondly. "Where the father goes," she looked above him to me, laughing in that knowing way which maddens me because I am never sure what it means, "the son must follow."

Oh my, oh my, I wondered, what is her thought? Where will this lead? This woman: she is another Lot, too smart for me. She may have the body of a baby whale, but she has the mind of a ravening shark . . .

Yet how could I nurse any worry at such a time? The dancers were beyond resisting. Now they were presenting a *hula* to the accompaniment of two different drums. With his left hand, Jared Pihana was beating out the major rhythms upon the *pahu*, the big sharkskin drum, set upon the ground before him, while with a little stick held in his right hand he tapped the lesser rhythms upon a small fish-skin drum strapped to his thigh. Above the intricate double cadence his voice sang clear and high:

> Thou art Hilo, Hilo floodgate of Heaven,
> Hilo has the power to wring out the rain:
> Though Hilo may turn here and turn there,
> Hilo is kept from her labors, is wet with rain . . .

When one song ended, another was begun. As one set of dancers grew weary, another took its place. Whenever the Kalani was especially pleased by a performer, she nodded vigorously or clapped her hands in the manner of Americans, calling out, "Good!" or "Well done!" By this acclaim the performers and her first chamberlain were given to know that more substantial awards would be delivered upon the morrow, in gifts of *kapa* or silk, of gold or silver, and sometimes of jewels or of land.

Eahou and I were entranced. Yet, mixed with my admiration for the excellence of her people was envy of her: they were the best in the land, all of them, and never again would I look upon my collections of ragged, raddled bumpkins without being ashamed. Oh, they are good enough, I suppose, for entertaining wanton foreign sailors and vulgar commoners, for adding more money to my treasure chests; but not since that night of the feast at Kahaluʻu have I been able to draw pleasure from the sight and sound of them. And those Spanish guitars, which once upon a time I thought were so nice: I wince now, when I hear them accompanying a *hula*. This is another lesson for the man who is falsely proud: at a time when I was most honored, by being her guest, then was I most put down, by being shown my commonness.

Gradually, as the torches burned lower and Mahina moved higher into the sky, paling the stars with her brightness, the pace of the music, the tales those dancers and chanters told, began to change. Rhythms quickened, verses which earlier were dedicated to praising gods and heroes now descended to telling about the lusts of men and women. Dancers who had moved like virgins now put their bodies into the motions of love. In those of us at Ke'elikolani's mat, as among the commoners below, the pulsing of the drums entered into our own bodies. More than the food and the rum I had consumed was heating my blood. Already, beyond the rows of gleaming eyes and flashing teeth which hedged us in, younger hastier folk in pairs were stealing away into the night. Ke'elikolani was leaning against her lover, sighing at the touch of his fingers upon her breast, the sharp little bites he addressed to the lobe of her ear, to the slope of her shoulder. "Ahh," she said, "this is the way to live . . . There will be much pounding of *pahu* tonight, long after the music is ended . . ."

I put my arm around Eahou, turning his face away from those masses of intertwined limbs. "Are you not sleepy, my boy?"

"No," he said, awake enough to outlast the night.

"Then drink this," I said, offering him my full glass of sweet dark rum. "It will warm you, against the cool night air."

He drew back with a frown. "But I am not cold."

"Drink it anyway," I insisted, hating myself for a liar. Desperate situations demand desperate remedies. "Later the air will be cooler, and I do not want your liver to be chilled." Obediently he took the glass, drank as if it held water—and coughed and spluttered, of course, when he was done. I was grateful for that, because it took his attention away from the words of the singers, describing in great detail and with unabashed frankness the mighty charms of Keʻelikolani and Eben. Good Heavens! What I heard of them, above my spanking of Eahou's back to ease the coughing, was enough to make even me blush.

Very unsteadily Keʻelikolani pushed herself upright and added her heavy-handed pats to mine. "Too bad, too bad," she crooned, "soon it will stop." Across his bent body she leered at me, "Too bad, too bad he is so young." Thrusting him into my hands, she set about with great determination to make a bed from the pillows around her, pounding them until they were almost flat. Seizing him from me, she pushed him down upon the pillows. "Here. Do you lie down here. You will feel better by-and-by." Tenderly, with a smile that masked her ugliness, she covered him with her cape. "Go to sleep now. You will feel better in the morning." What neither weariness nor I could manage, she and rum achieved. He lay still.

Before she settled back against Eben's belly, she summoned the chamberlain, whispered instructions into his bobbing ear. I gave this no further thought, intent as I was upon the dancers. By this time they were in a frenzy of lasciviousness, revealing the *hula-hula* in its very worst excesses—and at its sensual best.

In an instant of awareness I saw the scene before me as a horrified missionary might have looked upon it, discovering grossness in the sweating bodies, the writhing arms and thrusting hips, ugliness in the outflung hands of the men, seeming like monstrous spiders about to alight upon the women's jiggling breasts. But in the next instant the ugly image was gone, and I found again the beauty in this honest mating-dance, in the glistening perfection of those enticing women and urgent men. Eagerly I yielded to it, in every nerve and muscle. To Gehena with the missionaries! I said to my reason, while my responding body joined with those of all the other spectators in feeling that delicious stir of lust which is beyond stopping when once it is aroused. *"Ui-ha!"* I cried out with all the rest, urging the dancers on with wide-opened mouth and lip-licking tongue, aroused to the point where I no longer wondered how I could sleep this night in my lonely bed, no longer worried about how I could in decency walk away from this feast-mat when the dancing came to an end.

But she, the considerate hostess, had thought of this as well. The chamberlain returned, leading six dancing-girls of assorted shapes and sizes, whom he arranged before me. With a gracious wave of her free hand, Ke'elikolani said, "Take one. Take two.—Take all."

"You are very kind, but—" I bowed tipsily. How can I, with the boy here, I was going to say, until I saw him. He was asleep. "—but one will be enough," I pointed to a slim and comely girl who took my fancy, feeling no need to apologize for my restraint. After all, I have ever been a temperate man, at any one time. Immediately the girl came to kneel beside me, while the chamberlain took the other five away.

"Well!" said the Kalani, shaking with mirth, "some like 'em scrawny, it would seem."

"Different people like different things, my generous one," said Eben, pulling the skirt a little higher on her spectacular haunch. "This is the way things should be, don't you think?"

"I am thinking," she drew down his head, to nibble at his throat, "I am thinking that we should wait no longer for the things we like. Eben, my bed-man: let us go . . ." Clumsily they started to get up. Half-a-dozen lesser chamberlains, overjoyed that at last the moment had arrived for which they were condemned to wait, scurried forward to assist them, pushing, pulling, prodding, lifting, until the giant pair stood upright. My bedmate and I gained our feet without help. From her height the Kalani peered down at us. "Do you sleep well, you two, in my hotel," she said, winking both eyes. "And," she pointed at sleeping Eahou, "do you bring him back in five years.—Eben, my beloved, where the hell are you?" He was as close to her as he could possibly be, but in the tangle of arms and hands assisting her she had lost him.

"I am coming, my fragrant one, I am following," he assured her. "But do not forget, my love, do not forget to bid your people goodnight."

"Ah, yes, the people. The people. They are always with us. I thank you for reminding me." Turning grandly, as I imagine the earth does on its axis, she faced the people below. She did not need to speak. Lifting both hands toward them was enough. They understood, and were content. With a last nod from her to us, a warrior's clap upon my shoulder from Eben, they went into their house.

A steward asked if he could carry Eahou for me. Suspicious to the end, I inspected him carefully. He seemed man enough to be entrusted with the precious burden. "Do you lead the way," I said. I watched carefully until he placed the boy upon his sleeping-mat and departed. Not until I had covered the lad with a sheet did I turn to the girl, waiting for me on my mat.

We did not notice when the music stopped, when the torches burned out, leaving only Mahina to look down upon the village given over to love.

CHAPTER 15.

IN WHICH AN INNOCENT LAD IS MADE
ACQUAINTED WITH EVIL

L ate the next day I was well enough to leave. Perhaps
it was all that rich food thrust upon me during the
feasting, perhaps it was too much of that sweet dark rum.
Whatever the cause, I could not get up from my sleeping-
mat on the morning after Ke'elikolani's party. My head,
behind its eyeballs, felt like paper-mulberry pulp being
beaten into *kapa* by heavy mallets. My stomach churned
like the China Sea in a typhoon, with great waves of sour
fire crashing down upon continents of grease. And green,
ghastly green, was the color of my skin.

"What is the matter?" Eahou asked, bending over me
in alarm. I dared not lift my head from its pillow.

"I feel sick," I groaned, wanting only to be left alone
until I died.

"Ah, is this an evil?" he enquired eagerly, not yet
aware that there are occasions when the process of education must be held in abeyance.

After a long struggle, during which anguish made
war upon affection, I was able to mutter, "You'd better

go outside for a while." Obligingly he went away, mercifully I slept.

About midday, as I was awakening again, Eben sauntered into the house, accompanied by Eahou and a steward laden with bowls and bottles. "The boy tells me that you look like the flap of a dingy *malo*," said my brother-in-law heartily as he sat down beside me. "Indeed," he chuckled, while he felt my forehead, plucked at my eyelids, inspected my suffering body with those bright Forrest-green eyes, "the boy chooses his words well."

"Go away," I told him between clenched jaws, "come back next week with your unfunny jokes."

"Nah, nah," he said calmly, "you need not lie here that long. I know this sickness. And I have brought you medicines to cure it. First the gin and the *poi*," he said to the steward, who handed him the bowl containing this fine remedy. "Here, drink." He gave the bowl to me. "First we must quiet the uproar inside the fire-pit." I gulped the soothing draught, praying that it would stay down. As I fell back upon the mat, Eben continued: "Now for the pain in the head: '*uhaloa* tea. Drink!" This horrible bitter potion went down too, helped on its course only by my faith in its virtue. "Good," said my physician, "now we shall leave you for a time. You should be feeling better in an hour or two. Sleep, if you can. If you can not sleep, think pure thoughts—if you can. But do not be in a hurry to get up. You are welcome to stay with us as long as you wish."

His treatment was exceedingly effective: in a shorter time than I believed was possible I could see the world again through these precious eyes, could totter about on my own two legs. When Eben and Eahou returned I had washed and shaved and was dressed in city clothes. "Well, well," said Eben approvingly, with no hint of mockery, "the caterpillar has become a butterfly: a thing of beauty, ready to flutter away."

Eahou's worry fell from him like a dropped garment: he ran to me and hugged me, hiding his face against my chest. We knew what he meant by this. As I stroked the boy's head and shoulders I said happily to Eben: "Brother, if you are as good a physician to others as you are to me, you will never lack patients."

He was pleased by my praise. "The best physician is one who has tried his remedies upon himself. I am an expert in this sickness because of the way I live. But do not send to me a man with wounds that bleed or bones that are broken. I would grow faint at sight of him."

Understanding that I wanted to be on my way, Eben went to gain the chamberlain's help in speeding our departure. He accompanied the grooms when they brought our horses around to the door. "Your saddlebags are packed so full," he said, "that we have given Eahou a set of his own, with a saddle. In them you will find plenty of food when you are ready to eat again, enough to last until you reach Saul Bristol's place.—And Ruth sends you these, as parting gifts." Into my hands he put a bottle of gin, "for use as a medicine," he enjoined, as pious as that Irish doctor in Honolulu who sells glasses of "medicinal spirits" over the counter of his drugstore. Eahou received a loincloth made of rarest *kapa*, dyed with the light yellow hue which is reserved for the Kamehameha and stamped in black with a simple design of crescent moons. Although he did not know the meaning of the color, Eahou was impressed with the beauty of the finished *kapa*. "I can not wear it," he declared, "it is too fine. But I will keep it near me, to remember the Kalani by." For a boy who has nothing else to call his own, I thought, this is a good beginning—and a good omen.

"May we go to thank the Kalani for her hospitality, and to say farewell?" I asked.

For once I saw my brother-in-law shamefaced. After much looking about, to the right, to the left, anywhere but at me, after many false starts, he finally found some words: "No one will see her for a few days, I think." Assuming that she had come to that time of the month when, in accordance with the old *kapu*, she would confine herself to the menstrual house, separated from contact with all other persons "while Lehua shed her tears," I wondered why this grown man should be so unwilling to say as much. "Except for me," he went on. "Her face is swollen. I have given her some opium, to help her to sleep." Naturally, if only out of politeness, I expressed my regret at her indisposition. "Her nose," he mumbled, "it may be broken . . . " He looked down at me so intently that I was forced to examine his words for their meaning.

It came: a revelation. "You didn't!" I cried.

"Aye," he said, with a nod and half a smile. "She begged me. What else could I do?"

"Well, then. Let me congratulate you. This is proof of a great love."

"I am hoping so. Last night I thought it might be the gin and the *'okolehao* and the whiskey which made her entreat me so. But today I have learned otherwise. This morning she was full of thanks. Despite her great pain did she kiss this hand which inflicted the pain upon her."

"Strange, indeed, are the manifestations of love," I replied. And stranger still are the needs of women in love, I thought.

"Already she calls it 'Eben's mark,' " he said, "as if it were my brand I put upon her."

Aye, it is a brand, I said to myself: and now, because

of it, she will be beyond a doubt the ugliest woman in all Hawai'i.

"And I suppose it means that I will stay with her yet a while, before I must go home to Kealakekua.—Do you tell this to Rebekah, when she asks about me."

"I will so report, brother, only because you tell me to do so. But I think it will be better if I say nothing about this nose broken for love. That bit of news will set her tongue to wagging, and soon all of Honolulu will sound like a hen-yard threatened by a cat."

"You are a wise man, brother, and a forethoughtful one. Say only what you think is best." Taking my hand in farewell, he held it tight, as if to force into my flesh, too, the sign of a covenant. "Only one thing do I ask of you: remember your promise to me about Caleb."

We left Eben, strangely forlorn, standing in a ray of sunlight slanting down through the trees. Amid all this ease he was still uneasy, a man not meant to be tamed by indolence, a bull not knowing how much he feared the knife which would make an ox of him. Fishing he should be, at home on tranquil Kona's coast, with a son beside him; or hunting wild boars and wild cattle in the rugged uplands of Mauna Loa, with his son and a company of friends. Despite the pledge of love he had given Ke'eliko-lani, I knew he would not stay with her much longer: he would be the first one to tire of this useless life. Pitying both of them, the woman I feared a little less now that I knew her better, the man I respected more each time we met, I waved to him in sadness.

Not until we had almost left the village did I notice how empty of people it was. Not even the guards were out. "They are sleeping," Eahou informed me. "Uncle Eben said they might, because the Kalani would not be needing them. 'She will not be moving on to Kane'ohe for a few days,' he told them, 'so sleep, take your rest while you can.' He is a very kind man. I like him. This morning, when the two of us were walking—did you know that we went all the way down to the sea?—he told me about his homeland of Kona on Hawai'i. He said I must come to visit him there someday?"

"Indeed?" I said, striving to remember my compassion for Eben while jealousy gnawed at my liver. "And what did you tell him?" this man who is so easily made an uncle.

"I thanked him, and said I would like that very much, and I would ask you to take me with you the next time you went to Kona."

"That is a good answer," I said, rejoicing much more over his loyalty to me than at his tact with Eben.

"But tell me, Makuahou," he pushed on to something more important to him, "how is it possible for all these people to sleep through such a fine day? When there are so many interesting things to do."

"Perhaps because they worked so hard yesterday," I replied, straight of face, "and far into the night, also, do not forget."

"But they were enjoying themselves at the dancing, were they not?"

"Yes, of course," I said hurriedly, recognizing the need to guide this conversation in a safer direction. "Tell me: what did you think of the prayer to Mahina, as she rose above the sea?"

So we talked about safer things, about chants and musicians' instruments and the many kinds of *hula* (the more decorous ones, that is), the while I taught him the differences between one kind of *hula* and another, singing the chants for him, beating out the rhythms on the polished

gourd which held his present from Ke'elikolani, all but
dancing sitting-down *hula* in the saddle.

Scarcely noticing them, we passed through the mangey
village of Kahalu'u, crossed the swamps and mudflats of
Ka'alaea, where Ke'elikolani received her unforgettable
tribute from the old ones. To our left the Ko'olau mountains, the backbone of O'ahu, were decked with clouds,
still withholding their rain. Ahead of us, beyond Kanehoalani, great billows of dark smoke dirtied the sky.
Some of this smoke, pushed inland by breezes from the
sea, was soiling the rain clouds, was hiding completely
the peak of that perfect mountain which stands at the
head of Ka'a'awa's valley, the mountain whose *mana* is
so great that its name is never uttered except in prayers
addressed to the great god whose abode it is. Worry about
the meaning of the smoke troubled my mind, but rage
against the men who had lighted the fires almost choked
me. How can they do this to the god, I marveled. How can
they insult him with stinging, stinking smells? Where is
their respect, I asked, remembering how in the days of old
brush was burned only when the winds blew from the west
and the smoke could be driven out to sea. They will suffer
for this, the fools, I predicted, venting my anger. For, as
is well known to all but fools and foreigners, the gods—
patient though they are with weaknesses in men—will
never tolerate insult to themselves. When will people
learn that respect for the gods is the beginning of wisdom,
the foundation of all order?

We left the seashore and its foul-smelling mud, turning
inland a little to take the road across the firm earth of
Kiolea. We entered the rich district of Waiahole, which
adjoins the even richer district of Waiakane. Many are
the streams which flow down to the sea from the spine of
Ko'olaupoko, many are the watered patches full with

curly-leafed taro. Famed in song and story are Waiahole, the land of twisting water, and Waiakane, the land of the water of Kane. As is my way, I sang some of these songs for Eahou's instruction and my enjoyment. The best of these, and the most renowned, comes from Kaua'i, where Lono-of-the-Long-Clouds and Kane-of-the-Fallen-Rain are lavish with their bounty. This chant I saved until we came to the place dividing these two districts. To my pleasure Eahou joined me in offering this hymn to the greatest of our gods:

> A query, a question
> I put to you:
> Where is the water of Kane?
> At the eastern gate,
> Where the sun comes in at Ha'eha'e,
> There is the water of Kane . . .
>
> One question I put to you:
> Where is the water of Kane?
> There on the mountain peak,
> On the ridges steep,
> In the valleys deep,
> Where the rivers sweep,
> There is the water of Kane . . .
>
> One question I ask of you:
> Where flows the water of Kane?
> Deep in the ground, in the bubbling spring,
> In the crypts of Kane and Kanaloa,
> A well-spring of water, to drink,
> A water of magical power—
> The water of life!
> Life! O Kane, give us this life!

"Your grandfather did teach you well," I said when we finished the song, falling once again into almost unbear-able curiosity about this boy, about the grandfather who had taught him the lore which only a learned man's son would know.

"He spent much time with me, teaching me many things for when I should go among people. This one, he said, is the most sacred of all songs to Kane, because it is the most true."

"I agree with him. And I think that he and I would agree upon another thing: that it is the most beautiful of all poems composed in our native language."

With a timeliness that I felt must have been arranged by Kane himself, we entered into the shade of a grove of immense old *kukui* trees. A veritable temple to Kane is this grove of the tree-of-life, which itself is one of the manifestations of the god. Here in its shade we would rest for a while; and while we sat in peace, I thought, I will ask the boy to tell me more about his grandfather.

"And do you know why this is called the tree-of-life?" I called to Eahou as we were nearing a stopping-place.

Promptly came his answer: "Because wherever these trees do grow, the water of life is found in plenty. Because from its nuts is pressed the oil which burns, like unto the light from the sun. Because often these seeds are borne in pairs, enclosed in a single bag, which is shaped like the bag on the body of a man wherein his seeds are held. Because—"

All at once, with loud yells, three men ran toward us from among those sacred trees. In my surprise I could not think: all I saw were wide-open mouths and great dirty hands. Eahou, drawing upon Pueo's bridle, caused her to rear up, her forefeet pawing the air. Snarling and cursing, two of the villains dodged about, trying to escape those heavy hooves. The third slipped past them and rushed at me. By this time I was thinking again. Seizing my only weapon, I waved it wildly at the man, ready to use it as spear or as club, while Loke bucked and kicked, the man danced about, and I screeched "Where is your respect? Where is your respect for Kane?"

Scoffing at the weak foolish thing I was holding, he closed in. I saw the mouthful of stained broken teeth, the bristle of hair on his chin, the very dirt in the pores of his skin. Swearing even while he laughed, as if I were about to tickle him, he reached up and took hold of the umbrella. With a wail of dismay I felt the silken cover yield to his pull. With a cry of victory he ripped it from the shaft. But the heavy handle was still mine to wield. As I prepared to throw it into his face he fell back in terror. "Run! Run!" he shouted. "A spear!" Only then did I see the long bright sword that Mr. Wyllie had put into my hand.

Roaring now in my turn, I gave chase, wanting to slash them, to spit them one after the other upon this shining blade. But they were nimbler than I and they disappeared into the jungle faster than they had come. In the space of a breath peace was restored to the temple of Kane.

"Are you hurt?" I called to Eahou.

"No!"

"Then run!"

And down the road we sped. My fright gave way to fierce joy: in the bravery of Eahou, in the courage of myself, in the wonderful forethought of Mr. Wyllie, and, most of all, in the protecting presence of Kane, who had saved us from those evil men.

Even so, after about a mile of fast riding I had to stop. The effects of fear could not be outrun: the morning's aches and pains were rushing back into my body. I thought with longing of Eben's remedy. And, with guilt,

I remembered something that in my foolishness I had neglected to do.

We drew up beside a little stream, next to a field newly-
planted in sweet potatoes. The instant I touched ground
I ran to the nearest *ki* plant. Returning with two of the
precious leaves, I gave one to Eahou. "Here," I said, "put
it on. Had we been wearing them, that trouble would never
have happened to us." When I had slipped my leaf into its
proper place, I tore open Eahou's saddlebags. "Now," I
gasped, "for the sake of my galloping stomach, let us
rest."

While Eben's medicine wrought its cure I praised
Eahou for his bravery. "Was that bravery?" he replied.
"I did not have time to think. I did not know what those
men wanted, yet I knew that they must not touch me. Who
were they? What did they want?"

"Now you have seen evil, in evil men," I said, "and
now you have learned one form that danger takes. Who
they were I do not know. What they wanted I can only
guess. Perhaps to rob us of our money, or my city clothes,
or other things of value they thought we might be carrying. This is a terrible thing. Never have I known such a
crime to be committed by our own people. Usually they
are so law-abiding. But these are unhappy times, and no
longer, it seems, do some people heed the law. Lost they
are, lost in the shuffle, caught between the old ways and
the new, and not knowing which ways to follow. Once
upon a time, in the reign of the first Kamehameha, the
Law of the Splintered Paddle was enough. 'Here is the
law of the land,' he said, 'by which we shall be ruled:
let the aged man go and sleep on the roadside, let the
aged woman go and sleep on the roadside, and let no
one injure or molest them.' After that, bananas hung in

their bunches until they dropped with ripeness, sugar-cane stalks grew so long that they lay sprawled on the ground and rose up again, taros grew till their strength was spent and sweet potatoes till they were bleached in the sun, and no dirty-handed person dared to take them. They were protected by the law which Kamehameha did put upon the land and its people.—Alas, not this law, nor all the many new laws of the Kingdom, are respected by such evil men as those we met today. For this we must bow down our heads in sorrow."

"If this is so," the boy asked, "why does not the King appoint a policeman for this district of Waiakane, as Uncle Eben was the policeman for Kona?"

"But the policemen are appointed: the King has named them, one for each district. Do you remember the loud-voiced man in Kaneʻohe? He is such a one. But it is the way of evil men and of policemen to be far apart when laws are broken and people are molested. Today, when robbers lurk in Waiakane, the policeman is in Hakipuʻu perhaps, or in Kaʻalaea. Tomorrow, when he is in Waiakane, the robbers will be in Hakipuʻu or in Kaʻalaea, hopping about as fleas jump from one dog to another. And so it goes.—But good men, I tell you, need no policemen to make them good. And now we must go in search of such a good man. After this trouble we dare not go and sleep by the side of the road. Furthermore, here almost at the feet of Kanehoalani the cloud-snatching peaks are doing their work: soon the rains will be pouring down, and I do not like the thought of sleeping wet. We shall ask to spend the night at the first house we come to—if we can be certain a good man dwells in it."

"Then we have not far to go," he said. "There is a house on the far side of this field."

"Indeed! And has it been sitting there quietly all this

time? Or is it a ghost house, made of sunlight dappled with shade?"

"Do you not see it? It is a real house."

"Cha! These eyes of mine: they were not looking so far ahead, that is all, they were so busy peering into saddlebags. Tell me: is it lived in, this house?"

"Grown people are sitting in the yard, looking at us. Children are playing about. It is not a dead house."

"Then let us go there. A home with children in it is not likely to be a nest for robbers. But, to be sure of their respect, I shall not hide this umbrella pole of mine from the parents of those children."

With greatest respect, with eyes rounded in amazement, did the head of that household greet us when we rode into his yard. "Hiram Nihoa of Honolulu is here," I called, "and his son."

"And here stands Zorobabela 'Opunui, bidding you welcome," he replied.

He was a gaunt young man, still covered with the dirt and sweat of his labors. He had no big belly to warrant his surname, but he bore himself like a free man, and his *aloha* was in the eyes as well as in the mouth. While his two small sons stared at us from the refuge of their mother's missionary dress, I asked for their hospitality. "Yes, yes," said Zorobabela, seeing the sword more than he saw me, "you are welcome to sleep here. We have room enough. But you will be as ill-fed as we are: we have only taro leaves and minnows to eat."

"We carry some food," I said, "and we will share it with you."

"Then come in," he replied, smiling broadly. "Rare indeed is a traveler on this road these days. And never have I greeted one who brings his own fare.—But I beg you: do you put away that long spear. It might hurt someone, without your meaning to. What is it, I ask. A new kind of catcher for eels, perhaps? If so, it will not work without a barb on it."

This good man was as unacquainted with trickery as with swords. While his wife and the children went off to bathe in the stream, he helped Eahou and me to prepare our horses for the night. That was a chore I had not performed for many a year; and when it was done I was weary, quite ready to go with him and Eahou to steep like a bundle of *wauke* bark in the pool of the stream. Next time I am born, I told myself as I sank into the cool water, I shall ask to be a catfish, or a cat. Even so, I felt more like a man again after the bathing, and like a son of the land when I shed those city garments for my loincloth gained from Eben.

When we returned to the house Deborah had laid the food upon the eating-mat. A shy young woman she was, quiet and modest, not like so many of the loud, lazy, vulgar things you find in Honolulu nowadays, flouncing up and down, down and up the streets, looking for good times, instead of staying at home, where they belong. "We are grateful to you," said Deborah, kneeling between her sons. "Not for a long time have we eaten pork. And already these sons of ours are forgetting the taste of *poi*."

"Then let us eat, and eat well," I sang out, and was delighted when Zorobabela said, "But for me no water, please. I have had my fill of it." Yet he would not let us partake of that simple meal until we had given thanks to Jehovah for His bounty.

Afterwards, while Deborah cleared the leaves from the eating-mat—after saving the bones and the scraps "for to make a broth with"—and while Eahou was initiated into the pains and pleasures of playing with boys half his age, Zorobabela and I sat talking. When I felt the time had ar-

rived to speak of such things, I said: "That spear without
a barb: it is used not upon eels but upon men. It saved us
from robbers, and perhaps from death, only a mile or so
away from here."

As I finished my story he shook his head unhappily.
"Do not think ill of our men of Waiakane. Such a thing
has not happened in this district for as long as I can remember. It is not our way, to rob the traveler or to hurt
the weak. The Law of Kamehameha rules here still."

"Then what did they want from us? This is the riddle
I ask you to answer."

"Here is my thought: they were in need of food."

"Of food? How is it possible, in this rich countryside,
for so many people to be hungry at the same time? I can
understand how, with one or the other—as with yourself
—when a farm is between harvests—"

"Chah!" he cried, close to anger, thrusting his dirt-
stained hands before me, "do you think we are so stupid,
we who are farmers, that we can not plant our fields with
more care for the needs of our bellies? No, that is not the
reason. The food-gatherers of the Kalani Keʻelikolani:
they are the reason. They have passed this way of late,
with her." Hatred made his voice harsh. "Did you not
meet them on the way? They have taken from us almost every thing the land can yield. Only now are we of
Waiakane beginning to eat again. For a time we had
little but stream shrimps and bitter fern roots to chew
upon. And taro-patch mud to take the place of *poi*. And
these, as you see, have not put much flesh upon our bones."

I was stunned. But loyalty dies hard, and the memory
of Keʻelikolani (and of me!) at her feasting could not
rest in my mind if I did not defend her. "But do not the
Kalani's stewards pay for the foods they carry away?"

"They do, and fairly enough, I believe, for such high

and mighty folk. But can a man eat gold and silver? Can a broth made from foreigners' coins quiet the pangs of hunger? Every farmer in the district, I will guess, has a gourdful of coins buried beneath the stones of his house. But what good are these when there is nothing to buy? This is a good land, as you have said. The soil is rich, the water of Kane is abundant. Even so, they cannot make taro grow faster than Jehovah has told it to grow. The Kalani's food-gatherers are like caterpillars in a cabbage patch: where they have passed only the bare earth is left, and men must wait to eat again until the roots have sent up new shoots."

"Terrible, terrible," I said, hearing myself as though I were not there, as though Zorobabela of Waiakane talked with Abraham of Kaneʻohe while I listened to the round of woe. Lifted out of myself for that moment, I saw the unending misery of men among men, in a world where the strong preyed on the weak, the mighty ground down the lowly, the poor could never prosper. "Forgive me for being a stupid city man," I said, returning to my body, soft and wearied because it is no longer acquainted with hunger, or work, or need, "forgive me for having forgotten how worthless are gold and silver, how hard is the life of the country man."

"Do not blame yourself, my friend," said the tolerant farmer. "We have a good life in ordinary times. We know the land, we know the season for growing and the season for gathering. We can live well if we are but left alone to enjoy the harvest of our lands. Yet, as you have learned today so have we been taught again and again: although we can trust in the seasons, and in the good God who unfailingly sends them to us, we can not trust our fellow men. They are the bringers of troubles. And beyond fore-seeing are the comings and the goings of these troubles. I have learned to be as patient as Job, during the time of his trying. I do not complain. I endure."

Zorobabela was patient, indeed, and long-suffering to a degree I could never reach. When at sunset we went to our mats in that crowded grass house I was already half asleep. But sleep did not come either to me or to Eahou. An infant I had not seen, awakened by our moving about, would not go back to sleep, but fussed and cried, refusing even the solace of its mother's breast.

"And is the child sick?" I asked less peevishly than I felt, after a few minutes of this noise.

"Nothing important," Zorobabela assured me, a murmur of patience floating through the darkness. "Her arm is sore, I think, and she is a little feverish, from the pricking-of-the-skin against that foreign sickness which has not come here as yet. I forget its name."

"The smallpox, you mean?—She was vaccinated?"

"Yes, that is the name. All of us were scratched on the arm yesterday, by the foreigner who comes around every year or so to do this thing. 'Few Hawaiians are left now,' he warns us, 'we must do whatever we can to preserve the race.' I do not understand how it preserves the race, this vaccination, or what good it does. But because he is sent by our church I let him do what he must. If God works his wonders in such strange ways, who am I to question them?"

The baby's crying was as the music of wind harps compared with other torments which soon beset us. The creeping, jumping, flying farley in that house were beyond belief! Mosquitoes, fleas, lice, bedbugs bit for our blood; cockroaches nibbled at our hair and at the nails of fingers and toes; centipedes clattered frantically over the mats, every separate one of their hundred legs doing a *hula* to a different rhythm; mice squeaked in the thatch; rats rioted overhead and around the house, fighting over crumbs of food thrifty Deborah had thrown into the yard. Through all this bedlam Zorobabela and his family, even the feverish babe, slept the sleep of the pious. Eahou and I, tossing, slapping, scratching, itching, fretting, slept not at all.

Nor could we escape to the outdoors from that cageful of ravenous animals: if the savage rats had not attacked us, or foraging dogs, the heavy rains dropped from Waiakane's clouds would have drowned us where we lay. So we remained within, miserable and mean-tempered, longing for the dawn. If the Christians' Heaven is going to be inhabited by men like Zorobabela—and God must know how well he deserves it—then certainly their Hell will be full of houses like his. If only I could be sure that their just God would fill those houses with the souls of the foreigners who set loose these plagues among us, I would live and die a comforted man.

CHAPTER 16.

IN WHICH HOPEFUL MEN MAKE A COVENANT AGAINST DEATH

lorious was Hakipuʻu when we rode through it in the morning. As is the way with Lono-of-the-Heavy-Clouds, he went to rest for a while when the blazing eye of Kane came again to light up the skies. The earth lay cool and wet, every leaf and blade of grass, every spider's web and mossy rock, was hung with the fragments of a fallen rainbow.

Covered with lumps and bumps, creatures of scratchings and itchings, Eahou and I left by the light of sunrise, glad to get away from Zorobabela's populous household. Cold *poi* and cold water were our breakfast, served by a Deborah still dull with sleep, while Zorobabela saddled our horses. For their hospitality I gave them thanks and all the rest of the food which should have gone back into our saddlebags. Deborah accepted it with wordless exclamations of relief, but her husband went through the usual forms of protest. "It is too much. We are not worthy of such generosity." Yet, in the next breath, rushing on lest

I change my mind, he asked, "What will you eat, if you take nothing with you?"

For such a trusting man there is only one answer: "Oh, God will provide," I said, with the confidence that a full stomach gives to one who has not been hungry for many years. "And, besides, we shall visit the American at Ka'a'awa."

"Ah, that one," Zorobabela spat in dislike, "Pistol, that angry man. Perhaps he will feed you, perhaps he will not. But I would not count on him, not even for air to breathe."

"Well, then, we must go hungry until we find someone who will feed us. What of the people in Kahana?"

"Ah, they are from another breed of men. Those are good people, they are like us of Waiakane. And their taro, their dogs and pigs and chickens, should be grown enough by now to give you good eating. If they are not, the bay will offer up its fish."

So encouraged, we resumed our journey. "Being a city man has its advantages," I observed after we had ridden beyond Zorobabela's hearing. "In the city, as you shall see, we have other things to talk about than food. Country men, it seems, can think of nothing else, even when times are good."

"Are you never hungry, then, you who live in the city?" the boy challenged me, more sullen than I had ever imagined he could be.

"Forgive me for being an unthinking mind attached to a noisy tongue," I said, remembering too late. "You are right. There is nothing worse than a proudful city man when he is set down in the country."

Thus badly began the day which was to mark the beginning of my greatest misfortune. But I was not instructed by that ill-omened start. I am such a one as responds to the present, who sometimes learns from the past, but who does not always make the right guesses about the future. A teller of tales I may be, and a man who gleans wisdom from other men's experiences, as I amass money from other men's weaknesses. But as a wise man and a prophet I am a failure. I have been slow to learn this much about myself, and on the morning of which I tell I had not even begun to admit that I was in need of such painful schooling.

I was too happy to think about anything but the moment. I should have known, I can say it now, how jealous are the gods, how they play with the hopes of men. I should have done as Zorobabela does. But I was happy, and therefore I was blind, in more than my failing eyes.

The gods had given us a beautiful morning, Eahou rode by my side, I felt well again, our *ki*-leaf amulets were in place, I was confident of my ability to complete this mission for the King. What more could a man ask, in the way of pledges against the future? I sang, I teased the boy back into good humor, I answered his questions about whatever came to mind. I was foolishly, trustingly happy.

At the long curve of Kaneʻohe's bay, where Waiakane ends and Hakipuʻu begins, where the road turns eastward, below the soaring peaks of Kanehoalani, I was near to bursting with high spirits. "Look up, Eahou," I cried, "let us gaze upon the majesty of Kanehoalani." Up, up, up rose the mountain wall, massive at its base where it knelt upon the earth, thin as the crest of a helmet where its head brushed against the clouds. Like a warrior it was, offering homage to his lord, and like feathers upon his helmet and cape were the trees, the shrubs, the ferns, and the grasses adorning its sides.

"Give me a word," I called, thinking of a favorite pastime among people who travel in groups, "and I will make a verse around it, in praise of the companion of Kane."

"A wall, I see," he answered.

"The mountain wall of Kanehoalani
    stands strong against the wind,
    sheltering the god."

"A knee, I see."

"The knee of this companion of Kane
    is pressed upon the earth,
    honoring the god."

"An arm, I see."

"The arm of this companion of Kane
    points to him, the god,
    praising him."

"Two eyes, I see."

"The eyes of this companion of Kane
    look out upon the land,
    guarding the god."

"A head, I see."

"The head of this companion of Kane
    is lifted toward his lord,
    seeking him."

"Those eyes: how are they made?" asked Eahou, damming up my freshet of poetry. Perhaps it is just as well that our game ended there. For how could I have made poetry about the rump of Kanehoalani, when we came to it? Or the hump on his back, when it came into view? This Kanehoalani: in the flesh, he would have been a hunchback as well as a broad-beamed companion. The fever of poetry is like the heat of love: it makes a man blind to faults that others see too well.

Eahou, it seems, is a natural philosopher, not a poet. I sent up my apology to Kanehoalani before I answered the lad. "Often have I wondered about those eyes. In my boyhood people would tell me that those holes were made by the spear of Kane, that time he journeyed with his brother-god Kanaloa from one island to another. Because Kanaloa was taken so far from his realm in the sea, he was always thirsty. To quench his thirst Kane would thrust his spear into the earth, and lo! a spring would burst forth. —Kanaloa must have been thirsty indeed, for numerous are the springs which Kane did start for him.—In the days of my youth I believed this account. But now I think perhaps it may be a fable—may Kane forgive me for saying as much—and now, being a thinking man, I believe that those holes were made by wind and rain in places where the mountain is very thin. Perhaps earthquakes have helped as well, when, on Hawai'i, Pele writhes in labor. How is one to know? I am told, although I have not seen them, that similar holes are found on Kaua'i, near Anahola, and on Hawai'i, near Onomea." To tell the truth, I was going to say, I have always thought that these eyes of Kanehoalani are ill-placed: a very funny-looking companion he would be, with two eyes on one side of his nose and none on the other.

But a little thing chased this folly away. "Wait a moment!" I called, "we have an unwanted companion of our own."

"Where?" he looked about him, as though expecting to find the robbers returning.

"Right here," I said, plucking a fat little louse from the edge of his hair.

"And what can that be?" he enquired when I showed him the ugly, wriggling little beast.

"A farewell gift from the 'Opunui family. No doubt I have some too. We must take them off when we come to the sea." With that, overcome by itchings imagined and real, we could not reach the shore fast enough.

At the point of Kualoa, beyond the great fish pond of Moli'i, opposite the little island of Mokoli'i sitting in the sea like a peaked coil of aged dung, we threw ourselves, loincloth and all, into the warm water. The sea bath did not drown our guests, as some people are stupid enough to believe, but it did make them come to the tips of our hair, whence each could pick them off the other more easily. Fortunately for us, we had not stayed long enough in Zorobabela's menagerie to acquire a large population, and our search was soon ended. "Here is another reason why we are lucky to be Hawaiians," I said, explaining how the business of ridding themselves of lice was so much more arduous to foreigners, whose bodies are so covered with hair as well as with clothing.

This shore of Kualoa, with its sandy beaches and shallow reefs and the vast open sea beyond, with its splendid prospect of O'ahu's mountains, from Kanehoalani above to the cliffs of Waimanalo thirty miles away, was once the home of many people. But now few of Kualoa's families survive. The spirits of the dead have gone to sleep the long sleep of Niolopua, their houses on this earth have been blown away by the winds. The few people who remain live in loneliness, far apart from their fellow men. So must their ancestors have lived, in those distant times when these islands of Hawai'i were newly discovered, when the seafarers from Kahiki were newly arrived. Then they and their children thrived because death had not yet come among them, to kill them faster than they could be born. Then the land must have been full of life because the people were full of hope. The gods cared for them, and watched over them.

Now it was empty, this land, drained of life as well as of hope. Along all that coast, as far as we could see, no man or woman or child moved about under the morning's sun.

Neither did foreigners labor there. If they knew of Kualoa's wide plain, the filibusterers from California were shunning it.

In all the world only one man has put some value upon this abandoned spot. Two years ago Dr. Judd, the newspapers said, bought 622 of these worthless acres from the King, for thirteen hundred good American dollars. "Whatever are you going to do in that faraway place?" I had asked him, thinking of it only as being so remote from Honolulu, not knowing how dead it was.

"Hiram, my friend," he replied, smiling as his skin cracked in millions of tiny wrinkles, "I am still a farmer at heart, and I am yearning to put these hands of mine to a plow again, to draw my living from the earth, as my fathers have done before me. Some day, when I am retired from serving the King, I hope to start a farm out there at Kualoa. Or perhaps a sugar plantation. These islands of ours are well suited for growing sugarcane, as several people have proved on Kaua'i. And I am thinking of starting such a plantation at Kualoa. Our country needs more farms, more businesses, more money in exchange for the things it can produce. Why should we not make sugar and molasses from the lands of Kualoa? The soil there is good: I have felt it with these fingers. And rain there is plentiful for watering the crops."

He was another Zorobabela 'Opunui when he talked of the land. But he was as mad as a poet when he let his heart rule his head: "And the view! It is one of the most beautiful on this great earth." Never had I heard this usually sensible man speak so eloquently, or so foolishly. Even then I had gone away shrugging. Who would buy his sugar? And who can live off a view? Now, as I stood on Kualoa's point and looked up at the wide rump of Kane-hoalani, at the length and breadth of the dusty empty plain still untouched by Dr. Judd's plow, I was struck even more by the foolishness of his dream. Good money thrown away, I scoffed. It would be better spent on land nearer to Honolulu. Even Mo'ili'ili's swamps would be more profitable than this desert. At least they will grow taro.

After sea breezes and sunshine had dried bodies and *malo*, we girded our loins again in those wisps of *kapa* and resumed the journey. The swimming had whetted our appetites, and in hunger I regretted the haste with which after breakfast I had given away our lunch. "Let us push on to Saul Bristol's place," I said, "and ask him for a bit to eat."

"I am willing," Eahou patted his flat belly. "That *poi* did not last for long. But what if he is not there?"

"Then we will look about, until we find someone who is at home. If worse comes to worst, we can snare catfish and shrimp from the pond. A fine pond, fed by springs, lies just beyond the point of Ka 'Oi'o there." In truth, I was not worried: deep within me was the certainty that, in the most sacred land toward which we rode, the gods would provide everything we needed.

About halfway between the point of Kualoa and the point of Ka 'Oi'o we came upon a row of miserable thatched huts which were still in use. Fishnets hung on drying-poles; two small canoes lay upright on rollers, ready for going to sea at the cry of a fisherman; squid and small fish, placed upon racks made of driftwood, were drying in the sun. But not a person was to be seen.

As we approached the last of these hovels a man on a mule came out to the road. Seeing us, he stopped. "A foreigner," I exclaimed. "What can he be wanting here?" The only foreigner who lives along this whole coast, from Kaneʻohe to Kahuku, is Saul Bristol. But this small white man astride his mule did not match my memory of Alex's tall friend.

As is the custom, we exchanged greetings and called out our names. He was Brother Doison of the Roman Catholic mission on Fort Street in Honolulu. "Ah, then," I said, liking at sight this neat little man, with his brown eyes, brown hair, half-white's skin, and clothes of churchman's black, "you must be the one who is vaccinating our countryfolk."

"You have said it," he gave me an amused little bow, "but how did you know?"

"Zorobabela ʻOpunui of Waiakane has told me that you were near."

Falling into place beside me, he looked from one to the other of us and grinned. His teeth, alas, were half-white too—stained with tobacco and, I suppose, the sour red wine that Frenchmen drink wherever they go. "Ah, and you have spent the night in the house of that patient man."

"You have said it," I bowed in my turn, "but how did you know?"

Laughing now, he pointed to the red spots on our skins. "By these signs shall you know them who have been the guests of Zorobabela. I, too, have ridden away from his house with those marks—and other evidences as well. But only once, I can tell you. The wise traveler learns to visit with Zorobabela only on the outside of his dwelling, and only by the light of day."

"That wife of his needs a good beating, along with the mats," I growled. "There is no excuse for such slovenly housekeeping."

"No, no, you can not blame Deborah for that zoological garden. Just as it is with us, so it is with them: they are guests of Zorobabela by his invitation. He has taken to heart the humility of Job. Did he not say as much? I have argued with him on this subject, I have left him bundles of fleabane to sprinkle about and packets of sulfur to burn, but he will not use them. His reasoning is very simple, full of a certain cunning logic: 'If God sends me these afflictions,' he says, 'I must accept them without complaint.' He is like the people of China in this respect, although he does not know it. Like them, he feels that if he suffers constantly from little sorrows, then God will send him no great ones. Who can say? Perhaps he is right? Until now, at the least, he and his family are thriving, while all about them less patient folk are being visited with great troubles. Last week, for example, the influenza carried off two of Enoka's children, the brother of Kaula Hopu's wife was drowned off Mokoli'i, and the aged father of Puni Kuakea slipped in the mud of his taro patch, breaking a leg. All these people live within a short walk of Zorobabela."

"But the man does not think straight," I argued. "With one hand he spurns the fleabane you gave him. With the other he accepts the vaccination you bring. How does he explain this crooked reasoning?"

Rolling his eyes, shrugging his shoulders, Brother Doison said, "What man is ever consistent in his arguments with either God or the Devil? Was Job? Are you? Am I?"

Trampled flat by this answer, I could not raise even a squeak in rebuttal. "To tell the truth," he continued, "I think that, like so many of us, he does not fear things that he can see. The things that can not be seen, such as those agencies, whatever they are, which bring sicknesses: of these he is much afraid. Even so, when first I proposed that he and his family should be vaccinated, he would not submit to it. Not until, after much talking, I convinced him that this vaccination is a good thing, a new boon from God to ward off a new plague, did he agree that God was granting him permission to try this new gift. 'Only the foolish, ungrateful man,' he said, 'will reject the gifts of God.' And there, I do believe, he showed how wise a humble man can be. When a man has faith in God, God will keep faith with him. This is what I, too, believe, most firmly," he finished quietly.

O Kane, Ku, and Lono, I was thinking, all these men of religion are alike. So full of faith that they are fanatical, so fanatical that they are bores. Why did I have to meet this almost-priest, this mouther of pieties? Why couldn't my spirit-guardian have sent me an honest fisherman to talk with, a cackling old man of the country to gossip with?

"And what of you, Mr. Nihoa?" he asked.

"Me?" I said, trying to decide whether I should shock him to his Popish heart with an impassioned defense of our native gods or sear him with the fire and brimstone of Hiram Bingham's Calvinism.

"Yes. Have you been vaccinated?"

"Oh, that! I thought you were meaning—Why, yes, yes, I have been vaccinated, although it was done a long time ago. As a matter of fact," I saw how I could impress both him and Eahou, "I was one of the first of Hawai'i's people to receive those little scratches on the arm. A lad of fourteen then, eager to see the world, I had signed the articles as a cabinboy aboard a ship in the China trade. The captain, a Yankee, was a good man. Before we left Honolulu he insisted that all sailors recruited from Hawai'i must be vaccinated, to protect them from the smallpox when we reached Canton. He did this because on earlier voyages he had lost every Hawaiian in his crew from the smallpox in China."

"He was a most forethoughtful man. And did it protect you, that vaccination?"

"Indeed it did. When we arrived at Canton the smallpox was there before us. But not one of us, whether American or Hawaiian, was sickened, not one was lost, even though we went often into that vast crowded city, full of that dreadful sickness. It was a good thing for us, this scratching of the skin. It saved us, I have no doubt. Without it, I would not be riding here today. I believe in it, one hundred per cent."

"And what about your son?"

I had no need to ask. "No, he is not vaccinated."

"Then shall we do it now? To be safe?"

No! my spirit told me, do not do it. Quick to rise in me was a feeling of outrage that anyone or anything should mar the perfection of the boy's body. All the unthinking dreads were immediately remembered: to do harm to a man's body is to harm his *mana*: to weaken his *mana* is to weaken his body. Let well enough alone: to question the gods and their designs is to invite disaster. No! I wanted to cry out, leave him alone. The gods will care for him and protect him. But, being an educated man, a civilized man, I fought back those primitive fears, calling them superstitions, foolishnesses, fetters of ignorance. And, being a weak man, I did not want to be the one to decide.

"Are we endangered?" I asked, hoping for a sign in

his answer. "I have not heard that the smallpox is among us."

"No, it is not here—yet," he admitted, and I sighed in relief. "But always are we in danger of it. The pestilence rages now in America, along the whole coast from Panama to California. And, beyond all doubt, one of these days it will come, an unsuspected passenger on a swift ship from Mazatlan or from San Francisco—or from Canton. And when it comes I do not want to think of what will happen among our Hawaiians, who are so defenseless against all diseases from the countries beyond."

His logic was correct, his conclusion beyond argument. Remembering the horrors of the smallpox in Canton, and not wanting them to be visited upon Eahou; remembering how the vaccination, far from weakening me, had saved me, I quieted my fears, I yielded. "Then let us do it now," I said, showing with Zorobabela how much faith I had in the gifts of gods and men.

There, at the side of the road, in the shade of a *kukui* tree, did we seek in a covenant of blood and flesh to preserve ourselves from harm. Almost in the shadow of Paliku did that tree-of-life grow, of Paliku the steep-sided cliff, which is one of the most holy places in Hawai'i Nei.

My arm was the first to be scratched. Seeing that Eahou did not understand what we had been talking about and had no knowledge of the operation, I asked the little Frenchman, "And what of me? Should it not be done again on me, inasmuch as many years have passed?"

"Yes, it should be renewed, for your sake. Shall I do it to you first, then, as an example to your son?"

He placed upon a flat rock the little wooden case in which he carried the implements of his magic. With the deftness of a man who has done the same thing a thousand times, he laid out upon a piece of clean linen the metal canister which held those splinters of sharp bone. With a strip of linen he wiped the sea-salt and the sweat from the skin high on my left arm. As he lifted one of the splinters of bone from its container, I wondered where I had seen its like before. The Yankee captain, the physicians of Canton: they had used splinters of wood, not of bone . . .

While his left hand grasped my arm, to make firm the soft wrinkling flesh, with his right hand he rapidly pressed the sharp point through the skin, making many little punctures arranged in the shape of a small cross. He was a skilled man. I felt no pain. When he was done he released my arm and stepped back. "The Lord bless you and keep you," he said, making the sign of the cross above the wound, now weeping a little drop of clear yellow fluid. With his strong fingers he broke the needle of bone and dropped the pieces to the ground. Their *mana* was gone out of them, no more would they be of service. Staring down at them, I fretted because I could not remember where I had seen their like before.

Swiftly, in exactly the same manner, he performed the operation upon Eahou. And with the same prayer he asked Jehovah's blessing upon the twice-born boy. Only then did Eahou speak. "Tell me, please: I wish to know: what have you done to us?"

"An inquiring mind should receive an instructive answer," said Brother Doison. Holding up the needle of bone, he explained: "The tips of these splinters—they are called 'points'—were dipped into matter taken from sores on a calf sick with a disease known as the cowpox. That calf was sick in England, and the dipping was done many months ago. Even so, because the matter on these points was permitted to dry quickly, and the points have been kept dry thereafter, the matter has not lost its strength, its vital essence. Perhaps we can even say its *mana*. In faraway places like this it can be used still, in a simple operation such as you have just had, to put some of that vital essence into a person. That living contagion will grow now, in your arm, for a short while. And it will cause a little sore to form, a little cow-pock we might say. You will not be sick, or—at the worst—only a little bit sick. But when, after about a fortnight, the sore is healed, then you will be safeguarded against both the cowpox and the smallpox. A Dr. Jenner discovered this, many years ago in Beretania. And from his discovery the knowledge has spread, until today this vaccination is used throughout all the enlightened parts of the world, to save the lives of people who are threatened by the pestilence of smallpox. —Do you understand now?"

"No," said the truthful Eahou, "not everything.—But I must put my trust in your god."

"That, my boy, is what each of us must do, during every moment he lives," replied Brother Doison.

"One more question do I put to you," I said. "How does this vaccination help us?" His answer, delivered with headshakings and finger-flutterings, would have rejoiced Zorobabela. But it served only to baffle Eahou and to irritate me.

"Only God knows. Man can not know. It is a mystery beyond our comprehension. But men are learning, slowly to be sure, what they can do to help God help them, even in his mysterious ways. The observant Dr. Jenner was one of these men, I do believe. Your good Yankee captain was another. The officials of our government, who send me and others like me throughout the country, who buy from Beretania these portions of the vital essence, they too are learning. But the glory and the praise still belong to God.

Men are but his instruments, even as is this splinter of bone." He broke the sharp needle he had used upon Eahou, and dropped the pieces into the dust at their feet.

While he wrapped up his things and put them back into their box he said cheerfully, "If the sore itches, do not scratch it. Doing so will only make it worse. Wash it with salt water, if you wish, to ease the itching." To me he said, "The boy may be feverish after a day or so. Do not worry: it will pass.—And now I must bid you farewell."

"But do you not ride with us to Ka'a'awa?" I asked.

"No. Not yet can I leave Kualoa. A few families are living up there, among the trees at the foot of Paliku, where the spring is. I must call upon them, to count their number—you see, I am a census-taker as well—and to ask how many are in need of my vaccination since last I visited them. Farewell to you two.—Go with God."

So we parted, under the tree-of-life. We were with him for no more than fifteen minutes. Mysterious indeed are the ways of the gods.

CHAPTER 17.

IN WHICH TWO FEARFUL WANDERERS
ENTER INTO THE PLACE OF
ORDERED CALM

Beautiful is Kaʻaʻawa, beautiful beyond compare,"
I sang out as we came to the point of Ka ʻOiʻo, the
place which marks the end of Koʻolaupoko and the beginning of Koʻolauloa.

"High are the mountains which enfold it," Eahou continued the age-old chant, "but mightiest of all, most
sacred, is the one standing alone, the peak set apart, the
one which divides above from below. For there, there in
the heights, is the dwelling-place of the god."

Always it has been the custom, since descendants of
Hawaiʻi-loa first came to live on Oʻahu, for men to stop
at Ka ʻOiʻo, there to honor their mightiest god and to
praise the lovely valley wherein he abides during his
visits to this island. And always have I kept this custom,
since first I learned of it from my grandfather and the retainers who accompanied us from Kahana to Honolulu.
I was ten years old then, young enough to have been no
threat before that time to the power of the Conqueror,

yet old enough to be summoned to his court, where I would be watched lest any spiteful remnants of Oʻahu's chiefly families, of high rank or low, might rally around me in rebellion against him. Among all the families of Oʻahu's nobles, whatever their rank, only mine and one other were known to have a son who still dwelled in the country. All the rest were dead, killed in the battle of Nuʻuanu or slain upon the altar of Ku.

How ill-founded were the fears of the established King: after eighteen years of his rule Oʻahu's people were no longer interested in making war. And I could no more have led a rebellion, at any age, than I could have led uphill a river of water. But because no one knew as yet how unsoldierly I would be, Kamehameha's suspicion was my burden. A bird in the hands saves beating about the bush, he knew. This is why I went to live in the household of ʻIolani Liholiho, the son of the Conqueror who, upon his father's death, became Kamehameha II.

Across the years I remembered my grandfather's voice, speaking to me at Ka ʻOiʻo. And in his very words I spoke to Eahou: "The god will be pleased, to hear your voice honoring him." This is the duty of a parent, is it not, to teach the old ways to the young, to praise the young who learn this respect for the ways of old. What Eahou's grandfather and my grandfather had begun so well, I was continuing. Eahou understood this, better than I did when I was a boy. "I have waited long to offer up this honor," he said.

Only the rush of the wind and the roar of the sea could be heard as we looked across the mouth of the green valley to the mountains on its far side. Between us and those mountains, above the slight hill which impounds the swamp waters against the dam of the seashore, the brush had been cleared away in many places. In those scattered clearings, rich with green grass, cows and sheep were grazing. Gone, vanished with the dead, were the habitations of the people who once had lived in this peaceful valley. A forest of tall trees had sprung up at the place where once stood the great household of the Kanehoalani, the high chiefs who ruled over Ka'a'awa.

Nearer to us, less than a furlong away, was the spring-fed pond. Upon its surface ducks swam about, dipping for food. Just beyond the pond was Saul Bristol's house. Sheltered from the sea winds by *hala*, *hau*, and *milo* trees and by a high hedge of beach *naupaka*, it was a foreigner's house, made of wood, with a hip roof covered by thick shingles. In that setting the house looked as out of place as a grass shack would have looked in New England. Already its roof and sides had been weathered to the color of driftwood. About a quarter of a mile farther along the coast clusters of grass houses and outlying shelters showed where Bristol's ranch-hands and their families lived. Upon a little island of solitude, moated in by water and aloofness, this unfriendly man had set his castle.

In all that expanse of peace I found no evidence of free-booters from California.

Eahou gazed out upon the sea, rolling endlessly in upon the beach. He looked back, upon the distant crater of Ulupa'u, fashioned like a gigantic turtle, its head thrust out from the round shell, swimming forever through the waves toward the two little isles it would never reach. Beyond Ulupa'u, across the channel of Kaiwi, lay Moloka'i of Hina, gray in the haze. Last of all he looked up, straight up, at the soaring cliff, the right foot of prostrate Kanehoalani, rising more than a thousand feet above our heads. "In this mountain," he said at last, "my grandfather told me, there is a cave."

"Aye. It is there. The one called Pohukaina. Just up

there it is, in the very heel of Kanehoalani's foot. When we have gone a little farther along the shore we shall see it, behind that slope of fallen rocks."

"And is it a burial cave?"

"Perhaps. I do not know. I have entered only once into that big hole, when we took shelter from a rainstorm. We were very careful, I tell you, to stay only in its fore-part. We had no wish to go crawling around in the back, where it sinks into the mountain, narrowing like the inside of a ram's horn, as it goes underground. Yet they may be right, those tellers-of-tales, who say that Pohukaina is joined by long tunnels with caves in the southern side of this island. Would you believe it? They say that a man going in through Pohukaina's mouth can walk underground all the way to openings in the valleys back of Honolulu, even to some in Kahuku. If this is so, I for one would not like to take that dark walk."

"I would! And someday I shall see if it can be done, with torches to light my way."

"When that day comes, my active friend, I pray you not to ask me to go with you. I shall sit outside the entrance, basking like a lizard in the sun, with a good lunch, a good book, and a sleeping-mat, to pass the time until you come out again."

"But you have not said whether it is a burial cave."

This boy: he has a mind which fastens itself to a thought as firmly as a hook in the lip of a fish. "People say that Pohukaina is both a burying-place for bodies and a hiding-place for spirits. These are the very reasons why I do not wish to put even a small toe into that frightening hole. When I am dead, then I will learn the truth. For now all I can say is this: if it is indeed a burial cave, then the dead are well hidden. Only dust is there, on the floor, and cobwebs hanging from the ceiling. Not even so much as a piece of sennit or a shred of *kapa* did I see. Not even a bird's feather, for birds, too, shun the place. Perhaps the trusted ones who were charged with hiding the bodies of the dead built walls of stone between them and the eyes of the living. That is how they do it in other caves, you know."

"And the spirits of the dead? Are they there?"

"They are, indeed: one can feel their presence. The very name of this point is a witness to the procession of ghosts passing in and out of the gate of Pohukaina. And, in the deep silence of that cavern, where the noises of this world are shut out, one can hear them, whispering, sighing, rustling, as they move about. This sound of ghosts: it is frightening. The hair on my head stood up when I heard them. The flesh of my body rose up in lumps the size of goose eggs. I was so glad, I am not ashamed to tell you, when the rainstorm blew inland and we could start again upon our journey. The living do not stay willingly in this Pohukaina."

"It is as my grandfather said. 'A gateway to the land of Milu,' he called it. 'And one day,' he said, 'when your time has come to join me there in Milu's realm, I shall wait for you in Pohukaina.' "

"Aye, he would wish to be there, to help your spirit on its way," I said, disliking this kind of talk, yet feeling that it was what Eahou needed to ease his grief. "But not for many years will he be there. A long and happy life on this good bright earth is in store for you."

Before my eyes the boy seemed to wilt. With ashen face and quivering lips he wailed: "No! He is there now. I feel him near—"

The hand of horror gripped me, the blood drained from my own cheeks. I have seen such fear before, in the features of a man who died of it, because he was the victim of a *kahuna 'ana'ana*'s sorcery. There is only one way to combat such fear. To run away from the cause is to invite death. To stand up and fight the cause, to challenge the sorcerer and to win: this is the victim's only defense, if he wishes to keep his life.

" *'Onipa'a!*" I cried, pushing my own fear back into its dark cave. "Let us go up to this hole of Pohukaina. Let us give your respect to your grandfather, and say a prayer for the safe passage of his spirit through this gate to Milu's realm. If he is there he waits not for you: he waits for the gate to open wide."

Through chattering teeth the boy said, "Then do you show me to the path."

I led the way along the shore-road, until we were about halfway to Saul Bristol's house. From there we could see the rounded top of Pohukaina, like an evil eye peering out above the rampart of fallen rocks. The path to it was plain: the feet of the living have marked it out. "Now I will go alone," said Eahou, turning Pueo upon the path.

Unwillingly, most unwillingly, I let him go, because I knew he must go alone, for his sake. Ten breaths I drew, twice the healing number of five, before I followed him. In the stillness I prayed, into the listening silence I asked: who can it be who envies this boy his life? I could not believe that so cruel a spirit had dwelt in his grandfather. Then who else could it be? With the tenth breath I knew who it must be: that baleful crazy woman who had hated him even while she lived: she was the one who called.

Confident now of victory, I raced after him. A woman is a weak thing. Small, exceedingly weak, is her *mana*, condemned to defeat when it is met with the *mana* of a superior male. Eager now to confront her, to rout her, I charged up the slope to do battle with that thing of evil.

Eahou was walking slowly into the darkness. The immense black hole was opening up to swallow him. "Come out!" I yelled, "come back!" desperate to draw him out into the light of Kane before she could pull him beyond my reach.

Slowly, as if he moved in a dream, he turned around, looked up at me. "Come in," he called, sending me a reassuring smile, "it is safe." Rejoicing at the change in him, marveling at how easily that malevolent spirit had been vanquished, even from my distance, I leaped from the saddle and ran toward the cave.

"In the name of Kane!" I burst out. Laughing now as if I were the crazy one, I leaned for support against the cavern's wall.

"The living have pushed out the dead," he said, joining with me until the cave rang with our laughter.

The mad American of Ka'a'awa had made a bedroom out of Pohukaina. Against the cave's seaward wall, upon a platform of smooth boards evenly laid and firmly nailed down upon crosspieces of logs, he had installed furniture for comfort in this world: a narrow bed, a table and a chair, a set of shelves half filled with books. Like a captive wraith a mosquito net hung from a spike driven into the living rock above the Puritan's cot. From another spike, lower down in the rock, depended a paraffin oil lamp. A second lamp stood on the table, its flared shade of yellowed glass glowing as though the wick still burned. Precisely in the middle of the table top, edge aligned with edge, sat a book, as heavy and as big as a family Bible. Everything about that amazing refuge was neat, neat as only a fanatical *haole* could make it. Even the thick dust on the floor had been raked from rear to front. And a path of boards, laid from the cave's entrance to the platform of his unwalled room, permitted him to reach it without raising so much as a mote. "Ordered

Calm, indeed," I said, piling envy atop admiration atop scorn. "Behold! This is how one *haole* lives."

This Saul Bristol: a most remarkable man is he. My opinion of him leaped up: a man who reads books is a man I wish to know. Unable to resist, I crossed the path of boards to inspect those alluring volumes. They were well made, finely printed and richly bound. They must have cost him many pieces of gold, in any currency.

"What is this thing?" Eahou asked, plucking at the white counterpane, prodding the hard mattress.

"That is the foreigners' idea of a bed," I explained. "This man is a scholar," I pronounced, reading the titles on those books.

A few I knew, because I have them in my own secret library: romances by Sir Walter Scott and Fenimore Cooper, the tales of Washington Irving, books of travel and exploration, Hiram Bingham's account of his residence of twenty-one years in these savage Sandwich Islands, even a pair of which I am quite proud, the only two volumes of the *Hawaiian Spectator*. But most of them were strange—great big bulky things, or sets of several fat books, written by men who must have scribbled whole years of their lives away at their desks. Such tomes either awe me or bore me, and those I passed by, as I do in bookstores. But among them one slender volume caught my eye: *The Prince*, by Niccolo Machiavelli. Aha! I gloated, pleased by its being there: that sassy Lot is not the only one. Oh my! I wondered, worried by its being there: and why does Saul Bristol read this handbook for deceivers?

"What are those things?" Eahou reminded me that he, too, was there. In explaining to him what books are, and how worthwhile they can be to people who read, I mentioned of course the art of writing. In casting about for examples of written words to show him I opened the big book on the table, thinking it to be a ledger. I was expecting to see a ranch-keeper's account of his labors, the numbers of his cows and bulls, the payments he receives and the debts he owes—in short, the ordinary sort of ledger that any businessman must keep.

My schoolmaster's explanations died away at sight of the small neat script which filled the entire page, not with figures but with words. Inquisitive as I am, how could I not read them?

Saturday, January 1, 1853.

Wave upon wave the sea rolls in upon the sands of Ka'a'awa. Endlessly they form, endlessly do they fall upon the lonely beach. Upon this whole fetch of coast I am the only living thing. But the waves, the spray, the wrack of clouds seem more alive than I. They are moving, at least, coming from somewhere, going somewhere, while I stand, motionless as that log there, unyielding as this rock. I dare not move until I am wet and cold and as miserable in body as I am in heart. If I did move before that time, I would go into the sea, accepting at last the death it is forever offering me.

"Come," it says, "come with me," its foam as soft as a bridal veil, its caress as gentle as a bride's. "Come with me, and lie with me, and I will give you peace . . ."

But even a *niele* man has some scruples. Wanting to read on, to read all the pages in that revealing book, I forced myself to stop. Not only was I trespassing upon the man's property. I was looking into the private places of his soul. Suddenly ashamed, I closed the book.

"What does it say?" Eahou asked. "Is it a message from the spirit-world?"

I put the journal where it belonged, exactly in the position in which he had left it. "We must go," I said abruptly, "we have no right to be here." I could not hurry us out quickly enough.

Only when we were about to mount our horses did I remember why we had come to Pohukaina. "What of your grandfather?" I asked. "Is he here?"

He shook his head. "He is not here."

"And what do you think has happened to him?" I persisted.

"I think that perhaps in our talking down there, on the road, my mind was filled with foolish thoughts."

"I think perhaps you are right," I smiled at him, tousling his hair, tickling his ears. "And let both of us learn from this experience about the tricks a mind can play." The gods must know that I am the right man to express such a profound truth.

Now he was eager to continue the journey, almost as though release from fear had lightened his body as well as his spirit. When, at Saul Bristol's place, I turned Lokelani's nose toward the gate, he pleaded to ride on a little farther. "I want to see how Kanehoalani looks from this side," he said. To please him I was willing to endure the pangs of hunger for yet a while.

With each step we took a little more of the valley was revealed. The immense wall of Kanehoalani is even grander on this side: like a cathedral it stands, with heavy buttresses thrusting into the earth, with pointed spires reaching up toward the floor of heaven. Gone now is the image of a warrior-chief kneeling low before his god. From this side the eye is made to see a tremendous Christian church, raised to the glory of another god. But not yet has jealous Jehovah driven Kane from his home: with each step we took, more of his lofty dwelling was disclosed.

Almost, it seems, these two gods are met in friendship at Ka'a'awa, as though each is a brother to the other. Or, indeed, as some of our Hawaiian priests have declared since the American missionaries came among us, as though the two were one and the same, differing only in the names our two peoples have given them and in the ceremonies of our worship. This is a good and comforting thought, because I respect both of these great deities and do not like to think of one trying to drive out the other. Yet always, until this day, I had wondered whether, if these two gods were not one, they could live together in peace. I could not think of them living in peace any more than I could think of a noble, handsome, silent man being able to live peaceably in the company of a shrill and jealous wife. Now I saw that indeed it was possible for them, and for all gods, to dwell in amity. The sun, that most beneficent manifestation of Kane, stood at its height, casting only the smallest of shadows upon the ground. The wind from the sea sang its hymn of praise, Kanaloa in the sea brought his tribute to the shore. On the bosom of Papa-the-Flat-Earth, shrubs and trees and grasses bowed down in homage. And across the front of this valley of peace and beauty Eahou and I rode as in a world untouched by care or strife among either gods or men.

When we arrived at the exact center of the valley, midway between the mountain ridge on the left and the mountain ridge on the right, and the whole long sweep of it was opened up before us, from the sand at our feet to the peak of Kane, Eahou stopped. Slowly he dismounted, to stand upon the ground. Facing the sacred mountain, he lifted his arms in prayer. It sped from him alone, to the god alone. No other ear heard it. Just as no other ear heard my prayer, beseeching the god to be kind to the boy.

When he was done, he turned to me. "I thank you, Makuahou, for bringing me here. Now let us go back to the house of the foreigner."

CHAPTER 18.

IN WHICH THUNDER CRACKS OPEN
THE CLOUDLESS SKY

Dogs barked, chickens squawked and ran giddily about, goats bleated as we rode into Saul Bristol's yard. The field of grass, cropped close by the goats, was like the water of a green pond, lapping at the house standing high on stilts above it. *"Ui-ha,"* I called out, "may we come in?" Only the animal chorus responded. *"Aloha,"* I tried again, "is anyone at home?" Silence spilled out of the house, down the stairs, over the grass to where we waited. Almost I could feel it pushing us away.

"The house is empty," said Eahou.

Disappointed, I could only sigh. "We have come at a bad time, no doubt. I suppose he is working somewhere in the valley." Fervently did I hope so, for I could not have faced this frightening man if he had left the house in order to chase us out of his cavern-bedroom. "Do you wait here," I said, "and watch for his return, while I ride around to the back, to see if he is in the stable." I had in mind the cookhouse as well, for my empty belly was mak-

ing more noise than were all the beasts in Bristol's barnyard. Surely, I was promising myself, some cold taro
will be there, perhaps a string of dried fish hanging from
a roof-beam. And already I was wondering whether I
should leave a coin or a letter in thanks for those pro-
visions.

Loke and I had not reached the back of the house when
I heard Pueo's hoofbeats upon the turf. "Eahou!" I
yelled, "where are you going?" Needless to say, he did
not hear me. Hunger and weariness made me flare up.
"Damn it! Come back here!" I bawled, even as I lashed
Loke into a run.

We chased him at my angry man's pace across the narrow swamp, up the little hill, out on the level plain of
the valley. Eahou had slowed Pueo to a walk, and I caught
up with him just as he reached the grove of tall trees at a
turn in the path. "Damn it, boy!" I started on the usual
scolding which my sons hear when they have goaded their
patient papa into a fury. "What are you thinking—" He
stopped Pueo, but not in obedience to me. Come here, his
hand commanded me. With my tongue stuck to the roof
of my mouth, I obeyed.

Never in my whole life have I been so astonished!

For there, in perfect order and perfect repair, just as
it would have been in the olden days, stood the household
of a great chief. The high-ridged main house, the clusters
of lesser dwellings, work-sheds, storage huts were there,
the temple for the family's worship was there. Like a picture from the past brought to life was this splendid household, and I cried out in amazement when I realized what
it was and understood that it had not been allowed to die.
"How did you know?" I asked the boy, above the noise
of barking dogs and the squealing of excited pigs.

"My grandfather told me the way," he said.

An aged retainer tottered out of the nearest hut, to see what caused such commotion. His hand was lifted to wave us off when he uttered a loud cry and ran as fast as his unsteady legs could carry him into the main house. "And why should he fear us?" I asked, "who are so unfrightening." I even looked to see whether perhaps Mr. Wyllie's sword was poking out its sharp nose, but no, it was still wrapped up. "Come, let us go back," I decided. "We do not belong here. By lingering, we invite trouble. I know these great ones. They do not like to be disturbed." And I remembered, too, how Eahou likened great chiefs to pig-dung.

Forth from the main house came a man, a most noble man. Slowly, with great dignity, he walked toward us, pressing the folds of his cape at the level of his heart. Behind him came his wife, stately as he; and after her followed a man robed in the white loincloth and white cape of a priest. Recognizing them as the highest of chiefs, I hurried to stand on the ground, below the level of their heads. "Get down, boy!" I warned; "get down," I implored. From all sides, aroused by the old servant's alarm, retainers and children ran up to see who trespassed so boldly upon their lord's domain.

The chief came to within a spear's length of Eahou. Tall he stood, towering above me. Stern and haughty, he saw only Eahou, the defiant one who would not bow down before him. Close behind him stood his wife, her face twisted with unbelief, her mouth pouting little cries of annoyance over the boy's lack of respect. The priest scowled like a temple image, with lips drawn back to expose yellowed stumps of teeth. From the level of Lokelani's belly I asked their mercy. "Forgive him," I moaned, "he is only a country boy. He does not know." Ignoring me, the chief stared at Eahou, as if he were summoning up all the powers of his *mana* to blast the boy from the saddle. "Get down, boy, get down!" I made one last attempt to save him from destruction. This is how stupid I was, how unprepared, to the end.

The chief raised his right hand. Shuddering, I closed my eyes, not wanting to see the cruel sign by which he would command the servants to throw this boy to the ground, to break his back and beat his brains out with heavy clubs. "Forgive," I begged, kneeling in the dust, "forgive. It is my fault. Blame me, not him."

"It is he," the chief said. "It is he, in the flesh. He is—" The deep voice broke, shattered with sobs. I opened my eyes to see the tears spilling down his cheeks. Wailing with joy, the chiefess pushed past him. "He has come home!" she cried out even as she wept, "he has come home!" Seizing Eahou's leg, she kissed the knee, the shin, the foot, as she sank to prostrate herself upon the ground. Shouts of happiness, cries of thanks to Kane, went up from the retainers as the tears spurted from their eyes.

Weeping, too, in relief, in joy, in pain, I understood at last what was happening. It has happened before, it will happen again. But never, never in the history of gods and men, has a son been as worthy of such a homecoming as was my Eahou.

Gently, with trembling hands, the chief lifted the boy from Pueo's back, held him close. Mingling their tears, he touched his nose to Eahou's right cheek, to his left cheek. Only when this was done did he allow Eahou's feet to touch the earth. As soon as he was freed, Eahou took the chiefess's hands, helping her to rise. Weeping and wailing still, she held him close to her breast. Unable to watch

such happiness, I looked away. Among all the people assembled about this united family only the priest stood
apart, dry-eyed, expressionless. Who is he, to be so unmoved, I wondered, marking him for a man with a liver
made of driest dust.

Then Eahou did a strange thing. He removed the snaffle-
bit from Pueo's mouth, worked the reins free of it, while
we marveled that he should perform such a menial task
at so jubilant a time. Holding the bit high, for us to see,
he drew a golden ring from around the iron bar. Bright
it was, flashing like a piece of the sun, as he presented it
to his grandfather. The chief stared down at it, cupped
in his hand. "This is the marriage-ring of my mother,
who has gone to the land of Milu," said Eahou. "Now do
you please come with me to the temple."

The *heiau* was only a few feet away, on a prominence
which looked out over the valley, to the mountain of
Kane. A broad low platform of close-fitted stones, it was
made long ago by chiefs and priests and commoners
alike. No image of wood or stone, no oracle-tower or
sacrificial altar stood upon it: the great mountain was sign
enough of the presence of Kane.

Standing on the huge center stone at the edge of the
temple, Eahou lifted his arms toward the god, once again
invoking his help. Then, counting aloud as he went, he
walked upon the dark stones, so powdered with lichens
that they seemed to be strewn with salt. Seven stones to
the right he stepped, seven in toward the *heiau*'s heart.
There he knelt and lifted a flat stone from its bed. While
we gaped in wonderment, he brought from its hiding-
place a gourd container. Out of this he drew a roll of *kapa*.
Giving it to the chief, he said, "In this *malo*, which was
my father's, you will find his marriage-ring."

"There is no need," the chief replied.

"Please, it must be done," Eahou insisted, as though he obeyed a distant voice.

Slowly, with fumbling fingers, the great man unrolled the *malo*. "Aye, it is his, my son's," the chief's wife cried out, "I made it for him, long years ago." From the folds of soft *kapa* her husband lifted the golden ring.

"Read the writing in each," said Eahou.

"I can not," murmured the chief. "My eyes: they are dimmed with tears . . ."

"There is no need, my beloved," said the chiefess. "You are all the proof we need. You are the flesh and blood of our son: in you he walks again. He is lost to us, he too has gone to sleep the sleep of Niolopua. But you are here. You are all we ask—"

Eahou's proud neck bent at last, his determination broke before her tears. "Grandfather: Grandmother: I— I am happy to come home . . ." Once again we wept and wailed, overcome with our rejoicing.

At length, when tears would flow no more, and happiness shone in wetted eyes as the sun shines through mist, Eahou came to stand before me. "Makuahou," he said, "I thank you for bringing me safely home. Without you I could not have found the way so easily."

Now, after knowing the sweetness of rejoicing I tasted the bitterness of sorrow. Like a loyal *kahu*, I hid it under a brave smile, even as I knew that the rest of my journey, the rest of my life, would be a dispirited thing without Eahou.

Taking my hand, he led me to his grandfather. "Here is my guide, my teacher—and, for a while, my new father. Please do you make him welcome."

"He is welcome, indeed, who is the restorer of our

breath," said the great chief. "New life has he brought to us—" He stopped, puzzled by the boy's merry laugh, the delighted glance he sent to me.

"New life," the lad explained, "this is the name he gave to me, only a few days ago."

With this the chief was even more perplexed. "How is it so? Do you not bear a name? The name my son gave to you?"

"Yes, I bear a name. But my grandfather—the other grandfather who raised me—said I could not bear it rightly until I had won it. Only then, he said, would it be mine to use, forever."

"And what is this name you have been given?"

Lifting up his head, the boy pronounced the name which now was forever his. "Kane-i-ka-pule am I, son to Kane-lele, who was son to Kane-milo-hai of Kane-hoa-lani, high chief of Ka'a'awa, and of Maka-o-Hina, his wife."

As the noble names hung in the air between us I shook with fear at the power of Kane, who had inspired me so well, that time I gave this fatherless child into his keeping.

"And the name of your mother?" asked Maka-o-Hina, "of the wife to our son, whom we never knew?"

"Ahuki-o-lani was she, daughter of Ku-i-ka-pono of Maunawili, who was only son to O'ahu's King, Kalani-kupule, and—"

At the sound of that sacred name all who heard it fell down in awe, pressing our faces against the stones in obeisance to Kane-i-ka-pule.

For great, burning, exalted above all others, is the *kapu* of this highest of great chiefs, of this thrice-born son of the mightiest gods!

Beneath us the earth trembled. Above us thunder cracked open the cloudless sky.

CHAPTER 19.

IN WHICH IS RELATED THE SAD TALE
OF A PATIENT MAN

The remainder of that destined day was given over to ceremonies welcoming the young lord of Ka'a'awa into the company of his father's ancestors. The rites performed by the priest at the temple I can not describe, the prayers I must not repeat. They are too sacred for me to reveal. It is enough to say that, because Eahou-Kaneikapule and I, coming as we did from a countryside full of Christians and other infidels, were defiling the abode of Kane with our pollution, the priest insisted that the temple and all who stood upon it must be purified before Kaneikapule could be presented to the spirits of his ancestors and to their forefather-god.

When at last the cleansing was done the ill-mannered priest ordered away all the women and all males who were commoners. As they were departing he waved me off as well, most insolently, as though I were a fly hovering about his *poi*-bowl. Not about to be chased away by that arrogant one, I stood firm. I had as much right to be there as he did, and I was preparing to say so when Kanemilohai spoke: "He stays. Will the god who chose him to bring Kaneikapule to us mislike his being here now?"

While the priest scowled I bowed courteously to the chief, saying, "My family is not of your high rank, O Kanemilohai of Ka'a'awa. But always, since the beginning of memory, have the Kanehoalani of Ka'a'awa been served well and faithfully by the Nanahoa of Kahana."

"It is even so," he replied, "the very peak of Nanahoa on this ridge above us affirms the love and loyalty each family bore for the other.—Are you, then, one of the Nanahoa?"

"Nihoa of Nanahoa am I, grandson to that same Laha of Nanahoa who was your father's most loyal follower and his dearest friend."

"Is it so?" he cried out, embracing me. "Then you are doubly welcome, O grandson of the man who was a sheltering presence to my father. Let us together stand up before the god, to present to him the son we do share, to thank him for his part in joining our two families again after so many years."

Proudly did I stand beside him in the sight of Kane as the prayers went up, while the long roll of his descendants was recited as Kaneikapule was made known to them and to the god who was the founder of their line.

Kane himself rested upon the peak which is his throne when the name of Kaneikapule was pronounced. We could ask no greater sign of his blessing upon the boy. Reverently we abased ourselves before the fiery eye in the sun. Not until he had withdrawn behind the sacred mountain did we rise to our feet and, feeling still the holy awe, come down from the temple.

The feast that evening was very different from the one Princess Ruth had held two nights before. She and Eben lived in a different world. And yet I think that she, if not Eben, would have felt at home in the household of Kane-milohai and Maka-o-Hina.

Five of us sat at the eating-mat, we were well fed, and cool spring water was our drink. As befits a family which respects the gods and the sustenance they give, we did not fill the air with useless chatter. We kept a respectful silence, which permitted each of us to meditate upon whatever subject his spirit-guardian might put into his mind.

My *'aumakua* and I: we are not much given to meditation, I am afraid. Creatures of the moment are we, playthings of whim and sudden thoughts, for whom life may be unplanned but is never unexciting. This is perhaps the reason why at my house, despite the presence of Rebekah, our meals are never quiet affairs. Above the gossip and the laughter, the teasings and the screamings, the babble of babies and the merriment of children, no one can ever hear the sounds of chewing, even though anywhere from fifteen to thirty people are gathered around the eating-table. I like a happy meal shared with happy people, and there are no nervous stomachs among the folk who sit at my board.

But in Kanemilohai's house, even on that day of rejoicing, the habit was not changed. The priest, of course, was responsible for this holding to the rule. Sour as a batch of four-day *poi*, he sat grimly, eating sparingly, looking neither to the right not to the left. Although Kanemilohai was the chief and the head of the household, Hahau the priest was its master. The chief and his wife, accustomed to this relationship, did not seem to fret under it.

Kanemilohai and Hahau, I learned later, were half brothers, sons of the same father by two different wives. Hahau was the elder by two years, but because his mother was a commoner he was only a *noanoa* person, little better than a commoner, and did not approach the *wohi* rank of Kanemilohai, whose mother was a *naha* chiefess in her own right. Even so, Hahau would have inherited his father's lands if Kanemilohai had not been born. When the younger son arrived in this world Hahau was set aside. Instead of being brought up as a chief's heir he was dedicated as a priest to the service of Kane. This serving in a priesthood was the usual fate of *noanoa* sons in the days of old, yet it was only one among Hahau's disappointments. So undisguised was his resentment of Eahou that even I, the newcomer, could tell how the boy's appearance was only the latest in a lifetime of failures for Hahau.

This Hahau: there was something wrong about his person as well as in his disposition. And I needed many a furtive glance, much puzzled thought, before I figured out what it was. He was an ill-made man. Indeed, he was an unfinished man. It seemed as if he were born too soon, before he could be completed in his mother's womb. All the tips and ends of him, fingers, toes, nose, ears, teeth, were blunt and rounded, as if the shaping of them still remained to be done by some forgetful carver. The hair on his head was ragged and patchy: it did not lie down smoothly, nor did it end neatly at the margins. His skin was coarse and spotted, in several hues, as is the shell of a crab after it is cooked. The eyelids drooped, the voice was hoarse as if his throat was webbed with strings of phlegm. Oh my, he was an unlovely man. If his manner had not been so full of cutting edges and poking thorns, I would have been sorrier for him as a person.

And yet, such is the power of heritage, it was possible to see that Hahau and Kanemilohai were seedlings sown from the same gourd. Both were tall and lean, wide in the shoulders and slender at the waist. These, with the narrow head and curved nose I had remarked in Eahou, would have been the gift of their father, Kanehalo. And they were still young enough to be flat-bellied, not yet softened into fat. Kanemilohai, in spite of his graying hair, could not have been much more than forty years old. And, needless to say, he was the handsomest man I have ever seen.

Maka-o-Hina was the one who gave her eyes to Eahou, and those full lips. Although she was as plump as her husband was thin, as is so often the way among us for reasons I can not explain, she was still a beautiful woman, fashioned to bear handsome sons and lovely daughters. Seeing her, attentive to Eahou with a mother's devotion, I lamented the loss to her and to the nation of the children she had not borne. Why, I wondered, coming at last to brooding meditation, why are the women of our great families so barren, why are the men so sterile? Alas, this is a question no human being can answer. The gods, those inscrutable ones, those silent ones: they give, they withhold, they take away, as they deem right. And who is a man to ask them why?

When the eating-mat and the fingerbowls had been carried out, Kanemilohai spoke. "Tell us, son of our son, about the parents of your mother. Are they well?"

"I, too, wish to know this," said Maka-o-Hina, smiling fondly upon the boy. "And one more thing I ask: how could they bear to part with you?"

Only then did they learn, with many exclamations of dismay and sorrow, about the death of that ill-fated pair. This is their history, as we put it together from our knowledge of the times and from the things Eahou was able to tell us.

In the sixth month after the battle of Nu'uanu, while Kalanikupule and Pu'uhonua his wife, with two of their trusted retainers, were hiding from Kamehameha in the mountains of Ko'olaupoko, Pu'uhonua gave birth to a son. They called him Ku-i-ka-pono, which is to say, Ku-in-the-Right, or Standing-in-the-Right, as a reminder that he was the true heir to Kalanikupule's realm and the hope of O'ahu against the usurper Kamehameha. Because he was as much in danger as his parents, the infant was taken in secret to a lesser chief in Maunawili, to be raised until the time came when he could lead an army of O'ahu against the Conqueror. But the power of Kamehameha was too great, especially after foreigners settled in numbers on O'ahu and gave him their support. Kalanikupule, Pu'uhonua, and most of O'ahu's chiefs were captured and slain. The rebellion of O'ahu's broken people never came to pass.

When he had grown to manhood Kuikapono did not regret his lost kingdom. Gentle, interested only in helping the sick and the poor, he said, "Let us live in peace. Let us put behind the days of war and famine, let us forswear our enmity for Kamehameha. Is he not proving to be a just King?" As he wished so did it happen: the few who were loyal to him because of his parents sighed in relief, having no wish by then to wage a useless war against the established King. But no one was so loyal to Kamehameha as to tell him that a son of Kalanikupule lived in the land wrested from his father.

Thinking that the most public place was the safest refuge, Kuikapono made his home on the path to Nu'uanu's *pali*, where he could help people in their need. And there he dwelt as a commoner for almost forty years, known to his friends and neighbors by the humble name of Ahonui, the patient one.

Yet Pilihua his wife, a daughter of the chief who had raised him, could never forget his great rank or his lost realm. She kept his secret, but only out of fear for him. Proud she was born, haughty and unforgetting she remained. Too proud to serve common people, she would hide in shame when they sought her husband's help. He, the generous one, would attend them; and patiently would he suffer her sneers and revilings when they had gone on their way. Even so, during the years they spent in that embittered house, she bore him two sons and a daughter. The sons ran away as soon as they could, and were not seen again. Neither they nor their sister knew their lineage, because Kuikapono did not think them worthy of the trust. Ahukiolani the daughter, being youngest, was last to depart. The day came when she, too, fled over the cliff of Nuʻuanu, and they counted her as lost as were their sons.

But Ahukiolani needed them still, for one last service to her. Two years later, carrying a child in her arms, she made the perilous walk down the *pali* to Halfway House. Upon seeing this daughter with the child, Pilihua drove them away with curses and loud wailings. But Kuikapono followed them to the path, where it crosses the stream. "Take him and keep him here with you," she begged, putting the babe into his hands. "Not much time is left to me: I am dying of the consumption. My husband is dead, taken from me by this same foreigners' sickness." Speaking slowly, weak with the wasting disease and with grief, she told her father about the husband for whom she held such a great love, and how, before he died, he had asked a trusted friend to go to Kaʻaʻawa, to inform his parents of his death and to hide his marriage-ring in the temple there, against the time when his son would be grown enough to claim it and the birthright. He could not go himself because by then he was too ill to make the journey. The two together had not gone sooner to Ka'a'awa because his parents would not forgive his taking a commoner for wife.

"But that is not the truth!" cried Maka-o-Hina in great distress. "Seldom did we hear from him after he went away to Honolulu, to learn the ways of city folk. Never did we learn that he had taken a wife. Not even his friend, Punia of Kahuku, told us when he was here that Kanelele left a wife and a son.—We could not have been so cruel! —Did you, my husband, send this message to our son?"

Kanemilohai was as agitated as she. "I did not. How could I be so unkind to my only son?"

"Then how could he have had this thought?" she asked, "who could have put it into his mind?"

"Who can say?" the priest spoke, his voice rasping like stone upon wood, as he tried to soothe them. "Perhaps it was that foreign sickness which put this fancy into his mind. This is the way of sickness, I am told, of fevered bodies when the *mana* is weakened by foreign sorcerers."

"That is so, my dear," said Kanemilohai gently, while I nodded sagely as though I were as learned a physician as I am so excellent a spy. I can never abide sight or sound of grief, and, wanting to fend off more tears and wailings and futile regrets, I said, "Let us listen to the boy's story. Perhaps from it we can learn the reason for your son's mistake."

"This is what my mother said to her father," Eahou continued. " 'When my son is grown, or when your time is near to walk upon the path of evening, send him with my ring to Ka'a'awa, to claim his birthright. Tell him where to find his father's ring: it is the true mate to this one, as his father was true mate to me.' "

Adding their salt tears to the clear waters of the flowing

stream, they parted, she to climb the steep *pali*, her father to care for the precious son, whose lineage was known only to him. There and then, while standing in the flowing water, did Kuikapono give the child his great and sacred name, combining in one the *mana* of the two lines which were joined in him.

But grieving Ahukiolani did not reach the high pass of Nu'uanu. She jumped from the sheerest part of the trail, into the abyss. Kuikapono saw her as she fell, knowing, by the color of her dress, who had leaped. Her bones lie there still, near those of the warriors who were loyal to the grandfather she did not count as her own.

Thus did they live, the son and the great-grandson of Kalanikupule: modestly, quietly, not unhappily—for a while. Even Pilihua was almost happy, when she permitted herself to forget the past, especially when she looked upon the child who was her grandson. He was their comfort and their joy, for which reason they called him Ho'olu. And from him the forbearing Ahonui and the prideful Pilihua drew a belated peace.

It lasted until the boy's sixth year, when Ahonui was felled by a stroke. When he could not minister to travelers on the *pali*'s path, food ceased to come to their door. Then, in her despair, Pilihua's mind cracked. She would not work for food, she would not ask for it. All she could say was "Let us die. Trash are we, as trash is our name. We should be burned." Perhaps it was her way of showing her love for Kuikapono, perhaps it was her madwoman's way of hastening the end.

The boy tried to feed them with roots and fern fronds and stream shrimps, with taro and sweet potatoes stolen from the nearest farms. But never could he bring home enough food, and always they were hungry. Toward the end, Pilihua in her madness refused to eat, Kuikapono in his love gave most of his portion to the boy. Only when she was dead and he knew that his time was come did Kuikapono tell the boy who he was and what he must do to claim his birthright. This is how close Kaneikapule was to not knowing his lineage. This is how trusting Kuikapono was, with his faith in the gods. "He bade me go," said his grandson, "but I would not leave him there alone. I gathered the wood for the fire he wanted, I prepared the water of life, I waited to take his breath into me. This was when Makuahou came, sent to me I will always believe by the kindness of Kane."

"Great is the power of Kane," said the priest.

"And how well did Kuikapono know this," said Kanemilohai in wonder.

"Like the interwoven strands of a fisherman's net are the lives of men," I said, "bound one to the other, although each stands alone."

"It is ever so," Hahau agreed, for once, "but who is the maker of the net, who is the thrower? He is Kane."

When we had wiped the last tears of marveling and of sorrow from our eyes, Kanemilohai and his wife entreated me to tell the story of our journey from their grandson's former home to this new one. I gave them a brief account of the road we had taken and of the places where we had slept, saying as little as possible about our stay with the Princess Ruth. Hearing me, one would have thought that our evening with her was no different from the one we had spent in the Reverend Parker's stable. With something of his dead grandfather's wisdom, Eahou put aside his dislike for the family who had stolen his kingdom. "For a Kamehameha," he said, "she was very kind."

Kanemilohai was not so easily quieted in his fears of the ruling chiefs. In his mind now grew the same worry that bothered me: what would happen to the boy when the Kamehameha learned that he lived? The Conqueror would have ordered him killed at once, his flesh and blood and bones laid upon the altar of Ku. Yet I could not believe that Kauikeaouli or Alex would be so savage. Then I thought of Lot, another kind of man: he was the one to be feared, if ever he should come to power. Now I had two reasons to wish long life to Kauikeaouli, an even longer reign for Alex. Suddenly, in its searching to find a way of giving continued life to Eahou, my mind found the answer: a marriage of state between the boy and the daughter of Ke'elikolani. In this union between the only children of the two greatest families in the land lay the sole hope for Eahou's safety. With Eben's help I must seal this marriage which the Princess herself had proposed—even if the daughter proved to be as ugly as her mother.

Kanemilohai could not hide his fears. "And what of you, Nihoa of Nanahoa? Will you stay with us, to be *kahu* to our son, as you have been *kahu* to the Prince Liholiho?"

"How did you know?" I asked in surprise, for not one word about this relationship had I said either to him or to Eahou.

"Oh," he replied with a laugh, "we of Ka'a'awa may be far removed from you of Honolulu. But we are not so withdrawn that we do not hear some of the news from town, especially if it concerns our friends and neighbors from districts on either side. And if I have a way of forgetting some of these things, my brother reminds me of them when I should remember. To put your mind at ease: he is the one who told me that you were *kahu* to Liholiho. And surely I do not need to impress upon you how—" he hesitated, seeking the right words, "—how helpful to

Kaneikapule your presence here would be." He had found the right words to capture me, to offend Hahau. Beside him, the priest glowered, not hiding his dislike for me.

I was like an eel caught in a trap for lobsters: my new love for Eahou was surrounded by my old love for Alex. My new loyalty to the ruling chiefs was threatened from within by my family's old loyalty to O'ahu's kings. Like the eel in its trap, my mind flexed and coiled and darted about, not knowing how to join these loves and loyalties without hurting anyone. At last I found a narrow opening through which I squirmed to freedom. "Here is my thought: to live here in this household would not be good, but to be near by, within reach when I am needed, that will be both possible and safe—for all of us. I shall ask the King's permission to retire to my lands in Kahana, where I can serve both you and him, as is my wish, as is my duty. How does this plan sound to you?"

"It is the thought of a wise man," he replied. "For our sakes, I hope you will come soon to live in Kahana."

Pleased with his agreement, and attracted by the prospect of this new way of life, I said, "The sooner I start, the sooner I shall return. Tomorrow I resume my journey, knowing that I leave Kaneikapule in the best of care." As for you, you sour old bundle of envy and hate, I thought, not looking upon scowling Hahau, I shall dispose of you some other day, when I have the time.

By now night had come, the *kukui*-oil lamps were flickering. After the exciting day and our sleepless night before, Eahou was worn out and I was not much more sprightly. The boy, blinking sleepily, leaned against his grandmother's side. But I had one more duty to perform before we could seek our rest.

"Tell me a little something, I ask you, about the American who lives down by the beach.—I have a message for him, but before we meet I wish to know what kind of man he is."

The priest stiffened, bristling like an angry dog, but Kanemilohai smiled easily. "Kaula Pelikikola? Now there is one foreigner I like—even though he does not give me the chance to show it. We are fortunate to have him living here, in our valley. He is a hard worker, as you can see from the way he is changing the face of the land. And, unlike most other foreigners I have heard about, he does not hunt among our women to take them into his bed. He seems to have no interest in the pleasures of bed—which is perhaps the reason why he works so hard in the fields." Here was high praise, indeed, from a man of Kanemilohai's station, and I was ready to discard Zorobabela's opinion in favor of the chief's, when he continued. "But he does not like us, the people of our country. He shuns us, as if we were beneath his notice. 'The man apart,' I call him, and I pity him in my thoughts because he is so alone."

"Aye, it is even as my husband says," Maka-o-Hina shook her head. "I think that, in his heart, this man is a good man. Why else would he run about, when people are sick, taking medicines to them, bundles of food, words of advice—even though these are delivered with angry gestures and loud scoldings? To me he acts like a man much hurt, who shuns all other people now because he fears to be hurt again. I will make a guess that, like certain ones we have known among our own people, he was unhappy in love, and has fled to this place to forget his misery."

"Cha!" the priest cried in wrath, "you are soft in the head, you two! He is a man without liver or spirit. Less than a worm is he."

"Unfortunately," said Kanemilohai to me, "my brother

does not like this neighbor of ours. I think they have had some arguments between them."

"The fires he lights," the priest hissed, "the smoke he sends up into heaven: they are offenses to the god.—And that sleeping-place he has made in Pohukaina! Surely the spirits of the dead must haunt him for this abomination. I have told him that, for these affronts to our gods and to our people, the earth and its maggots will spurn him, and his body will be food for crabs in the sea." With clawed fingers, glaring eyes, Hahau begged the gods to smite Saul Bristol dead.

"And what did he say to this?" I asked, wondering if Hahau too might have read Bristol's journal.

"He laughed—and, turning his back upon me, he walked away. What else would you expect from such a thing?" Hatred such as I have never seen made the spittle gather on Hahau's lips, his whole body to quiver. "His presence here is an offense to us. Because my brother will not drive him away from Ka'a'awa, I ask the gods each day to do it."

Kanemilohai put up his hands in apology. With the same patient voice he must have directed a hundred times to the priest, he explained to me: "Without him and his cattle ranch, who would pay the taxes on these lands of ours? No longer can we pay the tax-gatherers of the Kamehameha in *kapa* and in taro and in pigs. Even if we could pay them in the fruits of the earth, as we did in the olden days, where are the people who would grow these many fruits? As you have seen, the valley is almost emptied of its people. Dead they are, most of them, or gone away to other places.—Gold is wanted now, and how else can we get gold except from Bristol's chief, the little Englishman called Hopakina? His gold keeps us here. Without it we could not have held this land for Kane.

Without it we cannot hold the land now for Kane and his youngest son. Now that Kaneikapule is with us, we must hold Ka'a'awa even more firmly."

"The foreigners are the ones!" cried Hahau, "they and their greed for gold. They are slaying our people, they are stealing from us our lands and our contentment. I say that we who remain should rise up and drive them from these islands before we are utterly destroyed. It is not too late—"

"It is late enough," decided Maka-o-Hina, stopping short an argument she must have heard a hundred and one times. "My grandson is tired, and the hour has come when all are ready for sleep. Do you in your prayers tonight offer to the gods our thanks for granting us this day of happiness. I shall do the same, on my knees, to the new god who listens to the prayers of women."

"Yes, Mama. You are right, as always," said Kanemilohai.

I could not help but smile. Men make noise, women make peace, as the old saying goes. In this lordly house, as in my carousing one, Mama is the boss. Without another sound the priest got up and stalked away, a greatly ruffled stilt searching for worms to peck at.

"Don't mind him," Maka-o-Hina told me quite clearly. "He is always sulking about something."

Kanemilohai himself escorted me to the guest house. It was clean and free of vermin, and the *kapa* sheets were fragrant with *maile*. But not for a long time could I fall asleep. The day had been too full of surprises, which I had to think about and understand before sleep could close my eyes and quiet my brain. And, let me confess it, I missed the boy. Tonight his grandmother and grandfather kept him between them. But how could I begrudge them that great comfort?

CHAPTER 20.

IN WHICH, LEAVING NOTHING UNDONE, A DETERMINED SPY PERFORMS HIS DUTY

A spy must leave nothing undone, I had convinced myself before I slept. A spy can indulge no scruples, I assured myself in the morning. Thus easily did I justify my return to the cave of Pohukaina. Saul Bristol's journal pulled me to it as whiskey draws a drunkard.

Our morning meal moved too leisurely for me, our farewells were too prolonged. I could scarcely spare the time for saying goodbye to my hosts, and I saw no need for sadness in taking leave of Eahou. Rested and happy, he gave me his hand in foreigners' fashion, as Eben had done when we parted at Kahalu'u. Holding it in both of mine, I gave him my blessing and a parting jest: "You will see me soon, before you have had time to forget the sound of my voice."

"I will never forget you, Makuahou," he said, hugging me this time. This promise, even though I had asked for it, I knew I could trust.

Kanemilohai tugged at my coat sleeve as I was about to climb aboard Lokelani. "Behold: Kaula Pelikikola rides into the fields." At such a distance I could see only

a man on horseback cantering across the pastureland toward the valley's far side. He might have been Ichabod
Crane or his headless horseman for all I could tell.

"Too bad," said Maka-o-Hina, "we have kept you too
long. Now you must follow after him with your message."

"No matter," I covered up my relief with the necessary
show of indifference. "I can stop to see him on the way
back. The message is not so important."

"And where is that old Hahau?" she looked about impatiently, already thinking of other matters.

"He keeps to his house," answered Kanemilohai. "You
know how busy with duties he is in the mornings."

"Even so," she tossed her head, "he should be here. I
suppose he is pouting still."

"Now, Mama," began her husband-slave.

"Farewell to you," I called, springing into the saddle,
"until we meet again." Joyfully I rode off, expecting to
return to them in a few days.

In high spirits I rode through Bristol's yard, congratu-
lating myself upon his absence, barking back at the noisy
dogs, and went at once to Ka 'Oi'o Point. Being a very
clever spy, I hid Loke in the tall shrubbery and walked up
the winding path to Pohukaina.

Everything in the cave was just as we had left it, he, the
trusting man, and I, the trespassing one. Today I suffered
no attacks of conscience: this is done for the King, I told
myself, aware even then that I lied. Sitting in Bristol's
chair, at his desk, I opened his book and quickly found
my place in that first entry:

...I am tempted, always I am tempted, some days more than
others. But I am not yet so mad that I can imagine warmth in
that traitor's touch, or love in that urgent voice...

"Cha! This light is bad," I grumbled. "This chair is
made for a long-legged, a hard-rumped man." I shifted

that high-backed, stiff-bottomed thing, to let the light fall over one shoulder upon the heavy book propped on my knees. Before I write down here what I read, let me say that I did not put it all into my memory. Good though it may be, it is not that well trained. Nor did I copy all this stuff down then, of course. The copying was done at another time, and in another place, as I shall describe later in this history—if ever I get that far. This is what I read:

—I do not yield. "Not yet," I answer. "Someday you may have this wasted life, but not now, not yet," even as I ask myself why I bother to resist.

I do not know why. Perhaps it is the example of Ulupaʻu, far to my right, many miles away, its outline dimmed by the spray: like an enormous turtle swimming in the sea, head extended, it does not yield to wind or water. Perhaps it is the quiet force of the mountains behind me, proud and unyielding, which sustains me. Or the long and lovely valley they enclose, in which I live. Other men would call them blessings, but I hate them.

Hating them, hating myself, hating life, I return to them each day after I have played my dangerous game with the sea. The waves have not quieted me, the sea has not washed me clean of despair. Yet each day I turn my back upon it, and come home again to the drudgery of life. Why, I ask myself, why?

Sunday, 2 January 1853

I do not know, I tell myself. Who can ever know himself well enough to account for his motives and his actions? All I can ever be sure of, about myself, is that something within me tells me to go on trying, to go on hoping. Hope, I guess it is, that silly, illusory, nonsensical sop to the stupid which Pandora hauled up out of the very bottom of her barrel. Hope that tomorrow will be better—no, not tomorrow, but next year, perhaps, or the year after. If I could not hope for time to bring an end to this period of doubting, as at home spring brings an end to winter, then I would lose my last link to reason, and my last defense against the sea.

A slave who has never been free could not possibly yearn for freedom as much as does the man new-come to prison. These kanakas here, who have never known the bleakness of winter: how can they pine for spring? Ahh, this is the heart of my trouble: I was happy once (or thought I was, which amounts to the same thing), until, all in a moment, my happiness was taken from me. How, then, can I not yearn to have it given back to me? —The waiting is an ordeal, the memories of my spring are tortures I marvel that I can bear. The road back is long and perilous, my progress is slow and wearying.

But I am making progress—I think. Let the sea be my witness: for three years I have resisted its siren call. Let this land be my witness: in two years I have broken it. Above all, this journal is my proof: I, who swore once that I would never write again, take up my quill now, resolving that this journal will be my passport out of despond into life.

For too long I have been mute, thoughtless, little more than an animal. Little better than the kanakas among whom I live, and whom I condemn for their brutishness. For too long I've wallowed in this slough. I did not know how to climb out of it until last Saturday, in Honolulu, I passed Hoffmann's Store. In the window some clerk had laid out a display of stationery, writing tablets, commonplace books, pencils, ferules—all the things a schoolboy needs to help him on his way to knowledge. The sight of all that gleaming untouched paper hauled me up short. I could almost smell it through the window-pane! Seized with a hunger I thought forever dead, I rushed into the store, intending to buy every piece of paper in the place. But one look at the clerk quieted me: prissy as a maiden aunt, he would never have permitted my raid upon his treasury, nor understood it. Chastened, I bought this enormous ledger, the largest one he had, two commonplace books, and a ferule. "No, no letter paper," I stopped him when he reached for some. I'm not ready yet for letters. "What about pens?" "I'm sorry, sir," he simpered, "those seem to have been left out of the last shipment. Terrible oversight . . ." "Never mind, I'll manage without," I cut him short, desperate to lay hands upon my purchases, impatient to be on my way home.

But the long ride to Ka'a'awa left me weary and melancholy again. I did not even strip the newspaper wrapping from these possessions until yesterday. Only then, as nervously I lifted the heavy ledger to the table and sat down to write—using a quill cut from the feather of a frigate bird, and sepia taken from the ink sack of a fresh-caught squid—did I wonder if I could ever bring myself to write a single word. For half the morning I sat before that blank page, terrified by its emptiness, while over and over again my divided spirit fought its arguments—

Not until evening, after I had gone for my lonely walk along the beach, and returned again from my combat with the sea, was I able to dip the quill into the inkhorn and begin.

Today the words have come more easily.

Saturday, 8 Jany 1853

You ass! You fool, you!—So you thought writing would be easier, did you, once you'd begun? And you thought, did you, to pull yourself up out of nothingness by writing down your daily little maunderings about yourself, a less-than-nothing?—O you pompous, fatuous, self-pitying, whining, whinnying monarch of all asses!

Go back to the fields, stick to your plow, drop your dung out there in the mud—if you can't find anything better to write about than your most precious, most boring, self. Don't come back until you've got something worth remembering.

Now git!

Tuesday, January 11

Dehorned 35 head of cattle today. Deballed 15 bull calves. Virtuously tired. The kanakas were very helpful, however, exhibiting little of their usual ineptness. Probably because I promised 'em those 15 pair of mountain oysters.

Thursday, Jany 13

Rained all the damned day today. Miserable!—Fortunately I finished plowing up the new pasture yesterday and got out most of the stumps. This rain will be good for the grass.

Friday, January 14

The rain stopped during the night, and today was sunny and clear. But everything outside is still too wet for work. So I saddled up the stallion and rode over to Kahana and Hau'ula to check the stock there. The streams were in flood, of course, and I got wet up to my butt in every one of 'em. But the cattle were safe, despite complete lack of attention from the kanakas. Those dumb brutes were still huddled inside their stinking, sopping grass huts, surounded by seas of mud. The cows, being smarter, had moved to high ground. The cattle thrive, the kanakas diminish. Small wonder. Good riddance. A dirtier, lazier, more shiftless lot of savages I have never known. Their emotions lie too close to the surface. The slightest fright will make 'em scream, the merest pleasure will make 'em shout. But, because of that same shallowness of feeling, the slightest trouble is too much trouble: they will do nothing that requires exertion, they would rather die than work.

As usual, I fussed at 'em, and, as usual, got my unvarying answers: broad smiles, universal shrugs, & a torrent of vowels, all meaning, more or less, that the waters will go away, the sun will dry things out again, and why should they go to the bother of moving if they are happy with things the way they are? When will I learn to give up my efforts to teach them the rudiments of civilization?

"Oooooohhhhhh, this goddam son-of-a-bitch!" I blew up, ready to tear the ledger apart, and the writer with it. "This goddamned sassy *haole*!—Why the hell doesn't he go back to where he came from, if he doesn't like it here? Why doesn't he go and drown himself in the sea?" Full of hate for him, who hated my people even more than he loved himself, I wanted to throw that vile journal of his against the wall of the cave.—But did I? No. His next entry drew me into it, as easily as molasses swallows flies . . .

Monday, Jany 17, 1853

Every now and then Charles Gordon Hopkins, my lord the Duke of Koʻolauloa, Grand Seigneur of this dismal demesne, of this my vassalage, is graciously disposed to commend to my hospitality those gentlemen from the great world who have thrust themselves upon his attention at Kahuku or in Honolulu. Poor man! Poorer me! The specimens of learning and culture who manage to penetrate this close to the edge of the world ought to be pushed over it, in my opinion, and I can't say that I blame Polly for foisting them upon me as soon as he can point their snouts away from him. But how I HATE to have them unloaded on me! I don't mind running the ranch at this remotest march of his duchy; I don't mind toiling like a serf for him from dawn to dusk; I don't even regret not being summoned to the revels at his manor house from one year to the next; BUT I sure as hell hate to be innkeeper to his guests too. When company comes in the gate, privacy goes out the back door. When fools come into the house, how else can I be but bored, *bored*, BORED!!!

Even so, old habits of decency die hard, even in old renegades like me—and when these jackasses errant turn into my place, worn and weary after the long day's ride from Kahuku, I haven't the brass to send them away. Mine is the only white man's house in 25 miles of Oʻahu's coast; and, shabby as it is, it is palatial compared with the flea-infested grass shacks and the luetic beds the natives have to offer between Kahuku and Kaneʻohe.

I've put up some weird folk in my time, usually single-minded, bespectacled natural philosophers determined to heap upon their pack-mules a specimen of every single kind of plant or animal or rock or shell or fish they can lay their grubby hands on; often enough a squadron of lewd young naval officers lurching from orgy to orgy in every native village along the way (and always yelping with pained surprised when the clap hits 'em before they're halfway around the island); but I must confess I'm not likely ever to see again such phenomena as I was host to yesternight.

I thought they were circus folk, or gypsies, when first I saw them, all got up in colored robes and broad-rimmed hats & huge leather gauntlets. Two of the Magi, on their way home from Bethlehem, was my next guess, until I heard their shrieks of laughter over my obvious amazement. "My God! Saloon girls," I snorted, immediately enraged. "What's Polly been up to now?"

Well, they weren't exactly saloon harlots, but they were a couple of dancers from the King's hula troupe. His Majesty, it developed, being weary of the disapproving missionary censors that oversee his every action in Honolulu, had escaped, with a few of his cronies, and his hula girls, and a mere hundred retainers or two, to the privacy of Hopkins' place at Kahuku. The bacchanalia having ended yesterday, His Sobering Majesty was wending his way painfully over the leeward part of the isle again, back to the clucking constraints of Honolulu and the glarings of his formidable spouse, who must know very well what he's been up to on this latest so-called Royal Progress. In the cold light of the Sabbath—if not *in mania potu* the night before—the Royal Head had nodded permission for the two girls to visit their families in Koʻolauloa before returning to duty in town.

All this I learned in the first few seconds after their arrival, before they'd dismounted. When finally they stood upon the grass I saw how small and young they were, little more than children. Their feet were bare. And, beneath the gaudy dressing gowns they'd managed to steal or wangle or earn from the King's Noble Companions, they were innocent of clothing, as they themselves told me with much laughing and exhibition of multitudinous teeth. "Kahana was so beautiful! We went swimming there. When we were finished we didn't want to get all dressed up again. So we put on these pretty things. Just like *paʻu* riders, no?"

Feeling both pity and disgust, I watched them climb the stairs and enter the house as if they owned it. When small Makana, wreathed in grins, came up to lead the horses away, I told him to get his mother to come and make the beds for Mr. Hopkins' guests and fix their supper. "Sure, I tell 'um," he answered cheerfully. "And you," I pushed him on his way, "you get those dirty thoughts out of your head. And when you've washed those filthy hands, you bring my supper up to the cave. I sleep in the cave tonight. You hear me?" "Aye," he mumbled, the grins effaced for a moment. These *kanaka* kids are too knowledgeable for their years, I muttered to myself, for at least the thousandth time, as I started up the path to the cave which is my refuge when the world is too much with me.

This morning the bitchlings departed while I was burning off the brush in the north side of the valley. When I returned to the house, expecting to find it ransacked and robbed of every portable treasure, I found it intact, and as neat as a pin. Makana's slovenly mother could never, even if she practised 'til she was ninety, achieve such a transformation. Well, they weren't such dreadful creatures after all, I was admitting, when, on the table in the parlor, I found a note. "Thank you, Kind Sir," it said, in a schoolgirl's scrawl, "from Agnes and Lovey." That's all, but—unaccountably—I was saddened when I read it.

Tuesday, Jany 18, 1853

The house stank so much of females last night—of female flesh and female powder and female perfumes—that I couldn't endure it—

No. In saying that, I fool no one but myself. If a man can't be honest with his journal, then why should he try to keep one of these pesky, nagging, demanding, alluring, irresistible things?

No. The house did not stink. It was fragrant. It was scented. With the beauty and the mystery of Aphrodite herself. I tried to sleep. I could not. The whole night was in league against me. No winds came off the sea to drive the lingering perfume from the house. Through my windows the full moon sent down her shafts to drive me mad. And mad I became, under the oppression of such torments as the night and memories brought to me. Mad with grief, not with desire, crazed with the awareness of what is and with the dream of what might have been, I abandoned the house to Melissa's ghost, and ran to hide in the darkness of the cave.

Friday, 21st January

Work: this is the only solace.
Time, they say, is the healer.
But, I ask: do some wounds ever heal?

Sunday, 23 Jan^y

This is the day when, by the law of this Christian land, no one works—save infidels like me. This is the day when, in universal conspiracy, the brown-skinned hypocrites among whom I dwell doff their perfidies and perversities, don their clothes, and, swathed in righteousness, float like massive chocolate angels to the neighborhood church. O Christ! what miracles of transmogrification are wrought in thy name!

Behold Kamanele, the mother of Makana. Who would recognize in this pious matron, enveloped by the decorous black Mother Hubbard, this valley's most assiduous harlot?

Observe the stalwart Pi'opi'o, the gallant spouse of Kamanele, the putative father of Makana, whose sire not even Kamanele can identify. Stiff in his hot black suit, he is upright on the Sabbath only. During the rest of the week he lolls on a mat, drinking homemade beer and cheating the village bumpkins at cards.

See the cherubic Makana, skipping happily to church, a sprite-ly herald of this model family. Forget, if you can, O Ye Recording Angels, what havoc this precocious cock doth wreak, indiscriminately, among cows and pigs and chickens, male and female alike, who fall within his grasp on any day of the week.

Lo! Comes now Pordagee Joe and his half-breed brood. Shaven and shorn and freshly scrubbed, hairy Joe barks like a noisy sheep dog at the horde he's engendered. The little lambs trot dutifully ahead, but Mama Ewe, long inured to Joe's nippings and his pawings alike, refuses to be hurried. Still carrying their last-born child in her arms, she's already full in the belly with Joe's next get. "One, two, three, four, five—and a half," I count them as they go past, as I always do, marveling at Joe's fertility and at his wife's durability.

"Morning, Joe," I smile toothfully at the fecund pair, "morning, Mrs. Joe," as they send their ritual smile at me. We hate each other cordially on Sunday mornings, a concession to the day of *agapé*. The rest of the week we hate each other at the top of Joe's loud and leathery lungs, because holy Joe resents my unrelenting determination to get an honest day's work out of him. If I didn't feel sorry for those half-caste brats of his, I would have run him out of the valley two years ago.

Last in the processional, and always after a bit of an interval, as if to signify that they are no part of the commonalty who have gone before, appear the valley's last Christian inhabitants, and its oldest. The valley is theirs, and I am the foreigner, the intruder, tolerated only because of the gold Milord Hopkins pays them for the right to use their land. They seem to be almost members of a different race, these two—tall, big-boned, proud as only exalted chiefs can be. These two I respect and honor, for they are not frauds and dissemblers like all the rest who come within my view. When Mr. Kanemilohai and his stately wife appear, I accord them the supreme courtesy: I take my feet from the railing, hide the bottle of brandy I've been sipping, and, almost mechanically, sit upright in my chair. Gravely he lifts his hat, regally she nods, soberly I bow. Then, when they have gone far enough along the path to free me from any threat of their disapproval, I address myself to my bottle of brandy, and proceed to get thoroughly drunk.

Thus passeth the Sabbath at Ka'a'awa.

Tuesday, 25 Jan^y

As usual, I was queasy in the stomach and aching in the head yestermorn, and sicker at heart. And, as usual, I resolved not to get drunk next Sunday, knowing full well that I've made the resolve often enough before and broken it as often. "Then why do you drink, Brother Ass?" I inquired solicitously. "Why, sir, to profane the Sabbath, Brother Fool," my sinister self retorted.

Pfaugh! I who rail at the kanakas for their hypocrisy!—I'm a bigger cheat than any of them. I can't even tell the truth to myself. I drink to forget. Most especially to forget the dreadful, dreary, grim wasteland that is the Sabbath, that gives a man time to think . . .

Wednesday, Jany 26

While I was preparing to shave this morning, I took a good look in the mirror, something I haven't bothered to do for many a month. A stranger stared back at me. Gone was the smooth-cheeked youth I've been thinking myself to be, gone was the innocent phiz, the wide-eyed gaze of the creature whose name I bear, whose thoughts I share. Skin and bones I am now, lean as a scarecrow, and as brown as a *kanaka*. The full lips which once Melissa kissed—Melissa only, and no other—are thin and cruel. The gray eyes, which once I thought were destined to gaze in delight upon Melissa's loveliness, are bleak now, cold and dead. The nose is a beak, narrow and bold. Not even my hair is unmarked: the long, black locks are shot through with white. Fierce as an eagle I look—but I feel, I think, I act like the youth I remember when I was wed to Melissa. Shocked at the mirror's revelations, I groaned.

For an instant, razor poised, revulsion rising in me like vomit, I was tempted to slit my throat. Only a greater revulsion saved me from the deed: the thought of the kanakas finding me naked and bloodied and *conquered*. No: the sea is cleaner, I remembered in time. Putting away the razor, turning from the mirror, I went unshaven for today.

Monday, 7 Feb^y

Went to Kahana and Hau'ula today. Everybody is sick with the influenza. Dosed them all with calomel & tea, just as I've done the past three days at Ka'a'awa.

Tuesday, 8 Feb^y

Got up with the influenza. Took a blue pill.

Wednesday, 9 February

Got up better. Plenty of opening medicine is the best thing for Influenza, if taken in time. The natives all experience a touch of ague with it, having alternate hot and cold fits. Every day that I live among them I become more & more convinced that they are a race in decay. Worn out, exhausted. In mind and body alike they seem to be destitute of vigor. I spent most of the day riding around, *forcing* them to take the medicine I brought them. I doubt if it will do much good. Some of them as much as said so, with their shrugs and scowls. Others simply walked away, spurning the *haole* medicine.—Or were they spurning the *haole*?

Saturday, 11 February

Travelers along this seacoast road are rare at the best of times, but since the influenza started two or three weeks ago no one has come past this house. What this means I do not know. I can't imagine everybody's being sick at the same time. Nor can I envision half the population—or even a quarter, a tenth of it—staying at home to attend the sick. And it is inconceivable to me that our efficient, our organized, our superbly intelligent officialdom in Honolulu will have told the people to stay at home, in order to keep the plague from spreading. That would make too much sense!—Knowing the lot of them as I do, I am left with only one conclusion: they're all in church, on their knees, imploring their Merciful God to spare them any more of his wrath. All I can say is, they'd better be careful. If their importunations should, by some strange accident, remind him that they exist, and he took one brief look at them, he'd have to—out of merest elementary justice—blast 'em all straight into hell for their crimes.

From the pleasant contemplation of such a Judgment Day I am not in the least deterred by the certainty that I should be plunged into the pit along with them. I am not comforted by the fact that most of the haoles here would accompany me—what a horror it is, to think of having to spend eternity with Dr. Judd, the very Reverend John S. Emerson, Polly Hopkins, and Porda-gee Joe, all of us wallowing in the same pool of flaming brimstone!—but I do draw some satisfaction from the hope that the Lord's justice, when it comes, will be impartial, finding sinners among the Pharisees and the Sadducees, as well as among the unanointed heathen.

While the road remains untraveled—O ye heavens! do I dignify it with the name of road? It is but a track across the grass and through the wind-shaped brush, a path worn into the earth by the tread of kanakas' wide dirty feet, the dainty plodding of horses or mules. No ruts are here to show that the wheel has ever been invented, because no wagon or cart could be drawn across those miles of mud and sand, fields of boulders and thickets of scrub, that lie between here and the declivity of Nu'uanu's *pali*. And a carriage would simply fall apart, at mere sight of the stony riverbed which purports to be the road down that perpendicular mountain!—while, I say, we here in Ka'a'awa are denied the sight and sound of passersby, we must perforce remain in ignorance of what passes for news in the splendid capital city of this kingdom of squalor and tawdriness. Not that I am especially interested in what's going on there, amid the dust & the bedlam of Honolulu. It's just that a man has a certain right to know, sooner or later, if the Hawaiian flag still flies over the land in which he drudges, or if some new crisis in Lilliput has brought another ship-of-the-line from across the sea, to train its guns upon Kamehameha's crumbling fortress and to run its arrogant standard up the mast. With Wyllie working for Britain, Judd conniving for America, and Dillon conspiring for France, one can entertain a legitimate worry. Not for myself, for I can always go as freely as I came, if I do not like the new regime. No, I worry for Alex, the only one in the Kingdom I've met who on Judgment Day would be worthy of a place on the right side of the Lord.

In the meantime, as we subsist in ignorance here, I am spared a number of aggravations. Not the least of these is the unwanted company of those learned gentlemen of science, in their everlasting scrabbling for specimens. Perhaps I should count my blessings, rather than fret over the lack of news. News would mean company, if only for a while, and I am not yet ready to *ask* for that.

One of the pleasures of solitude is the opportunity to read. I don't have many books here, but the few I've managed to round up, mostly at auction sales, I read thoroughly & well. Once again —for the third time—I'm pondering the message of Milton in "Paradise Lost." But Robert Burton is my greatest joy. Now there is a very model of misanthropes for me to follow! Such a wealth of specimens of melancholy he offers for me to imitate!— Yet, try as I do to anatomize my own, with respect to the paradigms he provides, I have not yet succeeded in finding my own particular place in his schemes. Am I so different? Lucifer's pride, which is not diminished by the arrogance of a Yale man, says Yes, I am. But a schoolmaster's common sense (or what remains of it) says No . . .

And, all of a sudden, perhaps because of my reading, probably because of my solitude, I want to write again. After years of unwillingness, my thoughts flow as readily as does the squid's ink from this quill. If only this readiness survives the morrow.

Sunday, 12 February 1853

Tonight I am not drunk with brandy. I am drunk with beauty —and with words.

It has been a beautiful day, all golden and blue over the sea, all golden and green in the valley. Never has Ka'a'awa been so fair. I had not the heart to spoil either the time or the place with brandy.

As usual, more out of habit than of need, I sat on the verandah to watch my neighbors make their promenade to church. I owed it to them, I told myself, not to disarrange their expectations of seeing me in my customary chair. "Thus easily does noblesse oblige assert itself," I explained to the chair, the railing, the air, and drowsing Belle, hung over a couple of sun-warmed steps, her belly swollen with the pups she is about to throw. I smiled primly at the libidinous Makana and his lascivious mother (giving them, in the instant, the tribute of wondering why I should be made so uncomfortable by their unabashed sexuality). Pordagee Joe was too harassed a *pater familias* to warrant even cordial hatred this morning: tenderly carrying one of his little daughters, still weak from the influenza, he gave me a wan smile that was like a plea for truce in our feuding. And when the nobility came past I actually stood up and bowed to them, calling out—needlessly, I knew, but in purest neighborliness—"How are you? Has the sickness come yet into your household?"

They seemed to be almost startled. Pausing for a moment, the splendid old man searched for English words he seldom uses. "No. No. The mercy of Iehovah: it is keeping us well." Then he continued on his way. Without stopping, she replied, "Mahalo . . . Mahalo ia 'oe . . ." Those soft words of thanks were the loveliest sounds I have heard in many months. Looking at them, tall and proud and perfect of their kind, I willingly conceded them a place beside Alex in their Jehovah's heaven.

After that I tried to read. But Milton's orotund verse weighed heavy upon my spirit. And the consolations of melancholickal Burton eluded me utterly: he was so sour, so grudging, so pontifical in his pronouncements, so pedantic even in his punning, that I snapped him shut noisily enough to draw a glare of reproof from Belle.

What to do, what to do? The bottle beckoned, but I resisted it. This journal called, but I spurned it. "Would you be a *scribbling* madman, too?" I snorted, "and in broad daylight?—No, that's Burton's refuge." A journal, I've decided sometime in my life, is a secret thing. And secrets belong to lamplight and the night.

I paced the porch restlessly, scanning the coast road hopefully, eager for the sight of a stranger. I was bored enough, and lonesome enough, to welcome a whole pack of gabbling naturalists, even a troop of unwashed Frenchmen in pursuit of whores. But the road remained as empty as ever, and no one arrived to divert me with annoyances.

Not a cloud dimmed the light of the sun, but in my mind a whole firmament of gloom was gathering. I recognized the signs, read the portents aright: if I allowed that gloom to grow into a storm of rage and recollection, it would rive me . . .

Snatching up the brandy, I poured a gobletfull. Overcome with loathing—for myself, not the spirit—I threw goblet and bottle into the grass. Scarcely knowing what I did, knowing only that I must get away from that brooding empty house, I hurried down the stairs, out from the shadows into the morning's sunlight.

Hating the thought of people now, even more than I'd longed for them only moments before, I ran up the path leading into the valley. Shunning the village beside the sea, with its Popish chapel, its mealy-mouthed Belgian priest, its pack of hypocrites gathered

around him like buzzards around a charnel-house, I fled by instinct to the only place where I could find peace.

At first I ran—up the winding path that skirts the swampy land
where the natives cultivate taro and mosquitoes, up the slight hill
that, like a glacier's moraine (in this island that has never known
the cold weight of glaciers), lifts the floor of Ka'a'awa's valley
above the reach of the sea.

And then, as I gained the top of the hill and came out upon the
valley's plain: oh, the beauty of it made me cry out in wonder!

I'd been there before, of course, scores of times, and I'd known
in a vague and unthinking way that it was a beautiful place, but
I'd never really stopped to look at it, to understand the reasons for
its beauty. Always I'd been too busy, intent upon clearing
pasture-land from the returning jungle, too determined upon
exacting an honest day's labor from Pordagee Joe and the kanakas, too preoccupied with my own sorrows and too full of lip-
biting rage to lift my eyes to the mountains.

But today was different. Today, at last, I saw them in all their
glory. The blazing sun, not yet at the meridian, limned in gold
the near-side of each soaring peak, each plunging cliff, each rock
and tree and blade of grass, and edged in deepest black the shadows they cast. Gold and green and black was the land, strong
against the dazzling blue of the sky.

On either side, seeming to be almost within arm's reach, the
mountain ridges loom, rising like cathedral walls for thousands
of feet before they taper into spires and pinnacles and peaks.
Waterfalls have so scored their flanks that each ridge appears to
be supported by enormous buttresses thrusting deep into the
earth. Peaks and buttresses stand up proud and high, walling the
valley in for about two miles, until, with a grace almost of things
alive, they sink to their knees, then fall prostrate at the feet of the
awesome, the perfect mountain at the valley's head.

In this land of many gods he is a great god. Even to me, the
doubter of God and of gods, he is a presence I can not dismiss.
Remote, withdrawn, perfect in feature and proportion, he stands
there, a pyramid of rock robed in vestments of green, observing
the deeds of men, judging them.

Long ago I decided that, some day, I would climb to the top of
the ridges that separate Ka'a'awa from its neighbor valleys.
Most of all do I want to stand where certainly few men have

stood, upon the very top of the arrogant peak which rises above my house, the peak closest to the sea. But not once has it occurred to me that I should climb the face of the god. I would not dare. "Great is its *mana*," Makua said, when once I spoke with him about that brooding thing. I believed him.

Today this *mana* was indeed very great. For reasons I may never understand, and scarcely can comprehend now, as soberly I try to remember how I spent the rest of this strange day, I was compelled to approach him. I made my way not in fear, not in awe, but in trust. It was a kind of interest, an *expectation* on my part, which urged me on, as if some message awaited me there, or even an angelic summoner charged to find me as I was ordered to find him. Usually, when I work in the valley, I saddle Beau or Drummer, and ride up by a different path. The path I followed today led me for the first time in months past Pordagee Joe's cluster of shacks, some fashioned of grass, others of wood, arranged helter-skelter around an open yard. Chickens, cows, and goats wandered at will, keeping the grass low, as they do in my place. All of them, more sensible than I, preferred to take their ease in the shade of orange trees and mango trees heavy with blossoms. Beyond a rock wall, climbing beans curled their tendrils around poles cut from guava shrubs, which grow wild on the slopes at the foot of the ridge.

Higher than Joe's house, higher than any house-site in the valley, past or present, is the ancestral home of the chiefs of Ka'a'awa. Today, as in the old days, the Kanemilohais live in a grass house larger and taller than are the thatched huts of ordinary men. At either side to the rear, arranged around the inner courtyard, are a dozen smaller shelters. In these are stored the family's goods, tools, and other possessions; and in some of them, I suppose, must live the aged servants who attend the chiefs. They never go to church, these ancient ones, less because of their age, I suspect, than because of their devotion to the pagan gods. Their hostile glances, their surly speech, when on rare occasions I encounter them, more than suggest how much they abhor foreigners. They give me no proof, of course, that they cling to the ancient religion, but anyone who is not blind can conclude as much from the care with which they maintain the pagan temple that adjoins the household.

It is a small *heiau*, a platform of rocks about six feet high, twenty feet wide, and thirty feet long. Its millions of rocks must have been placed there hundreds of years ago, because they are as speckled with lichens as a reef is covered with seaweeds. Unlike other temples I have seen, invaded by weeds and shrubs, ragged around their edges where the loose rocks have been knocked down by zealot Christians or by careless children, this one is in perfect order. It stands ready to receive its gods whenever they choose to return. The images and idols which, I am told, once rose above all temples, are not visible here. But I will wager that they were not destroyed when, way back in 1819, the kapus were ended and the gods of old were toppled from their positions. Swathed in *kapa*, hidden away in one of Kanemilohai's storage huts, the gods of Ka'a'awa sleep, biding their time.

Unlike most foreigners, certainly unlike the rigid demanding missionaries and their righteous converts, I do not condemn those natives who will not give up the faith of their fathers. I rather admire their stubbornness, if the truth must be told, the while I join them in asking what good the new and omnipotent God of the Christians has done them.

Anyone who stands, as I did this morning, before the *heiau* and looks out upon the valley of Ka'a'awa has the right to ask this question. From that vantage, where once chiefs and priests must have gazed out upon fertile fields and hundreds of happy people, today I saw only desolation. The people are gone, dead and vanished into the earth, and among the smothering weeds only the stone platforms upon which once their houses rose, only a few sagging, rotting grass huts, remain to show that this was a thriving community. In this half of the valley the only fields which show the husbandry of man are those I have cleared, the only signs of life are the brute cattle I have turned into those pastures to graze for the profit of my liege-lord, that lissome lisping Duke of Kahuku. Death and desolation fill this place. If I were a native, I would weep for sorrow, I would faint with despair.—How, then, can I castigate those who remain for laziness and indifference, for fecklessness and unconcern, when all about them they see these evidences of their mortality? I should not—but I do.

Being a Yankee, and therefore a creature of determination if not of predestination, I must nag them, fuss at them, stir them up, for their sakes. This is the only way, if only I could make them understand it, by which the few who remain can be saved from the same dreadful extermination which has already carried off most of their race.

Saddened by my thoughts, I wanted to go home in defeat. Wrathful more at the grim Jehovah who permits these hecatombs of sacrificed Hawaiians than at the poor victims themselves, I wanted to curse. Lifting my head to ready it for raging, I saw once again the patient brooding mountain, and—rising from the valley, as heat rises from embers—the beauty which paid it homage. Sadness, anger, despair drained away, deep into the earth where death is, and once more I began to walk—to the mountain, where life is.

Beyond the *heiau* and the ruined village, haunted by silence, no trail led to the mountain. I had to make my own way, first through weeds and grasses which fill the abandoned plantations, then, when I'd vaulted the last stone wall, raised long ago to keep out wild pigs and wandering goats, through the primeval jungle. Into the shade of giant *koa* and leafy *kukui* trees I passed, forcing my way through glades of ferns and fields of cool gingers. The mountain-apple trees were in full flower: from the crimson puffs gaudy birds of every hue sipped their fill of nectar. When intertwined masses of *hau* blocked my advance, I stepped into the cold waters of the stream, flowing clear and quiet and unhurried toward the distant sea. Like Adam in Paradise, I sought my goal.

Like Adam.—Suddenly I knew that I must not come clothed and sweating and befouled into the presence of the waiting god. Removing my clothes, I hung them from the limbs of a *kukui* tree. Stepping out of my wet boots and stockings, I put them upon a boulder to dry. The stream was too shallow to bathe in, so I fashioned a cup from a broad leaf of the *ki* plant, as the natives do, and with it lifted the cleansing water to my head, my shoulders, to every part of my body. When the lustral bath was done, I felt clean within and without. I was ready to approach the mystery.

In a few more minutes I came to the end of my journey. I entered into a clearing at the foot of the mountain. Others had been there before me, as I know others will come after me. But today I was alone, and alone I approached the hallowed fane. A small platform of rocks, beyond doubt a most ancient *heiau*, has been built at the very center of the mountain wall. The rocks were smooth and green with moss. No image rose from this *heiau*, but lying on its surface were several strips of red *kapa*. And from the base of the *heiau* flowed the water of a spring. Joining with the water from a dozen other gushing springs, it formed the stream which brings the water of life to Ka'a'awa. The water of life is the gift of Kane. Lifting up my head, I looked into the face of Kane.

Immense, a vast wall of moss and fern and green grass, he towered above me, filling my vision as high as I could see and as far to either side as my eyes could encompass. His head was lost in the brightness of heaven, while at his feet, dizzy from searching the inscrutable face, breathless with expectation, I waited for him to speak.

Fool that I was!—I wince now, when I think of that moment of weakness, as, quivering like a bride at her marriage-bed, I waited for the ravishment of knowledge. I sicken now at this long dithyrambic entry in this stupid journal, the while I comfort myself with the thought that, at best, it has given me some occupation at the end of this strange romantical day, that at worst no one else will ever read it. (REMINDER: Before I die, I must be sure that this treacherous thing is DESTROYED!!)

What did I expect from Kane, the god of life?—Why should I expect him to give me a sign, when the mightier Jehovah has steadfastly withheld his grace from me? Pfaugh! There's no fool like a skeptic who is weak enough to doubt his disbelief.

Yearning upward, trembling with need, I begged him for a sign, any sign, to let me know that something greater, something grander, than puny man exists in this universe. As I waited, even the birds were silent, even the springs and the soft breath of the wind were hushed. In utter silence we waited, all of us.

In utter silence, impassive, unmoved, immovable, he allowed us to wait. No sign did he vouchsafe, not even the dropping of a pebble from his garb. Nothing came from him to me.

I turned away from the cruel precipice and without a backward glance went to fetch my clothes. The birds started their chirping again, the springs their burbling, the warm wind rose once more up the face of the mountain.

I do not think that I will go there again.

Naked, I walked the long way back, tired and hungry, and

sorely puzzled. Only when I reached the desolate village did I dress, to spare the puritanical chiefs the sight of unclothed *haole* flesh. Only when I came upon the *heiau* near their house did I have wit enough to realize that it faces directly up the valley, turned as naturally toward the god it serves as sunflowers turn toward theirs. I wonder if its priests were more successful than I was at communing with their god?

Now, at midnight, the lamp burns low, I have worn out three quills and used up a hornful of squid's ink. And myself as well. Yet I could not have slept until I finished this account.

What does this day's experience mean? What does it mean? I have never known anything like it—

After my experience of the day before, I had no doubt about what his experience was intended to mean for Saul Bristol. The god was preparing him for Eahou's homecoming. This *haole* is not as bad a man as I was thinking, I admitted gladly, deferring to Kane's wisdom. Kane has seen this, and is gentling him. Now he will be a better man, more suitable a companion to Kane's son.

But what a strange, unhappy, sour man he is!—And this Melissa! Where is she? Whatever did she do to him, that has so unmanned him? Hoping to learn more about her, I plunged into the next entry:

Thursday, 16 February

After Sunday's orgy of overwrought nerves and words— Damme! if paper weren't so precious I'd hurl this ledger into the cookstove!—I've been tuckered out in the writing department. And, I confess, somewhat ashamed of both my behavior and my style. Such poet's posturing! Excessive, excessive—to a degree I did not think myself capable of. From now on, I promise, there'll be no more of this wild fancifying, either in thought or in word. Simplicity, good old New England directness, will be good enough for me. On Sunday—I guffaw at the thought—if Holiness Judd or ReverEND Johnny Emerson had seen me wandering naked in the wilderness, had read my mind, would they have taken me for a prophet, preparing the way of the Lord? Hell no! They would have clapped me into prison, the one for pagan obscenity, the other for Popish mysticism. All my assurances that I want nothing to do with either would have stood for naught. —And yet, and yet . . . Try as I might to forget it, the experience still haunts me.

Fortunately, other demands upon my time are helping me to recover my senses. The fine dry weather, unusual for this rainy time of year along this sopping coast, continues, and I use every minute of each day to improve the ranch. (Mind your fences, son, as Pa used to say.) We've cleared another large field for pasture, fenced it in with rails from trees we cut during the clearing, plowed the rich earth to give the grasses a chance to choke out weeds, hauled dung from the stables to manure it. We've worked like beavers, even Pordagee Joe, and not once have I had to swear at any one. Curiously enough, I haven't wanted to. Perhaps it is because the Mountain is there, clear and serene, to watch us. More than once, as I have looked toward it, I have caught the others doing the same. It is a better gang-boss than I, I'm convinced, far better than a conscience for these hap-hazard kanakas.

During the lunch-rest yesterday I asked fatherly old Makua what name his people give the mountain. For a moment he looked at me, not insolently but appraisingly, as though deciding whether I was worthy of knowing. The other natives ceased their banter, listening (I knew at once) not for the name but for his answer. Finally it came. "The mountain?" he shrugged. "It has no name." The rebuff was gentle, but I heard it. Among a people who have a name for everything, from the smallest seashell to the remotest stars, how could they not have a name for this most magnificent of all the things in their world? In my question, of course, lay my answer. Long before, Makua had given me the clue; now he and his countrymen gave me the proof. Great is its *mana*. So sacred is the mountain that its name can never be uttered. Thus it was with the Hebrews and their jealous name-less god, thus it is with the Indians and their Great Spirit. And so it is with these new-made Christians, baptized on their skins perhaps, but unchanged in their hearts. "Is that so?" I smiled, acknowledging their right to conceal the sacred name. "And the other mountains hereabouts: are they too nameless?" "Oh, no," he said, less guarded now, "they are well named." "Tell me, then, if you please," I pointed to the haughty peak rising above my house, "how is that one called?" "Ahh, that one: Puu o Ka 'Oi'o

it is called." The Peak of the Procession of Ghosts. Quite willingly he went on to name each of the summits in that gaunt ridge,
even to the last and highest of all, the one closest to the nameless
deity. "That one, the cloud-piercing one: it is called Kanehoalani." Just as I expected: the Exalted Companion of Kane. "And
those?" I indicated the ridge at the northern side of the valley.
Patiently I listened as he named then every one, starting from
the sea, I forgetting each as fast as he disclosed it, until he came
to the last, the one closest to the god. "Manamana is its name,"
he finished, smiling broadly, all but winking, to tell me that now
he knew I was prepared to guess the unspoken name.

Manamana: Divine Power. "Ahh, it is as I thought," said I,
"and now, indeed, I do know. But I will not say it, out of respect
for him who abides there. I thank you, Makua, for a lesson in—
in geography. It is good for a man to know the names of the
places in the land wherein he dwells." "Aye," he said, settling
back against his rock, "it is good to know." So did the others of
his people take their ease, at peace with me and with their land.
Only Pordagee Joe did not understand why we spoke no more
during that day's time of rest.

Here, all too soon for me, Saul Bristol's journal ended.
To my annoyance, the rest of the book and the rest of
Bristol's life remained blank. Sighing with regret because
there was no more to read and so much more to learn, wondering if now I knew any more about this peculiar man
than I did before I'd pried into his secrets, I closed the
ledger and turned to put it back in place.

Beyond the edge of the desk I saw the white loincloth,
the brown belly of a *kahuna*. Looking up, I stared into the
ugly face of Hahau.

CHAPTER 21.

IN WHICH THE POWERS OF EVIL ENGAGE MAKIA WELI IN MORTAL COMBAT

uwe! Auwe!" I yelped, scared halfway to death. "What are you doing here? What do you want?"

He looked down at me as a yellow-eyed owl does at a cowering mouse. "The question is one I put to you," he said, very calmly. "White men, it is well known, are very jealous of their property, and of their privacy.—Unlike *kanaka*."

Angered by the sneer, even more furious because—of all people—he should be the one to catch me at my spying, I sprang up, shouting oaths like a brawling sailor. Bristol's chair fell over with a crash, the cave echoed with my yapping.

"Stop," he hunched his shoulders, closed his eyes. "This noise: it is an offense to my ears, as you are an offense to my sight. Let us go outside, where you can not deafen me." Opening his eyes, he looked up to where the black rock was mottled with patches, as though ghosts hovered there. "Or disturb the spirits of the dead."

A mouse only too willing to run, I dashed across the

path of boards to the mouth of the cave. Just outside, lying on the grass, was a neat little bundle, wrapped in *kapa*
dyed in black upon white. Black is the color of night,
white is the color of nothing: together, they mean death.
I stared down at the packet in dread, knowing instantly
that it was a thing for doing evil.

Disdaining the board path, Hahau left his footprints in
the dust of Pohukaina. "Let us talk like men of reason," I
began as he came near.

"Aye," he agreed, "when you have told me why you are
here, instead of being halfway to Kahana, I shall tell you
why I am here. There is no reason why you should not
know, inasmuch as my purpose concerns you." The words
fell politely from his lips, but the face was a mask of
hatred.

"And how does it concern me?" I demanded, bold
without, quaking within. I was interested in nothing else
but me.

"Most closely," he said softly, ever so subtly, "as close
as the sweat on your body, as the hair on your chin. Can
you guess what I have put into this little bundle?"

How could I fail to guess? "Bait?" I croaked, like a
frog from which the legs are about to be ripped.

"Ah," he mocked me, "this city *kanaka* has not forgotten entirely the ways of old. Bait, indeed, is here. From a
man most careless . . ."

Squatting beside the bundle, he opened it, laying out
its contents as precisely as, only yesterday, Brother Doison
had brought out his canister of metal and splinters of
bone. There, for me to see and to shudder at, were my
cast-off *malo*, the limp *ki* leaf bent to the shape of my
loins, and—I had to look close to find these, smeared
upon a piece of sodden *kapa*—the black and white hairs

of the beard I had shaved not three hours earlier. Disbelief and fear crowded through the doorway of my mind at one and the same moment. While my heart jumped my mouth worked overtime: "Do you still believe in such nonsense? That superstition? Chah!" I spat at his feet. All my life I had heard of *kahuna 'ana'ana*, but not until now had I met one. And never, never have I been so afraid.

He rose to his full height. "Do you doubt the power of the gods?" Tall and gaunt, a thing of bones unsoftened by the fat of kindness, he loomed over me, with flared nostrils and lips curled in that hideous grimace which priests of old carved upon idols.

"No," I backed away, "I do not doubt the power of the gods. But your power to command them: this I doubt most strongly."

"I do not command, you foolish one. I entreat. They have listened to me before, they will listen again. Three times more I will ask them."

"Three times? And who will be your victims?"

"First, the least," he said patiently, as though I were a very dull pupil who needed to be told the most obvious facts. "You. Today."

"Why me? What have I done?"

"Because you are a bother to me, with your busy searching eyes, your sharp sniffing nose, your long wagging tongue. You must be removed first."

"And then?"

"That one," he snarled, pointing a blunt unfinished finger toward Bristol's house. "My patience is ended. I have tried every other way to drive him from this valley, but he does not go. Now I will open the way of death for him, as for you."

In a flash I saw the truth. "Blast your vicious tongue!

You are the one who has alarmed the King with your reports. Telling him of fires, and pirate ships, and armies landing on the beaches."

"I do not know what you are talking about. I have indeed told my cousin in Honolulu of my annoyance with this intruder and of his fires and their smoke, which are an insult to the god. Do not blame me if my cousin has carried these complaints to the Kamehameha. But what are pirates? I do not know these things. And about armies I have said nothing. Not even of the marchers of the night, when they go from and to this entrance to the land of Manu'a."

"You ass of a horse, you!" I jeered, "you foolish son of a bitch, you! All the trouble and worry you have caused!" Slack of mouth, glassy of eye, he stood there, understanding neither my insults nor my meaning. Seeing how stupid he was, I began to hope that I could defeat him in this pitting of his mind against mine.

But first I must learn one more name. Half knowing the answer, not wanting to hear it, I asked, "And the third victim?"

"That boy." The jaws snapped shut, the eyes glowed in malice.

"But why? What has he done to you?"

"He lives! Is that not reason enough? He is a danger to me, an offense—"

"How can he be a danger to you, a boy who has just come to Ka'a'awa? He does not know you, you do not know him."

"This valley: it is mine!" he shouted, flailing his arms in fury. "And the god's! I will not let the boy take it away from us. Just as I will not let the foreigner despoil it. Until the boy came, I had only the stranger to fight."

"Ah! Then you are the one who told Kanelele that his

parents would not forgive his marriage to a commoner?"

"Even so," he admitted. "And why should I not tell him this, when Kane himself would not forgive such a base mating as Kanelele himself thought he had made."

On and on he talked, about his great love for Ka'a'awa, his devotion to Kane, his loathing for Bristol, the unquestioned need for driving the foreigner away. The more he babbled the more I saw how addled in the head he was—and the better I understood that I must contend with a madman, and win.

But how could I do combat with a crazy man? What weapons did I have to rout him? Desperately I cast about for a way—and in my terror could not find a way.

"Why do you want Ka'a'awa?" I interrupted. "Do you have sons of your own who will inherit these lands?" If he threatened Eahou, I would threaten his sons. If he harmed Eahou, I would harm each one of them in the same way, down to the last piece of bone, the last shred of skin. I vowed it, forgetting in my concern for Eahou the fact that, within a few minutes, this vile sorcerer intended to make me disappear from the face of the earth.

"No. I have no need for sons," he sneered, "as I have no need for women. Long ago I gave myself to serving the god. For many years I have kept myself clean, undefiled by the touch of a woman, for the sake of the god."

Hearing this unbelievable argument, I hooted with laughter. "Then you, Hahau, are the biggest fool who ever lived. Never in the history of our race has Kane asked such a sacrifice. Indeed, he would be angered by such a sacrifice, he who is the giver of life."

"He does not ask. I give it willingly." With pride he proclaimed his belief—and in this pride I found his weakness. Always hit a man in his pride if you wish to break him: this is another lesson I have learned in growing old. Now at last I thought of a way by which I might defeat him.

"Hahau," I said courteously, as one colleague addressing another, "you do not know it, so in fairness I should tell you: I too am a *kahuna 'ana'ana*, although—"

He snorted. "How is it possible? A little fingerling like you? With no more *mana* in you than a taro-patch shrimp has? Cha! I can not believe you."

"You have your strengths, I have mine," I persisted, holding my anger in check. If there's anyone I can not stand, it is a man who scorns me for my smallness. By the gods of heaven and earth and sea, I swore, if I am to die I shall not die without fighting for my life and for the life of Eahou. "And I will contend with you, here and now, in this sacred place," I said evenly. "If you win, you can do as you wish with me. If I win, you must agree to give up your sorcery, forever. Is it a bargain?"

"I shall not lose. If you win, I do not wish to live," he said grimly, "I shall kill myself for shame."

"I do not ask that. To me a man's life is a precious thing. To you it is like dung. The gods see this. That is why I shall win. That is why I do not fear you."

"Talk," he snarled, "big mouth, little mouth," by which he meant that, although I talked big, I could do little to withstand him. "The power is with the gods, not with you, not with me. They will decide.—Let us begin."

"No, wait. Not yet. One more thing must be done, according to the god who directs me. First we must purify ourselves, by bathing in the sea. Then we must take a drink of holy water and a taste of *poi*, to strengthen ourselves for the long contest."

"I have never heard of such a thing. Weak you must be, boneless as a jellyfish, if you need such gross sustenance. My *mana* needs no *poi* to strengthen it."

"You have your methods, I have mine. You use bait, I use none. Who, then, is the weak one?"

For a moment he looked down at me, weighing his conceit against my meekness. "Let us do as you ask," conceded the man of pride. "It is a small thing, for a small man."

"You are a wise man," I was saying when he stalked off toward the beach.

With the briefest of dippings we washed away our defilement in the sea. Streaming wet and naked we started up the path toward Pohukaina. When we came near Loke's hiding-place I said, "Do you go ahead and prepare your bait. I shall get the holy water and the *poi* from my saddlebags." Without so much as a grunt he left me.

Swiftly I pulled out the weapons with which I hoped to defeat that dangerous man: the bottle of gin, the bowl of *poi* which, with other edibles, Maka-o-Hina had provisioned me, two coconut-shell cups, and my money belt. From one of the several packets in the money belt I drew a small pinch of golden powder, a portion no larger than my smallest fingernail, and dropped it into a cup. Wait a moment, I considered, if one is enough, two will be better. And three will be best. Into the cup went the third pinch of that magical powder, as a prayer went up to heaven: Let it work, O Kane. It is from you, for you.—And let it work fast, I beg you. Well did I know how much I needed his help, for in truth I have never been sure about the value of this golden powder. Along with several other things hidden away in that money belt, it is a keepsake from the days of my youth, when, in common with other sailors my age, I thought I could not live without it.

As I closed the saddlebags I chanced to touch the hilt of Mr. Wyllie's sword, sticking out like the gourd of a man from the rolled-up poncho. "A sign!" I cried, drawing the weapon from its soft sheath. Flashing in the light, the naked sword gave strength to my fearful purpose. If all else fails, I resolved, I shall spear him, this evil eel.

Hahau was sitting cross-legged on the grass, muttering prayers, the bait for malign spirits arranged before him. That bait was stolen from me: some of my *mana* dwelt in it still. And when I saw those things, and remembered his fearful purpose, I shuddered. O Kane, I prayed, O Ku, O Lono, O Kanaloa! O Jehovah of the Christians! Do not fail me in the time of my great need . . .

"Here is the image of my god," I announced, thrusting the point of Wyllie's sword into the grass between us. "Makia Weli is his name. I learned about him and his power in America."

From beneath hooded lids Hahau deigned to look upon the image of my god. "I have never heard of him. A false god is he. And yet you trust to him? Cha! Nothing good comes out of America. You should know this."

Touching the hilt, I made the glittering shaft to sway. Like a living thing it moved, like the head of a serpent swaying in its basket as the Hindoo piper calls it forth. "Be careful," I warned, "do not offend my god. Terrible is his vengeance upon those who anger him." Hahau shut his mouth as tight as the hole at the other end of his gut.

With much clapping of hands and writhing of arms, and a loud rendering of *Hail Columbia! Happy Land*, chanted in American for Hahau's confusion, I invoked the help of my deity. "Drink deep, says Makia Weli, drink deep of this holy water, of this spirit of fire," I chanted in our native tongue, the while I poured a huge slug of gin into each cup. The one with the golden powder I kept nearest me, the other I pushed toward him. "Drink deep," I invited, "drink to the bottom in one draught, else its blessing will not enter into you."

"Do you take me for a fool?" he said, in the way a city man speaks to the dealer of cards in a gambling house. "I know this trickery." His hand darted out to grab the cup near me. How well I judged my enemy. "When you have taken yours," he said, "I shall drink mine."

"The spirit of fire is the same in each," I replied. "You can trust me in this: I do not tell untruths." Slowly, with ritual grace worthy of a pope, I drained the cup. Bless my soul! How my fluttering stomach welcomed that good warming gin.

Suspicious still, he peered into his cup. "This dirt: am I to drink it as well?"

"It is not dirt," I assured him. "Would I serve you dirt, or me?" Among *kahuna 'ana'ana* it is a rule that always a victim of their rites must be informed that he has been chosen to be their prey. How else will he know that he must suffer? How else will he know in what manner his punishment will be visited upon him, and to what degree he must atone? I, a novice *kahuna 'ana'ana*, certainly did not wish to flout the law. "It is a powder," I informed him, "a powder prepared from the Spanish fly. Great, great indeed, is the *mana* of the Spanish fly. Drink it, and you will see the proof of its power. It will make things grow big, before your very eyes."

"Even you? Hah! That I can not believe. But if you are to grow big, I will grow bigger. Such is the power of my *mana*." He drank the potion in one gulp, down to the dregs. "Fire, indeed!" he gasped, as tears welled up in his eyes.

"Did I not say so?" I asked in the tones of a righteous man. "Behold. I show you the power of my god in yet another way." From an oilskin pouch in another pocket of that treasury of a money belt I drew a friction match, scratched it into flame on the sword's rough hilt.

"*Auwe*! That is something!" he said, impressed against his will by this new invention of foreigners.

"That is not all," I promised, putting the fire to the pool of gin lying in my cup. The faint blue flame was invisible in the sunlight. "Hold your fingers over this cup."

He permitted himself to indulge me and my god, and pulled his hand away faster than he'd presented it. "Ah, ah!" he cooled his hand in the air, "it burns!"

"Is this not proof that I do not tell untruths?" I said, most virtuously. "Now the *poi*," I decreed, placing the bowl between us. "Do you eat of it and I will do the same, both from the one source." We dipped our fingers twice into the sun-warmed paste before I pulled the bowl away from him. "Enough. Makia Weli is pleased that you have honored him by taking part in this ceremony. Now do you begin upon yours. I shall wait. I have lots of time."

"Do you enjoy it," he scoffed, cordial to the end, "the short time that is left to you."

Rising to his knees, he shut his eyes and started upon the weird wailing chant that called upon the malign gods and all the evil spirits he could command to wreak my destruction:

> O Ku! O Kama! O Nu'u!
> Hear me below, O you above, O you around.
> Here is the bait.
> Here is the victim.
> Seize him and bind him, the victim, the one to be killed:
> Break in the front, break in the back,
> Split open his head, rip out his guts.
> Enter his heart,
> Enter his liver,
> Enter his spleen,
> Enter his lungs,
> Enter his stomach,
> Enter his shrivelled gourd.

> Cause him to writhe, cause him to scream.
> Cause him to die a hurting death.
> Kill him! Kill him!

While he wailed away I sat there, stuffing *poi* into my mouth as fast as I could, helping the gin to calm the fear roiling in my belly. Perhaps it was Eben's medicine, rushing from stomach to liver; perhaps it was my confidence that I was more than a match for so ignorant a sorcerer: I do not know. Whatever it was, it sustained me, and within a few minutes I was settled in stomach and almost unafraid, listening with little more than an inquisitive man's interest to the horrendous curses he was heaping upon my body:

> May maggots crawl in your eyes, O Nihoa,
> Your mouth be eaten by maggots.
> Disease breaks through your throat, O long-tongued one,
> It is broken through by maggots, eaten by maggots,
> Maggots itch in your throat, O Nihoa the despised one,
> Disease cracks open your chest, O Nihoa,
> The chest is a mass of sores, eaten away by maggots,
> Disease breaks open your back, splits open your back,
> Maggots crawl in your back, the maggots crowd,
> The maggots move around, the maggots keep your back raw,
> You are broken open by maggots, disemboweled by maggots,
> Maggots dig open your back, O little man of little power.

So he progressed, through all my body's many parts and organs, from brain through butt and belaying pin to smallest toe, until I was supposed to be buzzing with flies, crawling with maggots, stinking and foul, a rotted corpse through which blind worms nibbled their way, in which rats dropped their dung as they tugged at my liver, wherein my spirit was forever imprisoned because its stench was too great for Manu'a to bear. Had I been a susceptible man I would have run away screaming with terror. I might have run for many miles, to get away from the sounds of those curses, I might have crawled into a hole somewhere, pulling earth and leaves and stones over me for a shelter, but I would never have escaped their black power. And, as he prayed, so it would have happened: within three days I would have sickened, within five days I would have died, as other men have sickened and died, slain not by his crawling maggots but by my own sobbing fear.

> This is the death I inflict:
>> he is to go and lie in the roadway,
>> and his back will split open,
>> a stench will arise,
>> and he will be devoured by hogs.
>
> A death I inflict is to start in him while he is here,
>> and when he goes elsewhere he is to vomit blood,
>> and die,
>> and his grease is to flow on the road,
>> and he is to be eaten by dogs . . .

But this disciple of Makia Weli is a clever creature, even if he is only a man of Oʻahu. Sooner than I expected, the gin and the magical powder took their effect. Hahau's chanting began to falter, his tongue grew thick, spittle filled his mouth, more and more the phrases of his evil litany were mixed up. Shaking his head in annoyance, he would stop after each error in this invocation and would repeat the words with the slow care of a man well on the way to being drunk. These mistakes alone were enough to comfort me, for everyone knows that prayers and spells lose their magic when they are not uttered without error. But he, the stupid man, must have thought that I did not know this power of words over power. Or perhaps he himself was so befuddled by Makia Weli's potions that he no longer thought straight, as befits a righteous priest. Who can say?

Sweat beaded his face, it poured from the armpits down the bony ribcase into the furrows of his loins. Whenever he opened his eyes he seemed to be surprised that I was still sitting before him, not yet a maggoty corpse lying in a pool of yellow grease. Then my pity for this crazy striving man would ebb, as I saw the hatred with which he glared at me. I would remind myself that, if I wished to live, if I wanted Eahou to live, and Saul Bristol too, I must be as ruthless with this mad sorcerer as he was with me, until he collapsed, broken in defeat.

Then I would reach out and set the image of Makia Weli to swaying again, as a message to Hahau, as a reminder to me of what awaited if I did not win this contest for my *mana* and my body.

He did not break easily. After half an hour he was still quavering away, and I was beginning to wonder if he had not managed to pray me into a hell of his own devising, where for all eternity I would be condemned to sit in brilliant burning sunlight while he screeched curses into my ears.

The evil words poured out, poured back and forth:

> Your legs bend,
> Your hands become paralyzed,
> Your back is hunched up,
> Your neck is twisted,
> Your head breaks open,
> Your liver rots,
> Your intestines fall to pieces . . .

At last I saw the signs for which I had been waiting. To his arm-waving and hand-flinging was added a new kind of motion, almost as though he were dancing a kind of *hula* which requires a certain suggestive movement of the hips. In plain language, he squirmed. Anguish twisted his mouth, worry hung in drops of yellow snot from that ill-made nose, in spittle dribbling down the unfinished chin. Often he lowered his hands, and I knew how much they yearned to scratch that part of him which long ago he thought was dead. Yet always he forced himself to go on with the incantation, commanding those hands to rise toward heaven instead of plunging to the spot where he felt the fires of hell.

Now was the time for my final move in this game of life against death. Not a little tipsy myself, between gin and sun, I brought forth a pack of cards from its place in the money belt. Like a bored gambler playing solitaire to while away an idle hour, I laid them out on the grass around the swaying sword of Makia Weli. But they were not playing-cards, those brightly colored pictures which I laid upon the grass.

Dizzy with gin, afire within, near to exhaustion and despair, he opened his red-rimmed eyes, searching for me. Irresistibly they were drawn to the display I had so thoughtfully arranged before him. The chanting stopped in the middle of a word, as he stared down at those paintings which every sailor in every port in the world can buy for a Spanish dollar. "What are you doing to me?" he cried, unable to tear his gaze away from those artful portraits of some of the most engaging acts in the world.

"These are the sons and daughters of Makia Weli," I said reverently. "And the Spanish fly is the food, the spirit of fire is the drink, they serve to his guests. Great, great is the *mana* of the Spanish fly," I intoned, tapping the sword into motion, staring steadily at the place where he burned with the fire that not all the water in the sea can quench. "And, as I have promised you, because you have partaken of this wondrous food and drink, you will see a great thing rising before you."

"No! No! It cannot be," he wailed. Even as he cried

out his spirit's hope, his animal self betrayed him. Pulsing and throbbing, following the rhythm of the sword I so faithfully kept in motion, the long-forgotten flesh was asserting itself. In truth, it was the only part of him that was not ill-made. At first he did not know what was happening. But in a few moments he could not deny, even in his despair, how the *mana* of Makia Weli had triumphed over his mortified body. He looked down in horror. "*Auwe, auwe . . . ,*" he groaned in dismay. Clutching with both hands at the evidence of his defeat, he screamed, "I burn! I burn!"

"Great is the power of my god, for he is but another manifestation of Kane," I said, feeling sorry for the poor man in this moment of Kane's victory.

He did not want to hear. Glaring at me with unalterable hatred, he snarled, "You have won!" He sprang to his feet and ran down the path to the sea.

"Hahau!" I shouted, "Wait, wait—" But he was too crazed to hear.

When I arrived at the shore, a trail of bloody excrement was all that remained of Hahau upon the sand. He was far out in the water, beyond the reef, beyond the breaking waves, swimming away from the Ka'a'awa he had lost forever.

On the beach, sword in hand, I watched and waited. He did not come back.

CHAPTER 22.

IN WHICH A CHASTENED VICTOR
CRIES OUT FOR HELP

Trembling like a man caught on a high cliff, whose fingers and toes are beginning to lose their hold, I sank into the shade under a *naupaka* bush growing from the sand of Ka'a'awa's beach. I lay there for a long time, afraid to move lest I fall screaming into a void of fear and madness. My ears did not hear the waves of the sea: they listened still to Hahau's curses. And even though they were closed shut, my eyes saw not Hahau the hating sorcerer, but Hahau the bleeding defeated man, running, running away to the sea and to death.

Now you are a murderer, my spirit accused me with each pulse of my blood. In vain did my reason protest that I had not meant to cause his death, that by destroying him I had saved three worthier spirits from being the victims of his hate. Stop lying to yourself for once, my spirit commanded me: you who said that you value the life of a man, you have caused a man to lose his life. Is there any defense against such an accusation? Alas, there is none from within.

When I understood this I wept, for then I saw how from this time on I would bear forever the burden of guilt. Whatever I did, wherever I went, the memory of Hahau would be with me. Of his vengeful wandering spirit I dared not think.

There, in the shadows of dread, I saw how, in choosing death, Hahau was striving still to destroy me. And I saw how I alone could never defeat him. The burden must be lifted from me by some other power, because the cunning malicious spirit of Hahau was beyond my reach.

Walking like a man recovering from a long illness, I went to stand again before the cave of Pohukaina. With arms raised and head uplifted, I stood in the light of Kane, beseeching his help:

> Hear me, O Kane: I pray:
> It is for myself.
> Forgive me this unwanted death,
> Free me of this death unforeseen.
> Hear me, O Kane, I beg:
> Guide the spirit of Hahau,
> Bring him to this gate.

Then, because this would bring Hahau's spirit only to the beginning of his journey down into the realm of endless darkness, I called upon Manu'a, the god of that realm of death to which Milu, the evil chief of Waipi'o, was sent for his foul deeds:

> Hear me, O Manu'a: I pray:
> It is for Hahau.
> Open wide the gate for him,
> Let him pass to the farther side,
> Let him descend to where Milu dwells,
> Let him find the way to forgetfulness,
> That we who remain above may live in peace.

In the heavy silence I waited for a sign to tell me that the gods had heard. The earth did not shake, the heavens did not growl, no cloud passed over the observing eye of Kane. In this way did he tell me that he did not reject my prayer. But what of Manu'a?

Hahau's loincloth lay where he had dropped it. Beside it on the grass lay the bait stolen from my body, and the weapons with which I had routed the sorcerer and killed the man. I lighted a match, touched the weak flame to Hahau's *malo*. "Manu'a," I called, loud enough for me to hear my cry returned as a faint echo from the cave. In the quiet air the smoke from the burning *kapa* rose straight up. "Manu'a," I moaned, "hear my plea . . ." But still the smoke went up, up toward the sky beyond the mountain top. "Kane!" I cried, imploring the greatest one.

And then—I swear it!—a wonderful thing happened. The hair on my head stood up at the sight. Above me, by a body's length or more, the wisp of smoke bent and broke and, softly, slowly, as if bowing to a command it alone could hear, it flowed into the cave of Pohukaina. Thus did it go, until the last fiber of Hahau's *malo* was consumed, until the last blue mote had followed all the others through the opened gate to the land of Milu.

Calling out my thanks to Kane and to Manu'a, I gathered up my possessions and fled. Mingled with my relief at such proof of Kane's power was my dread of Pohukaina. Never, never will I go back there. Not even if Lono should open up all the springs of the sky to pour rivers of rain upon my head, not even if Saul Bristol should leave written there the whole story of his life, will I go back into that hole for the dead.

Near Lokelani's hiding-place I buried the bait from my person, covering it so thoroughly with dirt and leaves and great rocks that not even a hungry hog could have rooted it out. Once again I went down to the sea to bathe. This time I washed away not only the dirt and the sweat from my body, but also the taint of fear upon my spirit.

CHAPTER 23.

IN WHICH, AT LAST, THE OGRE OF KA'A'AWA IS ENCOUNTERED

A new man, a forgiven man, a purified man—even though once again I was garbed like a missionary going home from a funeral—I returned to Saul Bristol's yard. All I wanted was a drink of cool water from the spring, before I went to Kanemilohai to tell him of Hahau's treachery and the manner of his dying. I did not expect to find Bristol at home, but there he was, walking toward his house from the stable as Lokelani and I rode through the animal racket. When he saw us he stopped short, as if he wanted to turn and run for a place to hide. The instant I saw him I recognized him, the man in the sea.

"*Aloha ia 'oe,*" I called, "greetings to you. May we come in?" Tall and thin, fierce and unsmiling, he had been when Alex pulled him from the water at Kaka'ako. He was no different at Ka'a'awa. I quailed upon beholding again the tight mouth, unwilling to smile, the haughty narrow face, those gray eyes fixed upon me in a blind man's stare. Oh, this angry stranger, I thought, he will run me out of here within the minute. Thank the gods he did not find me up there, prowling around in his cave.

Stiff as a fencepost he stood, and almost as weather-beaten. His denim shirt and trousers were so worn and faded that they were gray, no longer blue. His brown arms were like branches hanging, the brown face, muddy boots, and patches of sweat were like stained knots upon the skeleton of a tree. O Kane, I murmured, he's in a bad mood today, he expects to be bored . . .

"Greetings to you," he replied in Hawaiian as we drew near, "and what brings you here?"

No one of my race is ever so rude upon meeting a stranger. This high-hipped, tight-assed, close-mouthed Yankee, I thought, why is he so begrudging? Irritated by his ungraciousness, I refused to be my usual polite self. Pretending I had not heard, I set up such a flood of old man's gabble as would have silenced a grogshop full of sailors. "*Auwe, auwe!*" I complained, rolling my eyes, lifting my haunches as if I'd been in Loke's saddle for a week, "these old bones are stiff. This bottom of mine: it is made of aches and pains and tatters of bleeding flesh. I am thinking how perhaps I should lie down in the pond over there, and become a snail, or a shrimp, or a lazy un-moving catfish. Then I would not have to sit upon the bony back of this great beast for another day, another hour, another minute." Whereupon I delivered him a lovely toothless smile, pink with gums and rolled-up tongue. It is a trick I have learned, because it brings shrieks of delight from little children.

"Then do you rest here for a while," he said, breaking into such a smile as I never imagined upon that stony face, offering me his hand to shake. "Saul Bristol is my name. Come in, come in. My house is yours." He did not recognize me as Alex's companion that day at Kaka'ako. I was much relieved. How could he want to meet again a witness to his weakness?

With a stubbornness that interested me even then, I still did not give him my name. Bobbing and ducking like a gaffer twice my age, I cackled, "Thank you, thank you. You are kind to strangers. Strangers will be kind to you. But I do not wish to give trouble. I shall burden you with my company only while I sit for a moment in the shade of your *hala* tree, sipping a small cup of water."

"No trouble, no trouble at all," he insisted. "I was about to have a little something to eat. Please do you come and join me. Whatever I have is yours." He spoke Hawaiian quite well, a little slowly perhaps, and with something of New England's harsh sounds, but quite commendably, considering that ours is not an easy tongue to learn and that he had lived among us for only three years.

His invitation was beyond my ability to decline. Now that I knew so much about him, and so little, I was even more intrigued by this man of mystery. For my sake, not for the King's, I accepted the chance to stay. With a young man's attentive courtesy for a fragile ancient, he helped me to dismount. While he led Lokelani off to the stable I waited on the porch of his house, looking up at the mountains, thinking of everything that had happened in Ka'a'awa during the last twenty-four hours, wondering how much about these events Saul Bristol would ever know. Had he felt the touch of fear, earlier this morning, when Hahau's spite was turned on him? Would he know how closely Kane kept watch over his youngest son? And what will Bristol think of this son of Kane, when at length he meets the boy?

Out of the corner of one eye I discovered an impish creature peering at me from behind the open door. Not letting on that I saw it, I waited for Bristol by the railing. "Beautiful is the valley of Ka'a'awa," I said, as he came up the stairs, "and most fortunate of men are those who live here. This is the thought of one who has seen much, and pondered much—and who perhaps talks too much."

"I have thought so," he said. "About Ka'a'awa, I mean! —Not about you." His confusion was so boyish that both of us had to laugh.

To my surprise I found myself not disliking him, no longer afraid of him. I had been prepared to meet an ogre. I saw instead a good-looking young man, much as he had described himself in his journal, but also a young man with shyness in his bearing and great sorrow in his heart. His eyes were so full of grief and pain that I knew at once they yearned for the sight of his lost love. I would have known this, just as Maka-o-Hina had known it, even if I had never read his journal. All men must learn to live with sorrow, and most men can cover it up, bearing it within them, under layers of skin and flesh, finding a place for it within their bodies almost as if it were another liver or a second and aching heart. Yet a few men are denied this protection: they have no place to hide their sorrow because it consumes them, eating them out from within as a smouldering fire will eat out the soft wood of a log. In them the mind is the last to be consumed and, until it is gone, the fire of pain glows in their eyes. I have seen such men, in my grogshops and whorehouses, trying to quench this fire with booze or with love bought for the moment, or with both. Saul Bristol, I could not doubt, was such a smouldering man.

"I am called by many names," I threw away my stubbornness at last. "Niole is one my mother gave me, because when I was a child I ate so little, picking at my food with small appetite. Perhaps that is why I am so short a man. But Niele is the name I have earned for myself since I became a lad. You know what *niele* means?"

"I do indeed. We have a *niele* lad hereabouts. He pokes his nose into everything around, here, there, everywhere. I shall be undone if he is not already under this house, straining his long ears to hear what we are saying."

"No, not under the house." I sped to the door and, pulling Makana out by the hair, presented him like a magician drawing a rabbit from his cloak. "He is inquisitive enough to deserve our praise, for he will grow up to be a shrewd policeman. No. Let me make a new prediction for one whose mouth is so wondrously wide: Ka'a'awa's honorable member of the Legislature he shall be, I swear it." Grinning from ear to ear, the boy was not in the least discomfited.

"Talking man, listening man," Bristol laughed through his annoyance, "he is a pest. He is an affliction to me, as I predict he will be to the country." Hauling the urchin along by his shirt, he led him to the stairs, saying: "*O makana o makani nu*, O gift of roaring winds"—this was a nice pun, which both the boy and I enjoyed—"chase yourself home and tell your mother a guest is here for dinner. Now run!"

"Like the wind I go!" Makana shouted, galloping on his way, with arms held out like the yards of a ship under full sail.

"You speak our native tongue very well indeed," I complimented Bristol in his native tongue. "Most foreigners do not bother to—" He stared at me, while quite shamelessly I enjoyed his amazement.

"And you?" he found words at last, "how did you?— Of course! At Lahainaluna?"

"No, I was not so fortunate. That missionary school

was established for lads more proper than I could ever
be. No. I have been to other schools. My first teachers of
English—and of other subjects, as you might guess—
were sailors aboard merchantmen and whalers. I learned
the dirty words of the foc's'le first, the nicer language of
the cabin later."

"A hard school, for an excellent pupil," he said, "but
surely that was not all?"

The question pleased me as much as the praise: at the
least he was not being bored. "Oh, the polishing came
after that, when, tiring of the sea, I settled down in Honolulu. Then I learned to read and write, to do sums, and to
speak genteely enough to satisfy the teachers at the Chiefs'
Children's School.—Do not mistake me: I am not a chief's
child in disguise.—No. I learned my lessons at second
hand, so to speak, as I sat in attendance upon one of those
favored princelings. What he disliked, I wanted. And the
words of Mr. and Mrs. Cooke which fell upon his unwilling ears found their way into my *niele* mind.—The
gaining of knowledge, I submit, is one of the few advantages to growing up.—They did not know then, although
I have told them since, that I was their most grateful
pupil."

"Excellent, excellent," he applauded, lifting a hand
exactly as Mr. Cooke would do when he was happy with
a pupil's recitation. "Please come in. Let us be comfortable while we talk.—Dinner won't be ready for some
time, I'm afraid. My cook will be taken by surprise, because usually I do not dine at midday."

After we were seated in that stiff Yankee parlor, with
its torturesome chairs, as upright and unaccommodating
as church pews, I put him to the test. "I believe you know
the young chief to whom I was *kahu*?"

"Alex?" he asked, cocking his head, arching those black brows. The action was strangely young, very beguiling.

"Yes, he is the one."

"Oh, for Heaven's sake! Why didn't you tell me sooner?—How is he? Now there's a fine man." His affection was not pretended.

"He is, indeed," I nodded, as gratified as a father. "The despair of my middle years—and of Mr. and Mrs. Cooke's, I might add—has grown up to be the joy of my old age, and the hope of the Kingdom. He asked me to stop in here, to bring you his *aloha*."

For an hour or more, while Kamanele pattered forth and back from the cookhouse, setting the table, and her son squatted in a corner absorbing our every word, I regaled my host with news of Honolulu, giving my devotion to Alex and my malice to almost everyone else. Something about Bristol set me off on that gossip's path: for my self-esteem's sake I wanted to impress him, for his grief's ease I wanted to entertain him. Laughter is good medicine to the body, wit a tonic to the spirit. And I believe I succeeded in helping him, for a while: he enjoyed my assaults upon many a ludicrous foreigner, many a pompous chief. I was helped in this, of course, by my stolen reading in his journal, which gave me a better acquaintance with his prejudices than he realized. But his own humor, much more acid than mine, aided me wonderfully, and we chatted away as though we had been friends for years. Even so, there were perils to this frothy conversation: several times I had to curb my racing tongue, to keep from saying things I could have learned only from his journal. Once, when he cried out, "You read me like a book!" I feared he had discovered my treachery. Thinking fast, I shrugged, "But this is a common opinion," and slipped past that worrisome moment in the life of a talkative spy.

But he was clever too, this wary foreigner. He guarded his conversation so well that I learned almost nothing new about himself. If ever we need a school for spies in this country, I thought in admiration, he would make an expert teacher in the art of disclosing nothing.

Only one thing marred our pleasant visit. The food was terrible. Awful! Even sailors aboard a merchantman can eat better than we did. As with so many Americans, concerned more with their souls than their bodies, he had not the slightest interest in what he ate, as long as it rested heavy in his belly. That much-couched Kamanele took every advantage of him. She could have fried those slabs of beef more tastily; and with a little bit of salt and a couple of green onions she could have made the boiled potatoes and boiled cabbage more delectable. But no: being the slattern she most obviously was, a creature of bosoms and buttocks, but not of brains, she plopped those tasteless victuals down upon the table as though we were orphans dependent upon her charity. When I asked for salt she gave me the stink-eye as if I'd besought her virtue. "No mo'a," she declared, sailing away indignantly. Damn your lazy limbs, I grumbled, with a whole oceanful of salt at your very door?—Cha! What this poor man needs is a good woman to care for him.

Damn it! I turned my irritation upon him. And why hasn't he found a successor to his lost Melissa? A good-looking man, still young, with many nights of bed-love left in him, and here he is, living like a hermit sealed up in a cell. Another Hahau, denying himself the very thing he needs the most to give meaning to his life. A man's seed, as is well known, if it is kept over-long, will turn to poison, will send up harmful vapors to the brain and heart, changing his liver to dust and filling his bowels with bitterest gall.

Oh, these Yankees! I chewed tough dry beef rather than bare my teeth at him. They are so aggravating.—Always cherishing their griefs of the spirit, while their bodies wither away and grow old. Laden with guilt, thinking of eternity, they forget about the only life they can be sure of, they do not know how fast it fades away . . .

"What about the influenza?" he was asking. "We've had quite a few deaths out here, among the countryfolk. Is Honolulu as hard hit?"

"Oh, we've had a number of cases, as I recall, but not many deaths. Not enough to be alarmed about." Here spoke the learned physician, a veritable Dr. Judd, despite the fact that I had not the faintest notion how many of Honolulu's people had sickened or how many had died. For all I knew, they could have been as far away as Hilo, like Noah Mahoe, those sick ones, but still I would have discoursed upon them as learnedly as that fraudulent Frenchman Jean Rives lectured about medicines when he pretended to treat the ailments of the first Kamehameha. "But not because we are more virtuous in town," I lifted my hands in mock piety, "and therefore saved from Jehovah's chastising."

"Then why is it that no one has come along this road since the sickness began? You are the first one from outside Ka'a'awa I have seen in almost a month."

"This, too, is easily explained. The countryfolk from Kane'ohe and Maunawili are flocking to town, with pigs, chickens, taro, with empty pockets and big hands, hoping to make some money out of the misfortunes of Honolulu. Have they not learned from excellent teachers the virtue of being provident, the value of a dollar? They soon return to the country, bigger of paunch perhaps, yet just as empty in pocket, because they have spent all that money right there among the clever townsfolk who let them hold it for a short while. This, I suppose, must mean that Hawaiians understand the uses of money better than foreigners do. Foreigners strive to collect those little pieces of gold and of silver, Hawaiians delight in helping them to do so. And thereby everyone is made happy." Thus did I spout fables to delude him, this foreigner who despises my people. Why should I tell him the truth about my countrymen, starving because Keʻelikolani's food-gatherers were loose among them, bound to their homes because they were too hungry to go a-traveling? Out of shame I kept our secrets, out of pride I told him lies. I could imagine him dutifully writing all this down in his journal, thinking he recorded truth for posterity to read. So be it, I shrugged, even as I sneered at him. About such lies is history written, just as for other lies is history made.

My sarcasm floated right past his ears. A most methodical man, he ticked off the next item on his list of inquiries: "I thought, too, that it might be the filibusterers, if it wasn't the influenza. What news of them?"

"Nothing," I replied, carefully putting down the cup of weak tea, "nothing at all. Although some folk in town are talking about their coming back this year. I really haven't paid much attention, inasmuch as I am only a retired *kahu*, so to speak. Have you heard anything about them out here?" This was as direct a way to test him as I could contrive. But why I should trust him, this man who reads Machiavelli, any more than he should trust me, a complete stranger—and a *kanaka* besides—I could not say.

"Out here?" he whooped, "in this God-forsaken place? Nope. Nothing ever happens in this part of the world, this jumping-off place to oblivion. And if filibus-

terers—or anybody, or anything, be they wild men of
Borneo or polar bears from Alaska—were to land on this
fetch of coast today, I'd be the last to hear of it.—And the
most surprised.—But why should we fear?" Contempt
for the generality descended now to scorn for the particular. "When our mad, martial, melodramatic Minister of
Foreign Affairs and Minister at War is in a posture of
defense?"

Ahh, the pleasure of hearing wonderful words wonderfully used! Although I felt that I ought to say something
in support of poor Mr. Wyllie, I had to laugh—even as I
stored the description in my memory, to use sometime as
my very own.

Gleefully he finished Wyllie off: "That warrior with
words can drive any enemy from our shores simply by
talking 'em into a rout. As a matter of fact," he went on
with more heat than I'd thought he could ever display, "I
think this country is more in danger from fools within
than from enemies without. As long as this government is
run by a pack of feuding scoundrels, imbeciles like Wyllie, Judd, Keoni Ana, each more interested in his own
glory than in the welfare of the nation, none of them man-
ageable by that besotted King, so-called—My God! What
an insane state of affairs!"

"Now, now," this time I felt compelled to object,
"things are not as bad as you seem to think."

"Oh, no? That's not what I hear, when I go to town."

"Yes, but who do you talk with? Businessmen? American merchants and shopkeepers? All they can think of is
money—money and their precious property. Do they remember how Dr. Judd, without help from them, saved our
Kingdom for us, that time Captain Paulet took it away?
Do they see the problems of governing this country as the
King and his ministers see them? Be honest: how can

they?" I was hoping for a good argument in return, an exchange of opinions and prejudices such as genial conversation is made of. Shoot! He practically yawned in my face.

"You have a point there, I guess.—The truth is, both shopkeeping and the business of politics bore the wits out of me. For myself I don't care what happens to this whole asinine outfit. I could pick up and leave tomorrow, without regret, if the situation got so bad that I couldn't stand it. But I get all het up because I'm thinking of Alex. I just hope that when he becomes King he won't be stuck with this same bunch of dizzards for ministers, and a nation which is bankrupt. Not only financially, but morally, mentally, physically, spiritually. Dying if not already dead.—Alex deserves something better, when he comes into the Kingdom."

"On this subject," I raised the cup of tea in a toast to Alex, not in salute to this censorious son-of-a-bitch who treated me, my countrymen, and my beloved country as if we were trash, "from this subject, we can have no argument."

"Which reminds me," he looked me square in the eye, as a man does when he wishes to convince you of his sincerity, "be sure to give Alex my greetings when you see him, and my thanks for his remembrance.—And tell him, please, to call on me, if ever I can be of assistance to him, in any way. I say this as his most loyal friend, which is better than any subject can be."

"I shall tell him this," I said, believing him. "He will be pleased to hear your good words." How could I, or Alex, ask for anything more?

The repast came to a merciful end. "Goodness gracious," politely I covered up a resolute belch, "I must be going, if I am to reach Kahana before nightfall. This talking with a sensible man has been most enjoyable. Perhaps we shall meet again, when we are neighbors."

He pounced upon the word with an interest that pleased me. "Will you be living near here? Permanently?"

"Aye. This is the purpose of my journey. I go to Kahana, to ask my people to build me a house, where I shall spend the rest of my days. There, near the curve of Kahana's stream, where it meets the sea."

"A beautiful place. I know it well."

"Not so fair as Ka'a'awa, but more—let us say, more peaceful."

"Peace," he gazed past me to the green wall of shrubbery which sheltered him from the tumult of the world beyond, "peace. That is the principal product of this valley, of this whole coast. It is the reason why I am here."

Neither of us said anything about mud, or smart cows, or stupid, lazy, debased *kanaka.*

With unwonted efficiency Makana brought Lokelani from her rest in the stable. Already I was perched in the saddle when a parting thought came to mind. No spirit-guardian put it there: this was an idea of my own, brought up out of my wish to help this unhappy man. Deep within me, not grudgingly, I held a liking for him, as I do for all good men who strive and suffer. Crusty though he was, as is the wall of a cliff which is washed by the sea, underneath the cover of spiny thoughts and prickly words the rock of his true self was sound. He seemed to be an honest man, so I resolved to speak honestly. He needed a woman to live with him, to ease the desires of his body if not to fill the emptinesses in his heart. And, as my weighted stomach reminded me, to cook for him.

"One more thing," I said, smiling down at him. Such a handsome body should not be wasted: such a splendid sire as this should enrich the nation with splendid children. "Another message I almost forgot: *aloha* from two young ladies who remember your hospitality—and you— with highest regard." I'll bet they do, too, I said to myself, as I watched puzzlement give way to recognition.

"Oh, yes. Those two—those two dancing-girls. You know them also?"

I'd never seen them, of course, but such a little detail can never be a hazard to me. "I do. Agnes and Lovey are friends of my daughters. Very nice girls, of good families. They have wondered—as I do, now that we've met— why there is no wife in your house to make it a home for you." I was genuinely trying to help him. Had he showed the slightest interest in an arrangement with one of the girls, or with anyone, I would have offered to be his intermediary. I have done it for many another bashful foreigner, as a matter of business. Why should I not do it for him, as a sign of friendship? But no: this American was different. His expression of pleasure at being remembered gave way to disgust, loathing deepened into pain.

Seeing that I had failed, I rode away, leaving him alone in front of his house. For him it is more full of one ghost than is Pohukaina with many. "Some men are damned fools," I muttered to Loke as we turned toward Kahana. In this judgment I did not except myself for once, because I understood all too well how I had just made a very notable damned fool of myself. "I wonder what he will write about me in that journal of his?" I asked Loke the Wise, who knows when to keep her big mouth shut. "He will put me down for a pimp, of this we can be sure. And, what's worse, for even more wicked and debased a *kanaka* than all the rest." That's what hurt the most, to be so misunderstood—and so slandered. Are we wicked because we want to enjoy the good things of life? Are we debased because we do not see the need for working from dawn to dusk, six days out of seven? Seeking balm for my hurt pride, I looked up into the beautiful valley, to where Eahou lived, to where the mountain of Kane stood, wearing now a wreath of cloud.

Only then did I remember that I had planned to go to Kanemilohai. But turning back is bad luck, as everyone knows. And, besides, I could not face Saul Bristol again so soon. Very easily did I talk Loke and myself into a steady trot toward Kahana. Tomorrow will be time enough, I persuaded us, full of the best intentions.

That tomorrow never came. When my business in Kahana was settled I found many reasons for taking the longer road home to Honolulu. Why should I bring Kanemilohai such bad news? The bringer of bad news is an unliked sharer of misfortune. How can I tell the King that he should not worry about Kahuku, if I do not view it for myself? As long as I am out this far, why should I not ride along and see the rest of this fair island? I wonder how my old friend Lauwili is faring at Kawailoa? Should I not check the countryside around Waialua, that land of the two placid rivers? Filibusterers might come ashore there as well as they could at Kualoa, easier than they could at Ka'a'awa. And if I go back, the way I came, can I avoid Bristol of the smouldering pain? Or Ke'elikolani and Eben, and the hunger they caused? And the robbers of Waiakane? And the ghost of Hahau, in that procession of ghosts that comes and goes through Pohukaina? . . .

Under a mountain of excuses did I smother the little weed of unease, growing in me because I did not want to see Saul Bristol again, the creeping vine of loneliness spreading within me because Eahou had been taken from my side. Thus did I choose to ride sixty miles instead of thirty. And thus did I condemn myself to a lifetime of remorse and regret, because in my selfishness I turned my back upon someone who needed me.

CHAPTER 24.

IN WHICH A QUIETER AND WISER SPY ENDS HIS MISSION FOR THE KING

The journey home to Honolulu was dull. As Bristol might have written, I was bored, *bored*, BORED!!! No adventures happened, no willing women fell into my arms, no company joined me to while away the hours. I missed Eahou, and sang his name-song to thank Kane for guarding him so well. I worried about Hahau's ghost, hurling oaths and prayers into the air to chase it away if it followed me. The road was deserted, ahead and behind, the country was almost empty of people. Punia of Kahuku, Kanelele's friend who had hidden the marriage ring in the temple at Ka'a'awa, had disappeared, no one could say where. My friend Lauwili of Kawailoa had been dead for eight years, and few people were left to remember him. Needless to say, filibusterers and their fleets of ships and armies of soldiers were nowhere to be seen.

All this trouble for nothing, I grumbled every mile of the way, almost angry with those freebooters for their disinterest in so beautiful a land, so easy a conquest. Then I understood how Kauikeaouli must feel, when he is subjected to the disdain of captains and consuls from Europe and America. This little country of mine, this beloved land: is it only a thing to be laughed at, a thing not worth the bother of taking?

Making verses brought no consolation. All of them turned out as full of bitterness as 'awa root, as stinging as vinegar in a wound. Despite all his chatter, this old fool roaming on his mission did not really matter. When I came to that conclusion, on the misty plain of Leilehua, laughter went out of me, and levity, and foolishness.

Perforce, I did something I'd not found much time for in my past. I thought. Deep thoughts. Thoughts heavy as a leadsman's weight, as full of sorrows as those of a father who has lost his only child.

At last, near sunset on the twelfth day of my ride for the King, Lokelani and I reached home, tired, wet from the pelting rains of Ko'olau. The bones, the flesh and skin and guts of which I am made: they were the same when I returned as when I set out. My sons, playing at ball in the yard, recognized their papa when he rode through the gate to our house at Makiki. But within me the man who is Hiram Nihoa was not the same.

I greeted Rebekah with tenderness and our children with affection. They in their turn were unusually quiet, after their noisy welcoming, perhaps because of Rebekah's warning, probably because they could see for themselves how silent their father had become.

Gratefully I accepted Rebekah's care: the glass of medicinal rum, to keep me from catching a cold; the hot bath, prepared with water she had been heating on the stove for two days; the early supper served me in our bedroom; the clean, soft, sweet-smelling bed. "Ah, my dear. You are a very good wife," I said, pulling her down close as she tucked me in, giving her more than the usual husbandly peck. "And I am happy to come home to you. No more—no more will I roam." This, I thank God, is one thing I did right, one moment of happiness I gave to her in time.

"And I," she whispered into my ear, "I am happy you have come safely home. We have been worrying . . ."

One more thing I remembered to say before she put out the lamp. "Do not fret anymore about Eben. Soon he will be going back to Kona."

"Is it so?" she pressed her hands to her breast. "Ah, then Lukila, too, will be happy." This is my Rebekah, I thought, when she left me alone in the darkness. Always thinking of other people first, so little of herself. How slow I have been to learn this. How slow I have been to learn so many things.

The next afternoon I went to Hali'imaile, to give Alex my report. "My Father is ill. Please come to see me here," he had written in the note Abel brought home. We sat on the cool *lanai* at the shaded mountain-side of the house, while I told my story. Only the big green and yellow parrot on his perch could hear us, but he was not a danger because he understands only the vile language of sailors.

I told Alex everything he should have known about my journey. The one important fact I held back was the lineage of Eahou: I spoke of him as though he were the son of mere commoners. In doing this I was not being a traitor to the Kamehameha. Eahou was a problem apart, and I wanted to talk about him and his safety only when Alex was assured about the safety of the Kingdom. And in one lesser matter I was not entirely forthright: the manner in which Hahau was defeated. How could Alex keep his respect for me, and affection, if he knew that his old *kahu* trotted about the countryside loaded down with lewd pictures, bottles of gin, and packets of Spanish fly? No. There are some things with which friendship and statecraft need not be concerned. I let him think that the only weapons I had used against Hahau were my powerful *mana* and the pointed blade of Mr. Wyllie's sword.

Alex was frankly relieved with my conclusion that Mr. Wyllie's alarm had been aroused by Hahau's spite for Saul Bristol. He tried to apologize for having sent me on this wild goat chase.

"Do not even think about that," I stopped him. "For myself, I am glad I went. It was an interesting journey— and I learned much, about our people, about our island."

"You did, indeed," he said, "and I envy you those adventures. Who would have thought that, in this little O'ahu, where 'nothing ever happens,' as Saul Bristol complains, so much did happen to you?—But one more question I put to you, Kahu. Have you told me everything you'd like to say? Something is troubling you still. I can see it. You are so—so serious."

"Yes," I admitted, "there is one thing more." Leaning forward in my chair, I was about to reveal Eahou's secret when Lot came forth from the house, tying a *malo* about his loins as he approached us.

"*E*, Kahu," he said, "you're back. What did you find?" He slumped into a chair beside us, put his big bare feet on the *lanai* railing, while he rubbed the sleep from his eyes. The pattern of a sleeping-mat was still pressed into his cheek and the whole length of his side, from shoulder to ankle.

"A false alarm, a flash in the pan," Alex summed up my report. For some reason of his own—I can not help but think because he was irritated by Lot's sloppiness— Alex switched the conversation from comfortable Hawaiian to jerking English. "Nothing ever happens in our sleepy Hawai'i, it seems.—I'll tell you the details later. Kahu isn't quite finished yet."

"Poor Wyllie," said Lot, scratching his belly, not taking the hint, "what will he do now for entertainment?"

"Oh, I expect he'll find other causes to occupy him. I hear he's going to take on England, France, and America again, about those treaties. Are you prepared to go on another trip abroad, as our Minister Plenipotentiary this time?"

"Who, me?—You crazy, or what?—Nah, nah, I like it here, just the way it is. Let the *haole* keep their big, noisy, dirty world. I'll stay here, and enjoy the relaxed life of these quaint and easy-going Hawoyins, content with them to bask under a breadfruit tree, filling carefree days with laughter and song, my nights—Goddam! The crap these foreigners write about us, in their newspapers and books! Makes me sick . . ."

"My sentiments exactly, brother. Now, please, do you shut up. Kahu was about to tell me something important when you sailed in on the big wind."

"Sorry, Kahu. Don't mind me. As you see, I'm only a fishing-canoe, not a frickin' frigate. No guns."

No guns, perhaps, but a mouthful of sharp teeth, and fingers like daggers. With him there I would not speak of Eahou. "I am grieving over the death of our people," I said, driving the smiles from their lips, the young man's joy in life from their thoughts. "On this journey I have seen how they are living in ignorance and dying in hopelessness. I have seen how they are thriving in only a few places: at Kane'ohe, at Kahuku, at Waialua, and at 'Ewa. Why is this so, I asked myself as, between those places, I rode from one deserted village to the next. The answer was not easy to find. Not until I was almost back again in

Honolulu did it come to me. But now I believe I have the answer.

"Our people are thriving only in those places where a *haole*—a good *haole*—is caring for them, is watching over them. And where, I asked, are the chiefs who should be caring for them? Most of the chiefs are dead, or the few who remain are here in Honolulu, not knowing what is happening in the country. If, perchance, a chief is living in the country, he is as lost in the shuffle as are the commoners. It is a terrible thing, I tell you, to ride through valley after valley, district after district, and to find them almost empty of people where once people lived in plenty. The graveyards are full, but the villages are emptying or are gone, and weeds are the only crop in the fields. Except in one place, the old gods have gone away from us, their power is ended. But where good *haole* live, the power of Jehovah is strong. This I have seen with my own opened eyes."

"Granted," said Lot soberly, "the old gods are dead, never to return, and the people are dying. This we have known for a long time. You tell us nothing new. What can we do to stop this dying, before our race has vanished from the earth? This is the question we have asked of everyone, and no one can answer it. Have you, then, found the answer?"

"To this problem there are many answers. Mine is but one, yet it is also one which can be used immediately.— Here is my thought: we must do what those good *haole* are doing, the Reverend Benjamin Parker at Kaneʻohe, Mr. Charles Hopkins at Kahuku, the Reverend John Emerson at Waialua, and so on. We must teach our people how to work for themselves, how to care for themselves, how to live in the new way. The old ways, I have seen, are not good enough for these new times. Even worse! The old ways are being forgotten, if they are not already abandoned, and nothing new has taken their place. Now the people live in filth as well as in want. The wastes of their bodies mingle with the water they drink, the foods they eat. In their despair they have forgotten those *kapu* of old, which forbade them to defile the water of Kane, the taro of Ku, the fields and the forests of Lono. 'Why should we trouble to care for ourselves, we who are doomed?' one young man of Kawailoa cried out to me, with tears in his eyes and grief in his voice. This is a terrible thing to hear from the mouths of the young.—This is why I say that we must show them the new ways. If, knowing these new ways, foreigners can thrive here, why can not our own people learn to do the same?"

"Sounds reasonable," Lot agreed. "Yet for thirty years the missionaries have been trying to teach these things in their schools—"

"Schools are not enough," I interrupted, forgetting that I spoke to a ruling chief. "Too few of our young people are reached by schools, especially in the country districts. And a knowledge of reading and writing, while good in itself, does not teach a mother how to feed her baby, or a husband that he should build his house on high ground rather than on the mud beside a stream. These mothers: cha! They are still feeding their newborn babies in the old way. Not with milk from the breast, or with milk from cows, or with porridges and broths, as *haole* mothers do. Oh, no, that is too much trouble! With my own eyes I have seen a mother sick with the consumption chewing pork until it was soft, then spitting it into the mouth of her day-old babe. When I scolded her for doing this, she glared at me and said, 'This is how my mother fed me, and all her many sons and daughters.' And she would not listen when I tried to tell her that the new ways are better. Her child will not live to see the next full moon, I am convinced."

"But Kahu," Lot broke in impatiently, "the Legislature can't just pass a law, forbidding mothers to feed their babies in that disgusting old way."

"Wait, wait, let me finish my thought," I said. "Perhaps that way of feeding is not killing our people. But indifference born of despair: that is what is killing them. They are not lazy. Usually they are not stupid, as was that sick woman in Wahi'awa. They just don't care. They have given up the struggle to live. You can tell, by looking at them, sitting forlorn on their dirty mats before their sagging houses, in yards strewn with rubbish. 'Why should we care? Why should we put things away, for our children's sake?' they ask. And in this they are right," I said, looking at the two who were the hope of our race. "This is the saddest thing. The children have almost disappeared from our land."

"What do you think should be done?" Alex asked, "what do our people need?"

"What our people need today is what they have always needed. What in the old days they received from the chiefs and the priests, what today they receive only from a very few foreigners: example and encouragement. Where these are given, the people prosper. Where these are not given, the people are wasting away."

"Again I say your argument sounds reasonable," said Lot. "But I don't see what we can do to change the situation.—Or do you want us to tie *ki*-leaf bands around our brows and, like *kahuna* of old, go among our people, preaching to them the value of breast-feeding as opposed to the horrors of feeding from the mouth?—By the Balls of Beelzebub! What a career for the Kamehameha boys to take up!"

"Nah, nah," I was smart enough to laugh with him, "I know what you young fellows should be doing, but I do not think it is proper for me to tell you about it.—But for myself, I wish to go to Kahana. There I will do what Hopkins is doing at Kahuku, what Saul Bristol should be doing at Ka'a'awa. I will raise cattle, grow sugarcane, build houses in the foreign style for my people, above the streams and the mud. I wish to be an example to my people, and an encouragement."

"Good!" said Alex, his eyes shining. "And you will be an example to me as well: I shall follow in your footsteps, now that you have shown me the path."

"You know," said Lot, "that's the best idea I've heard yet, from anybody. I hate to admit it, Kahu, but you've made a convert of me, too. By the tongue of Nihoa! Never did I think that I'd spend my declining years being a missionary to my own people."

"And I know just where you can start, O apostle to the Hawaiians," said Alex, not concealing his glee. "Work on your sister Ke'elikolani. She needs a bit of exhorting. Kahu tells me she's been upsetting the whole countryside, out there in Ko'olaupoko and Ko'olauloa."

"An impossible task you set me, O my brother, but I hear you, I hear and someday perhaps I shall obey. But hearken, I pray you, to my thought: I think we should give up talking to Ruth. Just haul her into town, and lock her up in one of Kahu's hotels. That would solve all our problems." When our raucous laughter, and the parrot's very appropriate commentary, died away, Lot turned to me, most solemnly. "All of which reminds me, Kahu: what will you do with all your enterprises in town? You can't very well take them with you to Kahana. Nor can you close 'em down. The economy of Honolulu would collapse if you did." As I have said, he is a dangerous man.

With a voice and an expression that would have brought acclaim to the pastor of a Christian church, I replied, "It is comforting to learn that you are interested in matters of finance and business. But I foresee no problem of the sort you mention. Here, too, I have learned from foreigners. The income from my assorted enterprises in the capital will be used to support my interests in the country."

"Most laudable," Lot nodded, flicking imaginary ashes from an invisible cigar, "a Ministry of Internal Revenue, so to speak. No philanthropist should be without one.— But all joking aside, my honored teacher, if ever you want to sell out, let me know. I've had my eye on your hotels for quite a while—purely from the outside, of course, a form of speculation, as it were. Only my respect for you—and my extreme virtue, need I say?—have kept me from following this one of your sterling examples. Competition, as our Christian brethren teach us, is the life of trade. But I am sensitive enough to perceive that it is also the death of friendship."

Hah and hah! I wanted to huff, as my kids do when they are not amused by teasing. But I knew better than to risk any more jibes from this Machiavelli among princes. "What do you think?" I appealed to Alex. "Will His Majesty give me permission to live at Kahana?"

"Crissake, Kahu!" exclaimed Lot, "this is a free country. We're not living in benighted old grandpa's time. Haven't you heard of the Declaration of Rights?"

"I have indeed. But—"

"Let me, Kahu," said Alex. "What you don't know, Lot, and what I had forgotten, is this: when Kahu was a mere boy, our kindly old grandpapa ordered him to live in Honolulu, never to go back to Kahana without permission from the ruling chiefs. Grandfather's two sons, in their turn, continued this *kapu*. It stands to this day. Kahu, to his great honor, has obeyed it."

"But why?" asked Lot, for once in his life not knowing all the answers.

"Quite simple," said Alex. "Because Kahu is the highest of O'ahu's chiefs who survived the war of conquest. And grandfather didn't want any trouble to start out there in the country while he was living here in Kona or traveling around on the other islands."

"Well! Blow the man down!—That old land-grabber was a pretty clear thinker, I must say. The more I learn about him, the more I must respect him."

"But now those old days are ended," Alex brought him back to the present, "and we who are the usurpers don't have to fear that O'ahu's warriors will gather around Chief Nihoa and drive us back to Kohala—or into the sea, for that matter."

Lot missed the chance to laugh at the idea of me leading an army. "Bless me," he rolled his eyes up under their lids, pretending to look into the future, " a philosopher-king is coming next . . ."

Whereupon Alex threw a cushion at him, and they were boys laughing again, each a foil to the other. "Don't worry, Kahu," Alex said when their bout was ended, "I'll ask my Father. I'm sure he'll give his permission."

"One of the benefits of civilization," Lot assured the parrot. "Plucked of his feathers, the savage King is chained . . . Hey! That reminds me: what about the dukedom we promised Kahu?"

"Screw him!" shrieked the parrot, "avast there! Heads up! Heads up!"

For once I saw Alex embarrassed. "My Father's thanks

will be expressed in time.—As I've told you, he's been ill, and—"

Even more embarrassed for myself, I said stiffly, "No reward is wanted other than your thanks. What I did was done out of loyalty to you and to your Father—and out of love for our country. Is this not reason enough?" My goodness me! Even to my ears this speech sounded like something the spirit-guardian of Sir Walter Scott might have put into my head. But I meant it, every word of it.

"Good man, Kahu," said Lot, not teasing me this time. And I was pleased. This was a reward given from the mind, not from the heart. Lot does not give such prizes easily.

I picked up my hat, preparing to leave, when I remembered one last thing—a matter that had been bothering me since the day I started upon my mission for the King. "How did Mr. Wyllie know me, that morning?" I asked Alex.

"Wait, I will show you," he said, getting up from his chair. "I have been keeping this for you," he explained as he went into the parlor.

"Brace yourself," Lot warned, "there's a new kind of bait for *kahuna 'ana'ana* . . ." His voice died away, hinting at dark, sinister mysteries. "No one is safe anymore . . ."

"Bait?" I quavered, rising to his hook. "How did you know?" This is how unstrung I was, ready to believe that he was in league with sorcerers, even with the ghost of Hahau.

Alex returned in time to save me from making a fool of myself once again. "Do you remember the day?" he asked, putting into my hands an oval silver frame holding a piece of curved glass. Stupidly I stared down at the photograph of Alex and me, taken a few weeks before, in front of this very house. There we stood, stiff and unsmiling in the morning's sunlight, captured forever in shades of black and gray and white upon a piece of thick paper, like the images of spirits upon the ceiling of Pohukaina. That was the morning of Lot's twenty-second birthday, and His Majesty had invited Honolulu's only photographer to mark the occasion by taking pictures of the two young princes. I was hovering around the edges of the crowd of servants and gawking city-folk, laughing with them at the antics of Dr. Stangenwald, as he played hide-and-seek under his black silk shawl draped over the black box stuck up on three long legs, and commanded the bored youths to "Hold idt, hold idt . . . Do nodt moof . . ." Then, while the bustling little man was changing those big glass plates inside his magic box, and I was chatting away with Pilipo, the steward at Hali'imaile, Alex came and took me by the hand, saying, "Come on, Kahu. I want a picture of you with me, the two of us together."

Now, seeing the photograph for the first time, I said sheepishly, "Yes, I remember now. I had forgotten all about this new *haole* invention."

"Bait for the unwary," croaked Lot as I handed the photograph to Alex, "and an end to spying."

"No," said Alex, "this one is for you to keep. A gift from me to you, with much affection. I have another one, for me to keep in remembrance."

I could scarcely thank him properly, so great was the welling-up of happiness within me, that he should have been so forethoughtful. What greater reward for my mission than this did I need? This was my thought, and this is what I said to him.

Yet on the way home, as I walked the short distance to our house on Beretania Street, gratitude gave way to

grumbling—but not at Alex—so loud was the noise of a
new thought jeering at me from inside my skull:

> Can a husband hide from his wife
> Those diversions in his private life?
> Could she not, with camera and glass,
> Spy him out, and all his past?

Cha! I growled, kicking at a pebble lying in the road.
The photograph was heavy in my hands, and I resolved to
lock it up in my strong-box, where no prying spy could
ever see it, where no *kahuna 'ana'ana* could ever find it.
This is *not* the way things should be, I muttered. That
black box: those glass plates: they are inventions of the
devil. An end to spying, indeed!—They are the end to
privacy, to secret comings and goings, to doing as one
pleases. They are the end to freedom . . .

HIRAM NIHOA

at Honolulu, O'ahu,
  in the Kingdom of Hawai'i,
May 13, 1853.
at Ka'a'awa, O'ahu,
June, 1854.

SAUL BRISTOL

CHAPTER 25.

TRUTH OF A SORT

Hiram has told his story, as far as he was able to carry it before he had to put it down. Now I am to continue the tale by adding my part to it. I do not want to do this but I must because, as he would have written, "a promise is a sacred thing."

"But what good will come of all this scribbling?" I asked, trying to avoid the promise and to escape the labor. " 'Of making many books there is no end,' " I argued, knowing how he admired my learning, evidenced in the ability to trot out a pedant's tag suitable for any and every occasion. To him I am learned, but not wise, because learning is something gained from books, whereas wisdom is wrung from life.

Quick as the compiler of a concordance he recognized my argument. "And did his knowledge keep that man from writing a book of his own? *Vanity of vanities, all is vanity,*' he said, and yet this sour wisdom did not keep him from writing. And he did not write in vain, even though—like all writers of books—he wrote out of vanity."

Ah, this Niele! He has a way with words. And he has a force of spirit which never fails to astonish me. I have been an immovable object in my day, but he is the irresistible force which has kept me in motion since we met.

"Who will read it when it is written?" I veered off on another tack, "especially if you are going to keep your story locked up in a strong-box for a hundred years?"

"How can you or I know who will read it?" he countered, "and does this matter to us? Did Ecclesiastes write to please his readers, or to comfort himself? And that shrewd Italian, that Machiavelli: who was he pleasing, when he wrote his books in exile?—Nah, nah, stop your squirming. The reader does not matter now. The writer and the writing: these are what matter now. Therefore do you write your story to satisfy yourself, as I wrote mine to please me. When you have done your part it will be to mine as the last act of a play is to the first. Without your part my account will remain unfinished. Who would know then, a hundred years from now, about you, about me, about Kaneikapule? Yours is the burden now. My part is done. I can write no more." As somber as a man might be on his deathbed, he invoked the ultimate threat: "If you don't do as I ask, my ghost will haunt you after I am dead."

Not fear of him dead but fondness of him living made me submit. "Then we are agreed," he shook my hand solemnly. "The writing will be good for you, as it has been for me. And do not think about who will read it. Just write of things the way they happened. And tell the truth —the truth of events as they happened, not as you look back upon them now." He sighed, histrionic as always. "As, I fear, I did not always tell it. Then, when our story is completed, even a hundred years from now we will not lack for readers. Just as you and I like to learn about people of olden times in other places, so will those who come after want to read of us and of our times. And of the things that happened to us here in this lovely valley of Ka'a'awa, here on this beautiful island of O'ahu."

So, reluctantly, I begin. Once again I sit at my table, my ledger opened, quills sharpened, ink readied, everything in order except my reason's true consent. And I am overwhelmed by the task he has imposed upon me.

More than three years have passed since I wrote the last entry in this vainglorious thing I call a journal. I stare at it as though I've never seen it before. I read it as though I never knew the man who, enclosed in a cave and wrapped in a shroud of self-pity, wrote out those lamentations for his heart's pain and his vanity's pleasing. He was not a pleasing man, that creature of plaints and whimperings. But is he any better a man today? Ah, that is the question. I must think so, I must hope so, else I could never find the will to lift this pen.

"Tell the truth," Hiram has admonished. Easily said, hardly done. *Vanity of vanities, all is vanity*, Ecclesiastes has written for all men to heed, especially for those who look too closely at themselves. The truth is apt to be ugly and hurtful, as well as most difficult to find.

Yet there is truth of a sort in that last entry. I can't think of a better way to begin upon this accounting than to borrow a page or two from my journal, as Niele did:

Saturday, 19 February 1853

Niele, that curious little man, has started me upon a new use for this ledger. Before he rode into my life, and out of it again two hours later, I was content with an occasional schoolboy's entry in these great pages, dutifully recording, for want of other vent and utterance, my moods & humors, my boring chores & even more boresome bouts of the miseries. Because I live from day to day I have written all these entries in much the same narrow way, intent on the moment because I can find only sorrow in the past and hopelessness in the future. The present gives me occupation, if not forgetfulness; and I have been the prisoner of a thousand unvarying days because they made me weary enough to sleep through a thousand haunted nights. Work has kept me alive, if not entirely sane. Good Yankee that I am in this respect, I follow the model of all the half-mad saints who dwell in New England.

"Man appoints, but God disappoints," as Ma used to say. All of us, in that impoverished family of ours, learned well and quickly this bitter text and its many proofs. And, God knows, I have had reasons aplenty to remember it in the years since I fled from home "to make my fortune," as another Yankee adage expresses the eternal hope of everyone who ever scrabbled for a living in that inhospitable land. Want and struggle have been my lot for so long that I marvel I've endured it. But I have "fallen only to rise again," as some earnest hymn or other puts it, merely because, to my dour Calvinist spirit and hard New England body, a man can do nothing else if he must go on living. What self-respecting Yankee, even if he isn't a God-fearing man, chooses any other way?

Until recently I thought that in this new and kinder land, under this warmer sun, my lot was improving, and that my spirit was climbing out of the black pit in which it has wandered for so long. I should have known better. If Ma's grim axiom did not prepare me for the infernal round, then surely my studies should have done so. In point of fact they did prepare me—and only foolish trust in the healing medicine of time has led me to expect solace if not rescue. Oh, Demosthenes Junior! Add one more miserable man of melancholy to your grand summation: the weighted creature who cannot walk upright into the future because he is so much in bondage to his past. Oh, clear-sighted Calvin! Add one more predestined victim to the hecatombs demanded by your greedy God.

Even so, with the stupidity of the unknowing sacrifice, I thought everything was going well—until Niele arrived. Everything went wrong as Niele left. Oh, the bright Hawaiian sun still shines, of course, between showers of rain which have returned to water Ka'a'awa's pastures; the stock thrive on lush green grass; Belle's pups grow prettily; even those two purebred Angus bulls which Wyllie ordered for us from St. Julian in Sydney already have sired half-a-dozen healthy calves. Milord Hopkins, if he should condescend to pay me a visit—but may Heaven spare me such access of joy!—would find nothing to complain of in my stewardship. My exterior world proceeds well enough, and now the fortune I set out to make is within my reach. In another year or so I, too, can afford to buy for myself one of O'ahu's silent unpeopled valleys, and create from it a barony of my own. But why should I bother, I ask. For I am alone in the world. And my interior world, the place wherein my thoughts do wander, is black, is dark. An evil spirit has been sent by the Lord upon Saul to vex him.—And, I have discovered, there is no hellebore in Hell. Burton, bless his busy mind, did not think of that.

Niele, damn his bright eyes, his clacking tongue, his nosey nose, has done this to me. He's made me think again, about people, about events, I was beginning to cover over with scabs of forgetting. Under the scabs, the wounds still fester . . .

Damn him!—I can hear it still, that insinuating voice, asking, oh so slyly, why there is no wife in my house, to make of it a home for me. And my reply, rising too late of course, snarled after him as he rode away: "It's no business of yours!" And yet, as I hear him, again and again, during the day and during the night, I know that he put his finger upon my deepest wound. Damn him! To think that I liked the man—and like him still, when I am honest with myself. He is the most interesting Hawaiian I have ever met, for one thing, and one of the most entertaining wits I've known anywhere. We got along famously, until the end, and even that hurtful parting might have been avoided if he'd put the question earlier in our conversation, or in some way less sudden.

To me the most unsettling thing about the whole experience is the realization that I would have told him what he wanted to know, had we been sitting around the dinner table or even chatting on the verandah. If confession is good for the soul, then I must be ripe for unburdening. I can *feel* the whole putrid mass of thoughts and words and screams gathered in my breast, ready to burst out, like blood from the lungs of a man rotting away with the consumption. Of all the men I have known, Niele managed to convince me, he would be the most understanding and the least judging. A Yankee missionary, if ever I got close to one, would back away from me in horror before I could finish

my story. A Roman priest, if ever I could trust one, would con-
sign me body and soul to the flames of Hell. But Niele impresses
me as being a man of this world who doesn't worry about the
next—and who, therefore, might help me to find a way to peace
while I am still suffering in this one.

Because he left me so upset, I allowed two whole days to pass
before I worked all this out in my macerated mind and screwed
up resolve enough to go in pursuit of him. Not to confess—I was
not that addled—but just to talk with him, and to invite him to
visit with me, now that we're going to be neighbors. This morning I saddled Drummer and rode like a cavalryman the four
miles to Kahana. He was gone, of course. No one there could remember, in this Kingdom of the aimless, at what hour he had left
or where he had gone. At first they didn't even know who I was
talking about, because I asked after "the man called Niele." But
when I started to describe him they broke out in smiles and nod-
dings. "Ah, you are speaking of our chief," said Napuna, the
brainless headman at Kahana. "Nihoa of Nanahoa is his rightful
name. He was here, indeed. But now he has gone, riding to Kahuku, I think." "Nah, nah," bawled some of his fellow nitwits.
"To Kawailoa, he went." "To La'ie, he said." "To Waialua, he
told me." For them, who have never left the shelter of Kahana,
these alien places are not three filthy villages strung along the
same thin road around O'ahu. One lad cried, "To Ka'a'awa, to
the place of the angry *haole*," not connecting me with the one
they so distinguish from other haoles.

Only one fact could they agree upon. "Do not worry. He will
come back some day. See: we are making a house for him." They
pointed to a pile of stones they were gathering whenever the fit
grabbed them, and to a clearing where eventually they would use
the rocks to make the low platform upon which Niele's house
would sit. "A very sensible man is your chief," I took the chance
to instruct them. "He puts his house high on a hillside, above the
reach of the stream in flood." "A splendid house will it be,"
Napuna replied proudly, completely missing the point, "with a
fine view of the bay and of the mountains around, such as he asks
for. A house worthy of a great chief.—And a good place to watch
for schools of fish, swimming about in the sea."

This was the spark to set me ablaze. Furious with my misbegotten hope, that I could find comfort in talking with Niele or

discover common sense in any *kanaka*, I spurred Drummer into a leap, showering those complacent clodhoppers with sand and dirt. Not until I had rounded the point of Kahana and was racing along Mahie's level coast did I slow Drummer to a mere trot. But by the time I'd reached the work-gang, actually hacking away at brush as they should have been, the rage was somewhat abated. God knows I give these kanakas causes enough to call me the angry *haole*. Better to be thought angry, I suppose, than crazy. —If only they knew!

Nonetheless, my disappointment at having missed Niele smouldered until after supper. Then, in the dusk, as I walked up to the cave, the thought broke through at last: "There's your listener," it whispered. I accepted at once the premise that in writing out the story of my miserable life I would lighten the weight of its grief, and the promise that in this ledger I would find the perfect listener, patient, undemanding, and trustworthy. The promise pleased me, for I do not like to be obliged to any man.

And the premise beckoned. Begin at the beginning, I charged myself, striding toward the cave, as eager as an alchemist hastening toward his heated alembics. And tell the truth. Write this sickness out of your system. Let ink be your physick, the quill your bleeder's knife. Oh, what a perfect metaphor, I congratulated me, so taken with the conceit that I did not perceive my own.

Good humor even survived the revelation that, despite the taboo I have placed upon it, in the manner of these heathens, my sanctum has been invaded, my privacy violated. That damned-fool priest has been up here again: his big splay-toed footprints in the dust, the scar of a small fire burned into the grass before the cave, clearly show that he has been practising his sorcerer's rites for my sweet sake. The overturned chair and displaced ledger bespeak fury at his failure to make my possessions—and me—vanish in a puff of smoke. The old humbug! What a disgraceful specimen of priestliness he is. If he weren't so inept and bumbling a dolt, I do believe I would have been perturbed long ago by his resentment of my presence here in Ka'a'awa. But, with his wild gesticulations, gnashing teeth, and high screams of protest, he reminds me so much of your ranting Presbyterian, frothing away in a pulpit, that all I can do is laugh at him. Hahau is the comedian in my life, the only prod to humor. Next time we meet I must be sure to laugh all the louder, to let him know how much I relish his ridiculousness.

Fortunately my secret thoughts are safe. Nobody around here can read English, as I learned long ago when I took Hopkins' lease-papers to Chief Kanemilohai for signing. Although they can read and write Hawaiian well enough—as do most of this scholarly race, when they have a mind to read or write at all. Nevertheless, I think I shall keep this tell-tale book down at the house from now on, under lock & key. "Better to be safe than sorry," is another of Ma's helpful saws. I'd hate to have old Hahau burn this ledger up someday, in his righteous wrath. Such a waste of precious paper that would be, if not of beautiful imperishable thoughts.

And here it is, the end of the evening, and I've not yet begun upon my exorcism. I know why. I'm afraid to start. What will happen to me, when I untie this bag of memories? What will come of them?

But tomorrow, I assure me, tomorrow night I shall begin.

CHAPTER 26.

IN THE VALLEY OF LOVE AND DELIGHT

The morrow came, inevitable as death. Yet, with its mask of deceit, all painted in sunshine's gold and heaven's blue and earth's bright green, it offered the illusion of life. Men are dupes when they trust the wiles of day, forgetting that night must come, bringing its dark sorrows. Day is a painted strumpet, I decided, being a man as experienced as I am learned.—And night is the whore unmasked, I concluded, led to it by the sight of Kaʻaʻawa's night-hued harlot, pricking her way to church through Kaʻaʻawa's mud.

Oh, Lord, Lord! Another dreary Sunday. What to do, what to do? The excesses of the Sabbath before were not to be repeated. The wastes of today were not to be endured.—Possessed by boredom, I could feel it, sitting heavier upon my spirit than Monday's crapula upon my flesh, clogging the veins through which only blood should flow. The usual Sabbath procession of neighbors yielded neither novelty nor amusement. They too wore masks, and after a hundred performances of this rustic comedy I knew their lines by heart.

Don't be so critical, Brother Anger, I chided me. You are no different from the rest.—For what do I wear, if not a mask? One chosen years ago, from the very limited stock that New England provides. And now, even so far away from home, it has grown into the very skin of my face, it is so much a part of me that I can no longer take it off. Although I am dying of loneliness—I admitted this at last, bringing up the terrible truth as effortlessly as cattle cough up cud—I am unable to wear any other guise than that of an angry man. The mask has become the face, the actor has covered up the man. The youth is gone who once was so well liked, and people shun me for what I appear to have become.

And why should they not, I asked the vagrant breezes, for my humility's sake. Do you give them a chance to find the man of worth, the noble soul, hiding beneath your scowls and frowns? Of all the people you have met, during your years in this God-forsaken country, only Alex has seen that you are something more than an ill-natured foreigner, only he knows the reason for your rage. And only Niele has made you laugh in pleasure and forgetfulness . . .

Hungering for his company, remembering the sprightliness of his conversation, hearing the echo of our laughter—was I remembering aright? had he actually made me laugh?—I thought again of the genial little man, extolling his humor, forgetting his verbosity of course, and refusing to see that, after half a day spent with him or with anyone, I would be fully crazed and thrice as bored as when I am alone. All this was denied, as I sank deeper into loneliness. If a visitor had ridden into the yard that morning, I would have greeted him with hosannahs. A naturalist with his train of asses would have been welcomed like a pasha, a rancid Frenchman unacquainted with soap would have been hugged to my bosom. By Heaven! I'd have becharmed even a missionary straight from balmy Boston.

I was sporting with the idea of joining my neighbors at Mass, enjoying a vision of the sensation my arrival among the godly would precipitate, when Pordagee Joe and his tribe hove into view. I retreated into the house, not wanting them to feel my envy, reaching out toward them like the tentacles of a hungry squid.

I was hiding still when the chief and his wife came down from their hilltop. And I was touched to my blasted bleeding heart when, not finding me in my wonted seat, they stopped in concern. She said something, he replied with a shrug and a smile. Then, arm in arm, in a display of affection they'd never shown before, they went on their way. "Damn you!" I swore at myself, "even they are afraid of you." Flinging open the cupboard, I reached for the brandy.

One swallow of the stuff filled me with disgust. Pushing the bottle aside, I ran out of the house. I wandered around the yard, talking to myself just to hear the sound of a voice. The madness boiled up within me, close to bursting out in that flood of anguish which makes of me little more than an animal. How well I knew the signs, how much I hated the agony when it came.

Those dreadful bestial Sundays, when first I lived in Ka'a'awa, have scored forever my flesh and my spirit. Drunk with brandy and with desire, wild as a satyr, I would strip the clothes from my body. Stark naked, mouthing every foul thought and dirty word I have ever heard and have ever been taught to suppress, I would run around the circus of my yard, lashing myself with whips and branches, cutting my flesh with thorns and burrs. While my neighbors were on their knees in church,

easing their lots with soft mea culpas, I would be howling
in my private hell, punishing my body for its lewdness
and reviling my thoughts for their wickedness. Until at
last, streaming with blood and fainting with pain, I
found release from my need of Melissa in exhaustion
and escape from memory of her in laudanum.

But flesh and spirit can endure only so much torment.
Gradually, they have needed this anchorite's chastening
the less as the years have passed. Avoiding salt has helped
to calm me: just as priests in Egypt diminished their lusts
by shunning salt, so have I. By the beginning of my third
year at Ka'a'awa, body and mind seemed to have been
broken to my will—most of the time. But not yet were
they subdued forever. Grimly I remembered Saint Anthony, contending with temptations in his desert, just as
I fought with mine in this green valley. In this valley of
love and delight . . .

All unbidden, here in the desert of my trying, the
verses of the Shakers' song came into my mind. I had
thought them just and right when, in the spring of our
meeting, 'neath the greening willows beside the slow-
flowing Charles, sweet Melissa taught them to me. That
was the spring when, after the winter's long denying, we
found happiness in each other's arms. That was the time
when, in giving meaning to our lives, we brought down
damnation upon our souls.

Now, trembling with longing for Melissa lost, I stood
in the yard beneath these alien mountains and, the more
to hurt me, sang her song:

> 'Tis the gift to be simple,
> 'Tis the gift to be free,
> 'Tis the gift to come down
> Where we ought to be.

And when we find ourselves,
In the place just right,
'Twill be in the valley
Of love and delight . . .

Belle, ever the jealous female, could not abide my attention to another. She set up such an accompaniment of yelps and yowlings that I had to stop. "All right, all right, you win," I went over to her, welcoming the interruption. She lay just inside the stable door, with six healthy pups pulling at her dugs. "Well! I can sincerely compliment you on your choice of a husband, if not on your voice. You've married into a very fine family, indeed." I had half expected that the pups would look like lecherous Makana, but by now it was apparent that their sire could be none other than Chief Kanemilohai's big black pointer. Quite the purest-bred hound for miles around, he brought good blood into Belle's degenerate line.

I hunkered down beside her, commending the happy mother with pats and murmurings, but not really looking at her the while, or thinking about her either. Suddenly, as if conjured up out of sunlight and shadow, the most enchanting creature I have ever beheld walked into the yard. He needed only a moment to cross the greensward, but that moment was an eon which gave me more than enough time to see his beauty. Cupid's arrow, they say, is swift to hit his mark. I swear I could hear the pluck of his bowstring as he loosed upon me the unerring shaft.

I was pierced to the heart—and I knew it. Not with lust, for I am no boy-squeezer, but with an astonished kind of joy that a child so perfect should be walking upon the same earth that held me captive. I want one like him, I cried to myself. I want a son, a dozen sons, like him. In my whole life I have never been so surprised—or so cer-

tain that instinct spoke my heart's great need. Scarcely
able to hold back my wonder, I rose slowly, afraid to
move too abruptly lest, like a shy water-sprite, he be
frightened away.

Clad only in a loincloth, almost as free of raiment as
Cupid himself, he stopped a few feet away, smiling at
me across the moat of grass.

"Good morning," he said in soft Hawaiian, "may I
come in?"

"Good morning to you," I replied, still fearing that he
might be sent by Habundia, Queen of the Water-Nymphs,
to deceive me, "come in, please, come in."

"Kaneikapule of Ka'a'awa is here," he said, offering
me his warm, firm hand to shake. Only then did I believe
that he was real. "You are Kaula Pelikikola?"

"The same," I answered. "But you: if you are of Ka'a-
'awa, why have we not met before this time?" The elegant
head and lustrous eyes, the lean, strong, finely propor-
tioned body: I recognized them now.

"Because I am newly come to Ka'a'awa, four days
ago."

"Then let me say how happy I am that you have come
to visit us in Ka'a'awa.—And let me guess that you are
kin to the Chief Kanemilohai."

"He is my new grandfather," he replied, looking past
me to Belle and her family. "And what are those squirming little things?"

Taken aback by the question, I answered him in
English.

"Excuse me," he said simply, "I do not understand
what you are saying."

"They are the little children of this mother-dog.—In
English, the word is 'puppies.'—They, too, came to Ka-

'a'awa four days ago.—But have you not seen dogs before?"

As interested in the pups as I was in him, the boy knelt beside Belle. Panting with bliss, she permitted him a nearness to those precious infants theretofore granted only to me.

"Oh, yes," he said, "big dogs I have seen, but not little ones. In my other house we did not have a dog.—May I touch them? They look so soft. Like the moss on rocks beside a mountain stream."

Kneeling beside him, I picked up the sleekest, prettiest pup in the lot and offered it to him. "This one will be yours to keep, when he is old enough to leave his mother." Already full-grown in my heart was the favor of a father for his son. Already I saw in him the son I had always wanted, the son who, now that he was here, I would no longer be denied. He did not know this, but with the present of Belle's pup I gave Kaneikapule my devotion. —Nay. Why am I so unwilling to say it? I gave him my love.

"Can you do this thing?" he asked. "Will not the mother dog grieve over the loss of her child?"

"No, I think not. She will be happy if you care for him and give him a good home."

Only then would he take the pup. Stroking it gently with long, slender fingers, he said, "Then I thank you— and her. I shall be as a brother to this one of her children. And if she grieves for him she can come to visit us, with her other children."

"As I hope you will come often to visit her," I said, thinking not at all of Belle.

"I would like that. But I would like to come to visit you also. So many things are here which I have not ever seen.

Will you tell me about them?—I will not weary you by staying too long."

Rejoicing as Lot must have done, when the three archangels knocked at his door in Sodom, I assured the lad in the staidest manner of the most imperturbable Bostonian that he would be welcome at any time.

"And will you teach me the language of America? My grandparents are teaching me the reading and the writing of Hawaiian. But they say they do not know the foreign language well enough, that for this they would ask you to be my teacher. Will you do it?"

The mask of loneliness cracked into pieces, the shards fell away forever. "Most willingly. You have come to the right place for this. Although you can not know it, once, long ago, I was a schoolmaster in America. I shall teach you not only the reading and the writing. I shall teach you all I know about the great world beyond the sea." Milord Hopkins' cattle ranch could slide down into the ocean for all I cared, weeds and brambles could smother it—and him, too, if he objected. Already, in my mind's eye, the shack in which I lived was transformed into a schoolhouse, and in it sat the brightest pupil and the wisest teacher upon the whole wide earth.

"I shall like that," he said, much more sober in his expectations than I in my fantasy. "You are a kind man. My grandparents have told me this."

As gratified as Belle had been when he patted her, I could only act the pompous pedagogue: "Kindness comes easily to people who are treated kindly."

"Aye," he seemed to look through me with those astonishing eyes, "Makuahou taught me this lesson. I have learned it well—and I remember it."

I nodded sagely, as if, of course, all Hawaiian stepfathers, like all American schoolteachers, are packed full to the lips with wisdom. But I wanted to hear no more of grandparents or of stepfathers. I was captivated by the child, not by his lineage, and I would have been just as beguiled had he been the bastard by-blow of some commoner slattern like Kamanele instead of the grandson of a nobleman like Kanemilohai.

And yet the boy confounded me, too, in my prejudices. How was it possible, I wondered even as I admired, for such a superlative being to be living here in this remote valley, on this forlorn island inhabited by the miserable remnants of one of the most debased races on earth? Except for Alexander Liholiho—and, much more recently, Niele—I had met among the Hawaiians both in town and country only shiftless, feckless creatures for whom I held little esteem and less hope. I was angered by their laziness, aghast at their immorality, and appalled by the squalor in which they chose to live. I did my best to "teach 'em, treat 'em, and preach at 'em," but my mind despaired, as my body faltered, at the immensity of the task. How can a farmer harvest a good crop, when he has only tares to sow?

And then this child walked into my life, and I saw how hasty had been my judgment of his people, how quickly I had dismissed the nation as being worthless, even when I could see before me such splendid representatives of the race as Mr. and Mrs. Kanemilohai. At sight of Kaneikapule the scales fell from my eyes, the would-be teacher was taught another lesson.

He had a mind to match his body. While he carried the pup, we went on a tour of the stable. He was full of questions, quick to learn, easy to teach, yet he was surprisingly unacquainted with many things that were commonplace even to country natives. He'd never seen nails, for example, or a hammer, much less a saw or a plow. He could have stepped right out of the primitive past, before these islands were discovered by white men. I thought he must be teasing me, but he convinced me that he told the truth when he said, "My grandfather—the one in Maunawili— dwelled apart from other people. He lived in the old way. He did not like the new way."

"Yes," I conceded, "this is the manner of some grandfathers." My grandfather and my father—and I, no doubt —were formed in a similar mould. Grandpa, hard as the rocks in his fields, would not permit "them new-fangled whale-oil lamps" in his house, maintaining that if tallow candles "wuz good enough for my pa, they be good enough for me." Pa carried to even stupider extremes the family's boneheaded dislike for anything new and different. Friction matches were foresworn because "they stink of the Devil," most books—other than The Good Book—were proscribed because they were "snares of Satan." And he wanted to drive me out of his house when, having finished common school, I asked to go to the Latin School in a neighboring town. "No son of mine," he let me know in the instant, "needs any more larnin' than it takes to make a good farmer out of him. Git ahind the plow, or git out."

Taking him at his word, I left his cheerless house and went to live with Brother John in Boston. The fact that Brother John was making his fortune as a merchant in Boston did not alter by one jot Pa's attitude toward his sons at home. Nor did Brother John's willingness to send me first to Latin School and then to the college at Yale change Pa's estimate of me. The fact that in a very short time, sooner than any of us could have foreseen, Pa proved to be right about me is a hard truth I have accepted only lately. Just as, only recently, I have begun to wonder what mad forms my dislikes and hatreds will take when I gain the age of forty—if I should survive the years between now and that rheumy senescence. No matter where a Yankee roams, he's doomed to be a Yankee. If anyone should doubt me, let him look at Honolulu, a New England port town furbished with palm trees. Nay, by all the saints of the covenant: let him look right here at Ka'a'awa, where Pa's very spit and image is putting the Bristol mark upon this alien land . . .

"But this new grandfather in Ka'a'awa: he is different?" I said to Kaneikapule, observing the one little blemish on his body. Brother Doison's possessive brand was so well known that I did not need to ask the boy when Kanemilohai had arranged for his vaccination.

"Oh, yes," he replied, "we have many things in this new house which I did not see in the other one."

Having finished with the stable and its interests, we restored her pup to Belle and went to look at the pond. Only about an acre in extent, it is spiked around the edges with tall rushes, softened near the springhouse with pink and blue hyacinths I've brought from Honolulu. Small ugly native ducks swim on its surface, and fat lazy catfish sleep in its depths.

"And where is the spring, which brings the water of life to this place?" the boy asked.

While I pointed out the several springs that feed my pond, and discoursed upon the deep dark mysteries of water passing through the earth itself, we lifted our eyes to the pointed peaks rising high above the valley.

"Someday, when I am bigger," he said, "I would like to stand upon the tops of those mountains, to see the world from there."

"I too have felt this wish," I said, smiling down at him as I thought his gods must be smiling down upon the two of us.

"Then let us go together," he declared, "each helping the other."

"It is a promise," I said, "and I shall remind you of it, when the times comes."

A few months before, in one of my less practical moments, I had decided to try to raise mallards and swans on the pond, and herons or any other waterfowl which might prosper in this sanctuary. Although as yet neither bird nor egg had arrived to grace this preserve, I told Kaneikapule of my plans, flexing an arm to depict the grace of the royal swan, my fingers to shape its head and beak.

"My goodness!" he exclaimed, laughing in great glee as he imitated me with his whole body, "you look like a *hula* dancer . . ."

"And who ever allowed you to see such sinful things?" I cried, scandalized to my Puritan's core, when chickens began to squawk, goats to bleat, announcing the return of Mr. and Mrs. Kanemilohai. "When shall we start your schooling?" I asked hastily.

"You are the teacher, I am the learner. Do you tell me when to be here, and I shall be here."

Looking down at him, I wondered how I could possibly wait until the morrow. "Then tomorrow morning we shall start. When the sun has risen above the sea to the level of yonder ridge," I pointed to the mountains on the Kahana side of the valley. That is our town clock and church bell: when the sun stands at that height, we of the ranch know that the time has come to begin working for our absent lord.

"It is good," Kaneikapule offered me his hand, "I shall be here."

Mr. and Mrs. Kanemilohai were surprised to see us— and, I suspected, were embarrassed by the boy's native dress, in such contrast with their Sunday-go-to-meeting clothes. But fond smiles for him quickly chased away their frowns, and they were able to summon up a sedate "Good day" for me. I, unwilling to be left alone so soon, rattled on like a preacher at his church door, praising their grandson, expressing my pleasure at the prospect of teaching him, urging them to rest for a while from the noontime sun, until I plumb ran out of breath.

"We thank you for your kind thoughts," said Kane-milohai as soon as he could get a word in edgewise, "but, alas, we can not. Some other time, perhaps, when we are less hurried."

"Ask him about Hahau," his wife prompted him.

"Should we trouble Mr. Bristol with our worry, my dear?" he asked uncomfortably.

"And why should we not?" she demanded, tossing her head.

"If you think so, my dear," he patted her plump arm, as he turned to me. "We must hurry home to send our people in search of my brother Hahau. He has not been seen for three days, and we are much alarmed. —Have you seen him, perhaps, up there in the valley?"

"I am sorry to hear this," I answered. Hurt not one whit by the old fool's absence, I was indeed impressed by their concern. "Not for several days have I seen him. But do not worry: he has been up at the cave within the last day or two."

"Why should he go now to that cave?" asked Mrs. Kanemilohai.

"To smoke me out of it, I would guess," I said with a laugh, to let them think that I was not vexed by Hahau's amphigory or afraid of its effect.

"Alas! alas! Has he been so unneighborly?" said the chief.

"Tsk! This old Hahau!" exclaimed his wife, as annoyed with the peevish priest as I had been.

"Can I help you in your search for him?" I inquired. "Gladly will I go, and gladly will I send my men to help your people."

"Thank you," the chief said, "you are very kind. They will not mind working on the Sabbath?"

"How better to spend the Sabbath than in relieving a neighbor's distress?" I assured him. "We shall start out as soon as I can pry them from their sleeping-mats. Do you think that perhaps Hahau has gone up to the mountain of—" I caught myself just in time, leaving unspoken the sacred name.

"This was our first thought," the chief replied. "Hahau goes there often, as is his duty. Our people have gone to search, but no one has been there for a week." With utmost deliberation, he finished quietly: "Not since you walked there has the way to the mountain been trod."

These people! They know everything. And they are so patient with the intruder. Feeling as guilty as a schoolboy caught in a silly prank, I blurted, "I did no harm in going there?"

"No, no," he put up his hands, "not to us. And not to the dweller upon the mountain. But—forgive him—Hahau was very angry. 'Now the temple of the mountain must be purified,' he said. For this reason we were unworried when he did not return for two days. But this morning we are much worried. Four days is too long a time for a man as sickly as he is to be gone from home. Where is he, we ask.

If he is not at the mountain, or upon the way, has he perhaps strayed from the path, like a lost little goat?"

"Or, perhaps," suggested Mrs. Kanemilohai, "he is taken with the lung-fever, up there in all that wetness, and is too weak to crawl home."

"Yes, my dear," the chief said, with more patience than I could have found, "but I do not think that he would be taken with that sickness during these dry days. I fear that he has broken a leg, or twisted a knee.—This is why I wish for us to search along the edges of the valley. If you and your men will go up along the Kahana side, I and my people will go up along this near side."

"A good idea," I said, "we shall do as you wish."

Mrs. Kanemilohai, clasping her hands, said soberly, "We have prayed to Jehovah for his help to us. Now we shall ask Kane to help Hahau." The plan struck me as being as sensible as her husband's.

"How about you, my new-found friend?" I asked the boy. "Would you like to ride along with me?"

"Oh, yes," he replied, looking to his grandmother for permission.

"No, I think not," that positive beldame declared, "you will stay at home with me."

"Ah, please, Gramma," he began, just like any eager boy.

"No, I do not want you, too, to be lost up there, or to get all wet and covered with mud and then be sick with the lung-fever."

"On a day like this?" I ventured to protest, only to be ignored. Without another word one female demolished three helpless males. Who has said that Hawai'i is a Kingdom ruled by men?

"So be it," sighed Kanemilohai, turning the boy homeward, "Grandmother knows what is best."

Kaneikapule scowled, I ground my teeth. Like a mother hen with her chicks, she guided her men home.

During the long afternoon, as we hunted for Hahau in the far reaches of the valley, I thought I understood the meaning of my pilgrimage the Sabbath before. The same cloudless sky and brilliant light and worshipful earth told me that now, as then, a profound peace had come to Ka'a'awa. For me this was enough to know. If this peace was a benison from Ka'a'awa's god, then we mortals who lived in his valley were indeed fortunate. I did not make the mistake of believing in this neighborhood deity, or of thinking that this peace was given especially to me by the Jehovah I had revered once upon a time—before I learned too well how implacable was that jealous One.

Yet, in my simpleness I did imagine that Kaneikapule's god was smiling upon him, welcoming the boy to his new home. And, enjoying the pleasing fancy, I made a fool's leap into the future. Now I knew what I would do with myself for the rest of my years: I would live and I would work for the sake of Kaneikapule. With his coming, I foresaw, a new life was beginning for me.

We did not find the priest. But I was not thinking much of moping Hahau.

In searching for him, I found myself.

And I lost something that had been a part of me for so long a time. In the soft dusk, as we came down from the hills, and I saw how surpassing fair was this world in which we dwelled in peace, I finished in contentment the song I had begun that morning in sore distress:

> . . . And when we find ourselves
> In the place just right,
> 'Twill be in the valley of love and delight.

When true simplicity is gain'd,
To bow and bend we shan't be ashamed,
To turn, turn will be our delight,
'Til by turning, turning, we come 'round right.

This song was Melissa's last gift to me, as it was her first. With it, not with the painful ritual of my writing, did she free me of her ghost.

When, in the dark of night, I walked into my house, I knew that she was gone.

CHAPTER 27.

APPARITIONS AND PORTENTS

As I should have expected, my pupil did not keep his appointment the next morning. As I might have remembered, had I not been in such a dither, a man is a plodding blinkered jackass, lured on his way by a carrot of hope dangled from the stick of a perfidious Driver. With such a state of affairs I should have had no quarrel, had I noticed the stick rather than yearned for the carrot. But, despite my earlier experience with the faithless Driver, I was still the stupid striving beast of burdens. If there is a moral to my whole sad story it is this: a wise man keeps his eye on the cudgel, while a fool chases after the carrot.

The morning began dismally, after a wild and windy night, as torrents of rain fell upon Oʻahu. The cool trade winds had come back, ending the unseasonable spell of warm, dry breezes from the south. The bright interlude was finished, the raw wet weeks that pass for spring in this unpredictable clime were ushered in with trumpetings of wind, hurtling in from the northeast, and drumbeats of waves, crashing upon the beach.

Schooling is made for such a day. In my dank house, as I peered out the windows at the rain pouring from the sky, at the muddy water flooding the yard, I was reminded of home, of those dreary days in April when children are glad to stay indoors, huddling around cheerful lamps and warm stoves. I had not thought to put a fireplace in my shack at Ka'a'awa, nor had I missed it before this time. To make up for the lack I lighted every lamp in the house, as prodigal in my hovel as a Boston nabob in his palace, hoping that their glow would dispel the gloom, their warmth the chill. The very furniture was clammy, the paper was bloated in the commonplace book I'd brought out for Kaneikapule to write his letters in.

Eight o'clock passed, and still he did not come. Although scarcely surprised, I was disappointed. Thinking of my Tacitus, I wondered if this might not be an inauspicious start to a campaign which was designed to carry the light of American knowledge among the valley's dark barbarians. "Remember Quintilius Varus, Brother Ass," I rebuked me, drawing a wry satisfaction from chagrin, complacence from such erudition. Still the center of my universe, I thought that I alone was being warned, that only for me was the world gray and bleak. Dedicated scholar, eminent Latinist, weening magister of foolscap and ink-stains as I conceived myself, I was a very stupid man, without the sensibility to feel the clutch of dread, to see in that weeping heaven a portent of many tears to be shed on earth. Instead of asking for the return of my liberty, as once Caesar Augustus had cried out for the legions Varus had lost him, I embraced servitude instead. Instead of running away, even in the storm, I waited. I reasoned that the boy was late because he'd overslept, or dawdled at his breakfast, or couldn't come out into the rain because Grandma worried for his health.

Nervous as a schoolmaster whose whole class has gone truant, I sat in this pigsty house, smelling the unsubtle stink of mildew, seeing the dirt which neither Kamanele nor I ever noticed, feeling the stickiness of sweat and sea-salt upon the graceless furniture I had made. Even the roof leaked! In several places drops of water splashed upon the floor, collecting in little puddles which soon flowed to the ground beneath through cracks between the boards. Pfaugh! At last I saw the place as another person might—as Niele must have seen it, as I did not want Kaneikapule to see it. Niele was right: this place does need a woman's care, the presence of a wife to make it a home for me. "But how?" I demanded of his shade, perched there like a bird, head cocked, eyes alight, awaiting my argument. "How can I ask any woman to come and live with me in this—this ugliness? 'Come live with me and be my love,' I jeered, ever apt with the choice quotation, but never able to speak the truth. "Who can I ask?" I cried into the silent room, emptied now even of her shade, "who can take her place?"

These futile whippings of the spirit were interrupted by a heavy pounding at the back door. "Why didn't he come to the front?" I allowed myself to fret, now that he'd arrived, hurrying to let him in.

There stood an apparition of another sort—a creature resembling an enormous shaggy insect reared up on its hind legs. For a moment, in the dim light, I thought the rain must have washed it out of the sky.

"Kanemilohai sends a message," it spoke, the voice of a man muffled under the carapace of a gourd helmet. Through slits in the helmet's face glittered the whites of eyes, the brilliance of teeth—except for a startling wedge of blackness where one front tooth was broken off.

"Come in, come in!" I shouted, seeing now a man draped in a bulky rain-cape fashioned of overlapping dried *ki* leaves, from which water cascaded as from my shingled roof.

"Too wet," he said, putting up his hands. The cape fell open, revealing his torso, the brief loincloth, long muscular legs. Pale upon the warm brown skin, a jagged scar stretched half across his broad chest, as though lightning had struck him long ago. "Here is the message from the chief," he said. " 'My grandson is taken with a sickness. I ask you to forgive him.' "

"No trouble," I yelled above the bluster of wind and rain. "Tell him that I am sorry to hear this, and that the school will be here when the boy is well again." I was relieved to be assured that neither laziness nor forgetfulness had kept my pupil at home. So many natives are full of promises today which they do not remember tomorrow, and I would have been disappointed if the boy had shared this common fault.

The messenger was turning to leave. Rain beat upon the bald helmet like hail upon a pumpkin, hit upon the cape making it sound as if it were woven of hissing snakes. I should have let him go. Instead, stepping into the trap, I asked for particulars about the boy's sickness.

Sounding like a voice from a sepulcher, the man said, "He has a fever. His body aches. He vomits. We think it is the new sickness from Honolulu. Until now we have been spared this trouble." Mrs. Kanemilohai, he went on, attended the young chief, and had not left his side since the fever began, about lamp-lighting time the evening before.

"Does she have medicines for this sickness?" I asked, knowing the utter helplessness of natives whom I try to treat from my meager stock of potions and purges.

How can I say, he implied with the usual shrug. "She is the physician. She will know what to do."

With that he went back into the storm. Only when he

was gone did I remember that I should have asked about Hahau.

After mid-morning the rain moved inland, over the mountains. Out at sea, old Earth-Shaker was quieted for a while. But not until mid-afternoon would I submit to my concern. I did what I'd sworn never to do: I went unbidden to the house of the chief. Never, in the three years of my stay in Ka'a'awa, had that haughty grandee invited me to his palace. And, proud as only a stiff-necked American can be, I had vowed never to set foot in it even if he begged me to. But this pride was forgotten as, carrying my little leather bag with its stock of simples and pills, I trudged up the path.

A white-haired old man, wearing only a ragged loincloth, sat in the sunshine mending fishnets. In the enclosure formed by dwellings and work-houses, several other lightly clad folk were busy preparing foodstuffs, plaiting mats, folding lengths of *kapa* which had been laid out upon the grass to dry. Not a sound did they make at their labors: they seemed to be acting for my benefit a *tableau vivant* entitled "Domestic Scene in the Sandwich Isles, before the Advent of the American Missionaries." Many a panting white man would sell his immortal soul to gaze upon such an Arcadian prospect, but I was still too much the Puritan to take an honest look at honest nakedness. Regarding the toes of my boots as though they were the only protectors of my virtue, I followed them to the chief's door.

The old net-mender, in no great haste to rescue me from so obscene a stage, betook his wrinkled buttocks into the house. Acutely uncomfortable, as exposed to wickedness as a ship's figurehead is to scum, I stared out to sea, counting skipper's daughters until I was dizzy.

Kanemilohai was genuinely glad to see me. With a

courtesy that even this suspicious republican could not deem patronizing, he thanked me for my neighborliness and led me into his great house. Unlike the low, foetid, crowded huts of commoners into which I have crawled, the mansion of Ka'a'awa's lord was lofty and spacious, neat and clean. Also, it was dry, despite the morning's heavy rain.

The chief guided me to the far end of the vast room. Lighted by a single lamp, hedged around by wooden bowls, gourds, and piles of folded *kapa*, his wife sat on a mat beside the sick boy. She greeted me with a whispered *aloha* and a grateful smile.

Kaneikapule lay small upon his mat. Strips of *ki* leaves, like bands of dark green jade, were bound about his arms, wrists, and head. He was glistening with sweat, breathing rapidly through his mouth, scarcely conscious. He was far more ill than I'd imagined. I knelt beside him, felt the hot brow, reached with pity for his limp hand. All the jests about my diligent scholar and his tricks to avoid going to school, the little teasings with which I'd planned to lighten my visit, were stifled. I could only moan, into a dread too deep for screams, too enormous for anyone to hear in but myself.

At the touch of my calloused hand he opened his eyes and, recognizing me, tried to smile. The heavy lids covered those glazed eyes; he shuddered. "What is this evil?" he gasped through lips already swollen and crusted. From the bowls beyond him rose the reek of vomit, of excrement.

"Oh, he is so sick," Maka-o-Hina said, unable to hold back her tears, "never have I seen anyone so sick." She covered her face in the same piece of soft *kapa* with which she wiped sweat from the boy's body, vomit from his lips.

"Never before has he been sick, he tells us," said Kane-milohai.

"I—I am full of fear," sobbed Maka-o-Hina, bending low over the boy as though with her body she would shield him from the Angel of Death.

I tried to comfort them, sounding more confident than I felt. "Do not fear. Such is the manner of this sickness, when it begins. Many times have I seen it. And twice in my boyhood have I suffered it. But he will recover, as I did, as others have done. A fine strong lad such as he: how can he fare otherwise? You will see." Calmed by my false cheer, she lifted herself up, looking at me as though I were an angel of hope.

"What medicines have you given?" I asked. Talk about medicines always helps the family, a doctor once told me, even if the medicines are of no avail to the patient. " *'Uha-loa* for the aching," she replied, "*poi* for the upset stomach. But he does not hold them down for long."

"Exactly what he needs," I pronounced, as bold as any quack. For all I knew, they were just as good as the remedies I carried in my leather bag. Even my slight knowledge of the healers' art warned me that our medicines could bring little help to a child so far gone, in a contest with an adversary so unknown and so unscrupulous. "Give him more, as often as he can take them," I prescribed. "But the fever: it is the cruelest part of this disease. We must try to hold it down."

"How can we hold it down? Do you have a medicine?" she asked desperately.

Shaking my head, I confessed my helplessness.

"I am afraid!" she cried, rocking back and forth. "This is not the foreign sickness.—This is a sickness sent by Hahau!" she shrieked, "Hahau is the one! Because of his hate!" Lifting the boy, she held him close to her breast, anointing his head with her tears.

Kanemilohai moved quickly to her side. "Enough,

enough," he said, shaking her gently. "You are a silly woman if you harbor such foolish thoughts.—How can Hahau wish to harm our grandson, this boy who shares his blood and his *mana*?" Loosing her hold upon the lad, he laid him back upon the mat, while Maka-o-Hina buried her face in the sheets.

Faintly, below the sound of his grandmother's sobs, Kaneikapule spoke: "Kuku . . . Do not fear. The voice from the cave: it is not calling me . . ."

Maka-o-Hina lifted her head, staring wild-eyed at him. I turned cold at the sound of his voice, so weak, so thin, that it seemed to issue not from him but from his ghost, already entering that distant bourne.

"Quick!" I said sharply, as determined as she was to hold him to life. "Tell your people to bring water from the stream. Cold water!"

When the brimming calabash arrived I soaked a sheet in the water, wrapped the boy in it from head to foot, ordered more water to be fetched.

"Aye, this is a good thing," said Kanemilohai. "The water of Kane, the water of life: it will put out the fever's fire, it will save him."

CHAPTER 28.

THE WATER OF LIFE

For four days and nights we fought for the life of Kaneikapule. Helpless in our ignorance, furious in our weakness, we could do little more than wrap the boy in those chilling sheets, feed him with broth or with *poi*, a spoonful at a time, wipe the sweat from his face—and pray. Kanemilohai spent many hours lying prostrate upon the stones of the temple. I would have prayed to all the gods in the Hawaiian pantheon, had I known enough about them, or to the Devil himself, had I felt that he was reliable. As it was, I left the gods to Kanemilohai and the Devil to Hahau. Yet, troubled though I was, I would not refurbish the old petitions and address myself to omnipotent Jehovah.—How surprised he would have been, to hear such importunations from so unexpected a quarter! Since Melissa died he had received nothing from me save curses. Out of hate I spurned him, because I knew how deaf to prayers, how unworthy of trust, he was.

Fortunately for Kaneikapule and for us, the boy was unconscious most of the time—either from the unremittent fever or from the laudanum I administered each

morning and evening, after the first horrifying fit of con-
vulsions seized him. When it ended I knew that neither
he nor I could survive a second bout.

At my insistence, I attended him during the days, while
Maka-o-Hina took her rest. During the nights she watched
over him, while I went home to sleep. Even with the aid
of opium I slept poorly. Each morning, half-drugged,
half-dead, wholly determined, I hurried back to the
chief's house. Everything else in my life was set aside:
the ranch, its lowing herds, Belle and her pups, all were
put into the care of Makua and Pordagee Joe.

Whenever he was not making his supplications in the
temple, Kanemilohai would join me at the sickbed. We
seldom spoke, because there was little to say, and because we tried not to disturb Maka-o-Hina, sleeping beyond a curtain of *kapa* hung from a crossbeam at the
other end of the house.

Always, when the devoted old net-mender carried out
the slop-bowls to be emptied and cleaned, Kanemilohai
went with him, to watch over the burning of the soiled
napkins, the secret burying of the boy's thin vomit and
watery dejecta. "Dare I do otherwise?" he answered when
I asked him why he did this. "Perhaps it is indeed Hahau's
hate which brings this evil upon our grandson. He did
not like the boy's coming to Ka'a'awa. This we knew. But
I did not think that he would do harm to the child. Yet
Maka-o-Hina is certain that he is the one who causes this
sickness. 'What else would bring our grandson so close
to death?' she asks, he who has never been sick before?—
And if Hahau is not the one, why does he not come home?'
If she is right, then I must take every care that no more
bait for evil spirits falls into his hands."

After a long pause he went on. "The need to say this
against my own brother is a hurt to me. As I am hurt by

remembering how trusting of him I have been. Alas, perhaps we are too late now in our fear of him.—We have found one of the boy's loincloths in Hahau's house. If it was still there, what other things from the boy's body might he have stolen, without our knowing?"

While understanding his distress, I was unable to comprehend the reasoning which led him to fear the ridiculous priest. "But surely this is a superstition, is it not?" I argued, "a survival from the days of ignorance?" I could not believe that a man as intelligent as Kanemilohai, a man moreover who had been educated in missionary schools and was a convert to a Christian faith, could still be cowed by fear of evil spirits and black magic and malign priests.

He considered me with the patience one accords a newcomer. "Who can say? Can you be certain that our way of thinking is the way of ignorance? If evil spirits are not the cause, can you tell me what thing is making this boy so sick?"

"No man can say what causes this sickness, or any sickness," I replied, knowing how weak was the argument so firmly stated. It may well have made sense to a foreigner, but it was meaningless to a Hawaiian. Never before had I been so aware of the gulf that separates the native mind from the white man's.

"Then how can you be sure that Hahau's command over evil spirits is not the cause? Father Armand, Brother Doison: they are not as certain as you are. Often are they called upon by the people of the countryside to say prayers over sick people, sick animals, even over sick lands, to drive the evil spirits out of them. And always do they respond, with their prayers and their sprinkling about of holy water."

"By the horns of Satan!" I retorted, finger raised, ready

to charge full tilt upon the Whore of Babylon, that benighted pedlar of superstitions and ignorance, as every
Calvinist knows.

"Let me finish," he warded off my attack with a double
shield of fingers. "Nor am I so certain that Hahau can not
command evil spirits to do his will, I who have seen men
fall ill, or suffer misfortunes, or even die, victims of evil
spirits commanded by other sorcerers. Always I have
thought of him as being a priest of Kane, a saver of life,
not a giver of death. But now," he shook his head, a man
mistrusting his own uncertainty, "because I do not know,
I must give him no chance if he wishes to do evil. Yesterday, I am unhappy to say, I sent bait from Hahau's person
—a loincloth, some hair found on his sleeping-mat, and,
most powerful of all, his very navel-string, preserved in
our family temple since he was born—to a sorcerer-
priest who lives in Punalu'u, asking him to contend with
Hahau, if he is the one. If Hahau is indeed the one, then
we must put our hope in the greater power of that priest
in Punalu'u. If Hahau is not the one, then perhaps that
priest will tell us who is to be feared."

Opposed by such trust, I held my tongue. Who am I
to condemn him, I was forced to admit, I who am as ignorant as he of cause and effect. Who has ever seen the all-
powerful Spirit to whom I once prayed, the First Cause
and the Prime Mover whom my people believe they can
sway with their beseechings? I would accept any interven-
tion, be it gained by black magic or white, by prayers or
medicines or sheerest faith, if only it restored the boy to
health.

So, sustained by hope and little else, we went on, day
after night. Then, on the fourth morning of our vigil,
Kanemilohai was called away on a matter of great ur-
gency. Putting off his cape, clad only in a loincloth, he

departed in haste. He returned at midday, naked as a fisherman, and went at once to Maka-o-Hina. "Wake up, my dear," he called, loud enough for me to hear. "I bring good news—and bad." While she struggled into wakefulness, he beckoned me to join them.

"On the beach beyond Ka 'Oi'o, near Kualoa," he began carefully, "Hahau has been found."

"Ah, the gods be thanked," said Maka-o-Hina, "but what is he doing there? Who is caring for him so far from home?"

"He needs no more care from us or from anyone, my beloved. He is dead."

"Alas, alas. . . And how did he die?"

"No one can say—now. He has been dead for more than a week, we think. Perhaps he was drowned in the sea, perhaps he fell where the fishermen found him. We can not tell how his life's breath went out of him, or when it departed. Crabs had eaten of his eyes, sharks had bitten at his flesh, flies and maggots were devouring him. But it was the body of Hahau which lay there, upon the rocks, above the reach of the waves. I could tell."

"Alas for the poor man, to die so alone," wailed Maka-o-Hina, "alas for you, his brother.—But did you leave him there, lying on the beach?"

"Could I dishonor the body of my own brother? No. Respect for him is being shown. These hands have helped the fishermen of Kualoa to gather driftwood to place around that swollen corpse. These hands did light the fire, which now burns down there on the shore.—But do not fear: I have washed away in the sea the defilement of death, I have burned my loincloth in another fire than the one which consumes Hahau.—And later, when the fire has ended and the ashes have cooled, these hands will gather up the bones of my brother, they will carry him here, to his home. Even now the burial-stones are being lifted up beside the temple."

"Forgive me, my husband," she said, kissing his hands, "I should have known.—May his spirit forgive me my suspicion of him."

"Aye, that is the great good to come out of this sadness," said Kanemilohai.

"How is this so?" I asked.

"Do you not see? If Hahau has been dead for so long a time, how can we blame him for the sickness which has come upon our grandson so recently? No: Hahau was not at fault. I am much comforted, now my liver can lie quiet, because my mind no longer harbors unkind thoughts about him. Even more can I say. Since I left the burning fire on the beach, I feel in my whole body a promise that Kanei-kapule will not be taken away from us by this sickness. I can not tell you how I know this, but I know it. The knowledge of it causes my whole body to rejoice. Perhaps Hahau's spirit, standing near, is guarding us, is telling me this. Perhaps it is the water of life, falling this day upon Kanehoalani alone. I am full of hope, and I go now to the temple, to ask our god to make this hope come true." He touched his nose to Maka-o-Hina's cheek. "Go to sleep again, my dear. All will be well, you will see."

"My husband," she said, "how can I obey you? How can I sleep, when so much must be done?"

"We need no funeral-feast, my helpmeet. At this time, our people and our neighbors will understand."

"Aye, they will understand. But I am thinking of Hahau. To please his spirit, and to honor him, I shall make the *kapa* wherein you will wrap his bones. No one can say that Maka-o-Hina is lacking in respect for the brother of Kanemilohai."

"Let this be known to Maka-o-Hina," he said tenderly,

embracing her. "Deep, deep is the love her husband feels for her."

When he went away I followed him, leaving Maka-o-Hina with her happiness.

During that same afternoon, while Kanemilohai was claiming his brother's bones, Jehovah sent his emissary to assist the sick boy. If Kaneikapule had not been so ill, I would have been amused by this vying of deities, contesting among themselves for our gratitude. As it was, I felt a great relief when Brother Doison poked his head through the doorway. "May I come in?" he called cheerfully, arousing me from a catnap. The steady rhythm of Maka-o-Hina's mallet, beating out the paper-mulberry pulp to fashion Hahau's shroud, had lulled me to sleep. Even though the child was still very sick, the sounds of *kapa*-making and of other activities around the household, like Kanemilohai's hope, seemed to foretell a change for the better.

"A sick boy is here, I am informed," said the little Frenchman, coming like an ambulant shadow toward the circle of light where Kaneikapule lay. "Kanemilohai asked me to come," he explained, putting down his medicine bag and the flat hat I have likened since then to a black halo. Beyond the wall of thatch Maka-o-Hina's pounding stopped in mid-beat, as a servant brought word of the visitor.

Brother Doison talked to himself while he examined the boy, like a shopkeeper taking count of his goods. "Ah, the poor little man. Indeed, he is very—Ah, ah! Has not one seen this child before now? But yes, one remembers the occasion—High fever . . . Feed the cold, but starve the fever . . . La grippe, one can not doubt. Many are sick in the same way. One has seen so many . . ." When Maka-o-Hina joined us, he gave her greeting, commiseration, and encouragement, all in a quick smile and a bob of the head, without interrupting his soliloquy. "The vaccination: very good. Now it reaches the peak. As is proper . . ."

Finally he spoke to us. "Good, good. You have done well, with your care. The fever: this is the worst. And it has been tempered, one believes, with these wet cloths." Expert as an examiner, he was as helpless as we were in matters of medicines. But he did not let that worry him. Nothing could daunt his cheerfulness, not even death itself. When Maka-o-Hina asked how soon the boy would recover, he shrugged, as most Frenchmen and all Hawaiians would do. "He is in God's hands. He will live, if God wishes. If not . . ." Had he completed the thought, I would have hit him. "Be of good hope," he finished brightly, revealing bad teeth and a pair of unsuspected dimples. "The good God is with you. He does not fail those who trust in Him."

As with all missionizing Christians, his thoughts were directed toward things more important than mere bodies. "Has the boy been baptized?"

"No," said Maka-o-Hina meekly, "the sickness began before we could take him to Father Armand."

"In time of need," he reminded her, "any one of the faithful can do it."

I wondered how she would respond to this new predicament. After these few days spent in their company I was very much aware that, even though they went dutifully to Mass on Sundays, Kanemilohai and his wife were still heathen in their hearts every day in the week. Once I would have condemned them for hypocrites, and despised them for cheats. But that was before I came to know them. Now when I thought them the finest people I had ever known, I admired them for being sensible enough to take what was good from the new religion, the while they kept what was best from the old. Had I been in their position, I would have done the same.

"Then shall we do it now?" Brother Doison asked.

The poor woman looked from him to me to the unconscious boy.

"It can not hurt," Brother Doison said, "it can only help."

I knew what she was thinking, for I was fighting the same dread. Was this the Frenchman's way of telling us that the boy's life was nearing its end? And would she, by permitting his baptism and acknowledging its need, hasten him on his way to heaven instead of holding him here with us on earth? My heart cried out against the admission, at the need to express a choice. My cynic's mind tried to put into words its scorn for this Christian superstition of using spirits for bait, as benighted in its way as was the pagan nonsense about using bait for spirits. But when I looked down upon the boy my heart gave no room to scorn. As desperate as any man confronted with the terror of death, I grasped the promise of grace offered in those drops of water, those ritual words. His life was worth the yielding. Say yes, I wanted to cry out. But he was her child to give, to life or to death, not mine. Biting my lips, I made no sound or sign.

"Do it!" she commanded him.

He drew a small flask from an inner pocket of his coat. "What name shall we give to this boy, who comes now before the Lord?"

"Kaneikapule is his rightful name," she replied.

"And his name in Christ?" he persisted, most delicately.

"Saul," she said, without hesitation, reaching out her hand for mine, while my heart all but ceased its beating for surprise and joy. "Saul Bristol Kaneikapule Kanehoalani shall be his name before the Lord—and before men."

And so it was done. While the boy lay as still as an effigy upon a tomb, and his grandmother listened raptly to the formula of salvation, and I, the cynical renegade, snuffled like an old maid at her wedding, Brother Doison, with simple gestures and absolute faith, prepared the lad for life on earth as in heaven. "Amen," we said, the three of us, when the ritual was ended. The drops of holy water placed upon Kaneikapule's hot forehead vanished even as we uttered the magical word.

No angels descended forthwith from Brother Doison's heaven to drive the sickness from his body or to rout Hahau's demons from eating at his *mana*. No miracle, whether Christian or pagan, stayed the course of nature. When I went home that evening the fever kept its grip, the wasted body still fought for breath. I did not expect him to survive the night, but like a coward I fled from his side because I could not bear to be there when he died.

In the morning I returned with a heavy heart to the house on the hill. Expecting the worst, I was not prepared for the cries with which Kanemilohai and Maka-o-Hina greeted me. "He is saved!" they called out before I reached the sickbed.

"The fever has ended," she said, as I sat down between them, hearing their words, but seeing only him. "He sleeps easier now. And he has eaten a little something. But— thanks be to Jehovah, the Lord—he is cool again. Touch him. Feel him. You will see."

"Is it so?" I said, taking up the hand of the child who

was my given-son, knowing I was not worthy to touch even the sole of his foot, wishing I had the boon of faith so that, like a believer, I could lift up my voice in thanks.

"Life is restored to him," said Kanemilohai, "the gods are kind to us."

"As is the Lord Jehovah," Maka-o-Hina reminded us, most firmly.

We rejoiced even more as, during the day, each spoonful of broth and each sip of water gave strength and color to the boy's sallow flesh. "Soon you will be well again," we told him, less for his sake than for our own.

And we could find cause for comfort even in the misfortunes of others when, during the next few days, one by one, every single member of that household fell sick with the same affliction. Maka-o-Hina was the first to be struck down, followed soon by the old retainer who had assisted us so faithfully. The contagion swept through the people like fire through dry grass. The old retainer died, as did several other folk whom I had never seen; and Maka-o-Hina was so ill that I feared for her life. In the universal suffering Kanemilohai found further proof that Hahau could not be blamed for Kaneikapule's illness. "It must be something which entered into the boy while he journied from Maunawili to Ka'a'awa," we concluded, knowing no other explanation for this pestilence.

Of all the people in the household I was the only one to be spared. This escape I am inclined to attribute to the fact that I had suffered from the influenza twice before, although not nearly as severely as did the people of Ka-'a'awa. If Jenner's vaccination can protect one against smallpox, I reckoned, then why should not a seizure by the influenza protect one who recovers from it against a later attack with the same contagion? I am no natural philosopher, and thoughts of this kind are weighty enough to strain the processes of logic as well as my brain. In any event, as Brother Doison held, who can say with certainty, when it is God who giveth, and God who taketh away? I shall leave the matter for natural philosophers and other men of science to dispute—and to explain, if ever they can.

It is enough for me to confess that, from the suffering of others, I too found some cause for comfort: I was made acquainted with the virtue of humility, something I had not willingly met with before. Once upon a time I would have maintained that I was spared because I am a white man, and therefore superior, and that they were afflicted because they were kanakas, and therefore rotten and weak. I no longer kept this opinion. I needed no knowledge of natural sciences to tell me that I was arrogant in my pride, and more evil in this pride than old bumbling Hahau could ever be in his antics to keep me from despoiling Ka'a'awa with axe and plow.

Poor Hahau! The remembrance of him rankled most, because I could not prove to him how his family had gentled me. Making belated amends, I moved my things out of the cave at the first opportunity, putting them back into the house, where they belonged. I never believed the natives' tales about that hole's being a portal to their Hades, but for me, since his death, the cave of Pohukaina is haunted by my memory of Hahau's futile person. If I really believed in ghosts, I could most easily be convinced that Hahau's spirit inhabits the place from which he could not drive me while he lived.

In the midst of all this mingled relief and suffering, and in spite of the boy's undoubted improvement, one small thing continued to worry me. The vaccination sore on his arm had not reached its peak, was not abating as it should. Red, raised, as big across as a Spanish dollar, it was an ugly blotch on that reviving body. Seeing it, I could not but think of Thetis, and of her concern to protect her son from harm, when she held him by his heel as she dipped him in the waters of the Styx. To me the sore on Kaneikapule's arm was such a sign of vulnerability as that spot on Achilles' heel. According to my reasoning, it showed that the boy was still a prey to the smallpox, not protected from it, as was the intention of the Jennerian vaccination. And I dared not think of what would happen if the smallpox should be brought among us while the boy and all the members of his house were still so weak from the influenza.

I did not mention my fears to anyone, knowing that they had troubles enough to think about. I could only hope that the dreaded pestilence itself would not be unleashed among us before Brother Doison could be called in to prepare all of us anew, with fresh vaccine matter upon those little points of bone which were his weapons in the war against death.

The sore did not seem to hurt Kaneikapule. Weak, listless, uncomplaining, he lay on his mat, eating little and sleeping much. We were content, because he lived.

CHAPTER 29.

THE RIDE

When our contesting for Kaneikapule's life was won—this is how I thought of that long week, all but forgetting the others who sickened after him, even those who died—I went back to work for neglected Hopkins and his ranch. At the close of each day's labor I would stop at Kanemilohai's house, to learn what progress the boy and his grandmother were making. The chief and his wife had given me their affection and the freedom of their house. In my turn, I was grateful for the new place in the life of Ka'a'awa which their regard opened up to me. My loneliness had come to an end: now I worked all the harder, with unstinting purpose, because in my thoughts I toiled for them, not for Hopkins. I resolved that, in fact as well as in name, Ka'a'awa must belong once more to Kanemilohai and his grandson, as soon as Hopkins' leasehold could be ended fairly. And already I saw myself in a new role—not only the best schoolteacher and surrogate father a boy could have, but also the most loyal manager a landlord could ever find, running the best cattle ranch in the Kingdom for the sake of my new-gained family.

At each day's visit I found Maka-o-Hina improved in health.But the boy fared poorly. He ate little, spoke little, slept far more than was natural. When he was awake his sunken eyes showed nothing of their former brightness. It seemed as though, in his encounter with Death, those eyes had seen something which left him blighted. Maka-o-Hina, who was much more familiar with death and with the sorrows of living, did not have that look. One day I was struck with a sudden fear that his mind had been unbalanced, that the fever had burned him into blindness or into the dullness of an imbecile, as sometimes it is known to do. Yet when I questioned him carefully he was in possession of all his senses. Much relieved, I ascribed this slow recovery to an exhaustion of his vital humors, convincing myself that rest and food would recruit them in good time. If after another week his blood was still sluggish, we could send to the Catholic School at 'Ahui-manu for Brother Doison to come and bleed him. This simple operation, which I perform easily enough upon myself whenever my blood needs thinning, I recoiled from inflicting upon Kaneikapule.

My physician's acumen was confirmed. By the end of the week he was strong enough to sit up most of the day, to take a few faltering steps for the exercise of his limbs. Wrapped in a *kapa* cape and propped upon pillows against a sea chest, he resembled a fragile old man. "Hey, this is a gladsome sight," I said as I came in for my visit. "Soon you'll be frisking about like a colt. And you'll be able to bring home your puppy. He is growing fast, and he asks where you are." His lips shaped the smile for which I was pleading, but his eyes told me that he did not share my expectation.

Then came the afternoon when Maka-o-Hina was waiting for me outside the house. Sickness alone had not aged her. Worry unendurable had bent the straight back and made wan the beautiful face. "I am so afraid," she sobbed, clinging to me. "He is speaking of death. He says his grandfather waits for him now, in the cave of Pohukaina. His thoughts wander. He cries out in pain, in fear, even when he is awake."

"He is imagining these things," I said. "Who has been talking such nonsense to him?"

"No one," she tried to push back the tears with trembling fingers, "no one of this world."

He lay on his mat, silent and unheeding, just as though he had never risen from it. Beside him sat Kanemilohai, stooped and haggard, keeping flies at bay with a cluster of *ki* leaves. God in Heaven, I groaned, will this nightmare never end?

Beside me Maka-o-Hina murmured, "And the sore on his arm: it is not healing. . ."

"Damn!" I swore at myself, the complacent doctor, the unteachable fool. In my dreams of the future I had forgotten that imminent wound.

She lifted the sheet which covered him, carefully unwound the soft bandage she had wrapped around the vaccination. As the strip of *kapa* fell away I cried out in horror. Never have I seen anything so evil! A great band of festering sores, livid and raw and wet, completely encircled the thin arm. I imagined I could see the foul tetter growing even as I stared at it, could hear the sounds of invisible, insatiable smacking lips eating into the margins of healthy flesh—

"What medicines have you been putting on it?" I roared at poor Maka-o-Hina.

"Only water from the sea. As Brother Doison told him should be done."

"I did not scratch it," the boy said, faintly, as from far away.

"It is Hahau who does this," Kanemilohai declared, as

though he were stating a law. "I can no longer deny it. The flesh is split open. The fat of his body drips out. Soon the maggots will crawl . . ."

With a piercing scream Maka-o-Hina fell upon her husband's breast. "Do not say it!" she wailed, over and over again, while he, beyond heeding, beyond reason, continued his plaint.

"Hahau is the one. The spirit of Hahau is not at peace. His hate has entered even into the water of the sea, even into the air within this house."

Before this day I might have shaken them, like overgrown children, and shouted them into silence. But now I was almost as ready as they were to collapse in dread. Not Hahau did I fear, but that hideous, devouring wound. Never have I felt so helpless, so baffled, before an enemy I could see but did not know how to fight.

Reaching for my friends' hands, I strove to soothe them with protestations and arguments that we must accept if we were to keep from going mad. As solemnly as a pope on his throne I pronounced the dogma which was to save us: "This can not be the work of Hahau. To say so is to believe that evil men who are dead are more powerful than are good men who live. I do not believe this. How can you believe this?—How can you think that the *mana* of the dead Hahau is greater than the four of us who are present here in this house?" So, gradually they were quieted, were drawn back from the brink.

"This is only another kind of sickness," I insisted, "like a wound which must fester before it can heal. For such a wound a medicine can be found. I know it. I feel it.—Now hear my thought: I shall ride to Honolulu for a doctor. We will come back with medicines to heal this sore. We shall come back in the afternoon of the second day from now, or, if the doctor is slow, on the morning of the third day. Until we return you must put upon the sore whatever medicines you keep in this house or can get from other folk in the valley. Do you understand?" Like children they nodded, already brightening with hope.

Kneeling beside Kaneikapule, I said farewell to him. "Do not despair, my son. The doctor will come, and then you will be well."

"Do not trouble," he whispered. "My grandfather waits with Hahau at Pohukaina. The way to the land of Milu is open."

"You are mistaken," I said, drawing him into my arms. "We need you here with us more than they need you in the land of Milu. And our *mana* is greater, much greater, than is theirs. You will see. Now I must go. Do not fail me, my son. Do not leave me—" I kissed him on his sunken cheek, upon his brow, put him down upon the mat.

"I will be here," he said.

With that promise to sustain me I ran from the house, scarcely able to see. My fingers, stiff as sticks, were fumbling with Drummer's bridle when Kanemilohai came after me. "Kaula! Wait.—One more favor do we beg of you. When you are in Honolulu, please do you look for the chief known as Nihoa of Nanahoa. The boy asks for him. Bring him, if he can come."

"Nihoa? The little man from Kahana?—How does the boy know him?"

"Almost as a father. Nihoa is the one who brought him here to us. Nihoa is the one who saved him from death in Maunawili. This is my thought: if he did save the boy once before, he may have the power to do it again."

Here was another puzzle for me to ponder. Good God! How little I knew about these people, who had woven a net of love and need about my heart. "I'll bring him," I vowed, springing into the saddle.

"Our love goes with you," said Kanemilohai.

I stopped at my house long enough to snatch up a saddlebag and a fistful of coins. Kamanele was slapping things around in the cookhouse.

"Never mind supper," I shouted, "I'm riding to Honolulu. Be back in two days."

"Two days!" she bawled. "How can you do that? Are you perhaps riding through the air, on the back of a bird?"

She was still talking, urging me to eat, at the very least to take a little something to chew upon, for my stomach's easing, when I escaped. Kamanele, you sow, I blessed her as I ran, unlike you, I have other worries than those of the gut.

Because daylight was almost ended, I could not take the shorter route over Nu'uanu's pass. That merest suggestion of a trail, bad enough by day, is impassable by night. The only other route to Honolulu is the long way around O'ahu's northern point.

We stopped three times, not for my sake but for Drummer's: tough and spry though he is, the pace I demanded of him would have foundered a stronger steed had he not been allowed those hours of rest. Even so, I begrudged him the respites, cursed O'ahu's so-called road, the unnumbered swamps and gulches, the darkness of the night, the swarms of gnats and blood-thirsty mosquitoes, all conspiring to make our slow progress all the more infuriating.

We reached Honolulu at mid-morning, both of us jarred to the bone. As it usually is, the town was hot and dusty, raucous and stinking—my idea of Hell on a weekday. Had we arrived on a Sunday, more missionaries would have been abroad in this foulest of its precincts. To complete the picture, "the Devil was beating his wife," as the Irish say back home: when we rode through Palama, although overhead the sun blazed in full strength, clouds over the mountains were dropping their tears upon the plain. Into this humid stench of Honolulu, this Cesspit of the Pacific, I entered, a man in search of help. No over-arching sign warned me to abandon all hope, but no rainbow in the heavens offered its promise of grace.

Honolulu, more than any place I know, is a collection of miseries human and animal, wherein all the troubles and labors of mortal men, all their vices and vanities, are dumped, as in a midden. In the "Black Sea," that scabrous part of the town which lies between miasmatic Nu'uanu Stream and grog-soaked Nu'uanu Street, I left Drummer at a livery stable set amid a concatenation of shacks, tenements, saloons, and brothels, cheek-by-jowl with Chinese laundries, bakeries, tea rooms—and The Britishers' Mess.

My mind could not have been functioning at its incisive best when I permitted myself to give a second thought to that genteel Outpost of Empire. Nonetheless, because I had been admitted there a couple of times as the guest of Hopkins, that least prepossessing of Britannia's sons, I stormed this citadel of decorum in quest of its bathhouse. Enemy territory though it was, at least it would be clean —which is more than can be said for the public bathhouses in this New Sodom, infested as they are with cockroaches, centipedes, pimps, mahus, crotch-crabs, and the pernicious itch.

After one unbelieving glimpse of me, the frantic *Pake* who was in charge of the place started hopping up and down like a monkey about to be bagged. "No moa *kaukau*," he gibbered, trying to shoo me out of his empire of napery and silver, "no moa weesakee. You go nada place look-see."

The mere squeak of him enraged me. To have to waltz with such an animal, when every minute counted! "Look, you chittering Chinee," I favored him with foul breath and a very close view of teeth, shaking him until his pigtail swung out like a ratline in a gale, "I don't want any of your damned chow. I want a place to wash. Wash! You hear? Wash!"

"No moa washee oheah," he shrilled, "you makee missatake. Washee-close place ousside moa down."

For a moment, while this gabble sorted itself out in my ear, I examined the frightened face of Beretania's pygmy defender. Yielding at last to my sense of the ludicrous, I put his feet back on the floor. "Thank my English cousins for their hospitality," I drawled in an accent deserving of Hopkins' approval.

"Me no sabe, me no sabe," he was screeching as, unwashed, unshaven, and ignominious, I abandoned the field of battle. Me no sabe too, my Celestial friend, I muttered. That's life for you: a perpetual puzzle, which no one can savvy.

As if to drive the point home, there was that damned advertisement hanging above the door to a Chinese bakery —the one sign of all the many which clutter Honolulu's streets that I detest with a virulence amounting almost to frenzy. Although I know it's been dangling there for years, since long before Hopkins came to town, I've always blamed him for the dastard's deed, because it's just the sort of infantile thing he delights in doing. Sons-of-bitches, I growled, heaping infamy eternal upon the pedigrees of both Hopkins and the unknown damnfool *haole* —he must have been a Harvard man!—who has perpetrated this abomination upon us:

GOOD PEOPLE ALL . . . WALK IN AND BUY
OF SAM AND MOW, GOOD CAKE AND PIE,
BREAD HARD OR SOFT, FOR LAND OR SEA,
'CELESTIAL' MADE: COME BUY OF WE

Sons-of-bitches! I punched the board into a hanged-man's dance. One of these days, I solaced me, as I always do, I'm going to tear that stupid thing down, and bash it into kindling . . .

Like a beggar I washed my face and hands in a horse-trough, like a drunkard I broke my fast on lukewarm beer and jerked beef in the saloon of Joe Booth's National Hotel on Nu'uanu Street. Whereupon, fortified for the hunt if not presentable, I went in search of a physician.

Dr. Newcombe had not yet arrived at his rooms. Dr. T. C. B. Rooke was besieged with patients: natives sprawled about on the wide verandah of his splendid villa or on the lawn under the trees, foreigners sat primly in the parlor. Dr. Seth Andrews and Dr. Seth Ford were as engaged as Dr. Rooke. "Go avay!" shouted someone from out of Plutonian darkness at Dr. Stangenwald's place, "I am defeloping . . . Better you should come back later." I did not go back to discover what incubi and succubi he was conjuring up in that murky house. Dr. Hillebrand was ill, as usual, and Dr. Post was attending a sick patient confined to his bed.—The foul town held more doctors than trees, but where was the one who could listen to me?

On Merchant Street, of all places, I spied Dr. Judd, pushing toward his office in Honolulu House, the Government building. Long-standing dislike of the man and his policies made me look away immediately. The very sight of him confirmed my aversion: in the furnace of Honolulu, which he had ruled like a despot for ten years, he still affected the somber woolen garb of a New England deacon, he still stalked the streets like a preacher sniffing out sin. Instinct bade me run. But then good sense intervened: the old buzzard's a doctor, isn't he? What can you lose, by speaking to him?

Boldly I stepped into his path. "Excuse me, sir," I lifted my hat in seemly deference, "will you favor me with your advice?" He stopped perforce, glaring at me with his one good eye, while the other sought a way to escape me. I was only too well aware of my appearance: beneath the necessary painting of a languid broad-bottomed Venus and beyond the fly-specks, the mirror in Joe Booth's den of iniquity had shown me the bearded bum I had wanted to shed in the Britishers' bathhouse.

Carefully, with utmost faithfulness in the enunciation of every prolonged Yankee vowel and hard consonant, I endeavored to put the missionary at ease while I appealed to the physician. "Saul Bristol is my name. I am not drunk. Noa am I in need of charity.—I've been riding all the night. For a sick boy out at Ka'a'awar, who needs the attention of a doctah. But, try as I might, I cahn't get neah a doctah. You have no idear how hahd I've tried . . ."

The stern face softened, the one bright eye inspected me with kindness. "From Ka'a'awa?" He touched my shoulder with a paternal hand. "You have made a long ride, my boy.—Tell me how I can help you."

He listened carefully to my account of Kaneikapule's sickness, my description of that ravaging sore. Only once did he interrupt, to ask who had done the vaccinating. "Brother Doison?" he lifted an eyebrow. "A good man, the best vaccinator on O'ahu. I trust his work unquestioningly. The fault, then—if there is a fault, mind you—can not lie with him."

At the conclusion of my story I asked him to name a physician who would return with me to Ka'a'awa. He studied me for a moment. "You strike me as being a strong man, Mr. Bristol, one who can bear the weight of truth.—However, before I tell you my opinion, let us sit down. The truth is best received, I have found, when one can sink no more under its burden."

"You mean there's no hope for the boy?" I cried.

"No! That is not what I mean. Most emphatically I do not mean that. While a sick person lives, as every doctor knows, hope lives too. Come. Let us sit over here. Sitting will help me as well. My leg hurts."

A barrel of American flour served as his office chair. A bundle of cedar shingles from Oregon helped me to support heavy truth. Kindly, but unsparingly, he gave me his opinion. "Your son is suffering—if I understand you correctly, mark me. I really am most unwise to hazard a diagnosis on a patient I have not seen. But, under the circumstances, you perceive, there is nothing else I can do. —As I say—and, incidentally, I am basing my judgment upon the excellent description of the condition you have given me—as I say, I think your son is suffering from a very rare affliction. It is so rare that I have seen it only once in my life. At home, that was, in upstate New York. But it was so—well, let me say only that I have never forgotten it. The condition is, however, fully described in our medical books. Once in a great while, for reasons we do not understand, something goes wrong with a vaccination. The sore which, after a week or two, is supposed to stop growing, and to heal, does not stop growing, does not heal . . ."

Aye. There it was: the break in the armor of the skin, the vulnerability of Achilles. The truth pressed hard. My heart sank, hope drained away. I could not follow his discourse upon physicians' preferences about the name they should give this rare disease. *Eczema vaccinatum . . . Vaccinia gangrenosa . . .* Lovely, rolling, flowing sounds they were, like the names of plants, like epithets for ancient divinities. The crowds of people passing by at one side of us, the heavy oxcarts creaking along on the other; the clouds of dust; the incredible network of fine wrinkles in the man's face: they were more real to me than was this learned doctor's voice, pronouncing those scholars' words, all meaning only one thing, the one thing I could neither comprehend nor accept—

"And, I am sorry to say, unless it should heal of its own intention—as, of course, it may well do, you understand—there is nothing to stop the spread of such a sore."

"Nothing?" I sprang up, wanting to rage at him, at Kaneikapule's gods, most of all at the ingenious Jehovah who permitted such hideous diseases, who devised such terrible ways of dying. "You mean there's no medicine, no salve, no poultice, to put on it? *Nothing?*"

Full of pity, he shook his head. "Nothing but prayer."

"No! I can not believe you. There must be a way.— I have seen far worse wounds which have been healed."

"I grant you as much. But those are festerings of other causation. There are many different kinds of wounds and mortifications, as you must know.—And perhaps there is something, somewhere, a vulnerary of some sort, for this kind of wound. But what is it? And if it exists, do we have it here in Honolulu? Believe me when I say that we doctors do not know the cure for even the most common of afflictions. How, then, can we know the cure for a condition as uncommon as this?"

Looking beyond him, to the crowded busy street, I marvelled that all those people could be so intent upon their tasks, so concerned with the earning of money, when, if they should be wounded, if they should fall ill, the physicians of Honolulu had no medicines with which to save them.

"However, if it will comfort you," he was saying, "I

can send you with a note to Dr. Hoffmann for an unguent you might try.—And, my boy, let us not forget: it is entirely possible that I may be worrying you needlessly, with this diagnosis-at-a-distance." He pulled a crumpled envelope from a pocket, smoothed it out upon his knee, plucked the stub of a pencil from the band of his stovepipe hat. "On second thought," he put everything away again, "I'll go along with you to Brother Hoffmann's. He might have newer remedies about which I am not informed.—I haven't been able to keep up with progress in my profession during these last few years, I'm sorry to say."

At Dr. Hoffmann's drug store on Queen Street they talked their secret language, freighted with terms medical and chemical. To almost every suggestion from Dr. Judd his colleague, a fat little man of unquenchable levity, returned a jolly "No." To the few others he replied with finger-motions rippling off a descending arpeggio signifying hopelessness. The town's clown, its preeminent artist at the pianoforte, its music-maker and its dancing-master, the moving spirit of Honolulu's high society, could scarcely be moved by my little trouble. I hated him for his indifference.

At length, like merchants haggling over casks of mackerel, they settled upon a tincture of milk of lead and an ointment compounded of flowers of sulfur and powdered cinnabar admixed in lamb's fat.

While, in a very special concession to the moving spirit of all Hawai'i, Dr. Hoffmann himself measured out the medicines, I reminded Dr. Judd of the main purpose for my ride to Honolulu. Once again he boarded and scuttled me. "I know of no physician who would go with you on such short notice. Or at all, for that matter. Think of it, my boy: how can a doctor, needed as he is here in town by perhaps a dozen sick people per day, absent himself for the better part of a week, to take care of one patient as far away as Ka'a'awa? Cruel though this may sound, this is the way things are. In medicine, as in government, the needs of the many must override the needs of the few. —I'm afraid that you must be the physician to your son. —You and God—and I believe this—you with His help must heal him.''

"That will be two dollars American, please," said Dr. Hoffmann, placing the medicines upon the counter. One little round canister, one small glass phial, each meticulously labeled in a florid Germanic script I could not decipher. In them—and in God—I must put my trust. But what trust could I put in this Teutonic mountebank, whose pudgy little fingers picked up my money as easily as they tickled melodies from a keyboard? I hated him for his callousness.

Outside the show window with its hoard of writing paper, ledgers, and commonplace books which so long ago had lured me into Hoffmann's store, I thanked Dr. Judd for his kindness. I was trying to ask how I could pay him, digging in embarrassment for the right phrase, when he headed me off with a smile. "Don't think of it, my boy. I need no payment—certainly not in gold. I can only hope—as I shall pray, for your son and for you—that my suggestions will be effective.—But if you should entertain a sense of obligation to me, I shall ask you to do something for me whenever you think back on this day: do you stop, in your appointed round, to help a fellow human being in distress. I am old enough to have learned that Christian concern, not gold, is the most precious thing on earth.—But that is for the future. Now there is one more matter I must speak of, before we part. I dared not mention it in the presence of Brother Hoffman, for this is heresy to haoles.''

Like a conspirator plotting against his own government, he made certain that no one could overhear him. "Perhaps among the native medicines there will be one which can save your son. I myself have tried many of these remedies, in my early days here with the Mission. Most of them are no better than our American simples, and a few are downright useless, if not actually dangerous. But some are excellent for their purposes. When you get home send for the nearest native physician. He may well surprise you with his knowledge and his treatments. And you, of course, for your sake, you must leave nothing undone that, were it done, might help the boy." He took my hand in both of his. "I wish you well, Mr. Bristol, and I ask God's blessing upon you and your son. I hope everything ends happily for you.—For I know too well how grievous it is, to lose a much-beloved son."

When he went away I understood how earth must feel after a great storm has harried it: battered and blasted and bruised it may be, by thunder and lightning and wind, but it is also soothed by the merciful rain that follows, and it is quieted.

All the way up Fort Street I walked to the memory of a verse I'd charged my pupils to take to heart, but never thought to apply to myself:

> Of all the Causes that conspire to blind
> Man's every judgment and misguide the mind,
> What the weak head with strangest bias rules
> Is Pride, the never-ending voice of fools . . .

Yet hope, like pride, is not easily downed. Still ruled enough by bias not to heed the good doctor's word, this solemn fool wasted another hour in running after the unattainable.

The first charitable bleeder to whom I applied drew back as from a lunatic. "All the gold in these-heah Sammidge Ilins would not induce me to venchah across yondah mountins," he declared. "Now you git out from heah. Ahm late foah mah dinnah." The second Samaritan to the suffering reclined in a darkened parlor, drinking his dinner. While I put my request, he, bothering not to hide the bottle, thinking not of sharing it, improvised a secular oratorio from fragments of prayers and sailors' oaths, set to the music of sniffles, gurgles, and moans. "Grief, muh boy, grief," he intoned when I was done. " 'Tis the natural state of man. The world is full of it, these islands most of all. Never saw a people so willin' to die as these kanakas. A shame, too, a rotten filthy shame. 'Cause they're so— so damned beautiful . . ." Hoisting the whiskey to his lips with one palsied hand, he waved me off with the other. " 'What is Virtue but a Medicine?' " he was singing as I left him to his pickling, " 'and Vice but a Wound?' "

From far and near churchbells were ringing a glad midday. Having failed in my search for a dedicated physician among these quacksalvers and charlatans, I was left with one last hope. "Now where in this putrescent Hell will Niele be?" I asked the dust of Beretania Street. I got no better response from passersby, but a dealer in coffins and tombstones—who, generous to a fault, advertised the offer of a free bowl of coffee with each sale he concluded—happened to know him. "He's a busy man. Hard to say where he'll be. You'd best start by asking his wife. They live in that big house back there, on the corner of Richards Street. Look for the yard with the hibiscus hedge."

The house, a rambling assemblage of bedrooms growing out of a central cottage, looked more like an inn than a home. It was freshly painted in gray and green and black, not whitewashed (or neglected) as are most of Honolulu's dwellings; and the wide yard beyond the hibiscus hedge was as neat as the deck of an American ship-of-war. The size of the establishment unsettled me, for I had imagined that the little fellow would be living in a little house, tucked away on some nameless side street or other. A little house it should be, with a little silent wife in it, and tiny merry daughters, full of chatter and giggles. Like those two dancing-girls who were their friends. With Niele guarding their virtue, I jeered, as I mounted the flight of stairs 'neath the carriage-port, and knocked at the high front door of a mansion which could not possibly be his.

The verandah quaked as heavy footsteps made their unhurried passage from the back of the house. The great door swung open. Filling the entry was a formidable woman. Solid flesh swelled the gray calico Mother Hubbard, as square in the shoulders as a dory's stern.

"Yes?" she asked, not concealing her suspicion.

"Mrs. Nihoa?" I inquired, very politely, convinced I'd knocked at the wrong door, or, at the least, had stirred up some sullen abigail. She nodded, definitely a woman of very few words. My goodness me, I borrowed his favorite expression, how did he ever get mixed up with this Xanthippe? The severe lines of her unmistakably Hawaiian face were not softened by hard green *haole* eyes, by the sweep of amazing copper-red hair combed straight back from the brow. "Forgive me for this intrusion," I said, doffing my hat belatedly as I told her my name and why I had called.

"Ah, yes, Mr. Bristol." Her smile, the superb teeth, the golden complexion suggested some of the beauty she must have possessed when she was young. "My husband has told me of his visit with you at Ka'a'awa.—Forgive me for being so mistrustful. These days we don't always know who is knocking at our door." Her English was excellent, her manners worthy of a professor's wife at Yale.

"I can well imagine," I assumed my most rueful smile, determined to make up in politeness what I lacked in presence.

"Mr. Nihoa has just left, I am sorry to say, after an early dinner. He said something about having to go to the waterfront this afternoon. A shipment coming in, or going out, I can't remember which, they come and go so often. Have you tried at his office?"

"No, ma'am. I was not aware that he had one."

"Oh, he is a very busy man," she said with a laugh, a toss of the head, "at least this is what he tells me. Try to find him there. On King Street, on the *mauka* side, just *'ewa* of Bethel Church. Do you know where that is?"

"Yes, ma'am, that I do."

"If you cannot find him there, I expect him home at five o'clock. Shall we look for you then?"

"I'm afraid not, ma'am. I'm in a great hurry, unfortunately, and I must go right back to Ka'a'awa."

"Ah, he will be sorry to miss you, of this I am certain. But I hope you will find him now. He will be so disappointed if you do not."

"Thank you, ma'am," I said, backing down the stairs, "I shall go at once."

"*Aloha*," she called, "and please come again, when you return to town."

This Niele is full of surprises, I grumbled, as I pushed my way through the crowded streets. A man of substance, with a hotel for a house, an impressive wife, a thriving business, even an office. And all along I'd considered him a poor little man, "a retired *kahu*, so to speak," who lived on a pension from Alex. The more I thought the more I realized how many were the gaps in my knowledge about Niele—and how patronizing had been my estimate of him. Naturally, I put the blame upon him. The more I recalled the day of his visit, when he'd ridden exhausted into my yard, as though he had just that moment arrived from no less a starting-point than Honolulu, the more I suspected that the man had dealt me a whole pack of lies, from beginning to end. Not for the first time since I'd left Ka'a'awa I wondered about his absolutely incomprehensible silence concerning Kaneikapule and the part he'd played in bringing the boy to Kanemilohai. Now why did he make such a mystery of that, I snarled, growing all the more irked with the man's duplicity and with my inability to solve this puzzle. Just wait 'til I see him. By God! Look out for squalls!—I'll pull the truth out of him!

His office door, distinguished most elegantly with a shiny brass plate, proclaimed the worth of Hiram Nihoa, Esq. The big glass window repeated the message in letters of gold. Hanging behind the glass pane of the door a handwritten sign, full of flourishes and embellishments, its Cs looking like foresails bellying in the wind, informed the observant, in two languages:

OUT TO LUNCH
Will return at 3 o'clock

Very definitely a most busy man, I acknowledged, both amused and annoyed.

A couple of native youths—the kind who know everything and tell all, for a price—were lounging against the wall of THE HIRAM NIHOA BLDG, 1850. Their long locks were pomaded and combed to the last ornate curl, their bodies were stuffed into tight trousers of striped tweed and shirts of brilliant red flannel. But they were Hawaiian enough to forswear the extremes of foreign fashion: no stocks bound their throats, no shoes encased the big broad feet.

"And where does this great man eat his lunch?" I asked the excitable pair.

The one shucked off the effort of replying. The other hunched his shoulders and, with a leer, said, "Try Palama."

"Palama?" I echoed, not seeing the connection. Whereupon both broke into laughter, bleating like goats, and the garrulous fellow made a sign which means one thing only, the world around.

Damned little liar! I went off in a temper. I'll waste no more time or thought on him. As I hurried down King Street, back to the Black Sea and its wanton denizens, I came upon another native youth, as splendidly got up as were his peers. With a stick of charcoal he was calmly inditing upon a whitewashed wall a tender message to his lady-love:

EVA DA HOA
SHE LIKE ---- HAOLE

Ever the schoolteacher, I paused and tapped him on the shoulder. "Revenge may be sweet, friend," I counseled him in English, seeing that he was so proficient in the language. "But your spelling: between us, it wants something. The verb is spelled with a U, not an O."

"*Haole*, you make beeg mistake," he said coldly, surveying me from head to foot. "I no want be yoa sweet fren'. Mahus on da next street."

That's Honolulu for you, I muttered, retreating from yet another debacle.

Back again on Mauna Kea Street, I bethought me of one last errand, just before I reached the livery stable. Marching into the bakery shop of Sam and Mow, I placed a good American ten-dollar gold-piece upon the greasy counter. Even as both Pakes leaped to serve me, I walked out on them. While they watched in bewilderment, I ripped that damned sign from its moorings in a rain of rusty chains and dried bird-dung, and smashed it to smithams upon a hitching post. No Celestial screams hindered the act, no cries for earthly police followed the felon. Smiling broadly, thoroughly satisfied, I tossed the gaping pair a salute of purest good will, and continued on my way.

CHAPTER 30.

THE RETURN

As eager as I to leave the fleshpots of Honolulu, Drummer sped up the long valley of Nuʻuanu. But even he had to slow down to a Canterbury pace on the Kaneʻohe side of the trail: we wasted almost half an hour on that obstacle to travelers.—Some day when I have the time, I swear, I'm going to take a few kegs of gunpowder and blast out a passable road down that cliffside. Two hundredweight of powder, ten men to shovel away the loosened dirt and shattered rock, would give us a road along which we could drive a haywain. But nobody in the Government seems to have thought of doing this little favor for the few people who live on Oʻahu's windward shore. The needs of the many override the hopes of the few, as I've learned to my cost. That's why I myself will have to hack that road out of the mountainside.

At the foot of the trail, where Drummer and I stopped to wet our throats in the brook, the sour smell of wet ashes hung over the glen. Someone had set fire to the old grass shack there, abandoned even before I'd come to Oʻahu. Good riddance to bad rubbish, I thought. It was always a blot on the landscape, and should have been burned years ago. Already fresh green leaves upon the trees, long runners of vines and grasses on the ground, were healing the wound in the jungle.

Just so, I vowed, would we heal the sore on Kaneikapule's arm. We aren't defeated yet. First I'll try the medicines Dr. Judd is recommending. I'll call in every native physician for miles around and put every one of them to work. I'll pray, by God, I'll pray. With my prayers added to Dr. Judd's, how can that Omnipotent One deny us? And—the grim thought hit so suddenly that I reeled —if worse comes to worst, I'll cut off the boy's arm, at the shoulder. I've carved up enough sides of beef to know how to use a knife, to be able to find the joint, the tendons which bind arm to shoulder-socket. I'd seen enough amputations performed upon those pitiable sailors with gangrenous arms or legs, who lay screaming with pain upon the pallets of the American Hospital when I too lay among them, hoping to die of the lung fever. And, because I would have to do it all alone, I'd learn how to apply the cautery of red-hot knife-blades to the bleeding stump, in order to seal his severed flesh and halt the flow of his blood. For Kaneikapule's sake, I would do even this. Better a one-armed boy living, than a whole boy dead.

By the time we galloped into Kane'ohe I had worked out in my mind every detail of the grisly operation. A few days earlier I could not have borne to bleed the lad, but must whine about sending for Brother Doison to do it. Now, such is the power of the will, the strength of need, I was prepared to fight off Death with a butcher's knife for a sword and determination for a shield.

I'd planned to snatch a bite to eat in Kane'ohe, while Drummer rested for an hour or so. But when the filthy old Irishman who keeps the sole chophouse in that rickety hamlet wanted five dollars for two boiled eggs and a bowl of cornmeal mush, I told him where he could stow the lot and stalked out in a dudgeon. Not until we ran into a squadron of Her Fat Highness' tribute-collectors, clotting up the road, did I understand the reason for the publican's attempt at robbery. Doubly enraged by the thought of her depredations, I charged straight for the pirates, scattering them and their booty to right and left. It was a cheap show of disapproval, but I enjoyed the moment thoroughly.

Nonetheless, sight of all those victuals made me hungrier than ever. Slowing Drummer into a canter, as we approached the ramshackle encampment where Ruth the Gross and her latest stud wallowed in sin and luxury, I considered calling upon her to feed me in return for my hospitality when she and her locusts swarmed past Ka'a-'awa. But I knew that the stolen food would stick in my craw. Preferring honorable hunger, we dashed past her sleeping pickets. If Kane'ohe or Kikiwelawela had boasted such a thing of civilization as a whitewashed wall, I would have stopped to scrawl a borrowed message that would have rejoiced the countryside. It could not have told her people anything new, but it might have helped them to bear their misery.

Naturally, at He'eia the high tide was in. This meant walking Drummer either through the sea, where the water would rise to his cruppers, or through the marsh, where the muck would reach to his belly. I chose the cleaner passage through the sea. When we came again to the dry road, after almost a mile of slow going, we were exhausted.

We stopped at the point of Kahalu'u, where the bay curves inland. Far away, across the shallow lagoon, the gaunt ridge of Kanehoalani loomed like a fortress wall above the distant shore. Beyond it, as in Castle Perilous, lay my given-son, waiting for succor. With hard riding we could reach him soon after dark. But first we must rest. On the bank above the smooth waters of the bay we lay down for the hour I allotted us.

When I awoke the sky was saddening into evening. Three hours of daylight had been lost. Too dejected to curse, too angered to quit, I forced us on our way. The demons of darkness gathered around, filling me with foreboding. And up, out of the well of memory, came a fragment from Milton to taunt me:

> Now came still Evening on, and Twilight gray
> Had in her sober Liverie all things clad.
> They viewed the vast immeasurable Abyss,
> Outrageous as a Sea, dark, wasteful, wilde . . .

After Ka'alaea no light from earth or sky helped us in our passage across the dark waste: no fishermen's flares on the reef served to guide us, even the stars were hid. We reached Ka'a'awa long after midnight, and only Drummer saw when we came before my gate. Scarcely able to move, I wiped the sweat from the faithful steed, cooled him, bedded him down in his stall. Then, without breath to blow out the lantern, I sank into the haystack.

The roosters of Ka'a'awa must be the first creatures on O'ahu to herald the dawn of each new day. Saint Francis himself could not have enjoyed the matins which greeted this fiery morn. The sky, aflame with reds and golds and purples, seemed to announce a message of great import to the people of Ka'a'awa from their god. Looking out upon all that splendor, I read in it an omen for good.

Like a priest of Aesculapius, for in truth I thought of myself as such, I cleansed my body with a bath in the cool pond, scraped the dark beard from my face in the light of the unclouded sun, garbed myself in clothes taken fresh from the line. Breakfast, thanks to the providence of my sable Ceres, was properly vegetable, suitably spare: cold taro, overripe bananas, and water dipped from the spring.

Feeling like that purified priest from a temple of healing, I walked up the hill, bearing the medicines which were to heal Kaneikapule's wound. At the crest of the rise I looked down upon the placid sea, up to the life-giving sun, inland to the sacred mountain, so remote at the end of this beautiful valley and yet so near. On such a day as this, full of peace, full of promise, not knowing why I must go, I had made my journey to the mountain. Now I understood the reason: *he* wanted to test me, to learn if I were worthy of the trust he wished to place in me. Now, too, I understood how a primitive pagan must feel in the presence of awe. Saying the unsayable name, I spoke to him: "Give peace to your sons, O Kane." The answering peace in the valley told me that he had heard. Making the last concession, I lifted my face to the New God above: "Help him, O Lord," I prayed, "save him, I beg you."

As I approached the household of Kanemilohai the doubts and fears of yestereve were gone. The peace in my heart told me that all would be well.

Kanemilohai and Maka-o-Hina were sitting beside the boy. In the lamplight they seemed to be two statues, carved by an artist who had captured in burnished wood the beauty of love, the repose of faith.

"Good morning to you two," I called out, bringing my cheer into the quiet house.

"Ah! You are here!" cried Maka-o-Hina. "And the doctor? Where is the doctor?—Did he not come with you?"

"No, but—," I started to explain, holding out the medicines toward her.

"*Auwe! Auwe!*" she shrieked, "then is he lost to us!

Auwe . . . Auwe . . . ," she wailed, clawing at her cheeks, pulling the long hair down over her face. The horrid sight, the wild keening, froze the blood in my veins, drove the fatuous smile from my lips.

"The sores," said Kanemilohai. His flesh, too, had wasted away, the noble face was slack with weariness and grief. "The sickness: it has eaten into his mind. No more does he awaken."

Once again I sank to my knees beside that low bed. Wailing still, Maka-o-Hina drew away the sheet which covered the boy. Those insatiable sores had leaped from arm to chest and belly, were gnawing away his throat, his cheek, his eyes.

"The maggots," said Kanemilohai. "They are crawling . . ."

Seeing him lying there, his beauty destroyed, his life ebbing away beyond the rescue of medicines, beyond the help of prayer, I could not even moan. Beaten and broken, too betrayed to curse, I laid the useless medicines at his feet. Without a word I stood up and went out from that house of sorrows.

Stony-hearted, I sat on the verandah of my shack, waiting for the wailing to tell me when he died.

At midday, when the brutal triumphant sun stood at its zenith, he died.

Not wanting to go back, but knowing that I must, for the sake of Kanemilohai and Maka-o-Hina, I slumped in my chair, lacking the strength to move. Until the wailing turned to screaming, and a pillar of thick black smoke rose up from the house of the Kanehoalani.

Shouting now, in dread, I ran up the path. As always, I arrived too late. The great house was a mass of flames. Its grass walls were burning away. Through the sheets of fire I saw the forms of Kanemilohai and Maka-o-Hina crouched over the body of the boy. Tufts of burning thatch fell down upon them like searing rain, like fiery spit from the god who, disdaining them, destroyed them.

"Stop that!" I yelled at a wailing retainer, who was slashing at his back and chest and cheeks with a shark's-tooth knife. When I seized his hand to wrest the knife away, he slipped from my grasp and, streaming with blood, fled toward the temple. A few distraught servants were throwing water from calabashes upon the nearer huts. Others ran about aimlessly, screaming, pulling their hair, rending the strips of clothing still hanging upon their bodies.

Amid all this madness, one man stood apart, arms folded, calmly observing the raging fire, the crazed people. "How did it happen?" I asked.

"Kanemilohai did it," he answered. "With his own hands he struck the fire. 'Kane has spoken,' he said to us. 'Our line is ended. Why should we live?' With his own hands he carried the fire to the navel-thatch of his house. And we could not prevent him."

He started to walk away. But the truth flared too violently, even in him. Turning furiously upon me, he raised a hard fist. "You damned foreigners!" I did not flinch. Why should I, a man who cared no more for life? "The troubles you have brought upon us!" he cried, lips curled in anger, hands raised in wrath. The broken tooth and the jagged scar upon his chest told me who he was. In the midst of grief and turmoil I was strangely pleased to feel the hurt of his hate. It was savage, it was wounding, it strengthened the hurt swelling within me. Thrusting his big fist before my face, he snarled, "You will not rest until the last Hawaiian is dead."

I offered him the shark's-tooth knife, still wet with another man's blood.

He did not take it. He did not kill the intruder. He made the mistake that too many Hawaiians have made since the first accursed *haole* came to these islands. He turned away, and allowed his destroyer to live.

The fire burned the lashings which held in place the heavy crossbeams, the purlins, rafters, and ridge-poles. Slowly, grandly, as though it took pride in this last service to a long line of mighty chiefs, the great blazing house fell in upon the treasures it held.

Only then did I weep my grief for the family of Kane-milohai, for my given-son Kaneikapule.

As I went back to my empty house all the other thatched huts were burning.

And the people, daubed with blood and mud and ashes, were kicking down the stones of the temple.

CHAPTER 31.

THE MIDDEN OF THE SEA

I do not remember much about the next two days, and I do not like to think about the little I do remember. Most of the time I was sodden with brandy or dazed with laudanum. Driven inward upon myself, I brutalized mind and body in the need to punish myself because I grieved —and because I hated myself with a hatred far greater than the simple bitterness I knew that the people of Kaʻa-ʻawa must be feeling for me.

"The man who needs no one else is either a god, having everything within himself, or a wild beast." Thus spake Aristotle, long centuries ago. But I remembered him not. And, by denying both gods and men, even as I denied myself, I became worse than a wild beast.

I blamed myself for the death of Kaneikapule and his grandparents. My logic was irrefutable: if only I had not misjudged the vaccination, in its earliest stages, he could have been treated in time, he could have been saved. And I loathed myself to the depths of my soul because once again I had been foolish enough to give my love to someone, only to have it blighted and destroyed. "More fool, you," I howled, over and over again, as, during those days and nights of madness, I marveled that I could have been so trusting. "You should have known that everything you touch must wither, everything you love must die," I roared. "Once before you learned this lesson. But did you remember it? No, you did not. You allowed your mind to weaken, your heart to soften. And soon—oh, the shame of it!—you believed again in Heaven. You even fell so low as to pray again, crawling like a fawning pup, on your belly, before that faithless Kane, who would not lift a finger to help his children, to that jealous, punitive Jehovah, the most traitorous of all—" Pfaughhh! When I remembered how I had prayed, had *actually prayed*, to those implacable monsters, I bellowed in fury and writhed in an ecstasy of disgust, beating my head against the walls, upon the filthy floor, until blood mingled with my tears.

Raging at gods in whom I could not believe, and yet could not disbelieve, sobbing with pity for myself, crying for death, I smashed the furniture into splinters, ripped the pages from my books, drank to the dregs the poison of despair, but I did not die. Grief did not crack my heart, tears did not choke me. Nor did the gods I reviled blast me with lightnings or slay me with wrath. I did not die.

This is mystery enough for any man to ponder for a full lifetime. But I managed to cap it with another.

The moment arrived when the last drop of brandy was wrung from its bottle. Lifting the glass as though it were a chalice filled with sacramental wine, I said, "To Death. To Peace." With absolute certainty I knew that the time had come to end this wasted life. "Doomed," I blubbered, gulping down the salute to Death.

Gall and wormwood were in it, sulfur and brimstone, mixed with the heat of Hell. With it I tasted the greatest bitterness a man can know—the realization that, by his own deeds, he has cheated himself of happiness, robbed his life of meaning. Suffused with this bitterness, I saw again the course of my life and the cause of my ruin. By striving to be good, I have become evil. By giving my love, I have lost the ones I've loved. In seeking happiness, I have received only sorrow. In fearing God, I have denied Him. And in denying Him, I have shown my need of Him. And He has answered my need by turning His face away, by denying me His forgiveness and His mercy. "Doomed," I sobbed, not asking why, for I knew why I was accursed . . .

The sea beckoned. Wading through broken books, shattered chairs, pieces of glass and china, I went to hasten my judgment by keeping my tryst with the sea. Not with Melissa, for she was no longer there. But with Death in the midden of the sea. All the rubbish of earth finds its way into this cesspool sea, I reasoned. *Ergo*: it will take me. Unshaven, filthy, stinking, slobbering, a superlative specimen of the superior white race, I went to cast this attractive package of hair and hide and crap and corruption into the sewer of the sea. This time, I knew, it must welcome me.

Twice before had I been saved from the sea. For a man who is as in love with death as I am, one such deliverance might be reckoned an accident, and two rescues might be considered less a proof of my durability than a witness to the attention of bystanders. But what am I to make of three pluckings from the watery grave? Are they signs of the workings of grace, of a mercy I am too stupid to comprehend? Or are they merely evidences of an invincible ineptitude, before which all the laws of Nature bend, and for which a dispensation from their consequences is jesting Nature's recompense?

Upon this mystery too I ponder, for I do not yet know why I have been thrice saved. And I shall be a sadder fool, and no wiser a man, if before I die I do not learn the answer to this riddle. To learn it I continue to live.

The first of these occasions—Oh, my heart! Even now I cry out against the cruelty of it, and the pain! How can I bear to write of it?

—Helpless in the storm, our ship was driven by wind and waves toward the reef off Waikiki. Not a league from the harbor of Honolulu she would never reach, little more than a furlong from the safety of O'ahu's shore, she was hurled upon the adamantine rocks. She foundered within a few minutes. As the great breakers crashed upon her, sweeping her deck from stern to bow, we clung to the rails and shrouds, to each other, to life. Melissa was in the fold of my arm, our child was in her womb. I fought, I prayed, for them, for us. Until the immense wave came which, like a swipe from God's own hand, tore her from my grasp. She knew why she was taken away, she *knew*. Without a cry, without a struggle, like a mermaid borne on foam, she was carried backwards away from me. In the moment before she went over the side she sent me a smile of farewell, a last message of love. Weighted down by her heavy dress and the burthen of our child, she sank, she was gone.

It happened in an instant, but I remember it forever. And I remember too how the madness struck me. Crying into the face of Heaven, I cursed God for doing this to me. Then, willingly, I loosed my grip upon the rail, to follow her into the sea.

But I was not to escape so soon. The same great breaker which should have taken me to Melissa's side struck the ship with such violence that the mainmast broke above me. A falling spar knocked me senseless, and in its tangle of lines and sheets I was washed overboard. The flotsam carried me to shore, like a corpse in a canvas sling. And there, without my knowing, people on the beach pulled me back to unwanted life. I awoke in that wretched American Hospital in Honolulu, half dead, neither injured enough to die nor strong enough to return at once to the sea. Pretending to accept the condolences of other survivors and the sanctimonious comfortings of missionary vultures, I bided my time.

Weeks later—after recovering first from my cracked skull and the lung fever, then from the bloody flux which is enjoyed by every fortunate inmate of that foul hospice for the destitute—I was able to get up from the pallet of rotten straw which the American consul calls a bed. Little more than a scarecrow made of skin and bones and rags, I stumbled about, regaining the use of my legs, planning my reunion with Melissa. Never did I forget my resolve, never did I give up an iota of my hate, for life, for this foetid island, most especially for the God who had robbed me of my beloved.

No one noticed, because no one cared, when I left the hospital yard. I wanted to go to the beach where she had been taken away but, not knowing how to find it, I did not search for that special shore and looked only for the sea. I found it: beautiful and calm and warm, as alluring as the woman it was holding for me. I did not hate the sea, because she was in it. Filled with joy, thinking only of her, I stepped from the land into her embrace.

This sea! It is as treacherous as God, as unreachable as happiness. It called to me from the far side of a wide shallow reef. I did not see the reef when I made my hero's departure from the shore. Naturally, I was exhausted long before I could cross the coral plain to reach deep water. But where at last I fell there was water enough to drown in. Gratefully I sank into it. The lapping waves were soft and tender, like the touch of Melissa's fingers. Seeking her fragrance, her kisses sweeter than honey, I opened my lips, to taste her, to breathe her in.

Strong arms lifted me up. A deep voice asked, "Where are you going, my friend?"

"Let me go, let me die," I begged, trying to slip back into the water.

"And why should you die now, a man whose life has only begun?—When you are an old man death will come soon enough." Opening my eyes, I beheld the tawny youth who would not let me die. "Come with me," he said, drawing me toward the land. Without protest, without a thought for shame, I went with him. The luminous eyes, full of compassion, the gentle voice, the immense power emanating from him: I confess it: I thought he was a dark-skinned Christ come out upon the water to save me.

He called instructions in Hawaiian to naked companions standing near. Immediately they turned and waded to shore. There, in the shade of wind-bent trees, other naked men waited with horses and pack-mules. By the time my rescuer and I gained the beach the men had dressed and were saddling the horses.

After he was clothed, dazzling in white shirt and trousers, the youth came to me, where I sat drying out on the warm sand. "Feeling better?" he asked, holding out his hand. "I am called Alex."

"And I—" To my credit, I want to make plain, I balked at the falsehood, knowing that he was one who should hear only the truth, but forced by pride to continue the deception "—I am Saul Bristol."

"A good strong name," he said, "marks a good strong man." Not knowing yet how, to Hawaiians, words themselves are full of power, I wondered why he should say this of me, a man so weak.

He made me a guest in his own home, he restored my body's health and revived its sick spirit. I saw that where such a man lived I, too, could live for yet a while. But not until the second day of my stay, and not from him, did I learn that he was Heir Apparent to the King. When, not at his urging, he heard the part of my story which I chose to tell and understood my wish for solitude, he arranged with Hopkins for me to work on the ranch at Kahuku.

I stayed there for almost a year, because I liked Kahuku and the work. But whenever Milord Hopkins was in residence, time spent at Kahuku hit me like a season in Bedlam: he talks too much, for one thing; and, even worse, he has such a fondness for society that he is always accompanied by a crowd of gabbling friends and parasites, their harlots, jesters, dancing-girls, and servants. Before the year was out I could endure neither Hopkins nor his caravanserai at Kahuku. The moment he mentioned that he was thinking of adding the valley of Kaʻaʻawa to his dukedom, I jumped at the chance to manage this new venture for him.

Here, after more than two years of labor, during which I found a kind of contentment and was about to make a truce with grief, the month of disaster came, when once again everything I cherished was taken away. Once again the wheel had turned, and in turning had crushed me, as in India, they say, the wheels upon the great wagon of Juggernaut crush the victims in his path.

In the wreckage of my life, in the emptiness of my house, I writhed in torment, gnashed my teeth, macerated my soul with the sour juices of hate. Remembering Job, I searched in him for the meaning to his disasters, and to mine. Until I read:

Why died I not from the womb? why did I not give up the ghost when I came out of the belly?

Why did the knees prevent me? or why the breasts that I should suck?

For now I should have lain still and been quiet, I should have slept: then had I been at rest.

That was when I ripped up my books, so full of words, so barren of meaning. Those pages from Job were but the first to fall to the floor. All others of my meager possessions had been destroyed. The books went last because, always the clerk, I had thought they were the most precious. When they too were gone, I had nothing left to destroy but myself.

Raving mad, I rushed out from the shambles of my house. With the cunning of madness, I inspected the beach. This time, I was determined, no one would keep me from my goal. The shore was as empty and desolate as myself, as indifferent to my fate as the uncaring sun had been to Kaneikapule's. Beyond the narrow strand lay the open sea, its waves rolling endlessly in. Far to the right, Ulupaʻu fought its unavailing struggle against those pitiless waves, like a foolish man trying to survive in a sea of calamities. No wide reef was here, to deny me the embrace of those great waves. And Alex was not here, to save me with the delusion that someone cared. No one cared, on earth or in heaven. Ever since I had returned home from the flaming pyre of the Kanehoalani, I had not seen a single person. After that evening—when they left food for me on the doorstep, as though I were a beast in its cage, and I had kicked the stuff into the yard—that slut Kamanele, that whoreson Makana, had abandoned me.

No one cared. I was free to go at last, to give my eyes and ears and lips to the scavenging crabs, my corrupt and sinful flesh to the teeth of eels and sharks, my bones to those tiny creatures which would make coral of them, and sterile sand . . .

Without looking back at the valley of sorrows and griefs, I stepped from the land into the sea.

Well, needless to say, I didn't get wet above the knees. By the pitchfork of Neptune! Hawaiians, it would seem, make a veritable career, a lifelong ministry, of denying Saul Bristol the chance to drown.

The instant my feet were met by an incoming surge, Makana came whooping down the slope of sand and threw himself into the water with a noisy splash. In all my months at Ka'a'awa the imp had never been so bold. Suspecting the worst, I turned to look back.

Sure enough, out from the *naupaka* bushes came old Makua, trudging through the sand, sober as a gravedigger and twice as slow.

"Nice day," he said companionably when he stood beside me.

"What the hell are you doing here?" I croaked. "Why are you not working?"

"I am working," he beamed, not at all impressed by the notorious Bristol temper.

"Working? Here?" roared I. "When did I tell you to make pasture-land out of the ocean?"

"Oh," he said airily, "this duty is given to me by another boss. I work now for Kamanele."

Unable to believe my ears, I all but fainted in a surfeit of anger. "Kamanele? And is she now the chief of Ka'a'awa?"

"No," he looked me square in the eye, "she is not the chief of Ka'a'awa. Ka'a'awa is without a chief since you went into your house and did not come out again, roaring and thrashing about within it, like a wounded boar hiding inside its hole in the ferns. No, Kamanele is not our chief. Kamanele is only the one who has told us that we must watch over you, to see that you come to no harm."

The cesspit sea tugged at my feet, its stink of rotting seaweed and putrefying fish was strong in my nostrils, while Makua sang a siren's song from the land. 'Today is my turn to watch with Makana. And I am glad that I am the one to offer you my hand. I ask that you take this hand of friendship."

"How can you speak of friendship?" I cried, drawing back, "for me, the angry *haole*? For me, the hated *haole*, the bringer of troubles?—Go away. You tell me lies. Go away and leave me alone. You will soon be rid of me."

He nodded agreeably. "Aye, you have cause to think this thought. Once, perhaps, we did fear you, and speak of you as the angry *haole*. Can you wonder at this, you who were so hard of heart that you would give no love to us, you who were so proud of mind that you would take no love from us?—But that was long ago. Now you are changed. And so are we changed. We are not blind in our eyes, we are not deaf in our ears. And, although we may be unlearned, we are not small-hearted. We have seen how you cared for us when we were sick, how you have willingly taught us the new ways of caring for the land, of caring for ourselves. We who were without purpose in our lives are now given purpose because of you."

On his knees at our feet Makana scooped holes in the sand, which the waves almost immediately filled up again.

"But most of all we have seen how you did strive for the life of the grandson of our chief. And, in your showing of love for the family of Kanemilohai, we saw how we had wronged you by thinking that you were a man without love in your heart. Then we understood what long ago we should have known: that you are angered with us as a father is with children who do not heed his worry for them. That your heart is not hard but is empty, and yearns for love."

All this while he had been observing me closely, seeing how I accepted his argument. Now he looked away, to the land, to the high mountain peaks. "Why this is so we do not know. Nor do we ask. It is not our business to know why you are a man so burdened with sorrows. Yet such a burden is one which is known to us, because it is one which is carried by all men. Are Hawaiians any different from foreigners in this? Are you the only one who suffers? We can not think so."

He faced me squarely now. "This emptiness of the heart: it can be filled in time. It always is. That is the way of the heart, the most deceiving of all things. Like the squid, like the gourd of a man, it can be small and shrunken at one moment, and it can be large and full of strength in the next moment. But the pride of your mind," he shook his head, "alas, for this we can do nothing. This is a sickness which comes from within a man. And only that man can cure it. Perhaps this cure will come to you in time, perhaps it will never come. The medicine for this sickness we do not know with certainty. But I will say this for all of us who dwell in Ka'a'awa. I will give you this thought for your mind to think upon, as an opening medicine is given to a person with a costive bowel: we do not want you to leave us. We need you—"

"You *need* me?"

"We do. Now more than ever before."

"Why?" The mountains swayed, Makua's grizzled head was blurred, my legs trembled, not from resisting the pull from the sea.

"Who will be the father to us, if you go away? Who will guard us against the bad things that come with these new times? We ask you to stay, for the sake of the few of us who remain."

The stone of my heart began to beat again, the fortress

of pride opened wide its gates. "I am ashamed, Makua," I said, unable to look at him.

"Aye, that is perhaps proper," he said. "But waste no more than two breaths upon it. After those are spent, let the shame be gone: cast it into the air, to be blown away by the winds, to be purified by the sun."

"And I am made humble by your thoughts.—The pride of which you spoke: you have given me a medicine for it. And I am glad that you are the physician who gives it."

"Ah," he smiled broadly now, "such was my hope. And this medicine: is it also good for the heart?"

"A strange thing has happened to me, Makua: the one medicine seems to be a remedy for many afflictions. The heart is no longer in pain. It beats stronger now. It will not fail me."

"Those are good words to hear. They show how great is the *mana* in *aloha*.—Then I think we will leave you now, Makana and I. I think perhaps our work for today is ended."

"Wait, Makua," I asked for his hand with mine. "Let us go up together."

Let us go up together, to the land and to life.

CHAPTER 32.

THE PESTILENCE

Slowly, not without much pain, I returned to life. Like the people, I tried to exchange old ways for new. A firm resolution, founded on Makua's message, tided me through the bouts of despair which were the legacy of my sorrows. But habits are much more easily broken, I found, than is pride. Because now I was aware of the enormity of my pride, I chipped at it continually, as a mason chisels at a stone, dressing it to proportions more seemly, if not to a thing of beauty.

In doing this I learned something consoling: that despair and grief, like joy and love, are but different faces to the hard core of pride which lies at the center of each man's nature. What is happiness but the pleasing of pride, what is love save the most delectable indulgence of this gratification? And what is sorrow but the denial of this indulgence, what is despair if it is not the loss of hope that pride's demands will ever be appeased?

Having learned this much about the meaning of life, I found living possible to endure. I lived because, I saw, Life was but another aspect of Death, as the shadowed face of the earth is to the lighted. Now I saw that I could wait for this tiny sphere of my self to turn through its one little cycle, until at last, having turned and turned, it came out at the place just right, and gained the darkness of peace. Nothing mattered anymore, except the manner of waiting. And I waited, patiently and passively, just as at the height of each bright blazing day this valley of Ka'a-'awa, this little crack upon the globe of the turning earth, waits for the dark of night. When I am an old man, death will come soon enough.

No doubt prophets and philosophers have made this discovery often enough. And I suspect that, could I search among the mazes in melancholical Burton, I would find the same conclusion attested by a hundred tags and examples. With this lesson, as with so many worthy others, a man is like a youth: he can read about it or be told about it and be too dull to perceive it. He must learn it for himself, out of his own distresses. Now I wait to test the corollary: as pride diminishes, does wisdom move in to fill its place?

So much for the distilled essence of aging. If only so much vinegar did not come over with the spirit, the stuff might be more palatable to the young.—But what youth ever listened to his father?

In the shaping of my new self I was helped by work and by the knowledge—attested in deeds but never in words by the people of Ka'a'awa—that now we labored together for the common good. Although life gave me no joys, it did offer some satisfactions. These I knew would be the measure of my days, and I asked for nothing else. If I did not think much of life, at least I gave little thought to death.

The better to help myself, I never went to the seashore or to the place where the household of Kanemilohai had stood. In time I was able to look upon the mountain at the head of the valley and reduce it to nothing more than a thing of rocks and verdure, no different from the others which walled us in.

And the Three Fates, as I called the triplet of peaks rising above my house, still invited me. But not yet did I have the heart to climb them.

Thus did the quiet weeks go by. So, I thought, would pass the years, one after the other, without further trials either for me or for my friends in the valley. Behind the ramparts of Ka'a'awa's mountains we were almost completely shut off from the world beyond. We dwelled in a community much like one of those monastery villages in Europe after the fall of Rome. We were far from being a community of scholars, and most certainly we were not a society of monks. Two children were born to ranch families during those weeks: another girl-child was presented by his wife to Pordagee Joe, another son was slipped from Kamanele's commodious belly. This one took me utterly by surprise: I did not even know he was expected, until the moment Pi'opi'o called to announce his arrival. Sturdy Kamanele bore him between breakfast and dinner. All squeals and giggles, fuller of maternal delight than ever she'd seemed with the child, she was determined that I should miss no meal because of its birthing. While proud Pi'opi'o and Makana attended the babe, Kamanele prepared me my supper. I was too abashed to eat it.

Several other women were great with child. One of these was the wife of Linalina, the man with the broken tooth and the scar across his chest. Makua and he were my most valued assistants in our labors for the ranch. Even before I hired him—along with all of Kanemilohai's men of working age—I could tell from his manner that

Linalina nourished no hatred for me. That, too, had been burned away in the fire. The man who emerged was unalloyed gold.

Wanting for nothing, asking the world for nothing, we of Ka'a'awa dwelled in dignity and in peace. We enjoyed a good life, such as people everywhere might envy us.

But it could not last. There is no sanctuary from the world.

Late in May of 1853 a traveler along the coast-road told us that the smallpox had broken out in Honolulu. "From San Francisco it came, they are thinking," he said, "in the dirty clothes of miners sent to Honolulu to be washed. But, lo! More than gold dust has fallen out of those filthy rags." Within a week the first fugitives from town straggled into Ka'a'awa, some to stay with relatives or friends in our valley, some to move on to other refuges farther up the coast. Much as I feared these wanderers, I could not chase them away. I could only hope that they would not be touched with the plague.

A vain hope that was: two weeks later the scourge was loosed upon us.

"Alas," said Makua, when he told me that this new sickness had entered among our people, "this gold dust from California: it is a powerful thing, and evil. Now it has fallen upon us, like rain from a dry sky at sunset, and wheresoever it touches the skin small red sores are formed."

Much too soon these sores became filled with the gold of pus. And, overwhelmed with this unwanted wealth, the people suffered and died.

Kamanele's infant son was the first to go: a hideous screaming mass of sores, which lost their golden hue in turning bloody and black, he died three days after falling ill. Pordagee Joe's newborn daughter was lowered into a tiny grave. One by one, the families on the ranch, those in the village or scattered throughout the north side of the valley, knew the touch of death. The old perished as well as the young, the vaccinated along with those who had rejected Brother Doison's operation. Among those who succumbed were Pi'opi'o, the husband of Kamanele; Nohea, the aged mother of Makua; the pregnant wife of Linalina and their two children; and three youths from among my ranch-hands. Many a sinner escaped, while some of the saintly were taken. Wondrously distributed was the favor of Jehovah, surpassing all understanding was the election of his helper, the Angel of Death.

Once again I rode along the coast, from Ka'a'awa to La'ie, carrying my pouch of medicines, trying to treat the sick and to sustain the living. The medicines were useless. I was more successful at burying the dead. For many a family I was gravedigger as well as pastor. At some houses, where everyone had died and the corpses were too numerous for me to bury, I left them to rot on their mats. No one would disturb them, not even hungry dogs and pigs, and they had owned nothing that anyone would want to steal.

"*I will lift up mine eyes to the hills, from whence cometh my help*," I read over the shallow graves, for the sake of the living. Poor creatures. What else was left to them?

And for a whole month, unwilling to face a man whom haoles have robbed of everything, I went out of my way to avoid a meeting with Linalina.

I was not spared the experience of being harrowed to the depths of my soul. In the dying of every victim I was reminded of Kaneikapule's long dying. In the death of each native I saw the death of his nation. How could I answer the once-lovely maid who, as she moaned with pain, asked, "What have I done to deserve this death?" What could I say to soothe the once-splendid youth who, at sight of me, spewed out his heart's rage against me and all my kind? "You killers-of-men! What are you doing to me and my people? We have given you shelter. You have given us death." He cursed me, the accursed one, with his dying breath. I sat beside him until he died, and helped his weeping father dig the grave. But I read no message from my little black book over his body. As his father said, "his was not a natural death, but a death by outsiders."

Probably the only one to whom I brought comfort was a woman dying at Hau'ula. She had lost her husband to influenza a few months before, and an infant son to the smallpox. When I entered the house she was not too far gone to remember her only surviving child. "Take her," she begged, pointing to a half-starved, bescabbed little thing crouched in a corner. Why this three-year-old child should live while the mother died only whimsical Jehovah can say.

That was how little 'Opuhea rode with me, home to Ka'a'awa. I gave her to Kamanele, who welcomed her with vast hugs and sobbings of great joy. A plain, sad-eyed, quiet little girl, not too badly pock-marked, she became Kamanele's second shadow.

When, finally, in August we buried the last of Ka'a-'awa's victims, twenty-five of the valley's six-score inhabitants had died. Ka'a'awa's experience was repeated in most places throughout the Kingdom, before the pestilence ended in January of 1854. No one will ever know how many people sickened, or how many died. The Board of Health says that between 5,000 and 6,000 islanders perished, in the Kingdom's population of about 80,000.

But, as most of us are too well aware, these reports pertain only to towns and larger villages. The countryfolk who died in lonely homes and remote hamlets were never counted. In my opinion, the number of deaths was twice the official figure. The nation can spare none of them, and it will never recover from their loss. In 1778, when foreigners discovered these islands, about 300,000 people lived upon them in health and comfort, if not in a state of grace. Now, as I write, fewer than 70,000 Hawaiians remain. At this rate, the last Hawaiian will have disappeared from the face of the earth before this splendid century ends.

On a Sunday late in September, the King having declared it a day of national mourning and prayer, I joined the valley's Roman Catholic survivors in attending the services in Ka'a'awa's village chapel. I went not out of fear and trembling for an angry God, nor out of fondness for Father Armand and his mummery, but only to show our people that I shared their grief, if not their hope for divine clemency.

I had just returned to my house when Niele rode into the yard. I did not perceive him in the frail old man, slumped in his saddle, with silver-rimmed spectacles astride his nose, and a nimbus of pure white hair. Long before this day I had ceased to be interested in either the appearance or the conversation of wanderers who came through my gate. Even a good Samaritan wearies of his role. Wanting not to hear their tales of unvaried grief, I fed them, bedded them down in the stable if they wished to rest, and, as soon as was decent, sent them on their way. Not unschooled in woe, I have learned to succor the woeful with blinded eyes and deafened ears. If I was short-spoken, so were they, for none of us had any cause for cheer.

Thinking that this old man was only another exile from the city, I scarcely looked up from the book opened on my lap. Brother Doison had brought it to me, at my request, a week or so before. I was reading again the story of Job, this time in Hawaiian, seeking from him the secret of his patience. *Behold, happy is the man whom God correcteth*, Eliphaz the Temanite was lecturing at poor old Job, smitten with sore boils from the sole of his foot unto his crown, *therefore despise not thou the chastening of the Almighty. For he maketh sore, and bindeth up: he woundeth, and his hands make whole.*—You oily, slippery hypocrite, I was hissing into the ear of Job's comforter, when this other old man drew up at the foot of my stairs.

"*Aloha* to you, Saul Bristol," he said.

"*Aloha*," I replied curtly, not looking up from my reading. "Stop and rest a while, if you wish," I cocked a thumb toward the stable. Hoping he would take the hint, I lifted the book high, making it a barrier between me and everyone beyond its covers. *He shall deliver thee in six troubles*, I read, *yea, in seven there shall no evil touch thee.*

"Am I an enemy, then, a thing of evil, then, that you will not welcome me?" The old man's cracked and petulant voice seemed to come out of the pages of my book. Forced to look, I descried at last the person he wanted me to see, glaring at me from atop his nag.

"Land o' Goshen!—Niele!" The Bible slipped to the floor, I stood up, ready to embrace him. But even as I rushed down the stairs second thoughts swept away my pleasure. This philanderer who betrayed his wife, this man of many words who used them to hide truths from me, this master of deceit and duplicity: why should I be glad to see him, this man I could not trust?

"Welcome, Mr. Nihoa," I offered him a cold hand, a false smile. "This is a surprise. I did not recognize you."

"So I see," he said acidly, giving me the reins instead of his hand. "Do not worry. I do not have the smallpox. And I shall not burden you with my company for long. I remember how much you dislike visitors."

He dismounted stiffly, sighing with the aches and pains of a man who has been long on horseback. I was astonished to see how much he had aged in seven months.

Feeling sorry for him, I tried to make amends. "Don't be so tetchy, please. I apologize for not recognizing you.— And come in and rest a bit. Dinner will be ready soon."

He stared at me glumly. "You speak the same words as before. But now there is no heart in them.—Chah! I wish I could go back to that time and—by my words and by my deeds—choose another road into this time. Then perhaps you would find pleasure in this meeting, not dislike."

He was like a bantam cock, all ruffled feathers, talons, and belligerence. I stood there, dumb with confusion, unable to understand why he should be so contentious. I couldn't remember having done anything to offend him during his earlier visit. In fact—the more I recalled that occasion, the angrier I became—I was the one who should be quarrelsome, not he.

"Come in," I said instead, settling for amity. "You are tired. Later, when you have rested, we can talk more easily."

"Yes," he nodded, spectacles flashing in the sunlight, "we must talk of many things. For I do not wish anything to stand between us. Now, when we are going to be neighbors, I have been hoping—Chah! An old man's foolishness. Why should you care to be friends with a *kanaka*?"

Muttering to himself, he climbed the stairs, one step at a time. When I moved to help him, he waved me off. Sickness may have aged his body, I thought as I led his horse to the stable, but it sure as hell has ruined his disposition.

He was even more testy in the parlor. "For Heaven's sake!" he attacked, the moment I stepped through the door. Seated like a patriarch in my only chair, he pointed his sharp chin to right, to left. "And what has happened here? A bolt of lightning, perhaps? A wave from the sea?"

"I am going to make some new furniture," I said blandly, as though this were something I did with each change of the seasons.

"And all your books?" he demanded. "Burned up. Trash," I replied, not lying this time.

"No book is trash," he decreed, upright and fierce as an old owl.

I sat on the floor opposite him, leaning against the wall, determined to change the subject. With him in the house peace had dived out the window, fleeing for her life. "Tell me: how are things in town? What of the sickness?"

"Terrible, terrible. Worse than you can imagine, worse even than the most frightening of dreams. The yellow flag flies still, day and night. The death-carts roll through the streets, picking up the bodies of the dead—and sometimes of the dying as well. Smoke hangs above, as if the city burned. Smoke from wood fires, burning at almost every street corner, to purify the air, to drive the pestilence away. As the whole earth will be on Judgment Day is Honolulu every day. A City of Destruction. But God is not appeased. Fire and smoke, tears and prayers, death and wailing: they do not turn away his wrath. The pestilence goes on, people die each day by the score."

He was like a prophet out of the Old Testament, enjoying both his righteousness and the horrors of his tale.

"And through those streets full of smoke sailors run, gathering up the dead to bury them, lifting up the sick from their beds, to carry them to hospitals. Death-houses are they, not places where people are made well. At Punahou and Waikiki, at Kaka'ako and Palama. Few of the sufferers who are carried into those hospitals live to walk out from them on their own two feet."

The sailors, he explained, were "the one good thing to come out of these fearsome times. They are from foreign ships moored in the harbor when the plague began. Six of them were prisoners in the Fort of Ke Kua Nohu, put there for their part in that Sailors' Riot last November.— You remember it?—When our people sickened with the smallpox and died in such great numbers, when so many of our policemen and their helpers had sickened and died, or those who remained were too afraid to go near the dead, then those sailors sent a letter from their jail cell to Governor Kekuanao'a.—You know who he is? The father of the Princes Alexander Liholiho and Lot Kamehameha.— 'Release us from our prison and we will help you,' the sailors wrote to him, 'we are not afraid, for we have had this sickness before and we will not take it again.' Seeing those brave words, Mataio—that's my friend Kekuanao'a —released them. They did their work like heroes of old. We of Honolulu are forever grateful to them. They have been given their freedom, those helpful prisoners, as well as the King's own thanks. Later, he has said, he will grant them pieces of land to live upon, if they wish to stay among us."

I searched in vain for the old Niele, for the humor and malice and lively language that in February I had found so entertaining. They were gone. Merriness was replaced by bitterness, sprightly gossip had given way to a careful regard for slow detail, a scrupulousness mixed with piety, which was little short of dull.

Thus, when I asked about Alex, Niele could not merely answer that he was well. All during dinner I was regaled with a long and circumstantial report upon Alex's duties and responsibilities as a member of the King's Privy Council and especially as one of the Royal Commissioners of Public Health, of how he got along famously with Dr. Rooke, a second Commissioner, but was having endless difficulties with an officious third, whose name I never did hear. Niele was still *niele*, without any doubt, but only insofar as he was insatiable for details; and he poured out chatter as a stream in spate pours water over a mill-race, until I was about to sink in the flood.

Awash to the ears, glazed in the eyeballs, I scarcely listened after a while, occupying myself instead with recalling the topics I proposed to bring up, if ever he gave me a chance. On and on he talked, less like a travel-worn guest than a man terrified of silence. Undoubtedly, I reckoned, remembering that monumental wife of his, undoubtedly because he's treated to so much of it at home.

Finishing with Alex, he launched upon a story about how Dr. Judd had been forced out of the Government by irate townsfolk who blamed him personally for having allowed the smallpox epidemic to happen. Those absurd creatures actually had the gall to accuse him of being unwilling to spend money generously enough to vaccinate the nation's entire population after the pestilence had broken out! The whole slimy business was so obviously engineered by a bunch of Judd's political enemies, including several of his charitable colleagues in medicine, that I couldn't hear Niele out.

"That Committee of Thirteen," I barked, "the whole pack of 'em, ought to be run out of the Kingdom on a leaking ship. And those conniving, selfish, purse-milking physicians: they haven't done a fraction as much for the people here as Judd has. He's one of the finest men in the islands. And they know it. That's why they're so damned envious."

"My, my," said Niele, wrinkling up in a funny sort of smile, "is this bird singing a different tune?"

"I don't know what tune you sing, my friend, or whose chorus you join in town," I rushed on, completely misunderstanding him, "but mark my words: he'll be asked back into the Government when all this dirty politicking dies down, as soon as this pestilence is ended.—Those greedy bastards! They give me the gripes.—Let's leave 'em for more pleasant subjects. How's your family? How's your wife? Did she tell you that I was looking for you, one day back in March?" Oh, my immortal soul! Dr. Judd's enemies could not have been more subtle in baiting him than I was with the cheating husband of Mrs. Nihoa. *Wickedness was sweet in my mouth, though I hid it under the tongue.*

"Yes," he said quietly, "yes, she told me. When I came home from the office. She was much impressed with you. 'Such a well-behaved young man,' she said, 'and so handsome!'—I am sorry that you could not wait until I returned. As a matter of fact, I remember that afternoon very well."

To my annoyance, he seemed to be heading into another run of reminiscences, and, what was worse, to be evading the trap I'd set for him.

"I was down at the harbor, taking one of my sons to my brother-in-law. They were sailing for Kona at two o'clock."

Babble I could put up with, out of uncommon politeness, but I saw no reason to endure falsehood so brazen because so needless. "Damn it!" I slapped the floor, springing my trap, "don't feed me any more of your lies!" Oh, how I enjoyed the twitching with which he fought the noose, my own pleasure at snaring him for a cheat. "Or am I to believe that your good wife lied to me, when she told me I would find you in your office?"

"No, my wife did not tell you a lie. Rebekah could never say anything that was not true. But I do not understand why you are so angry. And neither do I tell you a lie now.—I have given up that game, but perhaps you have not noticed.—No. The explanation for that afternoon is very simple. I ask you to believe me. Caleb—that is the boy's name—is not one of her sons. You see, she did not know about Caleb. She was spared that knowledge, I thank God, until the day she died."

I fell back in dismay. "I'm sorry, Niele.—I did not know."

He looked down at me, sitting in the dirt on the floor, his eyes as hard as the glass in those spectacles. "Why should you be sorry? How could you have known?" Exacting his revenge, he set down his heel upon this venomous serpent. "The smallpox took her away. She was the first to go in my family. For this, too, I am grateful. She was not there to grieve when death came for our sons and daughters. It is not easy, I tell you, to bury nine children in three months." He was not lying. A man does not say such terrible things so softly and mean them for lies.

What does one say to a man so bereft? "Nine children?" I could scarcely whisper. "From the smallpox?"

"No. The smallpox took only four. Four others were burned when our house in Makiki caught fire in the night. I had sent them up there, to get away from the sickness in town, but even so it was among them when the fire came. No one knows how that fire started. But does it matter, now

that they are gone, and the faithful servants with them?—
And before that Abel, my first-born son: he was killed
when he tried to save a white woman with a runaway
horse. I know how that happened. A shaft of her buggy
pierced him, through the chest. They brought him home
to me in that same buggy. It is a strange thing. She was a
whore to sailors. Perhaps that is why she wept when my
handsome son died with his head in her lap . . ."

"God in Heaven!—How can you tell me all this so
calmly? How have you kept from going mad?"

"You are looking at a man who can weep no more. I
do not ask anymore why this happened to me. I do not
ask how I can go on living.—Oh, I shed tears at first, of
course, and I grieved. For, despite what you may think,
I am not a heartless man. Most of all did I sorrow for
Rebekah, not only because she was the first to go. And I
cried out to Jehovah, when he took my little Daniel away
from me. But when the fourth child lay dead my tears
dried up. Then I knew that the Lord was punishing me
for my wickedness. For all my sins, but most of all for
my pride. The fire, when it came, did not surprise me. I
will tell you why, lest you think me an unnatural father.
The runaway horse is the reason: it dragged me into the
dust, with Abel. Since then I have had no more pride, no
more willful wickedness. I am a broken man. But I remain, I live. Not happy—for how can I be happy?—but
wiser, I think, and less of a sinner than before. Not content, but waiting, in hope."

To hear him was to hear myself. He did not know that
the dung heap upon which he sat, dry-eyed and hard-
voiced, was big enough for the two of us. Nay, it was big
enough for the whole world of broken, cheated, hoping
men.

"But you still have a son," I tried to cheer him, "the

boy you sent to Kona?" Having blurted this out, I quailed.
If Caleb, too, had been taken by death, I would have
knocked my head against the wall, I would have wailed
like a native.

"Alas," Niele shook his head, "Caleb is no longer my
son, for I have given him to Eben—to my brother-in-law
—as I promised. This is one of Jehovah's jests, I think.
The boy I gave away like rubbish," he sneered as he said
the word, making it seem like something worse than rubbish, "is the one to be preserved. Whereas the children
I cherished, and would not part with, they are the ones
who were taken away, who were burned like trash, buried
like dung."

"Remember Job," I intoned, "who, by losing all,
gained much." I who had rejected Job and his ordeal and
his trust, when most I needed to remember him, I lifted
him up now from his dung heap, dusted him off, and solemnly presented him as the very paradigm of patient
trust. Pfaugh! I should have choked on my hypocrisy.
How little I knew about Job. How much less I knew about
Hiram Nihoa.

"That is why I am here," he replied. "I have learned
the story of Job, which I did not know before. Kauikeaouli the King, that man of sorrows, told it to me one night
when, alone and on foot, he came to my house to comfort
me. I have remembered his words, and I have remembered Job. And now I have come to Ka'a'awa, to receive of
Jehovah my reward. The hope of this reward is the only
thing that supports me. The knowledge that, living here,
in Ka'a'awa, safe from the world and its evils, safe
even from the smallpox, is the boy who—I confess it—
means as much to me as did all the children of my body.
Surely you have met him by now? The grandson of
Kanemilohai?"

Oh, God! The horror of that moment!—I wanted to run away, to sink into the earth, to hide, to be anywhere but in that house, when the poor man learned the unbelievable cruelty of this foulest trick which his Jehovah had played upon him.

"Yes," I forced myself to speak, "yes, I have met the boy. But," I drove myself on, preparing him for the truth, "what do you mean? Who is ever safe from the smallpox?"

"Why, the vaccination, of course," he said brightly, looking something like the old Niele as he leaned forward in his chair. "The vaccination I asked that Catholic brother to give to the boy. Back there at Paliku it was done, under the tree-of-life. Ever since the smallpox came to Honolulu I have been comforted by the knowledge that the vaccination I did not give to my own children was given to him in time."

In the instant, pity gave way to hate. Hate flooded up in me like vomit. "So you are the one who did it!" I pressed my hands hard against the floor, lest they kill him.

"Of course I did it. And why should I not? I believe in it, one hundred per cent. 'Niele,' I have told myself a thousand times, 'get on your knees and thank God that, for once in your life, you did the right thing at the right time.'—Tell me. I have been slow to ask, but eager to hear: how is the boy?"

What shall I tell him? What shall I give him, I asked myself, staring at him as a man stares at a worm writhing in dung. Shall I give him hate? Hate for a meddling fool, hate screeched at him so wildly that he will be forever hurt, as he has hurt me? Or pity? Pity for him, for me, for all poor deluded, striving, miserable creatures who, though they are little more than worms, think that they are men?

In the moment before my choosing I heard the high voice of 'Opuhea, as she trailed after Kamanele in the cookhouse, the low response of Kamanele, patient and kind and loving.

"Hiram, old friend." I was sick of hate, weary unto death with the miseries of men, resolved that I would add no more to them. "You did the right thing, indeed. The vaccination: as you say, it would have protected him when the smallpox came."

"That foreign discovery is a fine thing," he was agreeing, when my implication struck home. "What do you mean?" he sprang up. "What are you trying to tell me?"

Dreading the pain I knew must come, for both of us, I pushed myself up from the floor. Standing before him, I began, slowly, as gently as I could. "On the day after I searched for you in Honolulu, he—he went to join his ancestors in the land of Milu. And Kanemilohai and Maka-o-Hina: they went with him, on the same day. The influenza it was, which took them from us. The influenza, not the smallpox."

With head bowed, shoulders hunched, fists clenched, looking like a child being punished unjustly, he heard me till the end.

"*Auwe, auwe*," he moaned. "What did I do wrong?— Hahau has won, Hahau's spirit has won . . ."

The man who had no more tears wept. Feeling only pity, for him, for me, I put my arms around him, and gave him a place to weep.

CHAPTER 33.

THE NARROW PATH

Hiram did not like to live in his new house at Kahana because, he said, "grand as it is, it makes me sad. 'The rains gather at Kahana, splashing on the water of Lo'i-ke'e.'—That's from an old chant," he interjected, looking more lugubrious than the Tragic Muse, "telling of tears of sorrow falling on a shunned taro patch near my house. Always, almost since the beginning, it has been a place of sadness, that taro patch: this is why it is shunned."

I believed him, on the first occasion, having no reason then to suspect his veracity or his countenance. But when, under happier circumstances a few weeks later, he warbled the identical song and, forgetting his earlier fabrication, provided another interpretation that was downright obscene, I saw again how clever the man could be in bending words—and me—to suit his purpose. "Every Hawaiian song is full of phrases that have double or triple meanings," he was saying. "The closer you listen, the more you hear. Most especially is this the way with songs or chants that tell of rain, or mist, or water. Almost always these are love songs. No. No. The mouth has committed an error. Not love songs. They are songs about the act of love."

To establish the point, he gave me a phrase-by-phrase analysis of "the rains gather at Kahana" which raised blushes to my innocent's cheek and vehement protests to my Puritan's tongue. "Mercy me!" he snickered, "what a missionary you've turned out to be.—The trouble with you *haole* is that your nerves are sheathed in stone. Nothing excites you, not birth, not death, neither food nor drink, not even a good roll in the grass.—*Be not righteous overmuch*. How are *haole* maidens wooed? How are *haole* babies made? *E*?—And, besides, now that I think of it: what about that *haole* song you've been singing around here? That one about the valley of love and delight? *E*?"

The shock of sudden enlightenment has a way of muzzling even Protestants. Since then I've been very careful to think first before I criticize anything native, and to examine more than twice almost everything Hiram says. In more ways than one he has been very good for my humor —and a disastrous influence upon my notion of morality.

He does not actually "tell untruths" (he avoids the word lie, I suspect, as being too damning for one of his propensity), but often he comes perilously close to twisting truth almost beyond recognition whenever the distortion helps him to gain his end. In the beginning, as I say, I did not understand this and, being a credulous man (I won't agree to my being entirely a humorless one), I accepted him at his declared value. In time, however, realizing how he was using me, I found a workable formula to bring him back to a reasonable representation of truth —for a while. "I believe you," I would say, "fifty per cent," or "ten per cent," or whatever the case may call for. Never does he admit that I have caught him up. He will sigh, as with unwearied patience, or will favor me with a saintly smile, and say, "Trouble with haoles is, they have no humor." Nevertheless, thereafter for a time, perhaps for as long as ten minutes or so, he will hover more or less around demonstrable truth.

Before a month was out he spent more time at my place than at his own. Often he would extend "a call just for saying *aloha*" to a visit that would last a week or more. He needed my company so obviously that I did not have the heart to turn him away. I thought I needed him not at all. In plain fact, during most of those visits I was bored stiff with his chatter about the olden days, the involved relationships among the kings and the chiefs, the scandals of yesteryear and yesterweek, and, worst of all, with his zeal for getting into Jehovah's uncrowded heaven. Mercifully, I could flee to the fields, to the round of duties performed more for the sake of Ka'a'awa's survivors than for Olympian Hopkins.

But, by common consent, for reasons neither of us found strange, we never talked of Kaneikapule.

During one of Hiram's sojourns at his own house in Kahana, I stole the chance to climb the Three Fates. Although intending to go alone, I knew that I could not ride off without telling anyone my destination. Because neither man nor beast can scale those tremendous cliffs from below, I'd have to approach them from the rear, by ascending the ridge at its inner end, where it sinks before the sacred mount. And the ridge's spine is so jagged and so narrow that I would need at least two days to work my way along it, the first to reach those grim Fates, the second to crawl back to my starting-point near the valley's head. Having to spend a night up there added further complications: I'd have to carry food and water, as well as a blanket to keep me warm during the night.

When I told Makua what I proposed to do he rolled his eyes and puffed his cheeks, in a fine portrayal of a man who is hearing the unbelievable. Since that day on the beach, we two have been easy in our relationship, often to my entertainment, usually to my benefit. But this time he dug in his heels and laid back his ears, stubborn as a mule with a load too heavy for its back.

"And why do you wish to go up there?" he huffed. "Long is the way, and narrow is the path. Few men are brave enough to venture along that high road."

"Because I wish to stand up there, that's why, to see how the world looks from those heights."

"Chah!" he spat, as I'd known he would, "this is not a good reason. A wise man, such as I am, has sense enough not to put his feet in places where he is not supposed to walk. You would do well to keep your two feet upon this flat earth."

And this time I was irked by his manner. It was something more than teasing: it was worse than Hiram's abuse of my good nature. "Dammit, Makua! Stop treating me as if I were a child, and a stupid one at that.—If you must know, I want to go because Kaneikapule and I spoke about going up there together someday. Now, even without him, I wish to go.—As a kind of memorial to him." This was the truth. I had some silly idea of planting a flag up there, or building a cairn of stones, or doing something equally noticeable, as a sign that I had kept my promise to him.

"Ah, ah," he submitted at once, "this puts another finger in the *poi*-bowl. Then perhaps we can help you on your way."

"Not we. I wish to go alone," I insisted. I might as well have commanded the winds not to blow from off the sea.

"You can not go alone," he decided, once and for all. "Do you go alone, you will never come back. More than wild boars and high cliffs are up there, guarding the mountain of Kanehoalani. I shall ask Linalina if he will take you. Only he knows the way."

This was the first time I had heard so much as a hint that the ridge of Kanehoalani too was a *kapu* place.

Before dawn the next morning Linalina and I set out on horseback. As the sun was rising above the edge of the world, flooding the whole valley with light, we reached a small clearing in the forest. *Kukui* and mountain-apple trees lifted their leafy crowns to the new day, drops of night-rain clung to every leaf and fern frond, birds swooped and cried their alarums, the stream calmed them with its unchanging song. Beyond the tree tops the mountain wall rose up, immense, iron-black, forbidding.

We were still far away from the low hill I had assumed would be our starting-place, and I was not prepared when Linalina dismounted, saying, "We leave the horses here. —And our clothes. From here the way is *kapu*. As you did learn once, long ago."

"And how do you know this?" I asked.

"I was here, with Hahau," he said with a smile that eased my shame, "that time you went up to the mountain beyond. He wished to chase you away, but I asked him to let you go. 'Kane will stop him,' I said, 'if he does not want him near.' And Hahau agreed."

Never before, not even as a child, had I knowingly stood unclothed before anyone. Not even Melissa saw me naked, as I never saw her in the fullness of her beauty. The body is ugly, nakedness is sinful, we had been taught, and so we believed. And, when we drew together in the times of our love, we met in the dark, as if love itself were a sin, an act of shame.

In utmost embarrassment I shed my clothes. Like shrinking Susannah clutching her wisp of towel, I hid behind them until Linalina, having thrown his shirt and trousers over a branch, bade me do the same with mine. He, a natural man, happier unclad than dressed, as all Hawaiians are, was not in the least aware of my shame. When I found the wit to realize this, I hung modesty on the branch with my clothes.

Linalina was more concerned with tender *haole* feet. He tossed me a pair of sandals plaited of dried *hala* leaves. "I think you will need these, on the path above. But do not put them on until I say you can. And if you must piss, now is the time to do it."

The evening before, as we made our plans, he had told me to bring nothing for the trip. "We can not defile the mountain. To eat is forbidden. To relieve ourselves is forbidden. Springs will give us water to drink. And we shall come down before the night." Then at last I had understood that we were going upon a very serious expedition.

Gravely we emptied ourselves of defilement, staunchly we immersed ourselves in that cold stream, from head to foot, to remove outward pollution from our bodies. Wet and shivering, I stood like a bedraggled crane in a spot of sunshine on the far bank, while he tied some *ki* leaves into leis. "Here," he gave me one, as he put the other upon his shoulders. "To ask the protection of the gods, when we enter among the dangers above.—Now we are ready."

To my astonishment he took a path heading straight for the mountain wall. Almost immediately we came upon a small temple platform, its stones furred with moss. Within two minutes we entered a cave, much like the one of Pohukaina. But where Pohukaina burrowed into the ground, down toward the realm of Milu, this one wound upward, toward the realm of Kane. It was like a huge blood vessel in the mountain's side from which the blood had drained away.

When the darkness had closed in around us, Linalina stopped. "Wait here for a moment, until our eyes can see." Soon, high above and inward, nearer the mountain's center, we could discern the arch of sunlight which was to be our beacon. Up this long tunnel, at a steep pitch, we climbed. The dust upon the floor of the cave gave way to hard earth, to fine cinders packed hard by the tread of many feet, to bare rock. In some of the steepest places, shallow steps had been hewn out of the rock. Wherever the footing changed, Linalina's big hand in mine guided me. Near the top of this Orphic passageway water dripped from its ceiling, making the floor wet and slippery. And around its mouth, where daylight streamed in, ferns and mosses grew, springing from the sides and floor of the shaft.

My silent Virgil led me out from this dank hade into a forecourt of Paradise—a small sunken crater green with tall ferns and towering *kukui* trees. No trees of any other kind grew there: only the tree-of-life, sacred to Kane, was permitted to flourish in that hallowed grove. Many hundreds of feet above the valley's floor, this verdant bower lay in the lap of Kanehoalani, the highest peak in the ridge. Not even the tops of those ancient trees could have been seen from the valley below.

Putting a finger to his mouth, Linalina warned me not to break the holy stillness. He made an offering of leaves, plucked with his right hand from a *kukui* seedling, weighted them down with a small stone. Without hesitation I did the same.

He led me along a grassy path through the sacred grove and up its farther side, to the brink of the ridge. From that vantage we beheld the wide sweep of Kaneʻohe Bay and the long range of the Koʻolau. Warming winds rushed up from below, rustling the ferns and trees at our feet, stirring the leis upon our shoulders.

We turned to the left, toward the sea. In a few moments we reached the edge of the beautiful glade, where it joined the side of the next soaring peak. There, leading toward the seaward end of the ridge, was a narrow ledge, made when the mountain was formed.

"Now we can talk," said Linalina, "and from here you can wear the sandals." While I tied on those protectors of tender feet, he gathered fallen *kukui* nuts. "It is our custom," he explained, "to sow seeds of plants where none are growing. It is a custom pleasing to Kane and to Lono." He gave the seeds into my hands. After collecting more for himself, he started out along that narrow ledge.

It was almost a level path, and, despite the dizzying emptiness at our right, a tolerably easy one. I would not have found it for myself had I persisted in coming alone. In fact, knowing now what I do about that ridge, I would never have been able to get past the peak of Kanehoalani: it would have defeated me almost as soon as I started upon my journey. After a quarter of a mile or so, the ledge widened, the abyss beside us became less fearsome. Then, within a hundred yards, the shoulder of the mountain swelled, as if to hold up the heavy head of the peak above us, and the path became as wide as a road.

As we walked in Indian file along this high road, I allowed myself, for the first time in my life, to look undismayed and unabashed upon nakedness. Linalina's body, with its broad shoulders and narrow waist, its neat buttocks and long legs, was not a thing of ugliness or a cause for shame. The more I studied the play of muscles in that back and in those strong legs, the smoothness of his copper-colored skin, the very droplets of sweat forming upon the firm flesh, the more I saw how splendid a creation the human body is. Even my own body, when I considered it, was a cause for wonderment. Thin as it is, compared with Linalina's, and hairy, and *haole* pale in all those places which are so assiduously covered by clothing, so carefully hidden not only from the eyes of people but also from the eye of the sun: is it not a marvel of flesh and blood and bones, as it strides along this mountain path, without gasping for breath, without faltering or stumbling upon the way? How, then, can I despise it, hide it, deny that it exists? How, then, can nakedness be sinful? How, then, can Puritans be such fools?

Strengthened by sheer enjoyment of the sun's warmth upon my body, by the completest submission to the pagan pleasures offered by this glorious day, a suspicion grew into a conviction: the gods can not be prudes. Seduced by Kane, I laughed outright at New England's image of a bearded, frowning Jehovah, all wrapped up in voluminous robes. And found further cause for laughter in the picture that formed in my mind: of an angel despatched by that disapproving One, chasing after us, blushing in mien, with averted gaze—and with a large fig leaf in either hand.

Before mid-morning we arrived at the base of Atropos, the innermost and highest peak of the Three Fates, which I have given such an un-Hawaiian name. The level trail continued along its shoulder, but no path led to its top. Huge, barren, aloof, it rose above us for several hundred feet, as thin and hooked as a parrot's beak. A determined man such as I am could have found a way to its summit. Yet, as I marked out a possible approach, I knew that I would not try it. Fear did not deter me, but respect for the mountain. To scale it would be an act of vanity, a declaration of pride, and I was no longer that proud. A mere man, a naked man, can not be proud in the presence of a thing so ancient, so indifferent to him and to all other men.

"You wish to stand upon the top of Nanahoa?" Linalina asked.

"Once I did have that wish," I replied, "but now I do not. To stand upon the first one will be enough."

"You are wise," he said. "As you see, those of us who come up here feel the same way."

Beyond Atropos loomed Lachesis, the second peak, almost as high, just as terrible in its disdain for mortal men. As we approached it, and left behind the trees of many kinds which grow along the trail, Linalina cast a *kukui* nut to right or to left, wherever a little pocket of soil among the stones and sparse grasses would give a seedling a chance to take root. I did not part with mine, clutched in my sweating hands. I saved them for another place.

Long before noon we reached the base of Clotho, the peak nearest the sea, the one into whose heel the cave of Pohukaina is gouged. Little more than a hundred feet separated me from my goal: an ascent up its gentle slope would have been as easy as mounting the stairs to my house. Linalina stepped to one side, motioning me to go on.

"No, my friend," I said, stopping beside him. "I am humbled. No more do I wish to stand upon that peak. Its *mana* is too great for me."

"Again I say you are wise. In this you are one of us.— I will tell you a story about this mountain of Ka 'Oi'o. No one of us has tried to stand upon it since the first proud man went up there, long ago. The ghosts of the dead: they would not permit him. In their anger, they caused the mountain to shake, strong winds to blow, the rocks to crumble under his feet. He slipped, where no man should slip. He fell, where no man should fall. He rolled down this slope here, unable to stop, where now you or I could easily stop if we should lose our footing upon this path. And he fell, over the edge there, he fell down into the emptiness beyond. The stains of his blood and the fat of his flesh still mark the cliffs of Ka 'Oi'o, the sounds of his screams are still borne upon the wind. But even as he fell, brought down for his pride by the dead, Kane-the-Giver-of-Life was kind, and lifted him up for his daring. Even as he fell, Kane changed him into a bird, into a *koa'e-ula*. He and his offspring live now in holes high in those cliffs. Their red tail-feathers tell of the blood he shed, their cry is a warning of death to all men below."

Was it a myth he told me, or was it a warning of death? I can never be sure of his meaning when any Hawaiian speaks to me. Hiram had taught me as much, Makua had confirmed it. Now, as I searched for the hidden message in Linalina's story, I shuddered at the thought of myself falling, of any man's falling, into that void. And, suddenly, the fear gripped me, as I read one meaning to his fable: that he had brought me up here to take his revenge at last. Warily I backed away from him, as panic spread its poison through my very bones.

"Well, it's a good story," he laughed, "even if it may not be true. The living like to blame the dead, or the gods, for troubles which come because of their own faults.— But I am glad that you do not wish to be changed into a *koa'e* bird."

No more than now I want to be a part of a fish, or of a crab, or of a piece of coral, I thought. "It is enough to be a striving man," I said weakly, watching him, wondering what I should do if he turned upon me.

"Aye," he said, giving me one of his rare smiles. "You

are one with us in that. You are a part of us now. And that is better, is it not?"

With this the fear left me, as quickly as it had come. Linalina is not one who twists the meanings of words.

From our great height we could see almost the whole of O'ahu's windward coast, rimmed in golden sand and many-colored sea, from Kahuku at the north to Makapu'u at the south. Off Mokapu Head, the island's easternmost point, a ship under full sail, looking like a covey of gulls arrested in flight, made its way toward Honolulu. On such a day as this the prospect of O'ahu's mountains, valleys, and beaches must offer to mariners one of the most beautiful landfalls on earth. Beyond the channel, blue in the distance, lay Moloka'i; and beyond Moloka'i were Lana'i and the vast bulk of Haleakala on Maui.

"And there are Mauna Kea and Mauna Loa, on the island of Hawai'i," Linalina pointed to dark masses on the horizon that I had mistaken for clouds. "We are fortunate. They are not often seen from O'ahu."

From our eyrie we could look out in all directions, over many hundreds of square miles. Yet, so small were we, so broad was the mountain's back on which we perched, that we could see only the farther side of Ka'a'awa's valley and the ridge separating it from Kahana. My house, much of the ranch, almost the whole domain wherein I lived, were hidden from sight, as if they did not exist. I was aghast. If those extensive pastures and grazing herds were invisible, then how could I, the all-important I, be seen? I was affronted! I had not conceived, even in my most morbid broodings, that I who lived at the very feet of the Three Fates, who looked up to them as the most conspicuous features in my whole world, almost as the very keepers of my destiny, would be so beneath their notice.

To them I was less than a speck of dust on the valley floor: I was nothing, because to them I did not exist.

Linalina spoke my thought: "A small thing, indeed, is a man. Why, then, should he be proud?—The gods are very forbearing with us in our foolishness, I think."

"The gods," I mumbled, "how can they know that we exist? How can they see us, from their heights above?"

"Ah, my friend, there you are wrong," spoke the man of unbroken faith. "They see us. They know about us, because they do not always live in the heights above."

Some men carve their names upon mountains and monuments, to prove that they have been there, that they have lived. Others run up flags, pile up stones, strew their rubbish about. And some write books. Hawaiians sow seeds, and in that way gain a cleaner hold upon immortality. Linalina cast the last *kukui* nut down the stony slope at our feet.

I was about to throw mine after it, because this was the place I had kept them for, when he said, "It will not grow here, I think. Not enough water clings to this bare rock. I have tried before, and I try again today, but as you see—"

"What about the next slope back?" I asked.

"A better place," he said. "One little *kukui* tree clings there now. It asks for companions."

When we stood at the midpoint of the second saddle, I cast my *kukui* seeds down the slope, toward Ka'a'awa. "These are for Kaneikapule," I said aloud, not only to Linalina, "for Kanemilohai, for Maka-o-Hina."

"Perhaps Kane will favor those seeds," said my companion.

As he did not favor his sons, was the thought neither of us expressed.

By mid-afternoon clouds had gathered upon the peaks above us, rain was falling upon the ridges beyond Waiakane and Waiahole. Haze drawn up by the morning's bright sun veiled the windward islands. Now cool breezes rushed up the mountainside, and errant droplets of rain stung *haole* skin burned red by the sun.

Just before we arrived at the sacred grove, Linalina stopped in the trail, turned to face me. "Let us talk here, where we do not break the *kapu*. The time has come."

At my left, the abyss yawned, a void at which I dared not look. Leaning against the cliff, clinging to a clump of grass, I said, "The time for what?"

"I wish to go away from Ka'a'awa. My duties here are ended. My life here is too full of unhappy memories. I wish to go to another place, to start a new life."

My instinct was to argue, to try to persuade him not to leave the valley which had been his only home, not to leave the ranch, where his duties would never end. But what right did I have, to hold him back? "Aye, this I can understand," I said instead, "but I shall miss you, if you go. Especially after today." I valued this man, and I wanted him to know it. If he went away, I would be losing more than a good ranch-hand.

"But before I go, I need your help. You are the only one in Ka'a'awa who can do it, the only one who is worthy."

"Anything I can do to help you I will do. You have only to ask and I shall do it." Still the incorrigible white man, I thought he was going to ask for money, or letters of reference, or an arrangement with Hopkins for a job somewhere else.

"Makua and Kamanele: I have talked with them, and they say with me that you are the only one who can receive the burden."

"The burden?" I looked at him, rather than beyond him to the distant mountains, rather than below him to the depths. "What is this burden?" I asked, wanting no more burdens of any kind.

"Of being the keeper-of-the-bones of the Kanehoalani. Are you willing?"

"If I am worthy," I found myself saying, "then I am willing.—But what does it mean? Can I do it?"

"You can do it. You are worthy. I have thought so before today. Today you have made me more certain.— But do not fear: the burden will not be great, after today. Come. I will show you, what no man after you will ever see again."

At the edge of the sunken crater he stopped once more. "Because of their great *mana*, we can not walk into their presence. And we can not speak, unless they should speak first to us. Do as I do, and help me when I ask for help, with my hands, with my eyes.—Now the sandals must come off. Leave them here. You will not use them again."

"But who are 'they'?" I asked, bewildered by these instructions. "Who are we going to meet?"

"Wait. You will see," he said, leading me down into the silent grove.

We trod upon a different path, to a place whose position I can not reveal. Before a huge boulder fallen from the cliff above, he bade me to wait. Sinking to his hands and knees, he crawled into a fissure behind the rock. In the mysterious hush I waited, wondering at what was to come, fearing the nature of this burden he was about to pass to me. I was wary of burdens, I wanted no more sorrows.

In a few moments he returned, carrying a flaring *kukui*-nut torch, beckoned me to follow him through the narrow cleft behind the boulder. On my hands and knees, I crawled in after him.

Only his fingers held against my lips prevented me from crying out. We were kneeling in a large cavern. In the torch's flickering light the cave appeared to be filled with misshapen dancing goblins—until I saw that they were as unmoving as corpses. They were baskets woven of sennit and fine roots, each with a small head and a swollen body, but no arms or legs. Row upon row, dozens of them, they had been arranged along one side of the cavern. Their gleaming eyes, made of oyster shells with dark seeds for pupils, seemed to be fixed upon us in expressions of outrage. Only when I saw that some of the oldest of these baskets had rotted away, spilling their contents, did I understand that they held the bones of the dead. The bones of many generations of men and women and children were gathered there. Along the other side of the cavern, bundles of rotten *kapa*, spilling bones upon the damp floor, skeletons lying upon the bare rock, far outnumbered the woven ossuaries.

Linalina moved his arm slowly, directing the light upon different aspects of the tomb, allowing me to perceive other things: whole canoes, equipped with outriggers and paddles; barbarous leering idols carved from tree trunks, or fashioned with feathers, propped above the ghostly populace; wooden bowls holding remnants of rotted foods and mummified fruits; feather capes and helmets and fly-chasers; heaps of mouldering *kapa*; spears and carrying-poles of hard wood; *poi*-pounders made of stone; skeletons of pigs and dogs proferred in sacrifice. Among the things of old lay articles from the new times. Everything was grist to Death's mill: bottles of rum and glass beads and china dishes; bolts of dusty silks and dulled brocades; corroded pistols and rusting muskets; porcelain ewers and urns, even a child's painted chamber pot. Everything the chiefs of Ka'a'awa had used in life was assembled there to serve them in death, brought up with immense expenditure of labor from the valley below. The bodies of faithful retainers lay there as well, servants loyal beyond death, who had chosen to accompany their lords into the realm of Milu.

The still unmoving air stank of something more insidious than rot, more sickly sweet than the fumes of the torch's burning candlenuts. Cobwebs hung from the ceiling, the walls, the furnishings, the skeletons. And the roots of trees thriving in the sunlight above the cave, having penetrated soil and rock, grew like witches' brooms into the space above the dead, dripping water upon them which they could no longer feel, could no more drink.

Linalina swung the torch-light toward the cavern's entrance. Against the wall, not yet stained with mildew or broken open by decay, separated from all the others by a space broad enough to accommodate two more, sat four newly woven caskets: three large ones and, first in line, the last of his line, a smaller one. Its wide blind eyes filled me with anguish. Close to weeping, scarcely able to breathe, I crawled out from that crowded sepulcher.

Linalina scurried out after me. Allowing no time for grief, he signaled me to follow him up the side of the crater to the brink above the entrance to the burial cave. I saw at once why he had sought my help. The huge stones lying there were too heavy for one man to move.

Straining and pushing, white limbs helping brown, we rolled down scores of boulders, threw down upon them a wagonload of mud and grass and ferns, until the portal to the tomb of the Kanehoalani was sealed forever. No one but Linalina and I will know what lies behind that fall of stones and earth.

When our work was done we were covered with mud from head to foot, bruised and scratched and bleeding.

Linalina put up his hands: "enough." He shaped the words with his mouth: "it is good." He put his hands upon my shoulders, giving me a brother's thanks.

At the entrance to the tunnel which would take us down to the valley, we paused for one last backward look. Soft mist was drifting in among the crowns of the *kukui* trees. Not a leaf moved, not a bird called, nothing disturbed the silence of the grove. Beauty was there, such as I shall never see again. And peace was there, a profound peace.

The mouth opened to swallow us was black: the door of dark Hades is never closed. I dreaded the long descent through that unrelieved night.

As I should have known, Linalina was prepared for this, too. Tucked away in a recess just within the tunnel's maw were a sheaf of torches and a canister of matches, wrapped in oiled *kapa*. With torches to light the way, our return to the sweet air of the valley was swift.

Then I saw why Linalina had not used torches to help us in our ascent, why Makua would not permit me to blunder about alone on the ridge of Kanehoalani. Upon either side of the passageway, placed upon beds scooped out of the soft rock, lay more skeletons, more bones. In a few places, where the shaft opened up into caverns as vast as cathedrals or as small as chapels, or where tributary tunnels writhed in to join it, skeletons lay by the hundreds. The whole tunnel was one immense catacomb, and Linalina had withheld this knowledge from me until I had proved myself worthy of receiving it.

In the afternoon's waning light we reached our clothes and the horses near the ancient temple. Linalina broke the silence with a happy laugh. "Behold! Great is the *mana* of this mountain: one *haole* and one *kanaka* went up, two *kanaka* return."

But as we bathed in the stream he became serious again.

"Now you are the keeper-of-the-bones. No one else must know where they lie."

"I shall guard them, I shall keep the secret," I said solemnly. "But tell me: what if someone who is wandering around up here, in this part of the valley, should find this cave, should enter that long tunnel?" All the questions I had wanted to put to him while we were in the mountain demanded their answers.

"We need not worry about any Hawaiian, I promise you. If one of us should happen to find this tunnel and should see what lies within, he would run out of there so fast that he would look like a streak of smoke in a high wind. Ho! His hair would stand up. Bumps as big as flea-bites would rise upon his skin. He would leave pieces of his feet upon the stones, but he would not return to pick them up. And he would tell no one about what he had found. No, we need not worry about Hawaiians, because I do not believe that one of us would ever get close enough to that cave to poke his nose into it. He would feel the throbbing in his thigh bones out here, he would hear the warnings of ghosts, and he would know that this place is haunted, is forbidden.—But foreigners: they are the ones to worry about, the ones to be kept out, because—from what I have heard—they do not always hear the messages from the spirit-world, they do not always respect the bones of the dead, or the places where they are put. That is one reason why Makua, Kamanele, and I chose you to take my place. You will have the power to keep foreigners out of the valley. And when you are grown old, and your time to die is near, you must tell the secret to a man you can trust."

"Is that how you came to be the keeper-of-the-bones?"

"No. It was my duty, as it was the duty of my father, and of his fathers before him. The men of my family were the *kahu* to the chiefs of Kanehoalani: ours was the duty to serve them while they lived, to care for their bones when they were dead. We were the ones who watched over the separating of the flesh from the bones, and who put those bones into the caskets. And we were the ones who, in the dark of night, lighted only by torches, carried their bones, and the things the chiefs would wish to have with them in the spirit-world, through the tunnel to the cave above. Not even the chiefs knew where that cave is. The living said farewell to the dead when they were laid upon the stones of the temples down there, beside the household of the chiefs. And for this service, when they died the bones of the members of my family—and of others who served the chiefs well—men, women, and children alike, were placed near the bones of the chiefs. All those bones you saw in the tunnel, as we came down just now: those are the bones of our people of Ka'a'awa.

"So many lie there," I said, "I am astonished at their number."

"Do not forget: for many generations have our people dwelled here in Ka'a'awa, in peace and happiness. No battles were fought in this sacred valley, no sicknesses leaped like warriors among the people to strike them down. They were as numerous as are crabs upon the beach at night. This was a valley filled with contented families then, for always the Kanehoalani have been good chiefs, who cared for their people. Even in the time of my youth, many families still lived in this land.— But now almost all are gone."

"Those years before the foreigners came," I said, "they must have been times of happiness for the people of O'ahu."

He thought for a long moment before replying. He is the most honest man I know.

"I can not speak for myself, because I was not living then. Yet, from what my father told me of what his father told him, I believe that they were times of happiness. I have asked myself why this was so, and this is my thought: in those days the people lived with respect, with respect from each for the other, for their chiefs, for all their gods, the small as well as the great. Where there is respect, there is order. Where there is order, there is harmony. And where there is harmony, there is contentment. When the people cared for their gods, the gods cared for their people."

The cleansing water covered him up to his neck. Only his dark head showed, as though it rested upon a salver of shimmering gold.

"But when the people no longer obeyed the *kapu*, no longer heeded the gods, when they were no longer thankful for the gifts of the gods and wasted them and defiled them, then the gods could no longer care for them. I do not believe that the gods are dead, as some people are saying. I believe that the gods have gone away from us in sorrow, to another place, because few people will listen to them anymore. And without the gods to care for us, we wander in darkness, we are dying away. Hahau said, 'The gods are punishing us for our lack of respect.' The missionaries from America, the fathers from France, are saying, 'Jehovah is punishing you for your sins.' Perhaps this is so. I do not know. But I do not believe that the gods are so hard of heart. I think that we are a dying race because now we live in fear, not in harmony. Because we do not know what to do or what to believe. Because we have lost our respect for ourselves. This is the worst thing the foreigners have done to us: in so many ways they have made us to feel that we are ignorant and useless. In so many ways, they have taken away our respect for ourselves. The gods are not punishing us. We are punishing ourselves, and we are not wise enough to know this."

"You are as a voice crying in the wilderness, Linalina. Why do you not carry this message to your people?"

"I have done so, but they do not listen. 'Who are you?' they say to me, 'that we should heed you? Are you a priest, with the wisdom of a priest? Are you a chief, with the *mana* of a chief?' For so long have they listened to the voices of the chiefs and to the laws of the priests that now, when those great ones are heard no more in the land, the common people will listen to no one else. Now they are like crabs in a bowl, each pulling down any one who tries to climb higher up the sides of the bowl than the others.— Even so, I will try again, when I am in Honolulu. Perhaps there I will be heard. That is one of the three reasons why I wish to go to that big village."

"And the second reason?" I asked, guessing that he wanted me to do so.

"I wish to look for the bones of Kanelele. In his youth, and in mine, I was the companion to Kanelele, as my son would have been the companion to Kaneikapule, if they had lived.—This scar upon my chest: the wound that made it was put here when I ran between Kanelele and a wild boar which was chasing him. We were hunting with spears, not far from here, when that happened. He would have done the same for me. This broken tooth: I broke it off, with a stick and a heavy stone, in my grief when I learned that he was dead, for I loved him as a brother.—Of all the Kanehoalani, only his bones and the bones of his wife do not lie up there, with his ancestors. No one knows where they lie. Had I been with him when he died, they would be up there now, in their rightful place. But when he went away from Ka'a'awa I could not go with him. My duty kept me here, for by then I was the only helper to my father. And he was old, his time to die was close. Even stronger than the duty of a friend to a friend is the duty of a son to his father, and of a servant to his chief. So I stayed, and Kanelele went away—to his death. I do not have much hope of finding his bones in that big city. But if I should find them, I shall bring them back. And then you and I together will take them up into the mountain. We can not put them where they belong, but we can put them near to the bones of his fathers and of his son."

"How many generations of Kanehoalani were served so faithfully by your family?"

"Thirty generations of Kanehoalani lay in that cave, my father told me when he showed me the way. No one remembered, in his time, where the bones of the first Kanehoalani who came to Ka'a'awa were hidden. With Kanemilohai and Kaneikapule, thirty-two generations are brought together in death. And now their line is ended. Now the end has come, for them and for my duty to them. Only the gods can know why this is so. But now, I think, you will see why I do not wish to stay any longer in Ka'a'awa."

Yes, I could understand, weighted down with the memory of all the evidences of death I had seen that day, pierced with the remembrance of that one pair of unseeing eyes...

"And now," he grinned, "ask me the third reason why I wish to go away."

"And the third reason, my friend?" I asked, unable to understand how he could be so happy, how he could grin so broadly, after such a day, after a life so burdened with death.

"I wish to find me a strong new wife," he said. "And with her I shall make ten, fifteen, perhaps twenty children, to help preserve our race. That old shark, Nihoa of Nanahoa: he has the right idea. *Uiii-haaaa!*" he shouted, a man free of care, a man who would not despair, churning the water with his hands and feet until it foamed and fountained all about us.

CHAPTER 34.

A SERIOUS TALK

When Hiram stayed at my place—and while I was not on hand to be talked at—he would occupy himself in gardening, if the weather was good, and by reading, whatever the weather, in books carried in his saddlebags. Hapless Makana was conscripted, willy-nilly, to dig up an acre of turf and to haul swamp loam for Hiram's beds of vegetables and flowers. I was coerced into building coops for the chickens and pens for the goats.

'Ere long we had a weird collection of lettuce, carrots, beans, cabbages, gourds, melons, onions, and those juicy love apples which once I had thought were so poisonous, intermingled with gaudy marigolds, bachelor's buttons, sunflowers, wild tobacco, and almost every kind of flowering shrub they could drag in from miles around. But not a weed was allowed to survive: Hiram pursued weeds with a vindictiveness he never accorded to people.

In borders around the house he stuck herbs of various sorts, the uses of which I never suspected, along with banana trees, sugarcane, ki plants, and—a saddening touch—clumps of hibiscus bushes with their blood-red blossoms. He was as successful with plants as with words:

within a few months most of my wasteland of grass had been converted into a blooming garden. Straight as a staff, clean and trim, never sweaty or muddy with his exertions, he moved happily about in this sailor's haven.

Often, as I observed Hiram at those innocent diversions, I would puzzle over Linalina's reference to him as "that old shark." To me, in my innocence, he was nothing like a shark. He might resemble a lizard, perhaps, sleek and quick and sun-loving, or, at the worst, an eloquent macaw, but certainly he was not a sharp-toothed terror slinking 'neath the waves. I still had a few things to learn, it developed, about both Hiram and the subtleties of the Hawaiian tongue.

He did not confine his interests to the yard. One day, when he was overseeing Kamanele's energetic pretenses at housecleaning, he discovered under my bed the books from the cave, reposing in the sea chest in which they had been brought down from that monkish cell. Because they were hidden away, they had been spared the destruction suffered by the library more accessible to my barbarian's fury.

"Sure. Go ahead. It's a good idea," I agreed, when Hiram suggested that those tomes might better be set out in the parlor.

"And read them, too?" he inquired eagerly.

"Of course. Help yourself. You'll probably find most of 'em pretty dull, though, as I did."

As usual, I underestimated the man. The first volume he chose to read was old Nick's devilish difficult manual for princes, a thing I could never persuade myself to crack. Just incidentally, this Hawai'i-grown Machiavelli did not put my journal on the parlor shelf, to remind me that it existed.

For several weeks—and I am ashamed to record this

—I thought of him as something of a trial, refusing to acknowledge the fact that actually I was finding him very agreeable company. But, as the months passed, and sorrows faded in our memories, I finally conceded to myself —but never to him—that I fully enjoyed the old boy's presence. The sarcastic wit, the playing with words, returned to his conversation, along with those risible perversions of facts and phrases for which I prized him. I laughed at him while laughing at them, because in my supercilious way I thought them the mark of a show-off revealing his ignorance, the stamp of a *kanaka* Mr. Malaprop.

Then, one evening, came the awakening—and with a vengeance. He tossed off a definition of incest that left me spluttering: "That old Makakilo up there," he chuckled, hardly in disapproval, "he's bedding up on the wrong side of his get." At last I saw the expectant look in the face I thought I knew so well, at last I realized that he'd been playing tricks upon my complacent self since the day we met. *Haole* arrogance went down several pegs that night, huge chips flaked off spontaneously from this blockhead's pride.

We were sitting at the supper table, and Hiram was expatiating upon a favorite text: "Man is not bred to live alone," is the abridged version; "it is not meet for a man to live alone, with or without bread," is the longer. Theretofore I had heard, clearly enough, the wild mixing of messages, artfully planted among commendations of certain stale widows and unvernal maids, of all colors and an infinitude of shapes, who were notoriously in chase of husbands from among Honolulu's stampeding males. And always I had succeeded in shucking them off, as though I were as deaf as an old cannoneer left over from the Battle of Bunker Hill.

But this evening I was a willing, albeit helpless, victim of his machinations. He was at his entertaining best, having found new subjects for lightsome talk—an achievement of no mean proportion in a countryside where almost nothing happens which is not catastrophic. Thanks to him, the meal was the most appetizing Kamanele had ever managed to throw on the table: the beef was actually tender, neither bloody raw nor hide-hard, the vegetables tasty, if rather exotically flavored for my tongue. And, expert as a barkeep, Hiram had ladled into our tea mugs a very young wine he was brewing in a stoneware crock sequestered in his bedroom. A year or so before, Pordagee Joe—in one of those fetial gestures by which we softened our warring—had given me a couple of starts; and no one was needed to tell Hiram what to do with the clusters of Spanish grapes hanging heavy from the vines which threaten to engulf the stable.

"One of my many talents," he allowed graciously, responding to my praise of the wine. "I was never a temperance man.—A sip of wine is better than twine, for pulling a man together."

In the glow of tallow candles, also products of his industry, the ugly parlor, the whole shabby house, and I, the Ogre of Ka‘a‘awa, were transformed. I lifted my cup in a silent toast of gratitude to the urbane little man.

"It's ready now for aging," he judged, sipping the wine. "I've been looking around for bottles. There's a whole heap of sunken sailors out there in the rubbish dump. Wherever did they come from?"

Giddy with affection, not with wine, yet unwilling to confess my bouts of boozing, I said playfully, waving a hand above my head, "Oh, I don't know. From the spirit-world, I guess."

"What?" he yelped, dropping his cup. The wine flowed

like blood across the table top. "Oh, oh—I get you. Excuse me for being a nervous man." He mopped up the mess with his napkin. "For a moment I thought you meant they came from the cave."

Not until many months had passed would I understand the import of this incident. But in the days thereafter I noticed that he would not touch those empty bottles out in the swamp. His wine was aged in narrow-necked gourds, of the kind natives use for carrying water. The quality of the vintage suffered considerably, I fear. And my vocabulary forthwith lost a word: wanting to avoid reminding him of his departed dead, I took care never again to speak of spirits, of any kind.

That evening, begun in gaiety, ended in serious talk which changed the course of our lives. After Kamanele and 'Opuhea had cleared the table, and Hiram had begged and won his goodnight kiss from the delighted child, he sat in unnatural silence, smoking his little homemade cigar, while I worked cn the slender accounts I kept for Hopkins' sake.

"You know, Saul," he began tentatively, "you are doing here what I was wanting to do at Kahana."

"And what is that?" I asked, not looking up from my account books.

"Showing my people how to live in these new times."

Now I gave him my full attention. "Aye, this is something they very much need, don't you think? A few of Ka'a'awa's people understand this need, most do not. I reckon the people of Kahana are no different in this respect.—Why, then, don't you do what you wanted to do at Kahana?"

"I lack the strength, and I lack the knowledge. I was foolish for thinking that I could do it alone."

"Nonsense. With all your many talents?"

"Nah, nah, don't make fun of me. And let me, for once, face the facts. I am like that silly bird in the fable, who flits from nest to nest of other birds, but can not build one of his own. What do you call him, that useless *haole* bird?"

A cuckoo, I almost said, before I remembered that most certainly he was not a cuckoo. "A magpie?" the answer came, from an exile who has all but forgotten *haole* birds.

"Yes, that is the one. A funny name, for an unfunny bird. For an unfunny man.—I am a magpie. I can not do what you are doing here, what the missionaries are doing wherever they have settled. I can only talk, and flit about from nest to nest."

"Now, wait up a bit, my friend," I interposed for his sake, "you're not giving credit where it's due. What about all your business enterprises in Honolulu? Surely the Hiram Nihoa Company, Limited, was not founded upon mere talk?"

"Hah. They but prove my point. Every one of those businesses profits from the weaknesses of people. None of them does anything to help people to become stronger, or better.—I tear down, but you build up. You are a good man, I am not."

Inasmuch as I had not yet heard of his "hotels" and grogshops, I thought this a strange attitude for him to take toward his very profitable mercantile interests. "Tarnation! You sound as though the missionaries have got hold of you. I never thought to hear such mealy-mouthed—"

"Nah, nah, nah, they do not have to talk to me. With their example before me, and yours, what talk from them is needed? None.—And don't forget: I have had plenty of time, lately, to think. And I am a wiser man since I asked the King for permission to settle in Kahana."

"Did you have to ask his permission? Heavens to Betsy! I thought this was a free country?"

"Oh, yes. Yet with Alex speaking for me, and Lot also, it was not hard to get. Purely a matter of form. But," he sighed, "then I was weak when I should have been strong. Weak of will, weaker still in thoughts. You know how it is. While I was here, in February, I wanted very much to come to Kahana. But in Honolulu things looked different. Breaking away was not as easy as I'd thought it would be. The children did not want to leave the excitements of Honolulu for the quiet of Kahana. Rebekah did not wish to part with all her many friends. 'And what of the schooling for your children?' she asked, poking her finger into the pretty soap-bubble of my dream. Complaints, arguments, objections, childish tears: they fell upon me like rocks from a cliff, until the little spring of my mouth was covered up and choked off. This is the saddest thing: I knew what was right, but I did not do it, out of weakness. Had I been stronger, perhaps some of them, perhaps all of them, would be with me in Kahana today."

Oh, my body and soul! How well I understood these vain regrets, these unending recriminations. And how well I knew their uselessness. "Hiram, my friend," I said, the most constant comforter in all this wide world of dung heaps, "man proposes, but God disposes." This was the quickest way I knew to sum up the wisdom of believers and unbelievers alike, the wisdom of all suffering men, and the futility, compressed into the most crushing of laws. Then, seeing no contradiction in the question—for, after all, men are fools enough to live by hope—I pulled us out from beneath the turning wheel. "What did you propose to do in Kahana? And why can't you do it still?"

"What you are doing here, as I have said.—And more, because my people in Kahana have not had the help that

the people of Ka'a'awa have received from you. For much
too long Kahana's people have been neglected. Their chief
did not take proper care of them. Now he must make up
for the time he has misspent. And least but not last, he
must do this soon, for not many years of life are left to
him. Even worse. He must make up for the time his
people have misspent. Satan finds much mischief for their
idle hands to do. And their idler minds. The Devil's mind
is an idler's workshop. I am afraid that they copy—"

"Yes, yes, I know," I broke in, "that they copy our
nasty *haole* vices, when they should be practising our ad-
mirable *haole* virtues."

"Exactly," he said, looking surprised, "but how did
you know?"

"In the name of Christ, Hiram! That's the stock-in-
trade of every priest and missionary who ever set out to
bring salvation to the heathen anywhere. They must hear
that same unvarying sermon during every single day
they spend in their schools and seminaries and rookeries,
or whatever they're called, before they're shipped out to
do their duty. If only those black-frocked white men took
it as much to heart as they admonish the heathen to do,
they'd get more good done in this world, which needs it,
than they aspire to do for the next, which doesn't need it."

"Oh, shoot!" he said, wilting a bit, "and here I thought
it such an elegant way of giving the Devil his due."

"The Devil is always with us, my friend, as you and I
well know. And he will always take his due, without our
leave. How do we fight him, we who are not missionaries?
How do we save a dying people, we who are not physicians? This is the question before this convention of in-
tellects.—Now tell me, for Heaven's sake, and in detail:
what was your plan for Kahana?"

While he talked I was like tinder awaiting the spark.

Long before he was finished I had taken the fire.

"It is a worthy plan," I said when he was done, "and much better than my own for Ka'a'awa, because it is so much more generous." From him I learned how mean were my goals, how timid was my imagination. With him, I saw, I could salvage some good from my wasted life. With me, he could salvage what was left of his broken hopes.

"Here is my thought," I leaned forward eagerly. "If this world in which we live is to be improved, then we ourselves must begin upon the task. Let us do this together. Let us combine our knowledge and our money." To my chagrin, he did not jump at the proposal. Calm, inscrutable as the Three Fates above us, he sat back in his chair, drawing on his cheroot, while I rushed on, trying to convince him. The trust of Linalina, the memory of all those bones of Ka'a'awa's dead, given to death too soon, could be quieted in no other way. "The two of us together," I emphasized, "can do much more good than either one alone. And, best of all, we could start right away, right here, at Ka'a'awa."

"Ah, those are good words to hear," he said, looking like a poker player raking in his winnings. "I was afraid that I'd have a harder time persuading you."

CHAPTER 35.

KE EAHOU

So began our training school at Ka'a'awa. Although the idea behind it was not very original, even in Hawai'i, it was a different sort of school from anything else I've ever heard of.

At Hiram's suggestion, we named it Ke Eahou, The New Life. I thought this an appropriate name for a good cause, one which would represent our purpose to everyone, students, parents, government officials and missionaries, friends as well as foes. They warranted this assurance for, surely, never in the history of mankind has an institution of learning been founded by as unlikely a pair of sinners as Hiram and I. Two broken men, unable to recapture happiness for ourselves, we set out to tie it down for others, as the legend says Maui snared the sun for his mother.

Each of us assumed the duties most suited to his temperament and abilities. Hiram rode pink and plodding Lokelani up and down O'ahu's windward coast from Waiahole to Kahuku, telling the countryfolk in a prodigious verbal prospectus about our plans for the school, inviting them or their sons to learn the skills we proposed to teach. Many of the people laughed at our foolishness, saying, "Why should we learn new ways? Are not the old ways good enough for us?" Others grumbled, fearing an increase in taxes because of the school (despite the fact that we offered our instruction free of all charge), saying, "Do we not have schools enough, between the Calvinists at Kaneʻohe and the Catholics at ʻAhuimanu? Nah, nah, schooling we do not need. Just more fish from the sea, more *poi* in the bowl—and no tax collectors. That is all we ask." And some, the saddest ones of all, said, "Go away. Let us die in peace. Leave us alone, for the short time that is left to us."

"Shoot!" Hiram said to everyone who would hear him out, "These are the stupid folk, all of them. These are the unthinking ones, the complaining ones, who can not look further ahead than tonight's full belly. Wait and see. They will be the ones most confused, the folk most bitter, when in a few years they are lost in the shuffle. Then they will be the ones left out. And then they will not know why they have no pig to cook, no taro to pound into *poi*, not even the plot of earth in which to dig their ovens. You watch. Soon the foreigners will have all the land, and all the money, and all the knowledge. And Hawaiians will be left with nothing but air in their bellies. Then they will wail and whine, crying 'These are the days when the markets have nothing to sell, because there is nothing anywhere.' But they will be wrong. The markets will have much to sell. But they will have nothing with which to buy the things they will need from the marketplace."

But very few people, even after listening to Hiram's exhortations, approved of our plan. After a month of his gospeling, only six youths had asked to be accepted at Ke Eahou. Although we had hoped for ten, we decided to start with those six.

These were the subjects I taught: how to use foreigners' tools to clear brush from overgrown fields; how to harness a team of horses to an iron-shod plow; how to turn the soil with that plow; how to raise calves upon the grassy pastures until they were heavy with good meat; how to milk their lowing dams; and how to feed that rich milk to pigs until they, too, were full-grown and ready for the eating. Like all natives, those boys would not drink milk of any kind, so perforce it must go to the pigs. In all of Ka'a'awa, quite probably in all of Ko'olauloa, I was the only person who drank milk and ate butter.

We labored for both Hopkins and Ke Eahou. Although Makua and the ranch-hands assisted in every way, I longed for Linalina to return. With his quiet efficiency and many skills, he would have been the best possible example to our students. And then, one day, we learned that he would not return. He was killed in a brawl in Honolulu when, as a man who happened to be passing by, he tried to rescue a foreign sailor from some local thugs who were attacking him. Once again Linalina threw himself between Death and the intended victim—but this time Death took him instead.

Alas, for stalwart Linalina. Not even his bones will come home to rest in Ka'a'awa. Long before word of his murder reached us in this part of the island, his body had been consigned to an unmarked grave. When I went to the Fort to claim what was left of him, the Marshall's men could not even remember in which potter's field they had dumped him.—So much for thirty-three generations of devotion. So much for vaunted civilization.

Once we had claimed new pasture land for Ke Eahou, and Hiram had enlarged the vegetable garden, we progressed to even more novel tasks: we sawed wood from *koa* trees I had felled a year earlier; with the planks we built a house in the *haole* style, to replace the grass hut which had lodged the boys during the interval; and we made sturdy furniture to put into it. None of those boys had ever followed a plow, or slept upon a mattress in a raised bed; and most of them had not used any of the modern tools and implements which make life so comfortable for foreigners.

We worked hard, from sunup until near sundown, and with no complaint from five of our students after the first backbreaking week. The sixth did not stay to complain: he simply ran for home one night, taking his aching muscles and overladen brain with him. The rest of us agreed that we were better off without him. Makana took his place, spurred into it less by vaulting ambition than by the insuperable team of Kamanele and Hiram, one at either ear.

Our first class was an unqualified success—at Ka'a-'awa. "But what will happen when they go home?" I fretted, "how can our five boys change the habits of all their relatives and neighbors?" This was not the first time we'd discussed the usual worry of teachers. "Well," said Hiram, "we can only hope that each of them will share his knowledge, if only by example. After all, Jesus had only twelve disciples, and they changed the whole world.— And do not worry about the tools those boys will need at home. I shall take care of those, when the time comes."

On Graduation Day, at a farewell feast we held for our students and their families and for folk we wanted to impress, Hiram gave the shortest and most cogent Commencement Address I have ever heard: "These are now responsible men. They will not, like children at a game, sit down to 'open their mouths and shut their eyes,' and wait to see what God will send them. They have learned here that God helps those who help themselves." Whereupon, amid exclamations and applause from all sides, he presented to each disciple—except for misfortuned Makana—a written order upon Honolulu Iron Works Company for a complete set of farm tools, from anvils to yokes, and the address of the captain of a coastal schooner who would deliver those crated articles to the beach-landing nearest the boy's home. Each of them, again except for Makana, also received from Hiram a ten-dollar American gold-piece to spend during his visit to town. I gave each boy a small ledger, to keep his accounts in. Hiram, of all people, suggested this most impractical of awards. "You'd be surprised," he said, "how many uses can be found for a ledger." Makana, by arrangement between Hiram and Kamanele, received nothing but promises of rewards in some indefinite future, and—as a pretty poor sort of consolation prize, I thought—a shiny new money belt from Hiram. For a boy who doesn't know a copper cent from a pewter spoon—and what's more, who never will—this is the inducement least likely to succeed in its purpose, of all the bribes that I can imagine. But, as Hiram would say, "No matter . . . 'Tis the gift that counts, not the thought before it."

"I want them to see all the wonders of Honolulu," that master-manipulator said amiably when, before the ceremony, I had deplored his lavishness toward our graduates. "The wonders," I repeated, as if, of course, I concurred, the while I racked my brain to see if it could come up with just one thing in Honolulu that qualified for the distinction.

"Yes, the wonders," he continued smoothly. "Then they

will know how fortunate they are, to be living on this beautiful island of Oʻahu. They will see for themselves why it is named The Gathering Place. I want them to see Hoʻihoʻikea, the splendid Royal Palace, wherein live their King and Queen. And the noble Court House, wherein the nation's laws are made and its justice is dispensed. I hope they will stand before the mighty Fort of Ke Kua Nohu, wherein men who break the laws are punished. I hope they will enter into the great bare Stone Church the Protestants have built at Kawaiahaʻo, and into the long, pretty, painted Cathedral the Catholics have built on Fort Street, there to learn that Jehovah has come to stay with Kane, Ku, and Lono. I know they will see the fine houses in which city-folk dwell, and the wide streets crowded with wagons and carriages and with people of so many races other than our own. Most of all do I expect them to go into the shops and stores and marketplaces, filled with all the many good things foreigners have brought to us from all over the world. I want for them to covet some of those good things, to feel the bite of envy, the satisfaction of *having*. I would like for them to leave their rustic's innocence in the streets of Honolulu, so that when they return to the country they will never again be content with having nothing. I give them these gold pieces because— can you deny this?—they must know that money can buy comforts as well as spades, happiness as well as plows. They must realize that gold is a most necessary commodity in this new kind of life you foreigners are bringing to us. Until they learn this most important law of haoles, the law of property, how can they understand all the other laws which now govern us?"

"You win, my friend, as always," I retreated from a battle he'd won without even being aware that he was waging it. "Those shrewd haoles back home in New England can learn a thing or two from you."

"I am no niggard in the woods," he grinned, "even though I am only a simple country man, so to speak.— The only places I have told these boys not to waste their money in are the whorehouses of Honolulu. Why should they spend precious gold on shopworn pieces, I ask them, when they can get fresh goods free at home?"

Long before those boys left Ka'a'awa for the higher instruction afforded by Honolulu's stores and boulevards, Hiram was lining up their successors. Without telling me, he signed on a bunch of females as well. I was consternated when, very casually, he presented me with this accomplished fact. "Girls! Jumping Jehosophat! Where are we going to put 'em? Who's going to watch over 'em? And what, pray tell, do you propose to teach 'em?— Horse-shoeing? Bridle-making?"

"Nah, nah, stop rattling your chains. I've thought of all that. Teaching young women the new ways is even more important than teaching young men. Who bears the babies? Who cares for the babies? Who must learn the proper ways of caring for these babies, if they are to live? *E*?—Not the men. All they do, as perhaps you have read, is to plant the seeds." That dirty dig at my celibacy is just one of the many I have had to put up with —in anything but saintly resignation.

At his order, and as a climactic demonstration of their new learning, those six boys and I built a house for the young ladies. This one did not go up in the right place, on the hill: it went up in a corner of my yard.

"We shall watch over them with a fatherly eye, you and I," Hiram informed me, as he paced off the site for this vestals' domicile, "at least until you bring a wife into your house."

Letting that one go by for the moment, I inquired ever so softly, "And who is going to teach them?" About caring for children, I meant. Heaven—and the Devil—knew how they need no instruction at all in the manner of making babies.

"Who else but I?" he replied, as seemly as a nun. "Don't forget: I know a little something about the raising of infants, the preparing of meals, the many little tricks of domestic economy. And what I do not know the matron can teach them. Under my supervision, of course."

"The matron?" I repeated, assailed by thoughts of simpering, buck-toothed spinsters, of fat and frowzy widows, coming and going by the caravan, as calmly, unrelenting, Hiram sought among them the mate he'd choose for me. "Oh, no," I wailed, deciding to jump ship at first glimpse of a bonnet.

"Yes," he nodded, rather absently I felt, in view of the sacrifice he was requiring of me, "Kamanele. She will make an excellent matron, I do believe." At which I sank to the grass, stunned.

Needless to say, Kamanele has been a most excellent matron—untiring, loul-mouthed, sharp-tongued, softhearted, and as vigilant as only a woman of experience can be. Even a missionary wife could not find fault with Kamanele's tyranny. Lusty Makana, the other rutting, snorting studs in and out of Ke Eahou, have never had a chance. And—praise be to Kamanele!—neither have the girls.—So far. Knock on wood.

"It's not because we would object to a bit of innocent fornication between the boys and the girls," Hiram said at one of those discussions he likes to call Faculty Meetings. "It's just that they're here to learn new experiences, and we can't let pleasures interfere with education." That was not quite the way I looked upon the problem.

Matron Kamanele, nodding vigorously, precluded any statement from me to the contrary. A profusion of bulges and curves, stuffed into the skin of a calico dress, hands resting on massive thighs, toes locked around the legs of her chair, she was Alma Mater in the very solid flesh. "They are too young to be troubled with having babies," she declared, " 'Wait,' I tell them, 'do the work now, have the fun later.' "

"Excellent advice," beamed our Headmaster.

"I also tell them," Kamanele concluded debate upon this topic, for faculty or students, " 'Anyone I catch fooling around, I kick him in the ass. Hard.' " Praise be to Kamanele. That's the only commandment Makana and his ilk will understand—and obey.

Scarcely were the ten damsels installed in their convent when Hiram sat me down in our parlor one evening. I could guess from his elaborate circumlocutions that something big was brewing, something far beyond the ordinary. I was prepared for anything, from starting a sugar plantation, complete with mill (they were quite the rage that year), to something a little more taxing, such as a shipyard, complete with a wharf planted in our turbulent sea. " O. K., old friend, O. K.," I helped him, "out with it. What's it going to be?"

"I've been thinking," he began, as he does when he wants to tie me down for the branding. "The time has come to bring in the children."

For a long minute we sat in the silence of a childless house, each thinking of what might have been. I did not struggle.

"You are right, as usual. The time has come."

"But their house," he said, very firmly, "it must be made of stone."

"It shall be made of stone," I promised.

Now eight moppets, four boys and four girls between the ages of six and ten, occupy a stone house next to the young ladies' dormitory. Well, at any rate that was the way things were planned. The reality shows that even Hiram can't anticipate everything. The big girls spend all their spare time, day or night, mothering the kids. "And that is the way things should be, don't you think?" says Father Hiram, forgetting that he is quoting—very much out of context—the chorus from one of the most lascivious native songs ever to fall upon an astounded *haole* ear.

In themselves these kids, like all Hawaiian children, are an engaging lot. Yet they cannot be substitutes for the boy Hiram and I remember but almost never talk about. As Hiram once said of Kalanimoku, who was prime minister to the first Kamehameha, so it is of Kaneikapule: "when he died, there was no one to take his place." We did not say so, but I knew this to be the truth, for both of us: we looked upon Ke Eahou as our memorial to Kaneikapule.

Nonetheless, I like the kids well enough. I enjoy playing games with them on Sundays, and I dry their tears when they are hurt, take them riding with me across the fields or on hikes up into the forest for mountain-apples when they are in season. And I am the one who must dust their little bottoms, in the name of discipline, when they have been very naughty.

For most of us, however, the best times of all are the swimming sessions. Every afternoon at five o'clock, rain or shine, we go to the beach for our combined bath and laundering. The three members of the faculty, followed by Ke Eahou's entire student body, proceed in an orderly promenade to the shore. Once there, all decorum ends. Whooping and hollering, we rush into the sea fully dressed, and splash about in the waves and roll in the scouring sand until dirt and sweat have been worked out of our clothes and they are clean enough to don some other day. Then we take off the encumbering apparel, toss it up on the sand beyond the reach of waves, and, free as fish, swim, or dive, or "catch da waves" until each of us thinks he's had enough of such sport. As bare as turkeys ready for the spit, we amble up to the pond to rinse ourselves and our garments in fresh water.

Slick and shining, dressed in clean attire, the male contingent lolls around on the grass under a *hala* tree— or, if it's a rainy evening, in the covered *lanai* which is our refectory—chatting and joking, and teasing the small-fry, while Kamanele and the bigger girls serve the supper they've prepared during the afternoon. The boys and the smaller children do the dishes, under my rigorous scrutiny. Everybody shares in the work at Ke Eahou.

This custom of swimming in the native mode has grown up quite naturally. It all started, sensibly enough, when our first students and I went to the sea to bathe after each hard day's labor. Just before the girls moved in, I cornered Hiram to arrange a schedule by which they would swim at four o'clock and be safely off the beach when the boys and I arrived at five. For a very uncomfortable minute he looked at me, over the rims of his spectacles. "Absolutely not," he rebuked me, with unwonted asperity. "We shall swim together, all of us, in the manner of our people.—Pull down your eyebrows, my puritan friend, draw in your tongue. Remember where you are.—Do you really think that these boys and girls have not seen unclothed bodies before they come here? And do you honestly believe that their seeing each other unclothed will damn them forever? If you do, then you must be as smallminded as all those other Christians are."

While I tried to recover from that blast, he went on. "The surest way to cause trouble is to give these boys and girls reason to think that nakedness is evil. The surest way to avoid trouble is to give them no reason to be ashamed of anything. Of anything, mind you. Bodies, appearance, dress, thoughts, school work, house work, field work, dancing, singing, of anything at all. 'A sound mind in a sound body,' as that old Roman said: isn't this what we want our students to have?" Hiram can deliver a quotation correctly, when he wants to. And he can present a case in such a way that, somehow, I can find no ground for rebuttal.—I must assume that I've learned a few things since I left the College.

For me, personally, the best part of the day comes at the very end, after the dishes are done and the lamps are doused in the cookhouse. I wouldn't miss it for all the lures of Honolulu, this time when we "have dancing and singing" 'neath the *hala* tree.

The big boys and girls, without exception, know a great number of native songs and dances, of almost infinite variety in style and tunefulness, at least to my ear, and of no offense at all to my eye. Some, indeed, are very beautiful, extraordinarily graceful. I've been taught, in most agreeable fashion, that not all hulas are vulgar or lascivious.

These Hawaiians are amazing. They seem to have been born with the sense of music in their warm blood and supple bodies. I am impressed by the ease with which they make a song their own after hearing it but once or twice. Hiram's rollicking sea-chanties and more decent

tavern ballads, the few hymns and parlor ditties I remember, even Melissa's song, have been added to their
repertory. More wondrous still are the things they can do
with rhythm and harmony: they can make *Old One Hundred* sound as merry as a *hula* for a feast, a chanty as
doleful as a dirge. I am captivated by their music-making,
I envy them their ability.

And they have so much fun while they're at it. One of
the youths in our second group arrived with a Spanish
guitar hung over his shoulder and no other possession
save the shirt and trousers he was wearing—and the biggest, broadest, all-conquering smile it has ever been my
pleasure to see.

"Only the eyes have come," he said as he presented
himself to us, asking if he might attend our school. He
was not one of Hiram's recruits. Having heard of Ke
Eahou, he himself had decided to join us. Much to my
distress, Hiram started to laugh at him. This is not the
way to greet a convert, I was thinking, when Hiram said,
between chuckles, "From Ka'alaea, I will guess."

"Yes," said the youth, as laughter bubbled up in him,
out of him, through shoulders, eyes, hands, feet, until I
too was joining them, "a good place to come from. A very
good place to stay away from."

Even the voice of the boy, full of squeaks and break-
ings, was comical. We've been laughing ever since, all of
us, at the antics of this natural-born jester, this incarna-
tion of mirth. I will take an oath, on a stack of Bibles, that
I've never seen him serious. Much more than a brace of
empty hands came to us that day, when Poha Kealoha
walked into our school. When he sings or talks, even
though we can't see him, as in the dark of night, "we can
heah hees leeps smiling," as one of his small admirers
has said.

Where he found that guitar, how he learned to play it with such skill, in isolated Ka'alaea, I can not imagine. But then the same praise can be offered to Hiram, who is a master of the mandolin—and a very creditable baritone as well. To hear him "sing a yearning," one of those mournful laments Portuguese sailors seem to enjoy tormenting themselves with, is almost more than I can bear. Fortunately for me, he rarely is in the mood for such plunges into desolation.

Hiram, plucking away on that round-bellied mandolin, and Poha Kealoha, strumming on his guitar, provide the melody for our orchestra of gourds, calabashes, sections of bamboo, blocks of wood, pots and pans, clapping hands, clacking rib bones, stream pebbles, and serving spoons. Rather appropriately, I think, I have become a virtuoso of the overturned washtub, thumping it as if it were a big bass drum.

Poha is responsible for this evocation of my hidden talent. After putting on a great show, staggering across the yard as though bearing an almost insupportable load, he deposited the empty tub at my feet. "The biggest man," he gasped, collapsing beside the thing, while the girls squealed, the boys howled, "should make the biggest noise." I have obliged ever since, salving my self-esteem with the hope that Poha does not know the American proverb about empty barrels.

Everyone plays some kind of instrument. And everyone sings. They sing like a choir of angels. They dance as the Greeks of old must have danced before the temples of their gods. The girls, with their long hair braided and coiled, are as lovely as priestesses at the Parthenon. The boys, virile and strong, are as splendid as athletes at Olympia. Even Kamanele, who looks more like a female

Minotaur than a nymph, is as graceful when she dances as any of the girls.

By eight o'clock the stars are blazing in the black sky above, or the moon is casting her soft light upon us here below. The little ones are nodding and yawning and rubbing their eyes. Hiram gives his signal: "*Aia la, ua luluhi na maka.* Ah, now, the eyes are heavy with sleep." Caressing the tune from his mandolin, he sings our lullaby, while Poha, smiling blissfully over his guitar, upon all of us, devises happy little variations upon the theme:

> Look to your ways in Ka'a'awa,
> Look to your ways wherever you may go.
> Walk softly, commit no offense;
> Delay not, nor pluck the flower evil,
> Lest God in anger bar the road,
> And you find no way of escape.

As this sermon in song comes to a close, we stand while Hiram offers a short prayer, thanking Jehovah and his indigenous colleagues for their care of us. Then, to the sound of soft good-nights, we part in peace until the morrow.

Kamanele and the girls tuck the children into bed, the boys and I make a last round of inspection through the stable and the farmyard before I leave them at their house on the hill. Hiram studies the stars until the last lamp is snuffed out, and the boys and girls of Ke Eahou are safe in their separate beds for another night.

"All is well," I report to Hiram. "It is good," we say, each to the other, as we walk across the quiet yard to our house.

During the mornings, while the big boys and I work in the fields, Hiram is in his glory, presiding over the schoolhouse. There he teaches both children and damsels reading, writing, and doing sums—in English. His is the first secular school outside of Honolulu to instruct commoners in English. "Why should I teach them in Hawaiian?" he maintains, "when they know it already. Now they must learn English: that is the language of their future." Therefore the poor kids suffer an exposure to English, thoroughly admixed with fast-flowing Hawaiian when the foreign tongue proves to be too slow or too difficult. Often enough have I eavesdropped outside the schoolhouse to know that Hiram does not neglect his beloved country. "Breathes there the man, with soul so dead, who never to himself hath said, this is my own, my native land?" is as moving in Hawaiian as it is in English. Oh, the legends, the poetry, the chants and prayers, the history with which he builds up their pride in the past, so that they might carry it into the future. Each morning, when they recite the Lord's Prayer, I am convinced that they think of Kamehameha I as Jehovah, and of Kamehameha IV as his most beloved son.

Alex has been King since December 15, 1854, the day Kauikeaouli died. At the bedside of the dead King the new Sovereign took his place with these words: "Hear me, O ye Chiefs: I have become, by the Will of God, your Father, as I have been your child. You must help me, for I stand in need of help."

To Hiram's regret, he missed the great occasion when Alex became King. It all happened so quickly that he could not be summoned to town to witness the accession. Alex, it seems, like the other Kamehameha, required no coronation: he inherited the Kingdom upon his uncle's death, and no one disputed his right to the throne. But since that day both Alex and Hiram have made up for the lost moment.

On January 11, 1855, in Kawaiaha'o Church, when Alexander Liholiho made his inaugural address as Kamehameha IV, Hiram was there, resplendent in Windsor uniform embroidered in gold, ribband, and tricorn, standing proudly among the few great chiefs who remain. His was the right to be among them, for—as one of his first acts in the new reign—Alex had elevated Hiram to their station by creating him High Chief of Kahana and Ka'a'awa, and a lifelong member of the House of Nobles.

With that first speech the young King brought dignity to his office and new hope to the nation.

He spoke to his people in Hawaiian:

... Today we begin a new era. Let it be one of increased civilization—one of decided progress, industry, temperance, morality, and all those virtues which mark a nation's advance. This is beyond doubt a critical period in the history of our country, but I see no reason to despair ...

Then, in English, he spoke to foreigners, wherever they were, whether in his Kingdom or beyond the seas:

... To be kind and generous to the foreigner, to trust and confide in him, is no new thing in the history of our race. It is an inheritance transmitted to us from our forefathers ... I can not fail to heed the example of my ancestors. I therefore say to the foreigner that he is welcome ... so long as he comes with the laudable motive of promoting his own interests and at the same time respecting those of his neighbor. But if he comes with no more exalted motive than that of building up his own interests, at the expense of the natives—to seek our confidence only to betray it— with no higher ambition than that of overthrowing our Government, and introducing anarchy, confusion, and bloodshed—then he is most unwelcome!

The duties we owe to each other are reciprocal. For my part I shall use my best endeavors ... to give you a just, liberal, and satisfactory government. At the same time, I shall expect you in return to assist me in sustaining the Peace, the Law, the Order, and the Independence of my Kingdom.

Hiram has a right to be proud of his service as *kahu* to a boy who grew up to be such a noble King.

Each spring, when the Legislative Assembly is in session, we declare a long recess at Ke Eahou. Hiram is in Honolulu then, his Sovereign's most loyal liege-man—although not his most vocal one. He leaves that distinction to Mr. Wyllie, who is neither as poetical in utterance nor as practical in effect as Hiram would be. Hiram prefers subtler maneuverings behind the scenes. He and Prince Lot, an exceedingly practical young man, are forever conferring, arranging, contriving; and between them these "hands and feet of the King," as they are known throughout the islands, seem to be serving their monarch and the nation both honestly and efficiently. Even the foreigners are content, thus far, with the rule of Kamehameha IV. In consequence, there's been no more talk of filibusterers, either from California or from any other pirates' hideaway; and my perfervid compatriots from America have suppressed for the while—but only for a short time, I predict—their schemes to annex these islands to the United States.

In his concept of himself as Machiavel to Alex, Hiram has drawn me, too, into public life of a sort. Without my knowing, he put me up for appointment as a District Magistrate. My first inkling of this came when he handed me the official document proclaiming BY ALL THESE PRESENTS the fact that I am now charged with maintaining the majesty of the King's law in Ko'olauloa. I have submitted to this involvement with fair grace, thinking that if, earlier in his career, Hopkins was a Justice, I certainly can qualify as a Magistrate. But lately I've begun to worry over the possibility that, by being so amenable, I've left myself wide open for further invasions upon my privacy. "In two years, my boy," plotting Hiram announced the other day, "you will be ready to stand for election to the House of Representatives. And Makana will be your secretary. Who is going to teach him the fine points of politics, if we do not? Here he is, fifteen years old already, and we can't wait much longer to start him on his career."

I am not so certain that I shall stand for such an office, with or without Makana for a secretary. I am firmly of the opinion that natives, not foreigners, should run their government. And I am even more certain that Makana needs no instruction from anyone in the arts of persuasion. If I could have my way, I'd send that creature off to sea— did I not worry for the safety of his shipmates. He is the most accomplished persuader on this coast, as three tearful, hugely pregnant girls have testified before the exasperated Magistrate of Koʻolauloa. This annoyed Solomon is still trying to think of a wise solution to that problem in multiplication. If I were indeed Solomon, I'd cut Makana, all right, but not in half.—And I can't say that I approve of Hiram's attitude toward our jackrabbit-on-the-loose: "My goodness me!" quoth that pillar of rectitude, "when does he find the time?"

Hiram, it appears, is finding time enough for "riding sidesaddle," as the native expression puts it, despite his innumerable commitments here and in Honolulu. The truth will out. Gradually, little by little, with a name dropped here, a house mentioned there, I've discovered that Caleb, the lad he "gave away like trash," is by no means his only bastard. And finally I've learned—from Hiram's own pleasured self—what Linalina meant, when he spoke of Hiram as a shark. Once again, Hawaiian improves upon English: this old goat, as I would dub him in plain language, is very much of a shark, as natives call an

ardent lover. His raft of "*manuahi*" children—there's another charming euphemism, meaning "free" or "extra"
—has increased by at least two during the past year alone.
I should have guessed about this propensity of his, if only
from hearing him sing what he calls "my old school song,"
appropriately entitled "Gramma's Sin-tax." One line of it
will be enough to damn the rest: "Any chance to conju-
gate should never be declined." I can not bring myself to
write down what he has to say about conjunctions, copulas,
and propositions.

Job is coming into the fullness of his reward. Hiram has
recovered sufficiently from the loss of his Rebekah to be
weighing the prospect of marrying again. Not, he assev-
erates—and now I can understand why—"merely to enjoy
the felicities of the connubial tie," but entirely to safe-
guard his estates and his rank by passing them on to a
legitimate heir. "Who will care for my bones?" he asks,
although I'll wager he is at least fifty years away from
dying. "Who will be an example to the people?" he orates,
although I question whether a shark is quite the exemplar
they should heed. Candidates for his hand are not lacking,
he informs me, but he is being very choosy. No one less
than a chiefess will do—and these, unfortunately, are not
in plentiful supply nowadays.

"Lot has proposed his sister Ke'elikolani," Hiram has
told me, indignant and demure in the same breath.

"Surely only in jest?" I cried, scarcely able to see its
victim for laughing.

"How can one be sure, with that Lot?" he sniffed. "But
I tell you, I would rather suffocate in a flow of mud, than
be smothered in that mor-ass of fat. Can you just imagine
me—"

I could, we did, and together we laughed so uproari-
ously that I missed the one chance in a lifetime to shake

his hand solemnly and, with manly sincerity in voice and mien, congratulate him for being so greatly honored. But some day, I plot, waiting for the moment to arrive, I shall ask him what would come of a mating of such sharks . . .

I do not aspire to the Legislature because I do not want to leave Ka'a'awa. Hiram, that rolling stone, calls me "a rock weighing down a mat," which is to say, a homebody. The description is a nice one: I accept it without demur. He gathers no moss, I run no risk of being shattered. I have attained peace of a sort in this beautiful valley, and purpose enough in our little school. As it prospers, so do I. Just as my black swans from Australia thrive in their new abode, and my Muscovy ducks, Leghorn chickens, and gorgeous Indian peacocks, all *haole* birds, all at home with me here in Ka'a'awa.

Wild birds, also, come to our pond—and to our gardens—as to a sanctuary. Among them are the plovers, resting on their long flights across the ocean to destinations only they know how to find. In the fall of each year these koleas arrive, in the spring they depart, just as whalers come to Hawai'i's ports on their courses from northern fisheries to southern grounds. Yet one *kolea* has seen the foolishness of all this flying back and forth: all alone, unattended by kith or kin, he seems to be perfectly content to remain here the year around. He is a sensible fellow, much smarter than the rest of his gadabout species. In my thoughts I call him Saul. He and I are wise old birds. We know when we are well off.

Through Hiram's telescope I can detect, in the vale between the second and third peaks high overhead, the light green leaves of young *kukui* trees, grown from the seeds I sowed that time I made my walk with Linalina. In the years to come, when people will stop to wonder how the tree-of-life ever reached that windswept slope above those mighty cliffs, they will have to realize that the trees must have been planted there by the hand of man. I don't care if they will not know that I was the one who cast those seeds upon that slope, or that those trees, standing strong against the wind, were intended to be my private memorial to my given-son, whose Spring was so short, whose Fall came too soon. That intention has given way to another, in the years since Linalina disclosed to me the mystery of the mountain and made me the keeper of its bones. As he promised, the burden has not been heavy.

Not at all as I feared, I think very little now of the dead, because now I am devoted to the living. Linalina and Hiram, Makua and Alex, each in his different way, have helped me to turn my back upon death. And now I look upon those *kukui* trees not as a memorial to the dead, but as an encouragement to the living. The trees-of-life growing here, they proclaim for all to see who will see, were planted by forethoughtful men, and by no other agency.

Hiram grasped my meaning immediately when, one Sabbath day, I had to tell the *niele* man why I trained his telescope so often upon that one special place. With his usual facility, he converted the moral of my stolid tale into an epigram, which has become the motto of Ke Eahou: "As the tree-of-life flourishes above, so will the people flourish below."

The people of Koʻolauloa have heard this motto, and many have seen it on our school's banner, a pretty thing done in green and white (the colors of the *kukui*'s leaves and its blossoms), made by the girls of Ke Eahou. But, alas, the people do not flourish. Last year they died from another new disease, this one called the breakbone fever; this year they are dying from a recurrence of familiar intestinal fevers. And a new and horrible scourge is appearing among the people of Kaneʻohe. Hiram, who has seen some of them, has described its signs to the doctors in Honolulu. Dr. Hillebrand believes that it may be the Oriental leprosy. If he is correct in this opinion, God help the Hawaiian people.

To push myself into this picture is one more act of vanity, but I must do so because Hiram exacts this of me. I am content, if not happy. Kaʻaʻawa and Ke Eahou give me reasons to be content. Oh, I don't suppose we are doing anything here—except for the sinful swimming and the proscribed singing and dancing—that the missionaries are not doing for natives in their boarding schools at Hilo and Waimea, at Wailuku and Lahainaluna. But at least we are doing *something* to help preserve this vanishing race. If only half the boys and girls we are training here should survive, and if only half of their progeny should survive to bear children of their own, I shall count this a victory greater than any won in some bloody war. If only Poha Kealoha's line should endure, and his grand-sons can bring happiness to the people of their time as he brings it now to us, I shall be so busy laughing that I'll not feel the Devil's pitchfork when I get to Hell. And I would give my life, today, without a second thought, if by doing so I could wangle from the Fates a promise that Hiram's line would not end with him.

I am content. Happiness is beyond my reach. For that I need Melissa—or, to be truthful, I need to go back to the time before Melissa came into my life. Even so, although I never expected to see the day dawn, once again I can sing, without too much hurt, the Shaker song she taught me, not so long ago.

I can't be all bad, I think, each time I end this song, each time I look at Kaʻaʻawa and at our school. True sim-plicity has been gained, things are coming 'round right, in a way. But I am wary, still, of Atropos, the Fate that can not be avoided. I know enough about her to fear that all this can be taken away from me in the beat of a bird's wing, with a snip of her shears. She, not wisdom, governs our lives.

—Hell and Damnation! Truthful as I profess to be, I have not yet given up lying to myself—or trying to cheat Him. Atropos is not the one I fear. *He* is the one—and I live in dread of the flick of His finger. Twice before He has shown me His power, and twice before He has but toyed with me. Now I await the punishment He must yet exact of me. For I have sinned, and my sin is very great. And one day, sooner or later, this game He is playing with me must end. I do not need to be a magistrate to know that His laws can not be broken with impunity.

CHAPTER 36.

THE STRONG-BOX PAPERS

In June of 1856 Hiram was in a great ferment, preparing for another visit in Honolulu, this time to attend the wedding of Alexander Liholiho to Miss Emma Rooke. Although I've never met her, according to Hiram "she is a very lovely girl, very lovely. Even though, being part English, she is not of the highest rank. But she is just right for Alex. And how good their marriage will be for the nation—especially when their children start to come."

Knowing Hiram's jealousy for Alex's happiness, I accepted his opinion of Miss Rooke. Out of my regard for Alex, and because I could think of nothing better to offer the august pair, I was inspired one evening to compose an epithalamium as my marriage-gift to the King of Hawai'i and his bride.

It flowed easily out of my mind, through my hand to the paper. Florid, artificial, foreign though it may be in our time and in this place, it was faithful to its models. I thought it as happy a marriage between European poesy and Hawaiian imagery as I hoped would be the union it was intended to celebrate, between a maid half English and a King wholly Hawaiian. Admiring both the poem and its author, I copied it out in a fair hand. Bemused and befuddled and fatuate, I forgot where I was, relaxed my vigilance, betrayed my secret self, without so much as a cramp in the fingers to warn me against this folly.

When the copy was done I showed it to Hiram.

> Bind thy dark hair with gems, 'round thy slender neck
> Let glowing Rubies shine. Thy lovely form
> Assume the feather'd robe of Royal State,
> Bright with the spoils from twice ten thousand birds
> Robbed of their one sole treasure, yet not their lives,
> To form a mantle fit for thee, now become
> The true companion to the Lonely One.
> The luster of thine eyes will pale those gems;
> The rip'ning beauties of thy cheek outshine
> Those Rubies' beams, thy unbought grace of life
> Rival the free bird's wing on the mountainside,
> 'Ere yet its golden plumage was despoiled.
> Stand forth! Proclaimed the Queen of Loveliness,
> Fated to share the Throne of these fair Isles.

H*

"Beautiful," said Hiram, misting up a bit. "It is beautiful. They will be very pleased. You have praised her so prettily, this maid he loves.—But tell me: what does this H mean?"

"What H?" I barked, snatching the paper from his hand. There, plain as a wart on a nose, stood the rubric of my true name, the little starred device with which I signed the poems, essays, and pallid little tales I wrote in the years of my youth. "Oh, this H," I said, thinking fast, marveling that I could have been so unguarded, that I had not yet ceased to be the vain school-boy who forced his lucubrations upon an indifferent world and yet did not have the courage to acknowledge them as his own, "it's my *nom-de-plume.*"

"Ah, I see. But why don't you sign it with your real name? This H will mean nothing to them, whereas they will welcome the poem from Saul Bristol."

"Because I do not want Alex to think that I am trying to gain his favor." This was most certainly the truth, but even so, deep in my heart, I had wanted Alex to know that the poem came from me. Now, because of an unguarded moment, the poem was no longer mine to give. I was furious with myself for being so stupid. And I was also alarmed. In just such a heedless moment as this, when, with a simpleton's trust, I am least expecting it, disaster will strike again.

"Don't you breathe a word to anyone about who wrote it," I commanded Hiram, then and there. For once in his career—and on the one occasion when I really would not have minded his disregarding my instructions—he kept his word.

Somehow or other my poem got from Alex's hands into the clutches of Abraham Fornander, Honolulu's most busybody newspaperman, to whom nothing is sacred. Within six months of the royal wedding he rushed my epithalamium into print, in that fly-by-month magazine of his for which he and "Polly" Hopkins scribble so assiduously (and, may the Muses slay them, so asininely, so *dully*). Naturally they botched it up, calling it a Sonnet— a Sonnet!!!—and changing some of my words to suit their pompous idiocies. And naturally—oh, murderous blow! oh, Justice! to think that I should be done in by an H with no asterisk!—Hopkins got the credit for it among the dozen or so literati in Honolulu who read that *opusculus minimissimus* of Fornander's. Nothing could have riled me more. I gloomed for a week when Hiram brought that flimsy rag home and, without a word, showed me how my own cantankerousness had betrayed me.

The old pride survives still, among its dusty fragments. That is why I tell this ugly little story here, because, by Heaven, when a hundred years or more from now some other prying busybody reads this manuscript, I don't, by God, want Hopkins to get the credit for this corruscating work of art too.

That misbegotten little epithalamium has its place in this account for another and much better reason: it was the agent which started this whole flood of words, this whole swollen egregious exercise in egotism. If, before that day, anyone had told me that I—I, the one and only Bristol-thewed Saulitary, as Hiram-the-Birdwatcher has named me—was going to write an autobiography ere I died, I would have rapped him on the skull for the insult.

On the evening I swore Hiram to secrecy about the gift-poem, he sat in silence for almost a full minute. "You know," he began ruminatively, "you write very well. Very interestingly. Professionally, I am tempted to say."

"Thank you, sir, very kindly," I spat out the expression we both despise, and use only when we want to bespeak irritation. I was annoyed at such patronizing—and from a philandering gadabout, too! What the hell does he know about writing, I inquired of my truculent Muse.

"Simmer down, full pot," he said, not at all disturbed. My chief trouble with him, of course, is that he never indulges me in my black humors. He's so good-natured all the time that he's damned hard to live with. "I mean it," he went on. "About your writing, that is, about your use of words. I have read more of it than you realize. And I find it—well, intriguing . . ."

"What writing?" I huffed, supposing that he referred to my things which had been published in America, and that therefore he had seen this "H*" before.

"In your journal," he said, eyeing me warily, poised to run.

"By the Trumps of Joshua," I groaned, thinking of the secrets I had confided to those tattletale pages, "I am ruined . . . —But how? And when?"

"You said I could," he told me, revealing all those white teeth, that long pink tongue. "But even if you hadn't, I would have read it anyway. How could I resist? As a matter of fact—you may as well know it now—I did read it, up in Pohukaina, even before I met you, that day I came into this yard, into this house, for the first time."

"Well! Of all the unmitigated nerve!" I roared. "Oh, you double-dealing traitor! What a high-handed, what a damnable, what a sneaky thing to do!—Oh, what a viper I've been harboring in my bosom!" The fact that I couldn't quite remember what I'd written, had quite forgotten the journal itself, did not diminish in the least my fury at his crime.

"Ah, come off it," he actually laughed at me. "You're ranting like a lousy actor in a cheap comedy. I can see a better performance in that theatre on Hotel Street in town. —There was a good reason for my reading it, as I will tell you if you'll only be quiet long enough to listen.—No. Wait. Even better—"

While I fumed and swore, he scampered into his bedroom, came back lugging a metal strongbox. "I've been wanting to make a clean chest of this for a long time," he tried to calm me with another of his awful jokes, while he tinkered with a whole armory of keys and locks and seals and chains securing the holy writ within, "but not until tonight have you been kind enough to give me the opportunity."

At long last the box was opened. From it he lifted an oval silver frame, tarnished with neglect, holding a photograph he carefully did not let me see, and a packet of papers tied about with a cord of finely braided sennit. "Here is the history of my journey for the King," he said solemnly, putting the manuscript into my hands. "I wrote most of it in those last happy weeks before the smallpox came. This is the old Niele talking—or writing, rather. I have made a few changes and additions in it since I came here to stay, but most of it was written while my memory was still fresh, and when I had no reason not to tell the whole truth. I do not think that I would write it now in the same way. Now I think I would write it more with tears than with ink."

I looked down at the beautiful slender letters flowing across the cover-page, smooth and graceful as the sounds they denote, as elegant as is everything Hiram does:

KAPU   KAPU   KAPU   KAPU   KAPU   KAPU

KA

MOʻOLELO

NO HE

HUAKAʻI

PUNI

OʻAHU

NO

KA MOʻI,

KAUIKEAOULI KIWALAʻO, KAMEHAMEHA III,

I KA MAKAHIKI 1853.

KAKAU LIMA

NA

HAILAMA NIHOA,

O HONOLULU, O KAHANA, O OʻAHU,

I KA AUPUNI MOʻI O HAWAIʻI

KAPU   KAPU   KAPU   KAPU   KAPU   KAPU

"But it still lacks something," he was saying. "It is not finished. Please, my good friend: do you read what I have written there. And when you have read it, I ask you from my heart: do you write the part that will finish the history which only we two can tell."

The man is a devil! Even while my suspicions were warning me not to give in, my fingers were plucking at the bow of the cord. As *niele* as Hiram ever was, I could not resist that bait. Its title—The History of a Journey around Oʻahu for the King, Kauikeaouli Kiwalaʻo, Kamehameha III, in the year 1853—dangled before me like a baited hook before a hungry fish. Without answering him I started to read. With the very first sentence I was a fish on the end of his line, gulping hook and lure and greedy for more.

In two evenings I read the entire history, held in thrall from beginning to end. Also, I must add, instructed and enlightened—and chastened. I will not play patronizing Chesterfield to Hiram's Johnson by rushing in with praises that he does not need. It is enough to say that, long before I reached the last page of his manuscript, I was more proud of Hiram as a writer—and as a man—than ever I could be of myself.

He, of course, was fluttering about the house, nervous as a bird being stalked by a cat. Right on time, he came to rest on the arm of a chair, just as I put down the last page. "Well? What do you say?"

I studied my colleague, my teacher, my counselor, and my friend, seeing as though for the first time the lean, handsome brown face beneath the snow white hair, the black eyes bright beyond his spectacles. I admitted again what I had long since known, how dear to me he had become in the years of our friendship, I saw how doubly

dear he would be to me now that I had read his story. He is
no magpie, I thought, nor yet a sinister shark. He is an
'i'iwi, a quick flashing of plumage red and black and
white, swift on the wing, alert on the branch; a singer of
joyous song; a sipper of nectar from many a blossom, no
doubt, a wanderer from the nest most certainly, but a
bird which fashions a sheltering nest for his young. And,
alas, a bird found only in Hawaii, a bird doomed to die,
never to be replaced. Few, indeed, are the 'i'iwi now, in the
forests of O'ahu. And never, never again, will such a man
as Hiram Nihoa walk the earth among ordinary men.
When he is gone, there will be no one to take his place.

"Hiram, my friend," I think I hid sorrow well enough
behind the smile of approbation, "it is a wonderful story.
It is the best account of people and of places in these islands that I have ever read, because it is written from the
inside, so to speak, by a native of this country, instead
of from the outside, by some witless foreigner. I thank you
for letting me read it. Now you must arrange to have it
printed, for others to read, and—"

"No," he said quickly, "not for a hundred years can it
be printed. Not until the Kamehameha are no longer worried about their right to rule this Kingdom, not until they
can laugh instead of curse at my memory, and will bring
no harm down upon my descendants.—But let's not waste
time now on that far-off future. You haven't answered my
question. This history of mine: it needs to be finished. Will
you finish it?"

So we argued, back and forth, myself reluctant, he unrelenting. Whether with tongue or pen, he is a powerful
contender. He battered down every one of my defenses,
until at last he took me captive. "Good," he said, putting
me into bondage with a handclasp. "But be sure to tell

the truth. About everything. Even about me, as I have done with you. And most especially about yourself. That will be the hardest task of all for you, I think, as I did find it for me. Remember: we are writing a history of these times, not a silly romance for women to weep over. A man who writes novels writes lies. But a man who writes history tells truth—or tries to, at least, as best he can."

"All right, old friend, all right. I shall try to do it as you say. But only for you, I want you to know, would I bare so much of my life."

"Do I not understand this?" he replied soberly. "The writing will be good for you, as it was good for me."

When Hiram rode off to the wedding festivities, to drink in more than "the dun fuliginous abyss" of Honolulu, I found the time—and summoned up the courage—to begin upon my portion of our history. Once again, and much against my instinct—because something warned me that I was going to be the loser in this compact—I have become a Pen and Inkhorn man. I have tried to "tell the truth" as best it can be remembered, after the passage of three years or more. In order to do so I have described the events and my impressions of those times as I recall them, as I lived them before I knew what part Hiram was playing in the making of our history—and in the re-making of me. Alas! Remembering the truth has been easier than writing it down.

The only sop to my vanity, the one antidote to my unwillingness to write about my imperfect self, has been Hiram's assurance that these twinned chronicles will lie unread in his strong-box for a hundred years, at the least. I do not count upon a hundred years, knowing the ruthlessness of humankind. If only these pages of mine lie unread until after I am dead my present self will not complain. But if they should be burned, like trash, before ever they are read, at any time, my spirit, I promise, will dance for a moment or two amid the flames in Hell eternal.

~~FINIS~~

CHAPTER 37.

AN END—AND A BEGINNING

Ruthlessness present and personified: this is Hiram Nihoa. No one, a hundred years from now, a millennium hence, will ever be as hard to please, as *niele*, as irresistible, and as cruel, as is this demanding man who is now the master of Ka'a'awa and of me.

Hiram has read these chapters as they've come off my table. "Good! Excellent!" he has declared, "exactly what I've wanted. I, too, am learning much from this. I, too, am being humbled by some things you've written, made happier by others." His slavedriver's exactions mixed with such schoolmaster's praise have kept me going through many an evening of sighs and groans, bitten pens, and torn-up papers.

But a week ago, when—a few lines back—thinking I had come to the end of my indenture, I gave him what was meant to be the last word in the final chapter of our cooperative history, he was very critical, unnaturally severe. He turned from his desk across the parlor, where—half-hidden behind piles of newspapers and stacks of printed government reports—he is writing THE HISTORY OF

THE REIGN OF KAMEHAMEHA IV. Glaring at me above the rims of those fiery spectacles, he said, "It's alright, as far as it goes. But you have not told all. You are withholding some of the truth."

"Goodness gracious," I say, as meek as a dunce called up before his teacher, "I thought I had . . ."

"Far from it. You have left out some very important things. I have been waiting for you to put them in, but I do not see them."

"What things?" I mumble, unable to think of any important events in our joint account which have been neglected.

"Item," he snaps. "Why do you hate yourself so much? Why are you so afraid to love again? How is it that you can be so fair with everyone but yourself?"

"Some things are private, are they not?" I reply stiffly.

"Not to history!" he cries, shaking that deficient last chapter at me. "History wants to know *everything*!"

Outside, the wind is buffeting the house, rain is beating upon the roof, against the walls facing the boisterous sea. But within the house, where we sit in peace after the long day's labors, the candles glow as in a Popish chapel, the parlor is warm and mellow, I am in the presence of the man who knows me better than anyone on earth. It is a setting designed for extracting confessions. He knows this. I know it. And a part of me yearns to throw myself upon my knees before the man whom in my heart I regard as better than a father and more than a friend, to tell him all, to lift from me the burden which is weighing me down. But another part, rock-hard and stubborn and *private*, will not bend, will not ask for help. "Then you'll have to figure it out for yourself," I say, shutting me up, not him. "I shall say no more about it. And neither will I write about it."

"*Niele* as I am," he gives in, smiling like a cherub, "and thinking much about it as I have, since before the day we met, I have been unable to figure it out for myself. But I shall drop the subject for now, as you so sweetly request, and go on to something else. But I warn you: I shall come back again to that question, again and again if necessary, until you give me the answer. Item: Why did you and your wife come to Hawai'i? Surely history has a right to know this?"

"Aye, no doubt, no doubt." The least I can do for history, I suppose, is to toss it this morsel of fact. "A trifle for a short footnote: we did not plan to come to Hawai'i. We were on our way to the Oregon Territory, to start a new life there. After our ship rounded Cape Horn the winds were more favorable for Hawai'i than for Chile, so the captain made sail for Honolulu. We had no voice in the matter. Besides, I rather think he preferred the whores of Honolulu to the nuns of Valparaiso. His crew—and the four other passengers—made no secret of their desires.— Anyway, to make a long story short, we had fine weather during the entire voyage from the Horn, until we were a day out from Honolulu. Then the storm came up . . ."

"Ah, from such slender threads do our lives depend. Had I not met Brother Doison, how different would have been the fate of Eahou. Had you not sailed with a captain who lusted for Honolulu's harlots, you and Melissa would be together now, in Oregon."

Aye. That is the great question to which I await an answer. Is it Chance that rules our lives? Or is it Jehovah? "Perhaps," I said, amazed that we could be talking so quietly about treasures which had been given into our keeping, only to be taken away. "This is what I thought, for more than three years after—after I lost her. But now?—Now I am not so sure. Now I believe that, sooner or later, our punishment would have caught up with us."

As I expected, he sat up, all agog. "Punishment? For what?" History doesn't care a fig about such items of gossip as this, I have observed, but historians love them dearly. The least I could do for my friend was to share it with him, before he burst.

"For our sinfulness. For our crimes. You see, she was—" I faltered, putting off the moment of confession because, after it was passed, he must despise me even as I despised myself. "You see, she was my brother John's wife. I—I stole her away from him."

"My goodness me!" he gasped. "Oh, Lord, oh, Lord!"

For once in his life, I thought, definitely pleased at the effect, he is really shocked.

"And is this all that is bothering you?" he cried. "For Heaven's sake! Such a great fuss over so small a fault. What's the matter with you? You are so stupid. So—so innocent! It happens all the time. Why, I could name you a dozen couples—"

Now it was my turn to be shocked. "But Hiram: you don't understand.—You don't know what we—"

"What does it matter, so long as you loved her, and she loved you?—And you were wed, were you not? To please those evil-minded Christians, you 'made an honest woman of her' did you not, after you took her away from your brother?"

"Yes. But that happened later. After we'd killed him . . ." I was looking back, in all honesty, upon the terrible time, not as Melissa and I had seen it, but as a judge would have seen it, as the One who judges us all must forever see it.

"You *killed* him?" The ugly possibility did stop him, but only for a moment. Waving off the thought, he cried, "No! No. Not you. I can not believe that."

Relieved because both of us had safely passed this test, I finished my dismal confession. "Not with our hands, of course, but by our treachery. He shot himself, when he learned how we had betrayed him—in his own house, in his own bed. But his blood is on our hands, just as much as if we had murdered him.—And it was a great scandal in Boston, where he and Melissa were well known—and where I, too, was beginning to be known. People turned against us, and withheld their help. We could not blame them, but they would have hounded us to death, I think, had we stayed in New England. That's the reason we took ship for Oregon."

"And is this why you did not give us your real name, at Kaka'ako that time Alex saved you from the sea?"

"Item the next?" I said, glad to return to our shared history in Hawai'i. "Yes, that is the reason. Bristol is the name of the town down east where I was born. Because I feared that news of the scandal would have reached Honolulu before us, where we have kinfolk among the missionaries and the merchants, we hid behind this false name, to save them from disgrace, and to spare us their attentions. My real name—you might as well know it—"

"No," he stopped me, "don't tell me. I am not that inquisitive.—No. This is not the truth. The fact is, I have learned it long ago." He laughed at my astonishment. "Your *nom-de-plume* on the poem for Alex and Emma: that gave me the hint I needed.—Is it not the star-spangled H———, painted so heroically, along with the streaming flags and the grasping eagle, inside the lid of your sea chest?"

"God save us!" I clapped hand to brow.

"A veritable work of art that is," he sneered, "worthy of a place in the American Legation."

"The only one of my possessions which was salvaged

from the shipwreck, and you had to see it. Talk about spying!"

"Not spying. Just simple observation.—But tell me: didn't the people who rescued you—and that sea chest— link the name in it to you?"

"Not once, for they never saw it in connection with me. But if they had, I would have denied the name, with an explanation they could hardly question. You see, I'd thought it all out, before ever Melissa and I sailed from Boston."

"And the explanation?"

"Why, simply that I'd bought the thing secondhand, at a chandler's shop, wanting only a sea chest, caring not for the name."

"Sounds believable, even to me, the suspicious one.— But do not worry. I will forget that honored name, from this instant. Let it be your secret. Many a foreigner, if the truth were known, is living in these islands under an assumed name, for one reason or another. Let your old name be thrown away, lost in the sea with all your other belongings. You are known to us as Saul Bristol. As Saul Bristol you have earned our respect and won our *aloha*. Why should you worry anymore about that other man? Why should you not leave him, too, in the sea?"

"Alas, my friend. If only it were done so simply. But— as I have learned to my hurt—a man does not disappear so easily. Nor does he leave his past behind him when he changes his name and his dwelling-place. As I have been taught, so must I believe: *Because I have sinned, my heart is heavy. Tribulation and anguish must lie upon the soul of every man that doeth evil.*"

"In the name of God!—You are talking nonsense. You are spouting self-pity as a hole in the reef spouts sea-foam. I'll give you another quotation from that bookful of wisdom: *the guilty flee where none pursueth.* And another: *the Lord corrects him whom he loves, even as a father does his child in whom he delights.*—Why don't you look for solace in that book, instead of punishment? But no: because you enjoy suffering, you look for threats, you expect the worst.—You have talked yourself into this miserable state. You have put the hair shirt upon your soul, the chains upon your spirit. Can't you see this? You —you, not Jehovah—have put the knife to your balls, making you an ox instead of a bull."

Flinging the manuscript to the floor between us, he shot out of his chair, shaking a handful of fingers at me. "Damn it, Saul! You make me so mad!—When are you going to grow up? Here you are, a full-grown man, twenty-six years old, and still you think—and act—as if you were a lad in Sabbath School. When are you going to learn that you are not the only suffering man on earth, the only sinner who is being watched by the eye of God?—If I have learned anything at all in the course of my years, it is this: a man's life is his to make. No other man, certainly no god, will do it for him."

"You have your opinions," I said sullenly, rankled by his scolding, "I have mine." Never, since I've become a grown man, has anyone spoken so cruelly to me.

"Opinions, opinions! I'm not talking about opinions. You can have your crazy opinions, just as I have mine. Opinions are important only as they reveal the man beneath. And they should change, as the man beneath changes with experience.—I'm talking about deeds. We judge a man by what he does, not by what he says or how he looks. And what are you doing to help yourself?—Or, if you prefer, what are you doing to help God to help you? —I will tell you. You are doing nothing. Absolutely nothing. Meanwhile, time is closing in on you. Time is a hungry shark: it devours everything, especially the days of one's youth."

He pointed a sharp finger at me, slouched in my chair, confounded and annoyed, and beginning to be angry. "What is better? To sit on your butt here in Ka'a'awa, whining and whimpering, like a prisoner in chains, like a hermit mortifying your flesh, waiting for death to come, and the possibility of the reward of salvation for your suffering? Or to stand up, and walk about in freedom, and live like a man? To suffer, perhaps, but also to love? To weep at times, and to be in fear at times, but also to enjoy the things of this world which are given to us to be enjoyed?"

"I enjoy—"

"Yeah, yeah. Birds. Work. That is all. Why these things only?—Because they require nothing from you, nothing given from the heart. These things only do you enjoy. And one thing else, perhaps: the itching of that hair shirt, the rattling of those heavy chains. That's all. What about the other kind of itch a man should feel? It is dead. Despite the salt Kamanele and I have poured upon your food, it is dead. What about that thing between your legs? It is dead. Did I not see it every afternoon, and know very well that it is there, I would think you were made without one. Damn! I have been thinking that I should put a dash of Spanish fly into your milk, just to see if that could have any effect."

"Hiram!" I shouted, appalled at such indecent talk.

But he would not stop. "Had I not read about Melissa, I would think you didn't know what it was for."

"Hiram! That's enough!—Damn it!" I started to get up, heading for the stable, or for the cookhouse, for any place where I could escape this merciless man, "I don't see why I have to sit here, listening to your—"

"Shut up! Sit down! I'm not finished with you yet.—
That thing: it is there. I have seen it. A splendid ornament.
And, like all ornaments, useless. Limp as a dead eel. You
do not use it—except for pissing with, and a hole would
serve as well. Makana, the boy you resent so much: he is
more of a man than you are. He is alive. A snowman is
warmer than you are. He melts in the light of the sun. But
you: you are a block of ice, wrapped up in a husk of skin
and hair, beyond melting because you are beyond warming. You are worse than Hahau. You are an offense to
Kane, as he said, but not for the reasons that poor stupid
man gave. Shall I tell you why Kane gave it to us, that
thing?"

"I know what it's for!" I roared. "Damn you! Not
every man wants to be a shark."

"No, of course not," he made a little bow, grinning like
a mean little Punch, "not every man can be a shark. But
every man should want to be a father. What do you say
to that, *e*? Nothing, of course. Then if you will not use that
thing in pleasure, why do you not use it in duty? *E*?—
You write about the dying Hawaiian race. You bemoan
the loss of my people. Very touching. Very safe. But
what do they mean to you, those words you have written?
Is it only your concern for the benighted heathen that
makes you write those sorrowing words? Am I to think
that you, too, are a lying hypocrite, just as so many other
foreigners are?"

This was too vicious, even for me. My head went up,
ready for raging, his hands went up to quiet me. "No. Be
easy. I do not believe that you are such a hypocrite, at
least in this matter. I know this in my heart, from what
you are doing here in Ka'a'awa. I have had time enough
to study you, do not forget. And this is my thought: you
are not a hypocrite. You are an unhappy boy, lost upon

the way, unable to find the path to being a happy man."

"You live your life the way you want to," I said coldly, "and let me live mine the way I want to."

He shook his head sadly. "You talk like a boy, too.—Can a father stand by, watching while his son drowns, and not lift a hand to help him? Would you stand by, cold and useless and unconcerned, if your son were troubled? Your son, I say. Not the one who was given to you, only to be taken away, but the son you should have with you now, the son of your loins. Where is that son?—You wanted a son, you have written, you wanted many sons. With nothing you have written in your history could I agree more. Children are the best reasons for living that a man can find. A man without a son is a man without a shadow. A man without children has no claim upon the future. One way to get them, I point out to you, the man who reads books, the man of strong opinions—and one way to save my race from dying, I must add—is to make *kanaka* babies. If you will not make more *haole* sons in your icy image, then why do you not make *hapa-haole* sons? Half-white sons are better than none. And with you for their father, I can predict that they would be a good-looking bunch—even if they would not be very smart."

"Thank you very kindly," I growled, cut to the quick by this attack from the man I had considered my truest friend. For almost three years I had given him my trust and my affection, as I had given them to no one else. And now he was turning upon me, mauling me as savagely as if he were indeed a shark in the sea, and I a helpless swimmer. This is the thanks I get, I thought bitterly, this is the betrayal I've been awaiting. It has come, just as I knew it would, when I am least prepared . . .

"But I will bet," he tore into me again, relentless as a shark after it has tasted blood, "I will bet my last shining

American dollar that you've never once thought to take a Hawaiian girl for a wife. Or even for a bed-mate. 'White limbs next to brown,' " he jeered, slashing through *haole* skin and bleeding flesh, down to the glairy bones beneath. "The picture does not attract you, *e*? What a pity. You must be the only *haole* in all of Hawaii—except for the missionaries, may God give them joy in their wives—who is not busy trying to throw a *kanaka* into bed. Men, women, *mahu*, anything in between: they're all running about, in the town, in the country, in the fields, in the woods, with haoles in full chase, like hounds in a hunt. This is the national game of Hawaii, the people's pastime, the source of our income and the fountain of our happiness. And where are you in this sporting? Shoot! In your private hell, feeding birds.—Damn it! If you will not take a *wahine* into your bed, how about a *mahu*? Or a real *kane*?"

"Because I'm not that sort of man!" I bellowed, wishing I could punch him in the snout, to make him stop tormenting me with insinuations that were so unfounded.

"Are you sure?" he asked, very quietly. "There's more than a hint of interest on your part—in your writing, I mean, although not in your manner, I will say. That day you spent with Linalina on the mountain, naked with a naked man: was it not one of the happiest days in your life?"

Quivering with anger, I could scarcely reply. "It was. But not for that reason. There you are most wrong, you with your foul thoughts.—What are you trying to do to me?"

"I ask only because I want you to ask the question of yourself. But I do not press the point. *Kane*, *wahine*, *mahu*: I do not care. No one cares. In dark Hawai'i, if not in enlightened America, no one ever cares about how a man shows his love. The main thing is to love, and to be loved. But you: you will not love. And you will not accept love. You believe that you are afraid to love again. I say that you are too selfish to love again. Sometimes I wonder if you loved Melissa as much as you claim. Sometimes I think you loved yourself more. Just as now you love yourself so much.—And how do I know this? From seeing you, day after day, living, swimming, eating, singing, in the company of these beautiful girls here, any one of whom would make you a good wife. And you, with your averted gaze, your downcast eyes, you do not even see them. You do not even know their names.—How else do I know this? From reading what you have written. Those leering little essays on nakedness. Those proudful little sermons on pride. Chah! They are written not from the heart but from the scheming head. And they are written not to tell the truth, but to tell the world, a hundred years from now, how good, how noble, how virtuous you are, in the midst of all these gross and sinful *kanaka* temptations."

"They were not meant that way," I cried, dismayed to learn that I could be so misread, so misunderstood.

He rode roughshod over my protest. "Pride!" he hit me where I was weakest. "You are not proud, boy. You don't know the meaning of pride. That's something you've read about in your books, perhaps, but can not know from experience. Pride is big, it is immense, it is a noble thing that makes a man do noble deeds. It is a part of his *mana*, born with him, a bequest from his ancestors and his gods. What you are calling pride in yourself is a little thing, made up of even smaller things. Of little evil things that come from outside a man, not from within, of all the little uglinesses that make a man little and mean and ugly. As with all of us, you too are made of conceits and vanities, of doubts and misgivings, of fears about what other people will think, of dread about what God will think, of dirty secret longings, of malices and deceits, of envies and depravities. Yes, of envies. More than anything else in this world do you envy Makana, and "Polly" Hopkins—and me, even me—our 'pleasures of the flesh.' *U-iii*! Notice how delicately I phrase it. Out of regard for your refined sensibilities. I think you would fall into a swoon if I called it by its rightful name.—Sounded with a u, of course, I being such an educated man."

Never had I dreamed that this jesting little man could be so malicious, so full of scorn for me.

"No. You are not proud. You are small-minded. And you are certitudinous. Like all haoles, you are so sure, so certain that your way of doing things, of seeing things, is the only right way. But in this talent, believe me, you surpass all the haoles I have ever met.—Oh, boy! I don't know who this fellow Chesterfield is but, I tell you, you could give him lessons in how to look down a long *haole* nose at people of any color.—You are not proud. You are selfish. This is the word for you. A sassy, selfish boy who will not grow up to be a man, because he does not want to be hurt.—Search your little mind, boy," he whipped me brutally, "and tell me that I am wrong."

"Hiram, for God's sake! Stop! That's enough."

"No!" he shouted, stamping his foot, "not for God's sake. For your sake. For your sake, Saul. Answer me! It must be said, else all this grievous talk will be for nothing. It must be said, else it will lie within you, turning to hate, and I do not want your hate."

Sunk in my chair, chin resting upon chest, I would not look at him, would not answer. Where only a few minutes before affection and trust abided, I dug deep down for hate.

"Saul," he pleaded, standing before me. The legs of his clean white pantalons, the polished shoes on his small feet; my own long shanks stretching out, encased in rags, ending in misshapen boots stained with mud and dung: here is the difference, they declared in a language needing no words, between a man of pride and a proudful, selfish lout. "Saul. I have not said these things just to hurt you. Surely you must know this?" He was gentle now, and kind, kinder than he has ever been with this sassy selfish boy. "Surely you must know that for me, if not for you, your happiness in this world is a matter of great importance?"

As I looked at my boots, I saw myself as he must see me. Searching for hate with which to hurt him in return, I measured the smallness of my tight little heart, plumbed the shallowness of my arrogant little mind. How could I hate him for showing me the truth? How could I reject him, the wisest man I knew? He was right, in many of the charges he had leveled against me, if not in all. He had tied me down and cut me open, as a surgeon does with a sailor's swollen, festering belly, and he was showing me the foulness that lies within. The foulness and the falseness which I have known were there, which I thought were hidden from the eyes of men but could not hide from him. How could I hate him, when I was the one to be hated?

Yet selfish, proudful louts, full of wickedness and corruption, can feel the flush of shame, can run from the father who strives to correct them. I would not look at him, the while I wondered how he had endured me for so many years, without complaint or murmur, without long since having whipped me to my knees for my falseness. I could not speak, because I could find only loathing within.

The silence between us was like a swamp, sucking down

into its mud all the words I could find to say. He will take them for excuses, I told myself, he will hear them as whimperings from a beaten boy. What's the use of saying anything at all, I despaired, sinking deeper into despond, making no effort to escape. This is the end of our happy household, this is the death of Ke Eahou, I was thinking in one moment. The roof must be leaking again, I thought in the next, seeing droplets of water falling upon Hiram's shoes, upon the boards of the polished floor. Dispassionate, remote, as though I were observing them through a telescope and they were the most important things in the whole world, I watched them shatter and die, useless as drops of holy water upon the brow of a fevered boy. Lifting my head to trace the leak, I found that those were not raindrops falling from the ceiling.

What the water of Kane does for Ka'a'awa's earth, Hiram's tears did for me. From somewhere, I could not recall who had said them or when I'd heard them, the words rose up which brought me safe to shore. "I understand," I said, as much to myself as to him, "and I shall remember."

"Ah," he sighed, "those are good words to hear. This moment marks the end of a boy, the beginning of a man."

"I don't want your hate, Hiram, or your contempt—much as I deserve them." I was close enough to tears myself, my voice was strained, but the thought came straight from the heart. "And in the making of this new man, I shall take you for a model—in some matters." I tried to say this lightly, to prove that I bore no grudge, hoping to ease us back again to peace.

"My goodness me," he said, clearing his throat, busying himself with his glasses, "it is nice of you to say so. But I am thinking that a shark is not the proper example for a plover.—You have a better model to follow, I believe. And you have already found him."

"And who might he be," I asked dutifully, supposing that Alex was the one he would name.

"The man who was as a brother to you. The man who, out of his *aloha* for you, chose you to be his brother and his helper. The most honest man you know."

"Ah, yes," I nodded, "the very one," remembering how, long ago, Linalina had shown me that there was another way than the path I had chosen. "But you are the guide who has brought me to this path. For this I must thank you. Where might I not have wandered, if Hiram Nihoa had not come in search of me?"

"Could I stand by, useless and unconcerned, while you wandered in the wilderness? No, I could not. This is the trouble with a *niele* man who is also a loving man. To me, nothing is more important—nothing, I say—than saving a man from destruction.—Forgive me if I have hurt you with this talk. If I have kicked down, it is only to help you to rise up again, higher than before. After your unhappiness you deserve a new life, to go with your new name. You will find happiness again, my son, if you but search for it. I know it. I feel it."

His loving kindness touched me like a father's blessing laid upon my head. "Perhaps," I said, wanting to believe him, yet fearing still the touch of a heavier hand. How many times have I searched, how many times have I been struck down. How many times have I cried unto Him, out of the depths, in pain and in fear.

"We shall see," I said, wanting Hiram to believe me, yet not able to say so, because of that great fear. The least I can do for myself is to hope. But in me hope lies like a seed under winter's heavy snows, waiting for the spring.

And my soul waits for the Lord more than they that watch for the morning. Yet how can I trust that spring will ever come again for me, I asked myself in the eternal round, that He shall redeem me from all my iniquities? as I knelt upon the floor to gather up the sheets of paper scattered about Hiram's feet. He had flung them in anger at a selfish boy. Does a corrected man kneel now to pick them up, I wondered.

"I will try," I promised, putting away for the night the pens, the ink, the unfinished accounting of our sorrowful lives.

Only this evening, when we are at peace again, have I been able to bring this true history to its truthful end.

SAUL BRISTOL

at Ka'a'awa, O'ahu,
in the Kingdom of Hawai'i,
February 11, 1857.